Praise for
A Clearing in the

"*A Clearing in the Wild* is Jane Kirkpatrick at her finest. The story is quickly paced and engaging from the first to the last. One of the most difficult tasks for a writer—and Kirkpatrick's specialty—is to contemplate the lives of real people and to re-create a believable episode in those lives that is accurate yet interesting, to both inform and entertain. The dialog sings masterfully with perfect tone, building characters and pushing the story line in succinct phrasing that never overstates. Emma Wagner Giesy's story feels as genuine as if she herself were telling it."

—NANCY E. TURNER, author of *Sarah's Quilt*
and *The Water and the Blood*

"Jane Kirkpatrick shines her unique light on a fascinating episode of Oregon Trail history as she follows young Emma Giesy's struggles to prove herself a worthy wife and mother within the confines of her communal and highly patriarchal Christian community. This is a valuable read for those who appreciate having their history so fully and accurately imagined. Jane clearly knows her terrain, and by the time I finished *A Clearing in the Wild*, I felt I had lived through a damp winter or two myself in the rich but challenging country of the Willapa Bay of Washington State. This thoughtful and well-researched book will surely add to the numbers of Jane's well-deserved fans."

—LINDA CREW, author of *Brides of Eden: A True Story Imagined*
and *A Heart for Any Fate: Westward to Oregon: 1845*

"Jane Kirkpatrick has done it again! *A Clearing in the Wild* introduces us to a feisty young heroine who, by her determination, ingenuity, and faith, helps to create a home and a life in the wilderness. Readers are sure to fall in love with Emma as she weaves the story of her life, creating a pioneer tapestry and leaving us anticipating the next layer of her inspirational story."

—RANDALL PLATT, author of *Honor Bright* and *The Likes of Me*

"Through her careful research, Jane Kirkpatrick has captured the trials of those who are determined to settle a land that does not easily yield to civilization. She has brought to life another woman in our history whose faith, strength, and commitment is a testament to not only the pioneer spirit but the human spirit as well. Thank you, Ms. Kirkpatrick, for not allowing Emma Wagner Giesy to languish in obscurity."

—KARLA K. NELSON, owner of Time Enough Books
in Ilwaco, Washington

"Emma Wagner Giesy is brave, willful, and beautiful, and *A Clearing in the Wild* brings her to life without for a moment sacrificing her complexity. Kirkpatrick compels us to think again, and deeply, about the needs of the body, soul, and mind; and in these pages she proves once again that she is a gifted chronicler of the lives of women in the West."

—MOLLY GLOSS, author of *The Jump-Off Creek* and *Wild Life*

A Clearing in the Wild

a novel

A Clearing in the Wild

a novel

JANE KIRKPATRICK

WATERBROOK
PRESS

A CLEARING IN THE WILD
PUBLISHED BY WATERBROOK PRESS
12265 Oracle Boulevard, Suite 200
Colorado Springs, Colorado 80921
A division of Random House Inc.

This book is a work of historical fiction based closely on real people and real events.
Details that cannot be historically verified are purely products of the author's imagination.

10-Digit ISBN: 1-57856-734-3
13-Digit ISBN: 978-1-57856-734-8

Library of Congress Cataloging-in-Publication Data
Kirkpatrick, Jane, 1946–
    A clearing in the wild / Jane Kirkpatrick.— 1st ed.
      p. cm. — (Change and cherish series ; bk. 1)
    ISBN 1-57856-734-3
    1. Women pioneers—Fiction. 2. Social isolation—Fiction. I. Title.
    PS3561.I712C57 2006
    813'.54—dc22
                                                        2005035370

Printed in the United States of America
2006

10 9 8 7 6 5 4 3 2

To Jerry

CAST OF CHARACTERS

Emma Wagner   young German girl living
     in Bethel Colony

David and Catherina Sundell Wagner   Emma's parents
     Jonathan, age 18   Emma's siblings
     David Jr., age 11
     Catherine, age 9
     Johanna, age 7
     Louisa, age 5
     William, age 3

Christian Giesy   appointed leader of the scouts;
     Emma's husband

     Andrew   his son
     Catherina   his daughter

Wilhelm Keil   leader of Bethel, Missouri colony
     Louisa Keil   Wilhelm's wife
     Willie   his son
     Aurora   his daughter
     Gloriana   his daughter
     Several other Keil children

Andreas and Barbara Giesy   Christian's parents
     Helena Giesy   one of Christian's sisters
     Mary Giesy   sister-in-law to Emma and Helena
     Sebastian Giesy   Mary's husband; Christian's brother

Karl Ruge   German teacher in colony

John "Hans" Stauffer   scouts sent west
John Stauffer

Michael Schaefer Sr.
Joseph Knight
Adam Knight
John Genger
George Link
Adam Schuele
Christian and Emma Giesy

John Stauffer	returning scouts
Michael Schaefer Sr.	
Joseph Knight	
Adam Knight	
John Genger	
George Link	

Ezra Meeker	Washington Territory settler
*Nora and the gut doctor	couple at Fort Steilacoom
*Simmons and Marie	their children
*Frau Flint and Frau Madeleine	women at Fort Steilacoom
*An-gie	Chehalis maid
*Pap	her daughter
*N'chi	her grandson
Captain Maurice Maloney	commander at Fort Steilacoom

Sam and Sarah Woodard	settlers at Woodard's Landing
James Swan	early resident/writer of Willapa region

Opal	the mule
Opal	the goat
Charlie	the seagulls

*fictional characters

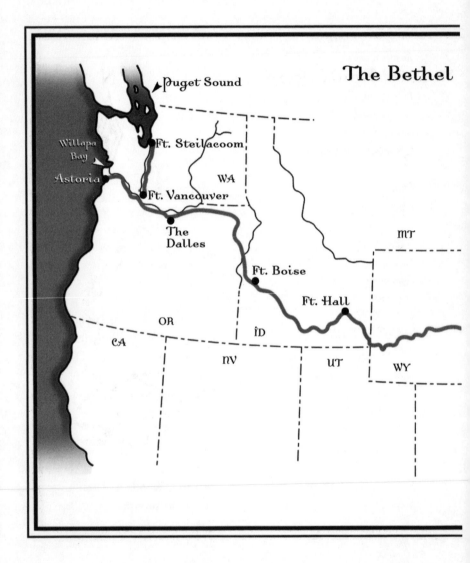

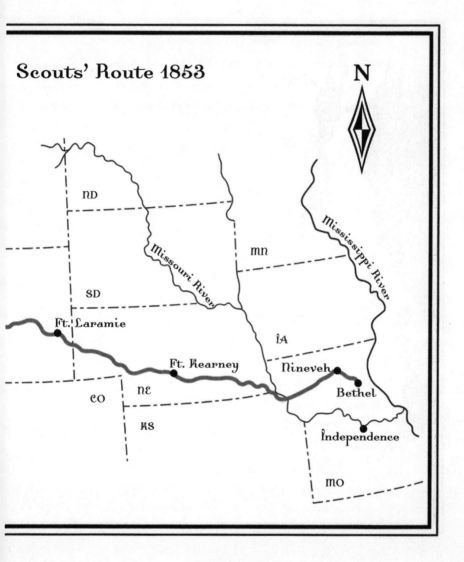

You can tell they're all related even though they're each unique. They resist exposing their tender innards. Something hard must happen to break them open; a foreign source invades. Then a knife slice and they unveil their treasures deep within.

ANONYMOUS, "On Oysters"

And the LORD God called unto Adam, and said unto him, Where art thou?...And the LORD God said unto the woman, What is this that thou hast done?...Unto Adam also and to his wife did the LORD God make coats of skins, and clothed them.

GENESIS 3:9, 13, 21

And all who believed were together and had all things in common; and they sold their possessions and goods and distributed them to all, as any had need.

ACTS 2:44–45, RSV

Part 1

1

The Thread of Love

Some say that love's enough to stave off suffering and loss, but I would disagree. Quietly, of course. Words of dissent aren't welcome in our colony, especially words from women. I should have learned these lessons—about dissent and love—early on before I turned eighteen. But teachings about spirit and kinship require repetition before becoming threads strong enough to weave into life's fabric, strong enough to overcome the weaker strains of human nature. It was a strength I found I'd need one day to face what love could not stave off.

But on that Christmas morning in Bethel, Missouri, 1851, celebrating as we had for a decade or more with the festivities beginning at 4:00 a.m., a time set by our leader, love seemed enough; love was the thread that held the pearls of present joy. It was young love, a first love, and it warmed. Never mind that the warmth came from the fireplace heat lifting against my crinoline, so for a moment I could pretend I wore the wire hoop of fashion. Instead of something stylish, I wore a dress so simple it could have been a flannel sheet, so common it might belong to any of the other dozen girls my age whose voices I could hear rising in the distance, the women's choir already echoing their joy within our Bethel church. Winter snows and the drafts that plagued my parents' loft often chilled me and my sisters. But here, on this occasion, love and light and music and my family bound me into warmth.

Candle heat shimmered against the tiny bells of the *Schellenbaum,* the symbol of allegiance my father carried in the church on such special occasions. The musical instrument's origin was Turkish, my father told me, and militaristic, too, a strange thing I always thought for us German immigrants to carry forth at times of celebration. The musical instrument reminded me of an iron weather vane on top of one of the colony's grain barns, rising with an eagle at the peak, its talons grasping an iron ball. Beneath, a crescent held fourteen bells, alternating large and small, dangling over yet another black orb with a single row of bells circling beneath it. A final ring of tiny bells hovered above the stand my father carried this early morning. As a longtime colonist, he walked worshipfully toward the *Tannenbaum* sparkling with star candles placed there by the parade of the youngest colony girls.

My father's usual smiling face wore solemn as his heavy boots took him forward like a funeral dirge, easing along the wide aisle that divided men from women, fathers from daughters, and mothers from sons even while we faced one another, men looking at women and we gazing back. All one thousand members of the Bethel Colony attended. The women's chorus ended, and I heard the rustle of their skirts like the quiet turning of pages of a book as they nestled down onto the benches with the other seated women.

Later, the band would play festive tunes, and we'd sing and dance and give the younger children gifts of nuts and apples, and the men might taste the distillery's nectar of whiskey or wine, though nothing to excess, before heading home to open gifts with family.

We began the Christmas celebration assembled in the church built of bricks we colonists made ourselves. We gathered in the dark, the tree candles and the fire glow and our own virgin lanterns lighting up the walnut-paneled room as we prepared to hear Father Keil—as my father called him—preach of love, of shared blessings, of living both the Golden and the Diamond Rules. He'd speak of loyalty to our Lord, to one another, and ultimately to him, symbolized on this day by the carrying of the *Schellenbaum* and the music of its bells across the red-tiled floor.

As my father passed in front of me, I spied my older brother, Jonathan, my brother who resembles me. He, too, is small and slender with eyes like walnuts framed by thick brown eyebrows set inside a heart-shaped face. I used to tease my brother about his chipmunk cheeks until the day I overheard Helena Giesy say, "Emma Wagner and her brother look like twins, though Jonathan is two years older. Such puffed up cheeks they share," she said. Our rosy cheeks bind us.

Jonathan held his lower lip with his teeth, then raised his eyebrows, letting his eyes move with deliberateness toward the front and the tall, dark-haired man standing next to Father Keil. Now my heart skipped. Jonathan lifted his chin, grinned. My face grew warm.

I never should have told him.

At least I kept the secret from the little ones, though Catherine at nine, wise beyond her years, would claim she was adult enough to know, but she'd have clucked her tongue at me for even thinking in the way I did. David, Johanna, Louisa, and William, well, they'd have blabbed and babbled without knowing what they really said.

The bells tinkled and the band struck up notes. Later, if the weather held, the band would move out onto the platform around the church steeple and play *Hark! the Herald Angels Sing* so loudly that perhaps the ears of those in Shelbina thirteen miles south would be awakened and our colony would intrude on them, but in a glorious way. We were meant to be set apart by our commitment to the common fund, Father Keil told us, and yet to serve. Lately, Shelbina and its railroad threatened us. My father said Father Keil grew worried that Shelbina's life might lure young men away. Father Keil would do his best to keep Bethel's sons loyal, separated, even though he said our passion should be to bring others to our fold, save others from God's planned destruction of our world, give to those in need, especially to widows and their children. We were to bring to the colony, through our acts of love, the women who wore white globes called pearls around their necks, the fine ladies who sought after jewels and gems that marked false loyalties to luxury over faith.

Neighbors. The people of Shelbina were good neighbors, I always thought. They bought our gloves, our wine, and our corn whiskey. But few of us really knew them. We had no way of knowing if they'd heard about the coming destruction or if they suffered from worries and woes. Our religious colony cherished lives of simplicity, sharing frugal wealth in common, all needs of colonists met, silencing desire for unnecessary passions. Whatever cash we earned went to the common purse. If we needed cash for some outside purchase, we went to that same coffer. Whatever we needed from the colony's yield, we simply walked to the storehouse to secure it. My mother said it eased all worry about the future; I saw it as one more person to have to convince to let loose the purse strings.

We colonists were different from those around us in Missouri; we were an island of our own. We worked to stay unsullied by the larger distractions of the world that Shelbina symbolized even while we attempted to bring others into the joys of our colony's ways.

Only the strongest of us could reach outside and yet stay faithful, Father Keil said. I smoothed my skirt and felt the ruffle.

The brass horns pierced the room, announcing Father Keil's beginning words. Angels' trumpets. Music is the perfect way to celebrate a glorious occasion, I've always thought. Jonathan played in the men's band. Not me. Not girls, not young women. Our music came from our voices raised in the choir or while beating rugs or dyeing wool or serving meals to men. I couldn't carry a tune in a candlestick holder, something else that made me different.

But separation from the women's choir or the brass instruments of music did not keep me from the joy of this day especially.

My father set the *Schellenbaum* on its stand, then took his place across from us, sliding next to my brothers, who then wiggled on down the bench, a place they always sat. We'd been a part of this colony for as long as I could remember. My father had been one of three scouts sent out from Pennsylvania by our leader to find a "place of separation" in the unknown territories, far from the larger world. I was five years old when we moved with other German families discouraged by the changes in George Rapp's colony at Harmony, Pennsylvania. We seceded first to Phillipsburg, then into Indiana, then into Shelby County, Missouri, where our leader imagined Bethel into being. It is a joyous place, Bethel, even though my father says many will be summoned in the morning to discuss reasons we might have to leave again.

Change never troubled me. I welcome change, newness, though I work to keep my pride in check about it. Pride is an evil thing, our leader tells us. We must not envy, must not lust, must not covet. So no one knows I've stitched a ruffle to my crinoline. It is a harmless vanity easily removed but one that warms my spirit knowing it is there, unique on this winter morning as crisp as a hot-ironed crease. I gaze without envy along the row of plain and simple wool dresses of Bethel's sisters on the benches.

Change has its richness in a colony where everything seems the same. At seventeen, I am of marriageable age, so change sticking its head inside my door will be patted like a welcomed dog on its happy head.

Before we left our brick home this morning, my mother cautioned me when I noted that this might be my last Christmas as Emma Wagner.

Next year, next Christmas, I might carry a new name and enter the festivities not as a child, but as a woman.

"He preaches of late, Father Keil does, that one should be devoted to the colony, not marry so young," my mother said as we readied to leave for the service. She combed Johanna's hair into a braid, brushed a crumb from little Louisa's face. "He says perhaps women should marry not at all. Tink of Saint Paul who advised, 'I say therefore to the unmarried and widows, It is good for them if they abide even as I.'"

"But he also said it's 'better to marry than to burn,'" I challenged. I could see my breath through the cold of our large house. I licked my fingers and flattened three-year-old William's cowlick as he sped out the door, then pulled on gloves made by Bethel factory workers.

"Paul says that, too," my mother continued, "but then tells, 'He that is unmarried careth for the things that belong to the Lord, how he may please the Lord: But he that is married careth for the things that are of the world, how he may please his wife.'"

"*Ja,* a good husband should please his wife," I said. "Besides, Father Keil married." I pulled on my woolen hood and tied the bows beneath my chin. "His nine children might say he either burned much or none at all."

"*Ach,* Emma!" my mother chastened. "How you talk. Young Father Keil married before he came to know the Lord as he knows Him now." Her hands shooed me out the door toward the rest of the family.

"He's been a colony leader for many years, and his wife Louisa still has diapers to change," I said, walking backward to keep chatting with my mother. My father held a lantern so we could see to walk to the church on the crunching snow, and he used it to signal me to turn about, gather up my younger brothers and sisters.

"Wiser now he is, so he shares his wisdom with us, and we must listen," my mother finished.

"Who is wiser?" my father said as we joined him beneath the stars. "You," my mother offered, taking his arm.

I didn't pursue the subject, but my disagreement with her and with our leader's view gave me yet another reason to be joyful about my unseen ruffle. After all, isn't part of wisdom thinking on one's own, doing not what everyone else does but making distinctive marks, as distinctive as…as a Turkish instrument carried by a German man?

Now we sat and listened to the bells of the *Schellenbaum* tinkle at this early hour service. Surely our leader didn't think young men and women would forgo marriage or families for the sake of the colony? How would it grow? Would he rely on new conversions of men going with courage into the outside world, men too strong to be lured into the world's ways?

The tall man standing next to our leader moved to center the *Schellenbaum* on its stand beside the altar. My heart pounded with anticipation. He was my father's good friend, our leader's emissary most recently into Kentucky and the Carolinas. His name was Christian Giesy, and it was him I hoped to marry, though I wasn't sure if he even knew my name.

Christian Giesy. I prayed I'd aged enough that he might see me this Christmas morning as a young woman and not just a snippet of thread tethered to the weaving of my parents.

He did not look my way but instead stared off as though he saw a glorious place somewhere far beyond this room, his eyes as shining as the lantern light flashed against the *Schellenbaum.* I swallowed. Perhaps he too believed as our leader did, that the finest way to honor God meant remaining celibate and unmarried.

I pitched away that disappointing thought.

Our leader raised his voice, large before us. Even errant thoughts of mine were pulled into the cymbal clang of his call to worship. His eyes were deep pools of churning water that nearly frothed with intensity and yet a kind of joy. We young women stopped shuffling our slippers. Men muffled their coughs. Mothers whispered quietly to their children, "Be silent, now." His oldest son, Willie, gazed up at his father as though he were a saint. Only the sizzle of candle wax and the fire's roar and the occasional tinkle of the *Schellenbaum* bells moved by the fire's draft interrupted our leader's words as he drew our faces toward him, toward the words my parents first heard in Pennsylvania, words that took us all in and changed our very lives. The fire waned in the brick church. I felt a chill. We remained awake in the cold and with *his* words. When he raised his voice, a mesmerizing sound echoed words I'd heard so often as a child from him and then from my own father, too, who preached, though without the fervor of our leader. I didn't need to pay attention now. But I willed myself to keep staring at him, to not let my eyes wander onto Christian Giesy.

A tinsmith, Christian, who also served as one of the missionaries our leader sent south to bring in new communal members, was a man one year younger than our leader but wiser and more handsome than our leader had ever been, though Christian's build was leaner, a sturdy pine beside Father Keil's squat oak. The recruits, whom we hoped would eventually convert, were usually people who could advance the colony: wagon makers, farmers, coopers. I wondered if we were contributing to their souls by making them colonists as much as they contributed to our coffers. *Sacrilege, such thoughts.*

My eyes ached from staying open. I refused to blink for fear the lids would overtake me and embarrass me with sleep. Maybe just for a second I could close them.

My head dropped onto my mother's shoulder. "Emma," she whispered. "Sit straight!"

Catherine pursed her lips as I wiped my drooling mouth with the back of my hand, hoping no one else had seen my lapse. Catherine was "too good" and would never sleep in church. Some unseen force moved my eyes to Christian's. I willed my face to heat no crimson blotches on my cheeks as I looked boldly at him. He stared, his dark hair as silky as a beaver pelt, no part, combed back. Long sideburns rolled up into a mustache thick and trimmed. Dark hair acted as a picture frame for a strong face, straight nose, and eyes as blue as the feathers of a blue-winged teal and just as soft. I sighed despite myself and my mother elbowed me. Had he seen me fall asleep? I hiccupped. My mother frowned. When I saw that Christian let his eyes rest on mine before he eased them toward our leader, I couldn't control the racing of my heart.

———

"Ve never neglect the children," our leader said when his sermon about Christmas joy ended and the children swarmed around him. My father said we American children were spoiled now, no longer having to fear the arrival of *Peltz Nickel,* the frightening, chain-dragging, bell-ringing companion of *Belsnickel* and *Christkind.* The former frequented the old country, prepared to punish us for wrongdoing through the year while we waited for presents from the Christmas hosts. Instead, we German-American children of the Bethel Colony witnessed our leader in the form of *Belsnickel,* who brought us goodies and who celebrated with tiny *Schellenbaum* bells instead of ugly chains. Still, I wondered whether even in this colony, because of our German history, joyous things came with the threat of later punishment and chains.

As children gathered around *Belsnickel,* I held back. But then the childhood lure drew me, and I rushed in to reach for the candies and raisins along with the little ones. Peppermints are my favorite, and our leader's wife, Louisa, had placed several inside little strips of cloth tied with hemp. Her youngest daughters, three-year-old Aurora and five-year-old Gloriana, pushed on either side of me, and I helped them forward, lifting Aurora to my hip, stepping in so my five-year-old sister, Louisa, could reach more easily too. The rest squealed in delight. Their voices sounded like tinkling bells and I loved it.

"Not so much with the little ones," my mother said as I pranced back to her, my young charges now on their own and my hands filled with little cloth bags of sweets I handed out to William, barely three, and to mother and others too embarrassed to reach in with the children. Wool swirled around my legs. She shook her head. "Spending time with the children is easier, I tink, than acting of your age."

"I might be unmarried forever, you tell me, so let my childhood fingers dip into *Belsnickel's* bag, please?"

"Ach," she said, brushing her hand at me dismissively, but she smiled and accepted the peppermint piece I gave her. "We help serve food now," she told me, and I gave Louisa and Aurora a candy. Both scampered to our leader, who lifted them high and nuzzled their necks with his beard, a dozen other children still clamoring at his feet.

Arm in arm, my mother and I walked to where the women uncovered tins of sausages and scrambled eggs kept heated in their tubs. Breads of all kinds and *Strudels* and moist cakes with nuts quickly covered the table. Steins of wine set like sentries along the white cloth overlooked the bounty. Our leader said these common meals following his sermons were celebrations of the Last Supper, served as though the Lord Himself were present, and it did seem as though our community was blessed this day with love in abundance and the spirit of grace.

Dawn seeped in through the tall windows, but outside the ground lay comforted by snow that didn't appear warm enough to melt. We'd have fine ice-skating later. I wondered what Christian would be doing. Enjoying his sisters and brothers and parents, I imagined, since he'd been gone so long. I sensed where he stood in the room. His presence filled a space, and I could see glimpses of him towering above many of the other men as I set tubs of *Sauerkraut* on the table.

The band played now, and Jonathan and Willie—our leader's oldest, my age—tapped their feet while marching notes rang out. Our leader didn't play in the band but sometimes brought out his harmonica. Now he clapped his hands as the children gathered around him for new treats he gave each one. The Christmas celebration proved almost as glorious as when we celebrated our leader's birthday on March 6. His wife's birthday and year were exactly the same, but it was *his* years we all cheered over. Louisa cheered too and said on more than one occasion that her husband was nearly as blessed as our Savior. I wondered if all wives see their husbands as such. She didn't even want us mentioning the day of her birth. My mother said she was a saint, Louisa was, and such a model of a wife and mother.

Perhaps.

The table now looked complete, and Louisa signaled to our leader the readiness.

"Christian will ask the blessing," he said. This surprised me that our leader would permit another to speak on such a spirited occasion.

Christian stepped forward and clasped his hands in prayer, holding them before his straight, strong chest. People in our colony did not kneel to pray. We stood tall, our heads raised, our loyalty and worship given freely, not because it was required as it had been in the old country, in the old religion, but because we believed in our Lord and our leader and stood ready to move to follow both as required.

Christian closed his eyes, and yes, I know I should have too, as did other Bethelites gathered in the church, but the opportunity to watch him, without any others noticing or later chastising me for my boldness, was a gift as precious as the peppermints and twice as sweet.

Christian's words came first in German, to make us feel at home, as one, though we are set apart. Then he spoke them all in English, for it was the language of our adopted nation, a language I'd just begun to learn. "The Lord bless this bounty prepared by grateful hands whose duty is set to minister to others. We thank the Lord for this provision, as for all provision. May we follow Your directives always to worship You and live in Christian love and not false luxury."

He paused then. I thought to add more of what our leader might have said about our colony. Instead, I watched as he turned slightly and searched the crowd. He found my eyes. He smiled, winked, nodded once, and then he said, "Amen."

———

The meal filled our stomachs. I watched as Helena, Christian's sister, laughed with her brother. I hungered as Christian clicked his heels in recognition of one of Helena's friends, closer to Christian's age than I. The Giesys were of Swiss descent, prudent, hard-working, and wise. I served meals and talked with friends, always aware of where my soul was anchored: to Christian, to his dark eyes, his promise of adventure taking him places far from Bethel.

I never once spoke to him. He was the favorite of so many. He never looked my way again, and so the wink became a question for me. Perhaps it hadn't happened.

Just before we'd set to leave, with Jonathan and David Jr. carrying out the *Strudel* pans, my mother and Catherine and Johanna bustling about making sure we left the church without a crumb beneath a table, and Louisa still skipping with Aurora, I noticed Christian Giesy stood beside my father. I straightened my shoulders, hoping it made me look older. I walked to the men then, bold as a bull calf, and heard my father say "trouble." I wondered if they spoke of Shelbina, but then Papa said, "move one more time," and I knew they must be talking of a new colony somewhere. Michael Forstner, a friend of my father's and a carpenter, had built up four colonies already following our leader, most in Pennsylvania: Harmony and Phillipsburg and New Harmony in Indiana, and then Bethel in Missouri. My father spoke often of the intricacies of keeping our colonists separated from the world's influences while still allowing commercial interaction that sustained us all. Our grain and gloves and whiskey were sold to outsiders. We sometimes even talked of mulberry trees and silk production just as those at Harmony did. Harmony was the colony where discord reigned, and my father seceded from it along with all the Giesys, eventually finding our leader to follow to Missouri.

Then I heard my father say to Christian something about "asking for trouble," and before I could lick the peppermint from my lips, that handsome friend of my father's turned to me. He clicked his heels as though a Swiss soldier and bowed at his waist. "Your father consents to my walking you home, should you concur," he said. "Though he warns me of the trouble."

"Trouble is the needle God uses to stitch us into finer quilts," I said before I could censure the spicy words as they rose through the tightness in my throat.

"I warn you," my father told Christian with raised eyebrows, but also with a smile.

We started off walking past the houses that inside were filled with celebrating Bethelites. I hardly heard a word Christian said, aware more of how close he stood, how the backs of our hands barely brushed, yet I could feel the heat of them like hot rocks my mother placed at the foot of our bed to warm the sheets of my sisters and me. Once I nearly stumbled in the snow, and Christian caught my elbow but in an instant released it, keeping chaste as required. He spoke a little of his journeys into Kentucky. I merely listened, hoping he'd not ask questions of me. What in my life was worthy of sharing with so important and so fine a man twenty years my senior? My feelings bounced like bells in a strong wind.

We sauntered toward the sawmill, past brick houses. Up the incline stood Elim, the large three-story home of our leader set up like a castle on a hill. We would walk to it later, and on the second floor, everyone would gather. Suddenly, our leader rushed out of the Latimer *Haus* toward us, his white napkin still tugging at his throat as he strode to where we stood.

"Chris, it is *gut* you have passed by. Ve have much to talk about. I'm finished eating here, so come, ve go to Elim."

Christian smiled at him. "Wilhelm, can it not wait until—"

"You rush along now, Emma Wagner," our leader said, shooing his hands at me as though I were his chicken. "Catch up with your father and brothers and stop bothering Mr. Giesy. He has little time to look after girls who fall behind their families." He tugged at the tuft of hair below his chin kept separated from his beard. "Go, then. See, your father waits now."

I wondered what Christian would do to correct our leader's understanding of my annoying him. *Annoying him.* I pushed my shoulders back straight as a knitting needle.

"Wilhelm," Christian began, but our leader already headed up the hill toward his home. He rolled his arm as though inviting Christian to hurry along, refusing to look or listen to what anyone else had to say. He left his wife and children at Latimers' to fend their own way home.

Christian smiled at me, eyes sparkling and wistful as a boy's. But he shrugged his shoulders, lifted his palms, then pointed with his chin to my father. "Hurry along then, Emma Wagner. There must be trouble I need to tend to."

"*Ja,* there's trouble," I said as I turned my back to him before I had to watch him do the same.

I reasoned something as I stomped away: Keil, our leader, pronounced his own name in the English as *keel,* the word that means the backbone of a vessel. He saw himself as a keel, that portion of a boat's structure which runs from bow to stern and to which all else must attach to form the ship. It is what keeps the ship afloat. But in German the word does not mean "keel," but "wedge" instead, something that splits, heavy like an anchor piercing the sea to hold the ship or keep it from moving forward. As I turned to see the back of Christian walking from me, I began that day to wonder if Father Keil would form a wedge in what I wanted for my future.

2

Dancing Over

"Remember the old German proverb," my mother said later as I sniffled about my budding romance so early thwarted by Father Keil. "Begin to weave / God provides the thread."

I nodded, though unsure of what that meant. Should I spend my time weaving and hope something good would come of my creations when I gave them away? Or did it mean that I should just begin, take my stand, and God would provide whatever was needed to serve His purpose? I let my mother wipe at my tears and cheer me as she said, "There's always the New Year's dance."

Waltzing is allowed by our leader, as are the colony's many festive days, though I suspect Father Keil didn't expect Christian to dance with the likes of me. I know that now. Following the wedge he placed between us on Christmas Day, I neither saw nor heard about Christian's activities for an entire week. I'd said nothing when my father raised his eyebrows as I caught up with my parents Christmas morning, and my mother merely handed me a handkerchief when I failed to hold back tears. But later, gaining rhythm, I threw off my brother's teasing that I'd been left behind like an old potato. "*Ja,* little you know about making stew," I said. "Potatoes, even old ones, give stew substance."

He wrinkled his brows. "What does—"

"Never mind," I said and hurried up the stairs to the loft room I shared with my three sisters, where if I was lucky and the girls played downstairs, I could smooth my rebuff in private.

But midweek, my mother's word of weaving brought hope. So on New Year's Day, with the Missouri winter pining for spring, I thought of dancing. We'd have a celebration later that evening with the brass band playing full force in Elim, the largest house in the colony, where our leader lived and where we often gathered for dances next to his octagonal music room. I had hoped, prayed too, that Christian might ask me to dance at least once, assuming he attended and hadn't been sent off again by our leader to some faraway place to gain additional converts. I revisited each thing he'd said, remembered the tingling of my skin as I recalled the closeness of our hands. Words formed into music as I beat our rugs beneath the opaque sky, then brought the handwoven carpets inside.

To touch the face / Of one so dear / Is like music / Falling on one's ear.
I knew the words were not at all like the elegant music of Papa's second cousin—mine too—Richard Wagner, who couldn't even hear his opera *Lohengrin* performed the year before because he displeased the German government. Franz Liszt conducted instead. Maybe music and dissent mixed in my ancestral blood, though it didn't help me carry a tune. But so mixed passion, too, as Cousin Wagner was a romantic man and so was my father. Even my uncle was an American ambassador to France, that most romantic of lands. My mother still wore beneath her dark high-collared dress a tiny strand of pearls my father must have given her. I'd glimpsed it once before she discreetly tucked it away, blushing as she did.

Later, after New Year's, I'd help my mother store the few Christmas decorations we kept up until Epiphany. I most loved the tiered carving of the Christmas story, each layer a circle, with wooden shepherds on the bottom, then on the shelf above them, wise men, and finally Joseph and Mary with the Christ child on top. The whole structure stood on the floor, and each level spun in circles by the heat of candles moving wooden flaps. My mother had brought it from Germany with her. I'd never seen one in any other colony home, and we were only allowed to display it during this season. Putting it away always marked the end of a celebrating time and then the beginning of the long wait for spring.

Sheppie barked, and I went to the window expecting to see a squirrel scampering. I instead delighted in watching Christian make his way through the melting snow to my father's house. I'd begun to think his little invitation to venture into "trouble" with me on Christmas Day was nothing but a *Peltz Nickel* treat with a twig attached: a promise of a treasure but with a punishment, too. But now, here he appeared, and me with dust fluffs hanging from my dress!

Seeing him stride up the steps onto the porch, his head almost touching the corner filigree, made me forget the punishment part. I pitched aside disappointment brought on by our leader's interruption on Christmas Day. The dust fluffs were forgotten too.

Christian struck the porch post, knocking mud from his half-boot ankle jacks, then he bent to unlace them. Sheppie barked a happy bark, his gray tail wagging like a metronome, his nails scraping across the pine floor, meeting my father approaching the door. The shepherd dog acted as though he knew the man when he surely didn't. But the dog's delight pleased me, and I felt myself emboldened enough to pull back the simple curtain covering our windows and stare out at Christian, willing him to look at me.

He didn't.

"Your beau's here," Jonathan said from behind me.

I turned and shushed him with my chin stuck out and a grit of my teeth. "He's here to see Papa, no doubt," I said, though I hoped I told a lie.

My father answered the door when Christian knocked, and for a moment I wondered if Christian would take offense at the lavish garlands of greens I'd woven dried berries into and hung around the room. I'd set candles in such a way that they, too, looked inviting and shimmered against the wooden cabinet in which my mother kept her good dishes that even today she had not pulled out. It was far from a simple great room, with the festive boughs acting like necklaces, candles flickering, and the fire crackling at the end of the house. Both Catherine and Johanna worked with thread and needles in their laps while Louisa napped. Books spread across the table and on the divan, and I wondered if that would upset him, since our leader didn't care much for books unless they offered practical advice for making better whiskey or gaining higher yields from fields. A colorful purple and green Wandering Foot quilt almost shouted its lavish comfort. Would Christian think us too worldly?

I stepped in front of the wooden Christmas tier to keep him from seeing its fine carving, just in case. My little ruffle, still stitched to my crinoline, seemed heavier. I had yet to remove it.

The smell of my mother's baked cinnamon buns permeated the air. At least good scents were not forbidden in a German colony.

Christian seemed not to notice any of his surroundings. He entered in stocking feet against my father's protest that the floor easily cleaned and he could keep his boots on. Instead, he set the boots with heels precise against the wall, then accepted my father's offer of ale. He didn't even acknowledge me as he bent to pet Sheppie.

My father ushered him into the dining room. "Come along, Jonathan," he told my brother, acting as though I were nothing but a candle stand.

Apparently, if I was to hear the conversation or even share Christian's presence, it would be as a serving woman unless I did something about it.

"I'd be interested in hearing what Mr. Giesy has to say about his travels," I said.

My father turned, frowned. "In the kitchen, your mother needs you."

"*Ja,* I'm sure," I said, "but—"

"Emma…"

Jonathan grinned as he marched by me and motioned to David and even little William to join him with the men.

I couldn't overhear them in the kitchen. When I brought in trays of tea to offer, they looked serious as I slowly served them, my brothers included, sitting stiff as bedposts. None of them even acknowledged my presence with a simple nod of thanks. All this men's talk apparently meant Christian truly had come only to see my father.

"They'll pass laws against communal living," Christian said. "And this will not be good for us."

"We're not like those…others," my father said. "We don't share our wives or husbands. We don't all live in one huge house. We're happy, giving to each other in a Christian way. Why should the government care?"

"Sometimes we do, though, live in one house. The bachelors who come with no family to stay with. And until we build them homes, new recruits and whole families do live with others."

"*Ach,* that is just family," my father said. "You have generations living in the Giesy house. It is nothing wrong."

"All we earn we put into one place, communally. All of Bethel's land is in Wilhelm's name, no one else's. This bothers some officials who see such commonness as…against the nation. They wonder if our loyalty is to our leader rather than to the country, and with the rumblings of war...*ja,* well, they might think we long to become our own country inside this new American state of Missouri."

"Wilhelm would change that in a moment if asked," my father said. "He does not keep the land for himself, only for the good of us all." My father's voice rose.

"I know this, David," Christian countered. He reached for my father's hand and patted it with assurance. Christian had fine, high cuticles, and his nails were white as piano ivory. "But outsiders, they don't understand. It seems strange to them, how we do things here. We are foreign to them, more German than American."

"When you recruit, are you able to win hearts for our Lord?" my father asked.

Christian nodded yes. "But it is harder to describe the necessity for all of us to live in one colony with one storehouse to fill and only one to take from. People wonder why our Lord asks us to live so... communally—"

"When all around us yearn for things, for new dresses, big horses, more fields to call their own," I said and continued before they could stop me. "We prosper by meeting those very needs we say we don't believe in. We sell whiskey and gloves and lumber to those who do not live as we do. I don't understand that either."

Even Jonathan's eyes grew wide. My father frowned. "Emma..."

"What she says I have thought too," Christian said. He sat straighter in the high chair and stared at me, elbows out as his palms rested on his thighs. "It seems a contradiction to separate ourselves and then to take gain from the sales to the fallen world."

He considered something I said important?

"But we do not get rich from it," my father protested. "Only enough to serve one another comes into the storehouse. We tend widows, orphans, no matter if they are colonists or not. That is our mission."

"But perhaps it's tainted," I said, pushing my good fortune. "How do we look to those we seek to convert? Maybe it appears as though we recruit to *our* way rather than to God's."

"Wilhelm's way has led us to our Lord well these years," my father said. He snapped the words out. He pointed toward the kitchen door. "Emma. Your mother has need of you."

"But, Papa—"

"Go."

I threw a glance at Christian, but he looked lost in thought, and once again he seemed unwilling or unable to challenge orders given me by other men. Never mind that one was my father, a respected elder, and the other our spiritual leader. Christian needed to stand firm, I thought, as the door to the kitchen swung shut behind me, bumping the ruffle beneath my skirt.

"I'll bake bread," I told my mother, slamming down the tea tray.

"Now?"

"It will give me something to push around and pound," I said, gathering flour into the doughboy and reaching for salt from the box.

"Well, a house can always use bread."

The fluff of the flour and the saleratus with melted lard seeped into the flour hole I'd made and kept me occupied, if not pleased. I tried not to think of Christian Giesy as being someone weak, easily overpowered by my father. He stood so tall, had brought in too many new recruits to be a weak man. It was even rumored that every day he lifted himself seventy-five times from the floor by his hands without letting his knees even touch. It took strength for such pushing up, strength that must reflect a man of character, too. Even Karl Ruge, the teacher, a highly educated man and a Lutheran still, chose to live in the colony because of Christian's enthusiasm and ability to express our views of love and service to one another. And everyone adored Karl—many admired his fine mind and his long clay pipe.

And yet, and yet, what is a man if he cannot put other men's wishes aside to tend to those of his beloved?

I imagined myself as Christian's beloved. *Ach,* I thought. *You are a Dummkopf.* That's what my father would say. I shook my head and knuckled the dough, imagining the conversation going on without me, imagining life going on without me, farther away, in Shelbina or maybe even Independence.

We Bethel colonists were asked to be in service, to treat others as we wished to be treated, and to go beyond, to help others live even better than we did. The Diamond Rule our leader called it, better even than the Golden Rule. And yet while women served, our voices were rarely heard except in music. Did not our Lord wash the feet of His disciples? Did not our Lord comfort those who grieved? Is that not what women do? And yet we are not invited into the halls of discussion, we are not asked to sit around the tables and talk with men making sense of a family's future. No, we are asked to influence *through* our fathers and our brothers and our sons but never *with* them.

"I hope that's not my head you're thinking of. You knead that dough with such vigor." Christian had stepped into the kitchen, his body dwarfing the doughboy table.

I wiped my forehead with the back of my palm. His height seemed out of place, but his voice fit here, low and calm and smooth as melted butter. "Or if it is, perhaps you'll exchange it for a chance at my feet this evening. Your father consents to my squiring you to the dance, should you be willing."

"And will something more come between us?" I asked, my hands on my hips now.

"Emma," my mother gasped. "Rude you must not be."

"She gives it fairly," Christian said. "I'll do my best to see I give her little more reason to express it."

How could I refuse?

———

This dance held a special tone as it announced the New Year, new beginnings. The year 1852 held prosperity, as Father Keil had already received orders for special wagons made for traveling overland to the Oregon Territory. Whole towns in the Ohio Valley and farther east had signed up to go west, and, hearing of our furniture factory and wagon-building and our colony being so close to Independence and even closer to St. Joseph, many commissioned us to build them sturdy wagons. Even colony women would assist with the construction in order to meet the demand.

It was our practice that as colony work required more effort, each set aside plowing or candle-making and put all hands toward the greatest need, men and women working side by side. "Ve build many vagons this year," our leader told us, and so we would.

Future prosperity lent a festive air to this occasion, and our leader charmed the crowd chattering and eating, paying scant attention to Christian and me. The band played and I watched Willie, our leader's oldest son, step forward and execute a solo on his horn. He twirled himself around so dancers stopped to watch him, including his father, including us. People applauded, clapped Willie on his back as he finished, and shouted out hurrahs from across the large room. A few men drank small glasses of our colony's Golden Rule Whiskey, and women not dancing or serving or watching after children sat in groups, their dark flannels reminding me of clusters of grapes waiting to be plucked.

Christian and I completed a *Schottische,* a pleasant dance with hops and easy twirls, but one that required a man place his hands across a woman's shoulders as they skipped side by side. Christian's hands felt smooth as river stones. The warmth that spread all through me as his palm squeezed mine surprised. He pulled me to him and smiled. I could have spent the entire night this way.

But after the fourth dance, we moved toward the door, where people coming in and out admitted a coolness. I couldn't help but notice the envy in the eyes of girls my age, as I'd spent my whole time with an important man just a year younger than my father. Even when men came by to talk to him, he allowed me to remain, didn't shoo me off, though most of the talk was of Christian's journeys and when he might leave again or about his tin shop and what work he could complete before he left. I never offered a single word, careful not to embarrass him. In our colony, listening was a valued skill, at least for women.

Willie played another solo, this one with even more gusto.

"People say one day Willie will be our leader," Christian said, leaning in to me as we stood still later with our backs against the wall.

"I doubt that," I told him. "He's too fun-loving, wants attention for himself."

"Possibly," Christian said. "But a leader needs to demonstrate enthusiasm in order to have followers. No one wants to be a disciple of a somber soul."

"Father Keil is far from…merry," I said. "Yet here we all are." I spread my arms wide.

"Wilhelm is joyous and kind, Emma. That's how we see him. He has the music, the band. He reminds us that we find abundance in living simply."

"Living simply," I said, disgust in my voice. I still had the ruffle attached, and I decided at that moment I would simply leave it there.

I'd wash it at home, not at the communal washhouse. No one would ever discover my interest in uniqueness.

"What else about Bethel distresses you?" Christian asked. He'd cocked his head to the side and had a wry smile on his face.

"You want my opinion?"

His eyes held mine and he sobered. I noticed that the color of his mustache bore tints of red. "I should know the things that cause unrest in you," he said, his voice as smooth as hot cider, "if you're to be my wife."

I felt my stomach fall into my knees.

Catching my breath I said, "The word *if* looms large."

"Indeed, *if* is larger. As with my dancing, I can step over that word rather than on it," Christian said, "and make the request without venturing further into what brings you happiness or strife. It surprises—"

"No, no," I said. "I want to be asked my thoughts. *Ja,* I do. Will my answers make a difference to the offer? It was an offer, *ja?* Or do I misunderstand?" My words twirled around, caught up now with my feelings like a kite string swirling upward in the wind. "Have you asked our leader? my father?" I didn't want to get my hopes up. I already knew Christian could be easily dissuaded by either of these two men.

"Your father has concurred. Wilhelm has not." I looked away. "Indeed, he knows nothing of it," Christian said, his hand patting mine in reassurance. "I did not wish to begin that…dance until I knew you would step with me. Your father's agreed first. Then if you say to proceed, I will approach Wilhelm. He is a kindly man despite what you may think, Emma. So I believe by his birthday celebration, we will be allowed to announce to all our marital intentions. God willing. You, being willing. You have yet to say if I can step over the *if.*"

"*Ja,*" I said. "I agree to be your wife, no ifs. But when the engagement is complete and we have answered our leader's probing, I hope you'll still be pleased with your offer."

"He doesn't interrogate, Emma. He asks to be sure that husbands and wives will be happy to be together for life. It is his duty as a leader to inquire."

"*Ja*, sure," I said, knowing it wouldn't be the last time Christian Giesy and his future wife would see the world through very different eyes.

We completed the evening with not another word about our future. It was hardly a romantic declaration, all wrapped up in talk of civics and ascendancy. And yet wasn't that what I'd been aching for, to have conversations between men and women, express words that did more than tease the mind? No, I'd been aching to be truly seen by Christian, to be known not as "one of the colony women wearing faded flannel and her hair parted in the center," but as someone another might pick out from a crowd.

Now that he had, I felt lightheaded: I might actually receive what I wanted. I'd begun to weave, and God had just handed me the finest yet most foreign of threads.

3

A Ring
Around the Fire

Youth claims perfect pitch and often fails to note disharmony. When I
told my mother of Christian's intentions, she smiled and held me, her
apron comforting with *Sauerkraut* smells. "I know," she said. "Your
father forewarned me, though he didn't tink what you might say."

"You never saw my interest?" I asked my father later as he drank
strong tea at the head of the table.

My father merely raised an eyebrow, his "well, well," look, the same
he gave me when as a child I asked some question about why sheep's
wool held heavy oils or when I urged him to tell me something I didn't
already know. I suppose he welcomed my inquisitive nature, knew in
advance the challenge Christian's life would have for me, both encouraging it and tempering it.

Jonathan sounded the only sour note I heard. "What's Christian
Giesy see in you?"

"*Ach,* Jonathan," my mother cautioned. "Be happy for your sister,
ja?"

Jonathan grunted as he cut his sausage, popped a section in his
mouth. "He's a tinsmith with the gift of gab," he said. "Think of how
many girls he's been exposed to. Why would he settle for you?" I don't
think he meant to hurt my feelings, and in truth, he said out loud what

would have eventually made its way into my consciousness. But until then, I saw Christian's interest as an answer to my prayers, as a tapestry God saw fit to stitch together: two hearts, two hands, two souls hemmed by faith.

"Do you think Father Keil will forbid it?" David Jr. said. He held his fork midair above his egg. "There is something noble in being a bachelor, I think."

"Why should he?" I asked. "Papa's approved. And Christian is beloved by Father Keil. He wants him to be happy."

"He didn't think of it himself, though," Jonathan said. "Father Keil likes to be in charge of all things. A good leader is, sister. Willie told me that."

My father corrected. "It's a leader's duty to have authority, but this does not mean power used for personal views. He doesn't think he must order everything, Jonathan. Maybe Willie chomps at the reins the way young men do. Willie's time will come."

"It will be a strange marriage with Christian leaving again soon," Jonathan said. "That's his way, his work."

"I'll not hear any more contrary thoughts." I put hands over my ears. "Not from you or anyone else." I left the room.

Christian and I agreed not to say anything outside our families until receiving our leader's blessings. I didn't know what the Giesy family thought of me, though it seemed that Helena was more distant in the classroom, where we helped Karl Ruge, than she'd been before. She acted more formal, but I might have been imagining that. I have an active imaginary life, which led me to wonder if Christian's absence after New Year's was planned or happenstance. Either way, Jonathan proved himself clairvoyant. Christian and I had had no time together since he stated his intentions. But then, he was a busy man, had always been.

He met with our leader and the men's council, a group of twelve who advised about the happenings at Nineveh, an offshoot colony near Hannibal, where we ran a ferry and a steam mill that powered huge textile looms. The men advised about work at Bethel too. Christian was often gone, but I felt sure he'd return for our leader's birthday. It was always a grand affair. I prayed for patience.

Two days before our leader's birthday, Christian again knocked on our door, Sheppie's happy wagging tail expressing my thoughts completely. That day, I asked Christian about what my brother and sister said. We sat at my parents' house on a hard bench set before the fireplace while my family discreetly kept us within sight but out of hearing, my mother spinning and my father polishing a bridle to keep the leather soft. The boys stayed outside, and my sisters whispered in the rooms above us. I could almost imagine them hovering over the opening that allowed heat and sound to rise up through the ceiling. Christian had first spent an hour with my father, telling news that he'd gathered on his travels, leaving me to eavesdrop.

Outside our great-room windows, tiny buds of crocus pushed their way up through the soil, and already robins sat on the porch rails, watching for early worms. The dog slept at my feet. Then at last I had him to myself, after a fashion.

"What did I see in you to make me want you for my wife?" Christian repeated my question. "Your kind spirit, indeed. And your willingness to question even when there might be…consequences. These are good qualities. Necessary for learning, my friend Karl says, necessary for change."

I hadn't thought of myself as unusually kind and said so.

"Remember New Year's Day?" Christian told me.

How could I forget? "It was the day you asked me to be your wife."

"Yes, yes. But more," Christian said. "In the corner of Elim where we gathered sat a woman with three children huddled around her. She was not of us."

I thought back. Yes, there'd been a woman who piled her hair on top of her head in an Apollo knot, the false hairpiece standing up behind the center part instead of in a chignon at the back as we colony woman wore ours. She wore fancy clothes, cloth with new dye, something else that made her different. The rest of us dressed in flannels or woolen dresses, clean but well-faded. New cloth was seen as a luxury we made and sold, unless one had worn out a dress and had already turned it into strips for rugs or repatterned it for a child's gown.

Louisa Keil, our leader's wife, pulled her dark woolen shawl tighter around her as she knelt at that woman's feet. She patted the woman's knee, talking quietly to her. The woman nodded, wiping at her eyes with a handkerchief. Louisa looked up, and spying Christian and me— had I detected a frown?—she motioned us over.

"You're good with *Kinder*," she said to me, nodding to the children. "Help them join in with the others, give their mother a bit of rest."

I remembered that the children's mother wore bruises on her cheek and lip, and I assumed she was one of many women whom the colonists took in to help as they made their escapes from harsh men. Some remained and joined us; others recovered and moved on, often returning to the men who'd harmed them, a choice I never could fathom. I'd taken her children and we'd played Ring-around-the-Rosy, with all of us falling down in heaps, serenaded by their peals of cautious laughter.

"I remember the woman's bruises," I said. Sheppie's tail thumped the floor at the sound of my voice. "I wonder at times if our offering help to such people makes us suspect to other Missourians. We colonists step into the middle of a fray, act as servants to those in need, but such work can cause resentments."

Christian nodded. Missouri was a slave state, but on the border with freer territories, and many people didn't own slaves here. There'd been talk of repealing that compromise that allowed Maine to enter as a free state and Missouri as a slave. Perhaps Missourians feared our colony would harbor escaped slaves, since we rescued broken women. I wasn't sure that we wouldn't. Maybe that was why there'd been discussion about the colony moving again. We danced around issues, and sometimes we stepped on someone else's toes.

"The children, they were so frightened; so many changes."

"You answered Louisa's call without hesitation. You were selfless. This is good. It tells me you can see beyond your own needs to those of others. I had seen this before in you."

His praise warmed me to my toes, and I vowed to give him more reason for such words, though vows among the young are often soon forgotten. "And what else?"

"Those questions," he said. "You ask…pointed questions, a sign your mind keeps working. Just as now, about slave and free. And you're persistent when you want a thing."

"Stubborn, my father says." I felt my cheeks grow warm.

"Indeed." Christian smiled and lifted my hand, placing it in his. I waited for him to give me an example that I could cherish ever after, but instead he said, "And you are beautiful," the words a whisper. "Beautiful as God has made you without adornment. So my admiration for your form, my filling up by looking at you, watching you float across the room as graceful as a swan, causes no challenge to our need to set aside all but simplicity and what is useful. You cannot help how you've been formed." With his other hand he drew his finger around the outline of my lips, an act so surprising that his touch sent shivers through me, past the chignon that gathered at my neck. I swallowed and thought of Saint Paul's words about marriage being better than to burn, about the rocks that must surround such fire or it would flame across a field, taking everything in its path.

My mother coughed, and he dropped his hand from my face as though he'd been stung.

Some days later I told Jonathan that my intended saw the good in me, a loving heart. "Ha," Jonathan said. "The man is blinded then," but the sparkle in his eyes told me he teased.

"By my beauty," I told him, flipping my fingers at my ears. It was an idea still settling in my mind.

My brother softened then. "That you are, sister. That you are."

My only regret from my conversation with Christian was that I wanted to share what in him appealed to me, but he never asked.

Fireworks marked March 6, as always, it being Father Keil's birthday. Our leader chose it as the time for our discussion of our marriage.

It was to be a simple declaration of our intentions so that we might begin to tell others of our plans. I saw myself as a person seeking the sonata rather than the dirge. I held on to those notes now.

I knew the rules, of course, about unions among the colonists or outsiders. Father Keil raised few objections, however, if a man became engaged to marry an outsider, as it was believed she would eventually join the colony, accept the colony's ways, and consent would be freely given to their nuptials. She would move in with his family until a home could be built, but at least the couple could begin or continue to work without the colony having to take time out to build a house for them. The man almost always had a meaningful job within the colony already, or he wouldn't be a Bethelite. His intended bride would soon find her place in worthy work.

Women finding men outside created a different problem: even if Father Keil approved their marriage with the man's intention to join us, the building of their house would take labor from other valued work: farming, the furniture factory, our Bethel Plow manufacturing, and this year, building wagons. And should the couple later choose to leave, this new man who had not contributed all his life nor had a family do so before him would require compensation, something our leader offered anyone who later settled out. Men received money for each year of service to the colony whether or not they'd brought wealth in to the common fund; married women received half of what men received for each year of service.

Christian assured me that since we were both of longstanding families, Father Keil would have little objection to our marrying.

We arrived separately to put off wagging tongues. I spoke with Louisa on the main, or family, floor as she mended little Aurora's torn skirt. She didn't ask me about my appointment. Neither did she raise her eyes when, with the arrival of Christian, I stood and climbed the center staircase to Elim's third story.

Once there, Christian and I sat on tall hardback chairs and faced our leader in his office. The large room served as his laboratory, too, where he grew and experimented with healing herbs. People were healthy in Bethel; few had even a sniffle. When they did, our leader offered relief with his blends of teas or things to swallow or rub to bring about cures. Many in the surrounding community even asked for his slippery elm brew or peach tree bark concoctions. They all called him "Dr. Keil," a name that always brought a smile to his lips. It was rumored he'd once had a magical book that held healing potions, written in his own blood. But that was earlier, before he led us as a Christian colony.

Light streamed down through the clerestory windows that from the outside reminded me of an Indian's eyes, narrow. Those third-story openings were barely a third of the size of those on the first and second floors, and they were high above so we couldn't look out through them to the spring beyond.

Father Keil's chair, on a platform behind a heavy walnut desk, would have resembled a throne if the desk hadn't been there. Leaders in Germany lived in castles, had thrones…it was expected of a colony leader, not something meant to be ostentatious.

Or so I told myself.

His forearms rested on the desk, hands folded as in prayer.

It was my first visit to this room. A single bookshelf held titles about medicines and plants. Wooden bowls and pestles perched neatly on a long table off to the side. The room felt almost steamy on this warm March morning, what with all the plants and earth readied to be set out as soon as any threat of a freeze had ceased.

Our leader's eyes looked tired as we waited for him to begin. I thought perhaps as this was his fortieth year, he might be weary of the celebrations of his birth and the fireworks that crackled every now and then. Men seem generally less interested in fusses made over birthdays, or so my father always said when my mother tried to do something special on his day.

"So," Father Keil began when the last singing hiss of a firecracker faded. "You wish to marry."

I knew enough to remain silent until after Christian spoke, though it surprised me that our leader already knew. Christian must have told him. Or rumors spread despite our trying to keep it quiet. Christian told him about conferring with my father and then with me and now with him, how he had prayed about this union and felt God answered after all this time his desire for a workmate by raising me before his eyes.

"You might have talked to me first, Chris," Keil told Christian. "It would have saved this…disharmony now, as you will surely see it." He looked at me for the first time.

My heart began to pound. Fear like a startled cat pounced on my chest. I hoped I didn't whimper out loud. Our leader sighed deeply, turned back to Christian. "I see no good thing to come of this union, Chris."

I nearly bit my tongue through to hold my words in my mouth. I hiccupped. Both men looked at me, then Christian went on as though he hadn't heard what our leader had said.

"She has a loving spirit. I've seen her kindness. Indeed, I've watched her grow into a young woman of substance. Even my sister Helena comments on Emma's good way with the children. She helps with the *Kinder,* so my sister sees firsthand this woman's strengths. 'Suffer the little children to come unto me,' our Lord said. Children know a person's heart, Wilhelm."

"But they lack judgment, *ja?* Until they've grown. Emma is not grown, and she will bring your work down as you must pause to raise her."

Could smoke come from one's ears? Could a heart explode like the firecrackers outside?

"She will be a good mother to my children," Christian said, his eyes lowered now.

"But this is exactly my concern, Chris. You are nearly my age, and to begin now with a family will take you from the work you're called to just when we need you most." He said the word *just* as though it were *yust,* and for the first time I wished we were speaking in German instead of English and wondered why that was so on such an austere occasion. Maybe he knew I had trouble understanding English, even more to speak well in it. Did he intend to demean me before my beloved's eyes? "You will have a woman to worry over, a family. There'll be the need to build a house for you when you should be off recruiting."

He actually thought I would interfere, that I would not support my husband's work? He didn't know me or know my heart. I started to speak, but he held his hand up to stop me as though I were a mule pushing too close to the one in front of it.

"Chris, you are a good man whose strength lies in your compassionate spirit toward our people and a fire that burns for God." He switched to German now. "That fire brings new people to His way. Your life tells the story again and again to people seeking to live according to the Golden Rule, to give one's all to God, and through that, to each other. Look whom you have brought to this colony. Karl Ruge, among others, a man of great wisdom whose practical teachings enhance our youth. He nurtures ideas of invention, just like how we solved problems when we lacked a way to bring water to the fields. Remember? You helped design the special drills to bore holes through the center of the logs to act as pipes. As inventive as the Romans and their aqueducts. But this takes a singular mind of care for others. I know this. I must keep my own family's needs as well as the entire colony, and it is a trial, *ja,* a trial. One our Lord has given me, and only a strong man so anointed can endure. Now, more than ever, with the words of Daniel coming closer, telling us how human conditions will end, we need you and only you to continue as a singular flame for God, Chris, not as a man burdened with family."

I hated that he called him Chris, as though he did not deserve the full use of his own name, as though our leader could ignore a name given at his birth that spoke of who he was and would ever be, Christian. The scent of green plants growing in this warm third-story floor seemed suddenly overpowering. The smell of earth, while usually so inviting, smelled of decay to me now. Our leader stood, revealing his long black coat hanging funereally to his knees.

"She may be good with the *Kinder,* but it's because she is one." He acted as though I were one of his plants that could neither hear nor feel. "In the glove factory, she makes games and distracts. I have seen her toss turnips in the fields as though they were balls for the dogs to retrieve. She is too interested in those who travel to Shelbina, too interested in what is not here at home. These are signs too, Chris, signs I cannot ignore. I tell them to you out of love. For you both. Your union would be wrought with fractures no glue could repair. At the first sign of a trial, you would seek to separate, and this would not be a good witness to the colony."

I wanted to tell my part, defend myself, and reassure Father Keil that I could be in service to my husband and this colony. Disagreement wasn't a sign of rebellion, only wisdom. Were not we Germans known for seeking knowledge? And what of joy? We held dances, our band played for entertainment, so what was wrong with my donning gloves like a rooster top to hop around the factory floor? People laughed, and what was un-Christian about that in the midst of work?

Christian leaned forward, his hands folded together, his forearms resting on his thighs. My heart pounded. He remained silent, and it took all I could not to stand up, say what I wanted him to say. But I had agreed and would show my discipline was as good as…our leader's.

A clock ticked in the silence. Then Christian stood, eye to eye with our leader. He turned to me. I saw a pain there I hadn't seen before. I felt my heart pound, sure that he would say now that he agreed with our leader and dash my hopes for a long and abiding love.

But Christian addressed our leader, though he held my eyes. "I believe you are in error, Wilhelm. I believe your error comes from a good heart, one that honors me with your confidence that I do good things. But I do so with God's help. Indeed, I did not bring in Karl Ruge to teach our children English. God did. I did not bring in new Scots-Irish recruits from Kentucky and Tennessee. God did this. And I believe that God has given me a future wife in Emma Wagner, whose father you so entrusted with our colony that you sent him out to find this Bethel, this "place of God," this "place of worship," as the Hebrew word translates. She's been raised in our ways and knows them—"

"She challenges them," our leader said.

"But she will keep the vows and understands what I am called to do," Christian countered.

Our leader puffed up his chest then. "You will defy me, Chris, over this…this trivial thing?"

"Wilhelm, please. I have no wish to drive a wedge between us. There is a compromise. Emma turns eighteen on the twenty-seventh of this month. We would set the date for then and pray you will be the one to officiate. We will discuss this again when you've had time to pray and consider. Come, Emma. Let's go, give Wilhelm time to prepare for his celebration."

How I wanted to have my say, but for once I chose to be right in silence. And my intended had stood firm and had even named a date, though I would have preferred to have some say in that. To witness a birthday and a wedding anniversary on the same occasion robbed a woman of one celebration. And in a world where there were few, I meant to have as many as I could.

I followed Christian out, feeling the eyes of our leader boring a hole into my back. "We can announce our wedding, then?" I said when we reached the empty second-floor gathering room.

"No," he said. "I want Wilhelm's blessing. It will be better if he comes around, if he sees that we have chosen and he cannot stop us. The colony will be the better if he too is in agreement."

"And if he doesn't ever give his consent?"

On the stair landing, he pulled me to him and kissed the top of my forehead. It was the first touch of his lips upon my skin. "We will marry, Emma. But we'll keep this quiet for now. Agreed?"

"*Ja,*" I said, not wanting to be the first to pull away from the firmness of his embrace.

I'd remain silent, but I went home and sewed another ruffle on my crinoline.

4

Choose Life

Right after our meeting, our leader sent Christian on a mission that took him away on my birthday and on the supposed wedding day. But he encouraged Christian before he left by telling him that when he returned in April, we could discuss our marriage possibility again. I suspected he would use the interim time to watch me, so I wore my best behavior. In the glove factory in the afternoons, I stayed to myself, working hard to finish off the deerskin gloves with the finest stitches. Our colony's gloves had won awards in competitions at exhibitions back East, and I liked to think my work contributed. Father Keil made a fine time of hunting the many herds of deer in this part of Missouri, having the meat for our common meals and the hides for the factory. I thought again how blessed men were to do the things they loved yet name their acts as practical and thus always permitted.

Secretly, I didn't mind not having the wedding on my birthday. I could be open about the date as long as the event would happen. Being flexible about accomplishing a thing was always optional, I felt, as long as everyone could agree upon the outcome. Half the time people argued over how to do a thing more than whether it should be done at all. I thought the latter to be the topic of greater importance. If only people would take the time to voice their desires, others could assist them in achieving them; that was my motto.

Christian's absence made me think of him all the more. During the noon break at school, I prompted Helena to talk of her older brother, but she spoke instead of her own choice long years before, to give up the love of her life, the son of the man who would later design the Brooklyn Bridge and who later built his own suspension bridges.

"He was a good man, but we were not well matched."

"But you loved him, *ja?* Isn't that match enough?"

"He chose not to join the colony," Helena said. She swept the tile floor as we talked.

"Christian and I have no such barriers," I said. I wiped the face of a small child whose berry jam smeared across her face, then sent her on her way.

"True, you both share the faith," she said.

"Couldn't you have married Mr. Roebling anyway?" Her story was a legend in the colony, that she had chosen service to the colony over love. My sister Catherine especially admired Helena.

"Yes, but if two people do not share the same hopes, then discord will reign. They will be unequally yoked, as Scripture says."

"Nothing will rain on Christian and me," I chirped.

In silence she stacked the slate boards the children used, making a pile at the edge of the desk. She turned to me then, and I could see Christian's thoughtful eyes reflected in her face, his high forehead and strong jaw. "It does cause concern, your youth compared to his…experience. He's gained so much and given much, not being…hampered by a wife and children. He's important to the colony, Emma. Almost as much as Father Keil. If he marries you, Christian will have little time for…peevishness. We have been successful all these years because our leader knows how to put self aside in order to serve. I hope you consider this." She walked stiffly from the room.

I tried to remember when I had been peevish or irritable with Helena or any of her large family; or when I'd done something to suggest I didn't put others before myself. Nothing came to mind...except the ruffles that she knew nothing of and were of so little import, I couldn't imagine them being any real barrier to the safety of my soul.

I decided not to be peevish and argue after her. There'd be time enough to change her mind when I lived with the Giesys after we were married, while our home was being built.

At the second meeting with our leader, silence again became my first task, while our leader spoke a long prayer, seeking guidance and wisdom in this matter. Then while Christian and our leader quoted Scripture to each other, I bit my lip and stayed stiff as a boot hook. Our leader liked certain Old Testament words, and very few chapters from the New, except those that supported the common fund such as in Acts. He used them repeatedly in his sermons but always emphasized neighborly love, self-sacrifice, and prayer, and apparently he believed our marriage would do nothing to enhance those colony virtues.

Self-sacrifice. I knew that was what he wanted from Christian and from me. He wanted us to be like Helena, married to the values of the colony rather than each other. Sitting there, seeing those fiery eyes that made people believe whatever he said, I realized what he expected most of all: obedience. That we'd come a second time to even talk of our marriage must have challenged him. Few ever did. In that instant, I knew he'd never approve this union no matter how we felt. Convincing Christian to marry against our leader's wishes would be the greater task before me. He was second in command. Would he dare defy his spiritual leader?

This second inquisition without my being asked my opinion nor allowed to speak told me all I needed to know about what course I'd take next.

But then our leader turned to me. "Emma Wagner," he said, "I must speak to you of something you know nothing about but is important should you ever wish to marry." *Should I cajole him? Should I defy him? He holds more than authority here; he holds power.* "Do you understand the trials of childbirth, the pain of laboring, and the demand that follows?" He drew a hand up to silence Christian, who began to intervene. I sat like a rabbit with an owl above it.

"Of course," I said, gaining my voice. "I've helped at birthings."

"But not to watch the child agonize into the world," our leader said. "You were too young to see or to assist as your brothers and sisters arrived, too young to gain experience except to comfort little *Kinder* in the household. So let me advise." He made a tent of his fingers, leaned back in his high chair. "The infant presses against the smallest of bony places, where blood pours to weaken the woman as she writhes in pain. She pushes to bring forth this child, rising above the arc of searing torment." He lifted his eyes to the heavens as he spoke, raising his long arms to sweep over the arc he described. "I have witnessed nine such trying times with my own beloved Louisa. All this pain is created to remind women—even devout women like my Louisa—of their early sin. Sometimes," he almost whispered now, "small women do not live through this. Even with poultices to stop the bleeding, they die. Sometimes the infants die. The sins of the father are meted out onto their offspring and death results. You have not witnessed this, Emma Wagner. You are not prepared for this. I cannot have Chris marry a woman whose needs will overpower his work, a woman who could not endure the trials of Eve's first sin."

My face grew warm. I had no choice but to let my tongue speak out. All would be lost if I didn't; it was probably lost before I started. "Perhaps this childbirth pain suggests some flaw in God's design if the birth canal is so much smaller than an infant's head."

He gasped. "You blaspheme," he hissed, his eyes like black coal burning.

There was no going back. "I've heard that your herbs help relieve a woman in her time," I said, holding his stare. "Are you interfering then with God's design for the capture of each woman's soul?"

"Not now," Christian interrupted.

"You're quick with your words, Emma Wagner. But quick wit does not prepare you for life's tragedies. And these will come, mark my word. Mark God's words from Deuteronomy: 'I call heaven and earth to record this day against you, that I have set before you life and death, blessing and cursing—' "

" '—therefore choose life, that both thou and thy seed may live.' Deuteronomy 30:19." I finished the quote, ever grateful the words had not escaped my reading just that morning.

He actually stepped back. I didn't know what Christian might think of my quoting Scripture to our leader; I hesitated to take my eyes from those black accusing coals.

We heard shouts of children playing below us. Our leader's little bottles of tinctures rattled as he stepped from around his desk.

Christian cleared his throat. "You see, Wilhelm, she is called to be my wife and to bring forth my seed. She will look to the good of things and choose life. Is that not what we need? Is that not how the colony will truly grow, not just by new people coming to see our ways but by raising children up in the 'way that they should go'? This too is scriptural."

" 'Be fruitful, and multiply,' " I added.

Christian gave me a look, and I dropped my eyes. To our leader, I said, "I only meant to say that just because one has not experienced something doesn't mean one can't rise to meet the challenge when called to. I am up to the challenges of being a good wife within this colony."

Our leader's eyes focused on something high and behind us. "We may not have long life in this colony," he said finally. "I've told you, Chris, of my concerns, of the work we must do to ready our people. This woman will distract you."

"This woman will renew me."

Our leader clapped his hands then, startling both of us. At least I jerked in my seat. "You vill do vhat you vill do," he said. "I do not give my blessing. It will go against my belief about the rightness of this, but I vill not stand in your way. Marry in Shelby County if you are so inclined to set aside my visdom on this matter. But you may have the party here, at Elim, and have the marriage recorded in the membership book. On April 22. So be it. I have spoken."

"*Danke,* Wilhelm," Christian said, standing. "Thank you, so much. Come, Emma, we have taken up enough of Wilhelm's time."

I rose, confused. Father Keil withheld his blessing and would not marry us here in Bethel, yet he'd let a worldly judge pronounce the vows and then offer us a celebration later in his own home? The last surely marked some form of consent. Did it save face for him, show that he stood firm by refusing to officiate at a marriage he felt was doomed, yet allow him to be generous and showy through a party in his home?

My intended husband acted satisfied with this configuration, as twisted as a pig's tail.

I would not complain. The outcome would be as I wished it: I'd be Mrs. Christian Giesy and show our leader that one young and inexperienced woman could withstand the pangs of bringing forth new babies into life.

———

We married in the Shelby County courthouse. I had long imagined myself walking down the red-tile aisle of Bethel's church, Christian at my side, the colony as witness to our union. But the courthouse served us well, one of those adjustments to the stepping stones along a trail, if not the final destination. My family came with us, as did some of Christian's fourteen brothers and sisters—but not Helena. Even Karl Ruge stood there for Christian. Good friends and family then witnessed our vows and the new dress my mother sewed for me. She even allowed blinker curls to coil on either side of my rosy cheeks. A short muslin veil covered my face, and I wore gray so as not to appear too worldly.

Because my father had preached and helped found the Bethel Colony, he asked the blessing on our marriage and spoke the prayers when the justice of the peace finished our short vows. And later, at the dance on Elim's second floor, our friends and the rest of Christian's family, too, gathered for the meal—including a goose—that made it almost as festive as Christmas. At Elim, where our leader ruled, Father Keil even clapped Christian on the back and nodded politely as he became, he announced, "the first to call her *Frau* Giesy." He wasn't, but I didn't correct him, grateful he'd chosen to acknowledge my married state.

I looked for Barbara Giesy, Christian's mother, and when my eyes found hers, she smiled. She and I were both *Frau* Giesy now, along with another Barbara and a Mary, already her daughters-in-law. I'd reserve the term *Frau* just for his mother, though. She served food behind the long table, her gray curls brushed tight against her head, as though to hide the flair of their waywardness. Secretly, I hoped our daughters would have such curly hair rather than take after me with my straight strands.

Christian and I hadn't talked of living arrangements, but I assumed we would have Christian's room at the Giesy house until the colony could be freed up to build a house for us. Those worldly people heading west and needing wagons had yet to taper off, even though most pilgrims tried to be at Kanesville, Iowa, some miles west, by May 15 in order to cross the mountains before any early snows. But soon we could set about to make bricks enough, and meanwhile I could learn about the Giesy family and his many other brothers. Helena was his only unmarried sister. Living with them would be my next step as a married woman, one I welcomed.

On my way to *Frau* Giesy's side to help serve, people stopped me for good wishes, admiring the tiny stitches my mother put into my dress. Willie Keil wished me well, as did Louisa Keil, of course. She held my hand extra long and nodded silently. Several of the Nineveh families had come for the celebration too. I trusted the joy each expressed in their words and on their faces. These were good people in this colony who had chosen to follow our leader, to express their faith through actions and works. I belonged among them. Having won my objective to be Christian's wife, I could even allow a softening for our leader. After all, this was his home, and he remained at this gathering for us, which offered a blessing of a kind. Perhaps all would turn out well as Christian insisted.

Then *Frau* Giesy put her arms around me, an embrace of warmth and grace. "Christian has chosen a lovely bride," she said, patting my back as she pulled away.

"Nothing I take credit for."

"Well said," she answered. "I will thank your parents, then."

"As I thank you, for giving me this good man. And for welcoming me into your fold."

"That we do." She brushed at the blinker curls at the side of my face. "We're not so fancy, though."

"Just for special occasions," I said, pulling the curl back behind my ear.

"I hope you aren't too disappointed that you'll be remaining in your parents' home for a time. Until a house can be built for Christian.

And for you. Here, Edna, take this last piece of raisin cake. It's so good. Luella made it, brought it all the way from Nineveh." She so easily wove in words of hospitality to women across the table that I wasn't sure I really heard her other words.

"Excuse me?"

"We thought it best. For so long Christian has served the colony, and I have tended him as his mother and as a colony member when he returned home. That will all change in time, but for now, I'm pleased you found no objection to this plan of you remaining with your parents."

Christian and me living with my parents? Where? Perhaps the boys would move out into the woodshed so my sisters could take their places. It could be arranged. It wasn't what I wanted, but I could adjust. It was one of my strengths, I decided, this ability to move across the trail, back and forth, crawling over rocks laid in the way. No one could set me off the path, at least, and I chose not to let *Frau* Giesy know her news came as some surprise.

"*Ja*, it'll be strange to share my room with him," I said. My sisters would be in the room next door, my parents below us. "But my girlish things I need to put away."

"*Ach*, you have time," she said. "There is *Strudel* at the table's end," she told Willie when he approached, raising his empty plate. "Let me get it for you." He followed her along like a puppy. She served him, then returned.

"He'll stay at home until your house is built. Then you can join him. That way he can continue his work while you'll be with what's familiar and none of your family is inconvenienced."

I kept my face without reaction, pretended that this wasn't something new to me, that my husband and I reached this conclusion together, not that he'd talked of it to everyone but me.

"We all thought that was best, especially since he still must travel."

We all thought? My parents, too? Was everyone in league to keep us separated even after we'd been wed? Or was it yet another test composed by our leader to see how willing I was to support my husband's work?

Well, he would discover—they all would discover—when something truly mattered, I could conform.

———

We did spend our wedding night at my parents' home, and I chose not to bring up the larger issues of our living apart. I didn't want to spoil that night. We'd planned no bridal tour, and if what *Frau* Giesy said was true, then this would be our only evening together for a time until I could convince my husband otherwise. We settled beneath the goose feather comforter, our bodies barely touching as we lay, eyes wide open staring at the board ceiling. He clasped my hand in his, and it felt sweaty, or perhaps it was merely mine. "Emma," he began. *Will he tell me now what I already know?*

I noticed a strange smell in the room, something from Christian's boots, perhaps. I heard scratching at the door. Whining followed, then yipping barks until I rose, and when I opened the door, Sheppie ran in. The dog sniffed wildly beneath the bed. I couldn't imagine what was under it, but the dog squeezed himself under the slats as Christian, standing in his nightshirt, held the lantern high. "A mouse?" Christian ventured as the dog's tail thumped the floor, waking my parents, I was certain.

The dog backed out with a deer leg bone, fresh meat still attached, the pungent scent now filling the room.

"Indeed."

"Jonathan! David Jr.!"

I heard my brothers laugh from beyond the wall. My sisters giggled. I opened the door and shooed Sheppie out, bone and all.

We settled back. "Emma," Christian began again. He lay on his hip, his arm up over my forehead, twirling a lock of my hair.

"What was that?" I heard something swish against the window. Could it be raining? The weather had been fine. Then what sounded like hail hit the panes, followed by the rapping of a snare drum, and then the tubas and the french horns and trumpets woke up the neighborhood. The colony band stood outside our window. A charivari they called it. It was a French event that we Swiss and Germans adopted, meant to celebrate newlyweds on their bridal night. I sighed. Nothing would do now but that we invite all the musicians in and anyone else who made their way through the moonlight to our door, where they would be served wine and cakes and would chatter until they had their fill and went home. Hopefully before dawn.

"At least your mother has cakes to give them," Christian said as he pulled on his britches. "Or who knows what pranks they'd play on us. In some places they kidnap the bride and ask for a ransom of sausage on the bridal night."

"I'd make them pay you to take me back," I said. Christian laughed. He walked to the window and waved at them, but the music didn't stop. "Maybe they'll make us both go with them like on New Year's, *Belsnickel*ing until dawn."

"*Ach,* no," he moaned, but I could tell by the smile on his face as he turned from the window that he was pleased to be chosen for this silliness by his friends and brothers. Most men married younger than he was now, and I think it made him feel welcomed to the fold to have been chosen this, regardless of his age.

"I hope they don't make us go from house to house playing and eating with them," I said. "Or we'll never get to sleep."

"*Ja,* sleep. Or whatever else, *Liebchen,*" Christian said. He'd never used a lover's name for me before. *Liebchen. Sweetheart.* He kissed me then, and I wished this silly charivari could be waylaid until another time. He released me, letting me go first, patting me on the back the way his mother did. I vowed then to make him love me as one who would hold me tight forever, and that one day, I'd be that lover filled up enough to step away first but not far or for long.

"We may as well get this over with," he said to Jonathan's pounding on our door, the younger ones laughing and the dog yipping beyond. Even my father was thumping something on the floor. A broom handle perhaps, thrust against the ceiling.

"Let me help you finish dressing."

Such a wedding night, I thought. Such adjustments I was asked to make!

Christian set the lantern down to help me put my crinoline on. "What's this?" he asked.

Only then did I remember the double row of ruffles he now held, the pale cloth cascading over his wide hands.

"Just a little luxury," I said. "No harm meant." He grunted. I kissed him on the end of his nose. "I choose life," I added. "Remember?"

5

Sent Out

We separated the next day. Oh, not over the ruffles. Christian laughed at those when I told him when they'd been sewn on. "That's a good thing to do when you feel overcome by rules," he said. No, we separated because our leader knocked on our door early in the morning, reminding Christian of a meeting scheduled. My husband leaped from his bed, performed not seventy-five pushing-ups but seventy-six, then dressed and left. When my husband returned, he told me he was being sent out and would be gone some weeks.

"But what of our home? What of our plans? Can I go with you?"

"Now, *Liebchen,* you knew this was a part of who I am."

"But we haven't even talked of where I'm to stay while you're gone or even considered that I might go with you."

"Out of the question," he said, though he kissed the top of my head. "Be restful, *Liebchen.* My going tells Wilhelm that our marriage will not interfere with what needs doing here. Or wherever he sends me."

He assured me he would not be far away and that he'd post letters. "South," he said. "I'm going back to the hills of Kentucky. The government leaves people alone there. Or maybe the hollows of old Virginia." He stopped, thoughtful for a moment in the midst of pulling on his boots with the jack. "Did you know that when Virginia colonized, only the Anglican Church was recognized there? But when the Scots-Irish Presbyterians and Calvinists came south from Pennsylvania, the Virginians let them have their preachers so long as they settled in the hills and acted as a buffer between them and the Indians the aristocrats feared. Isolation served them well, and it will us too. They're hard-working, these potential converts, and not interested in gaining wealth through owning land. They just want to lead faithful lives and hunt and fish and worship as they please and do what is right for their families. They are whom we wish to bring to Bethel."

"How long will you seek them?"

"I don't know. But you're in safe hands here," he said. "Taking care of each other while one is gone is another gift our colony gives to one another." Then he kissed me soundly, picked up his valise, and left.

Perhaps I was naive and inexperienced, as Helena suggested, but I had a sense that Christian's leaving had been purposeful, meant to separate us. But it would not be a wedge between us unless I let it. We'd married. Our leader would one day have to come to terms with that fact.

In the weeks that followed, I began to pay more attention to those married in our colony, how they tended their families. *Frau* Giesy and I often met at the storehouse, where we would pick up flour as we needed. I took more time to listen to young wives expecting a child, knowing one day I'd be there, cherishing this precious gift of life. Mary Giesy, Sebastian's wife, wore a loose dress, but I could still see that she was pregnant. She never stopped her working, and it seemed to keep her healthy, unlike stories I'd heard of women in Shelbina who stayed in bed while their babies grew.

I watched my parents more closely to see the tender ways my father expressed affection with a touch to my mother's waist as she stood at the tin-lined sink washing potatoes. At night, when their soft laughter rose up through the floorboards from their bedroom, I let it comfort me, to soothe the ache of missing Christian and the humiliation of a married woman still sharing her bed with two sisters. One day, I told myself, my husband and I will laugh beneath the comforter again, just us. *It will be my husband's warmth I feel against my back and not my younger sister's knees.*

Summer came and with it the outdoor work we all contributed to. We hoed and weeded the large cornfields that surrounded Bethel town. My father said Bethel was arranged, as in the old country, where people lived next door to one another, farmers and butchers and tailors. They knew their neighbors' business and could also help in time of need. Even though farmers rode their carts out to their fields each day, they weren't separated from other families by miles and miles, each living on isolated farmsteads, making their ways alone for weeks at a time. It was that way in many frontier settlements, with farmers not aware of town concerns and town people thinking they had little interest in the ways of laborers far away. They didn't come to help when a man was injured by a bullock or when a wife had trouble giving birth because they didn't know of the need. In Bethel, farmers rode out together to their fields and returned back each night. We helped one another. And like disciples of old, we went out to transform the world around us.

Christian had been "sent out." The other Bethelites who recruited in the South were all single men. I saw advantage to that now as I ached to start my life with Christian but couldn't.

Autumn pushed in through the steaming summer, bringing with it flocks of geese migrating south that sometimes settled in our cornfields before we could hurry them on with our shouts. Once the corn shocks were in our barns, we let the geese waddle over stubble. For me, everything seemed more vivid that autumn: the sounds of the geese calling, the scent of pork being smoked, the taste of apple cider on my tongue after a day helping with the harvest. My mother said this happened when a woman fell in love; the world seemed brighter, more intense. "Maybe I fell in love after I married," I told her.

"*Ja,* it would be like you to find a contrary way."

The colder nights and river fog in early morning brought bursts of color change to Bethel. Near the gristmill's pond, the maple trees turned red and yellow and all shades in between, and reflected like a mirror in the water. I held my breath one day walking past, and Mary, Sebastian's wife, bumped right into me as I stopped to stare. "Such beauty in this place! I wish that I could paint it," I told her. "So I could hang it on my wall one day. The white walls of the mill a mate to the blue water—"

"*Ach,*" Mary said. "You shouldn't covet such things to hang on your walls. Only portraits should hang there or maybe your stitching."

I wondered if I blasphemed to think that man's creations could enhance what God designed. Or if wanting to remember such beauty could truly be a sin.

We Bethelites heard much about sin that fall, and our leader referenced "coming troubles at the end" that stirred his words to such frenzy at times that when I left the church I felt beaten as an egg. He'd give no date, unlike some communal leaders, my father said, who would tell their followers to prepare for Christ's coming on a certain day and then find they had to retract and explain when the date arrived without incident. Our leader spoke of ends, but he always finished with what I suppose he thought were hopeful words, saying God would provide a way out for us, a way for His followers to begin again. I could never tell if he forecast a heavenly change or if he referred to possible political disasters right here in Missouri.

How I wished that Christian sat beside me on the porch so we could discuss our leader's words. I had to write instead. When Christian wrote back, I took his missives to my room, pushed the little ones out the door, and savored them, alone.

He wrote with precise characters marching along the pages, his words providing details of what he saw and heard and even of the weather. He honored me with political talk, of how men in Carolina spoke less of slave and free than the idea that there might be aggression from the North, that one state could somehow impose its will upon another. *Even men who own no slaves will take up arms against the North should they invade,* Christian wrote. *Most living here are as poor as slaves, but they resist ideas imposed by aristocrats, Bostonians, New Yorkers. Yankees. Indeed, for them this disagreement isn't about slaves at all but independence, life without intrusion, something we at Bethel understand.*

But what I treasured most in Christian's letters was that he told me how he felt, how the sound of the Ohio River gurgling in the morning while he fixed coffee over a campfire made him think of my laughter. He described the elegant elms soaring up to blue sky and that the sight of them as he rode through their cool shade reminded him of my compassionate embracing arms and the strength I would give our children one day. He wrote of picking up a walnut, saying it was the color of my eyes. He wrote of missing me. *For so long I missed no one while I traveled, or so I thought. You often came to mind as I watched you grow up, Emma Giesy, and I imagined you as a loving niece who would one day find joy with a husband like Willie Keil or one of a dozen other young men smart enough to see the strength in you.*

Willie Keil? Surely Christian suffered a fever to ever imagine such a union as that.

That you should choose me, Liebchen, *and that I should at last see you as the woman you are instead of only the daughter of my friend, is truly one of God's great gifts. An old man I am and yet not too old. But I might have passed you by if not for your eyes meeting mine on Christmas Day and the prayer I saw in them that only God could answer.*

We became closer by this separation, something I suspect our leader hadn't planned for, and I wondered if I didn't get to know Christian better this way than if I'd moved into his parents' home and heard their stories about him. This way, I learned to tell my own.

I loved the way his words flowed across the page, and I read them again before I slept at night, hearing the low tones of his voice, feeling the quiver of my skin as I imagined his hands upon my body. I could hardly wait for his return, for then I imagined my life would truly begin.

———

I prepared for another Christmas without Christian. I worked hard not to hold resentment toward our leader. It would do no good to blame another for what was, only keep me filled with irritations that would grate at my soul like a file. In his letters, Christian gave no indication of when he'd return, but I hoped he'd come north as the geese flew south. I'd memorized a poem in English called "The Night Before Christmas" that I planned to recite to him, but I'd settle for brothers and sisters and my parents as my audience if no one else. I'd stitched a special pair of gloves for Christian, helped tan the hide myself, and they were wrapped in brown paper tied with ribbon. We called the Christmas Eve gift bearer Kris Kringle now, who'd leave his gifts snuggled within the branches of the tree. Our leader said it was more American to do it this way, and he wanted anyone who might ask or wonder to know that we Germans were loyal to the country.

It was Christmas Eve, and my father called to me to hurry down, to bring a candle so he could restart the fire. I mumbled something about letting it go out and Jonathan or David being capable of such, but I did as I was bid, only to be swung into the arms of my husband, who nearly smothered me with kisses.

"You're back!"

"Rode all last night," he said. "And through this day, which the Lord blessed with sunshine instead of snow. It is good to be home."

Christian brought me fruit and raisins, and when we opened gifts, he took from the branches of our tree a wooden box that had my name on it. It was a pair of woolen mittens like every other pair available at the colony store. I hid my disappointment at wanting something just for me, something purchased on his travels to reassure me that I'd been on his mind. But I soon pitched that thought, grateful he was home for this holiday. *That* would be his gift to me, that he'd arrived. He unwrapped his gloves and admired the special stitching. "I could have used these," he said. "The days are cold alone in Carolina."

Upstairs, as we prepared to bed, he pulled out another package from his pack. He removed the twine covering it.

I held up a new crinoline, one with rows of ruffles circling the skirt.

———

I never wanted to stay in bed so much as I did on Christmas morning. We lingered in each other's arms. "It's our bridal tour we never had," I told Christian as I ran my fingers through his now-full beard, tinted auburn. "Taken in my own bedroom where I grew up." He squeezed my hand, kissed the palm. Then I asked, "Did you come back on your own, or did he call you back?"

"Both. I said I thought it time to return and brought several families with me. He did not protest and so I'm here, to stay now for a time. To go back to tinsmithing and begin my life with you."

My family had already left for worship, and because we'd found it difficult to leave the comfort of each other's arms, it was nearly 4:00 a.m. before we'd crunched over the snow and reached the church. Like schoolchildren caught after the bell, we separated and slipped onto the benches, facing each other across the aisle. The service had already begun, with Willie carrying the *Schellenbaum* this time and standing beside his father, though a step below.

Christian looked toward me often. At first I wondered if he minded that last year he'd been standing beside our leader, and now he sat across from me. But then my face grew warm as I read into his eyes not the envy of a man replaced by our leader's son, but the memories of our sweetest holdings from the night before.

Father Keil's sermon soon stripped away our dreamlike reverie. He talked of change, of needed change. He spoke first of literature, not biblical verses, telling us that *Uncle Tom's Cabin* was a book that caused consternation and would swirl the world as we knew it and this was as Daniel said and John wrote and there would be a terrible war between good and evil and it was our duty to prepare and to protect our families.

It seemed a convulsive text to preach on Christmas Day, harsh words disgorged to pit against tender skin prepared to dwell on charity and love, on God's gift of grace and precious treasures already opened on Christmas Eve, and the peppermints and fruits that would follow with *Belsnickel's* good cheer. I hoped that Christian wasn't taking our leader's dark words too much to heart. I wanted nothing to intrude on this sweet new beginning promised earlier that morning in my husband's arms.

The dance later brought friends to talk with Christian, and I was included in the Giesy gathering of sisters-in-law and their chatter. No one raised the issue of Christian staying with them until we built a house, so I assumed our time apart had erased that plan. I served with *Frau* Giesy and smiled quietly at jokes made about my one day bringing forth a baby as Mary soon would. For me it marked a recognition of my married state, a recognition I felt I'd never truly had.

We heard the pounding on the front door early the following

morning. My father answered, but it was my mother whose "Oh, no!" sent chills through me. Christian slept, and I eased myself from beneath his arm, pulled a quilt around me, and slipped downstairs.

"What is it, Papa?" I asked.

"It's Mary Giesy. Her baby comes too soon," my mother answered as she grabbed for her cape.

"Should I come with you?"

"*Ach*, no. Your father takes me. You tend to your husband and your brothers and sisters should they wake."

But before I could fix potato pancakes for the household, my parents returned. My mother yanked at her bonnet and tossed it in a heap on the table, something I'd never seen her do before. Jonathan looked up in surprise. Catherine's eyes brimmed with tears. I shushed the little ones. My father took her cape and shook his head at us. She pulled at her soiled apron, couldn't get the bow undone, and when my father attempted to help, she slapped at his hands, and then he turned her to him and held her as she sank against his chest and wept.

"I could do no ting," she said. "No ting at all."

"You did what you could, Catherina. It is all we are asked to do."

"But his words, *Herr* Keil's words. I have never heard such a ting, to say that the baby died because of some sin of the parent. Why does he say such tings?"

"The words are biblical," my sister said, her voice soft.

"But are the words meant to bring Mary relief when she lies with her body having given all that it can? Those words have no comfort, and they cannot change what is. The baby has died. Now the parents are asked to bear guilt as well as grief?" My father stroked my mother's back. She pulled away from him, looked at his face, tears wet upon her cheeks. "I don't understand this, David. I don't. Biblical words like these...out of all he could choose...no. These are not the words our

Lord would say, not when He so loved children. He would grieve with Mary and Sebastian, not prolong their pain."

She left us then, but I could hear her quiet cries from behind their bedroom door.

By mid-January, our leader called us all together for a major decision. Women were told to gather too. "There is free land in Oregon Territory," our leader told us. "If we claim the land and live there before the end of 1855, we can each have 160 acres that could start our new colony. Married couples can claim twice the amount. Scouts I send, as Joshua did, send them into this foreign land. They will spy for us and bring back the word, and then we will all go, those who wish to leave here and be in a new protected place where the trials of the larger world will not intrude. No one will be forced to leave, but many will wish to. I wish to," he said, "when the right place is found. These spies—nine I send—will leave with no wagon, only their horses and pack animals. As soon as it is spring here, no later than April. They will do for us what we cannot do for ourselves, be good servants who will save us in the end."

"Is this necessary?" Karl Ruge, the teacher, dared to ask. "You've moved so often, and this is Bethel, a place of worship. We have been here not yet ten years. Are we in such danger?"

"Our young people fall from our ways," our leader told him. "Parents have been letting them grow up in a blasphemous and unspiritual life. It is time we found a new place where government does not wish to interfere with us and where the rules are not yet so bogged down in political mud that we can still make paths through to homes of our liking. No one will care if we have communal coffers from which we draw to take care of ourselves. No one will question how we conduct our business. No one will be lured into sinful ways."

I wondered how the new recruits that Christian had brought back with him would take this. They'd uprooted their families, and while they had no homes of their own yet, they were settling in, finding out about the charity of this colony. Most stayed at Elim's second floor. None wanted for food or clothing or shelter, and each found work to fill their days, even through these winter times, and so had already begun to feel a part of who we were at Bethel.

I wondered what Christian thought with his efforts to find new land south suddenly set aside. Would he see his efforts as failures? It might be a high price to pay as I saw it. But if he had failed, then he'd be unlikely to be sent out so soon again.

Our leader narrowed his eyes at Karl. "We will miss the coming storm if we go to Oregon Territory, while those here in Missouri will be in the center of it, mark my words."

Silence filled the church, a place I now thought our leader had chosen for special reasons. Usually our gatherings were at Elim, not in this sacred space. To defy him here, to disagree with the way he saw the world he'd define as blasphemous, would take strong courage.

"Who do you send, Wilhelm?" my father asked. "There are many willing to follow you and to trust in your vision as we have before."

Our leader nodded appreciatively at my father as he began. "Joseph and Adam Knight. Good brothers. They will go. Stand, please," he said. "Adam Schuele. John Stauffer and John Hans Stauffer, father and son. John Genger." I looked at John Genger's wife. She sat straight as a knife. Each man stood slowly, and I wondered if this was the first they'd known of our leader's choices. I looked down the aisle at the women in their lives. Stunned looks crossed their faces. The weight of future separation formed lines to their eyes. I felt my own heart begin to pound. "Michael Schaefer Sr., George Link." I counted. *One more to name.*

My father hadn't known who would be called to go; at least I didn't think he'd been planted to ask the question of our leader. But now I looked at him, and he chewed his lower lip, perhaps in disappointment that his name had not been called, perhaps in hopes it wouldn't be.

"And one last," our leader said. My father looked up, expectant. "Christian Giesy."

I jerked my head toward Christian. He bent over as he stood. He would not look at me, but I knew he heard the silent *"No!"* screaming from my speechless throat.

6

A Woman's Lot

I should have known, and I suppose my heart did know before my head, and that was why it chose to pound as I watched those men stand. Did their women feel as I did? A blend of pride and pout, a disappointment for us while carrying honor reflected from our husbands and sons.

Adam Schuele had located the Bethel property with my father; he'd been sent out before but never quite so far and to such a wilderness. None of them had ever been gone so long. It would be at least a year, more likely two, before they returned. My father's mouth drooped; my mother patted his arm. She looked relieved.

"You've given enough," I told Christian later in our room, my voice a whisper so as not to let my parents hear. "Doesn't our leader see that these separations are not good for families? Why does he insist we find a new colony now?"

"We've grown closer with our separations. You said this yourself."

"Do you want to leave Bethel? You bring people to it and then you leave? What must they think?"

"They didn't follow me, *Liebchen*. They followed their hearts. Their belief in God brought them to this place. They won't harbor anything against me. Why do you?"

I tried pouting, but he pressed my lower lip with his finger and smiled.

"I'll go to him," I said, "and tell him you must stay home now and that we will start our family."

"*Ach,* you talk like a *Dummkopf,*" he said, throwing up his hands. "You can't change this, so you must accept it."

"*Nicht jetzt.*"

"Yes, now," he said. He raised that one eyebrow that I'd come to see as a warning for me not to press too far.

I flopped on the edge of the bed, arms crossed. "He wants me to endure the pangs of childbirth as my wage of sin. So he should let me have time with my husband…so I can later suffer."

A sad smile crossed his face. "How you talk," he said. "A mix of stubbornness and spirit. May it one day be converted into faithfulness and strength when you grow up." He turned away from me and didn't see my mouth open in protest. "It is an honor to be selected. We won't be gone long. Only a few months out, and then we find the land, and then we come back."

"But when you find the perfect spot, won't someone need to remain there to hold the land until the rest of us can arrive? Who'll stay?"

"The leader will stay, I would guess," Christian said, but he wrinkled his brow as though he hadn't thought of that before.

"And who leads?"

"Wilhelm hasn't settled on this yet. We all meet and make plans, all the men and those chosen to go. We know what we look for. Isolation. Good timber for homes. A mild climate without hard snows. Fertile soil for our farms. Maybe a few settlers there so we will have others using the gristmill but not so many people that they poke into our business. We'll find such a place. Already people coming back from the gold fields say Oregon Territory is where the real treasure is, all that free land."

"All that is claimed goes into the colony, *ja?*"

"As at Bethel and Nineveh. It is our way."

"My father would go in your place if you asked him," I said. "He looked so disappointed when our leader failed to call his name."

"Emma." He turned to me as he sat at the side of the bed. "This is not something you can control now. I will go and I will come back, and you will continue as you have until we travel out together with the colony. Then we'll begin our life."

"I want to start our life together now," I wailed. "People don't always come back. Something could happen to you."

"Last year more families traveled there on wagons than ever before. They have new lives there, new chances."

"We have no need of new lives. This is a good life here in Bethel if I could ever begin it with you. If there is something wrong, we can make it better. Our leader can solve the problem that sends us on our way. I'll tell him so."

"Not one word of your protests to Wilhelm. Not one word. Your interference in this might cause him to prevent my going, my doing the work I'm called to do."

It occurred to me only then that perhaps Christian had the wanderlust, that quality of some men who never settle in one place, who are always seeking other hills to climb. His preaching and recruiting gave him reason to roam. He might never stay at home even if we had a child of our own. I felt a chill go through me.

That momentary insight changed the way I looked at him, altered how I thought he saw our marriage too. Like a woman riding on a pillion behind her husband, we traveled the same road but arrived at our destination with very different views. We had different hopes, it seemed, save that we each said out loud we wished a family.

That's what I'd have to focus on, then, making sure we were together no matter where he chose to go, so we could begin this holy work of raising children. I'd either have to convince him to remain here while others headed west, or that he should take me with him.

———

Routine laboring in the colony continued without change through spring. Only the chosen men spent extra time with our leader making plans; only the wives and daughters and mothers of these men moved between pride at their men having been chosen and their own trepidations at being left behind. At least Christian remained with me in my parents' crowded home. At least I could watch his morning ritual of pushing-ups, even if the rest of the day I felt more like a sister and daughter than a wife.

The colony would provide for all the families while the men were gone, that was not a concern. But seeing them go, not being sure if they'd come back or when, that's what troubled, I suppose, as it had women who watched their whaling husbands set to sea or waved a last good-bye to the backs of soldiers as they marched away. We'd memorize their profiles, the outlines of their backs, and cling to these fading memories long after the taste of their last kiss had dried upon our lips.

We'd also dream of a home in the new land, one that would be more glorious and grand than the ones we had in Bethel. That wouldn't be hard for me, not having a home of our own. I'd be left to help my mother with the children and share my bed again with sisters.

I sought a plan. I could show myself as someone needing reining in. If our leader thought I couldn't be left alone here, without a husband to control me, he might then require that Christian stay in Bethel with me.

But when I thought of what I might do—talk overly loud at Elim gatherings or slack off at the glove factory or act peevish with Helena—

the efforts appeared so childish that our leader and maybe even Christian would just laugh and tell my father to keep his thumb on me while Christian headed west. Or worse, my parents would be shamed, and Christian, too.

I considered raising dissent among the newcomers. It might not be difficult, as a couple of the Kentucky families newly recruited had already left us by February. Christian said they'd found nothing wrong in Bethel but that they realized they wanted to claim ownership of land, be able to plant what they wished when they wished, hunt when they wanted. The process at Bethel told them well that this would not be the case as a part of the colony. Our leader decided such things, and most of the men went along with him. Those who didn't, left.

I could be vocal about not understanding why people left. We lived in America, after all, where we ought to be free to make choices. I hoped my words would find their way to our leader and perhaps he'd suggest to Christian that he best stay here to keep my tongue in check.

"You've been encouraging dissent," Christian told me in our room that March evening not long before my birthday. We were readying ourselves for bed. "I hear of it."

"Nothing others aren't saying out loud," I said. "We're free to have our say, even us women. I'm surprised anyone listened."

"You don't know the hardships of women who alone with their husbands and children try to claim a land. *Ja,* they end up with their names on a document. But they alone must do the work, as there are no others invested in their success. If their crops fail, they have no storehouse to deliver grain for their families. It is not all roses, *Liebchen.* You do a disservice when you tell people only of the difficulties of the colony and only the joys of settlement on property alone."

"Many of the newer recruits came from small farms," I said. "They know the trials." I picked up my hairbrush.

He sighed. "You are destined to cause me pain."

"I only want people to know what we're about, and that we are not all perfection, as our leader would have us believe. We do have tragedies here, too. Look at Mary. And our leader blamed her for her baby's death. Do you think he was right?"

Christian shook his head no. "But there is a time to disagree, Emma, and a time to keep silent."

"I'm not well-versed in keeping silent," I said. I pulled my brush through the long strands, rolling the loose hair from the brush into a tiny ball that I could later weave into a wall hanging. Maybe I'd tie a ribbon around it and slip it into Christian's saddlebag so he'd remember me after he'd gone. I forced myself to stop thinking that way. He just had to stay here with me.

"Your words bring suspicion and discord where it need not be, Emma. Will you stop it, for me?"

"Stop talking about the virtues of owning one's own land?" I said.

"About your view of life here. It…unsettles people to hear you speak such things while I'm away."

"Perhaps you shouldn't go, then," I said. "Or maybe in my own house, I'd find a better way to see things."

"Any new home must go to the new recruits, Emma. You have a fine place to reside. It would be selfish to live in your own home alone, a waste of colony labor to build for us when we are leaving."

"That's the point, though. *I'm* not leaving. You are."

His galluses hung loose at his side, exposing his shirt, his wide chest. He took in a deep breath and clamped his jaw shut. His fists rolled up tight, then released. He exhaled a long, slow breath. I stepped back from the force of him. "You will stop talking in the way I've asked, Emma." He'd never given me a direct order before.

"Or?"

"Or face consequences I do not wish to name."

"Because?"

"Because you are the wife of the leader of the Oregon Territory scouts. And you must act accordingly."

———

As leader, he'd remain behind in the Oregon Territory once they found the new land. That meant more than a year before I'd see him again, more likely two. Here's where I'd stay, beneath my father's roof, never in a home of my own.

Pray? I suppose I might have tried that route. But our leader always led our prayers during worship; at home, my father did. We read the Scriptures and did discuss them, but most of Bethel lived content to let our leader set our spiritual tone and be the intercessor for our needs. Our leader would hardly offer prayers for my contentment. I was on my own and beginning to wonder whether my prayers, like my voice in the colony, were ever heard.

I'd have to make Christian want to take me with him. I imagined what miracle would make him do this, what intervention would cause him to set aside the dangers or demands of such a journey so he'd include a woman in the undertaking, one woman, his own wife.

I'd have to press the shared goal we had to begin our family. He'd turn forty this year, 1853. It was time he had a son. I needed to remind him of his mortality and his duty to his wife. Ruth's words from Scripture came to mind: "Whither thou goest, I will go." Perhaps he'd listen to that.

I packed a basket of food. We'd taken a horse cart to the center of town, which offered a kind of park. Keil had laid out Bethel beautifully, with wide streets and trees planted on either side. At the park, a bandstand offered a sheltered place for concerts in the summer. It was deserted in March except for an early crocus poking up through the earth and a wild goose or two. Sheppie trotted on behind us, chased at the geese. Then he panted, waiting for Christian to finish chewing on the chicken leg, sure my husband would toss the skin to him.

Christian wiped his beard with a napkin. "No women on this journey," he said when I raised the issue.

"But you said yourself that more families headed west last year than ever before. Whole families. Including women and children."

"They took wagons, Bethel wagons, sturdy and well built so they had plenty of supplies. And there were others in the party, other women. Ours will be a fast journey of all men, horseback. We've had special saddlebags made to carry what we need. It's not a trip for a woman."

"Those missionary women, that Narcissa Whitman and Eliza Spalding, they rode sidesaddle all the way to Oregon," I said, "years ago. They had no wagons."

"They hooked up with a fur trading group from Hudson's Bay for protection. We'll travel as light as we can to move quickly, act as our own protection. Indeed, God as our protector." He chewed again. "No, Emma," he said to my open mouth. "No women."

"But that will mean another year or more before I bear a child for you. Another year of my dawdling as though I'm married without any of the accoutrements of marriage: no home, no child, no husband at my side. What am I to do?"

He took pity on me and held me. "You're young," he said. "You have plenty of time to have things go your way. There are many who need your help while I'm gone. You can serve them; prepare yourself for when the whole community crosses the plains. Let your kindness rise like cream."

"Cream sours," I said. "I don't just want things to go my way. I want you to have what you said held meaning for you. A wife and family, both."

"*Ja,*" he said. "I have a wife. A generous one. I'll settle for one out of two."

———

By early April, having made no progress with Christian, I took my case to a higher authority, asking for an audience with our leader. I was visiting Mary Giesy when Willie stopped by and said his father would see me then.

"We'll talk later, Mary," I said. Her face blotched from the tears she still shed daily over the loss of her son. Just a few more weeks and he might have lived. So small, so tiny, smaller than the palm of her husband's hand. Being with her reminded me of my mother's outrage at our leader's condemnation of this woman. She'd done nothing wrong that I could see. While I believed that our leader had God-inspired visions that led him to the faith and the way we practiced it in Bethel, I also thought his humanity clawed through sometimes, tearing up what God intended. Finding Mary and Sebastian Giesy responsible for their infant's death tore at my sense of fairness and the image I had of God. The God my parents shared with me offered hope rather than the picture of One who stunned His followers with tears over unknown sins so powerful they could cause their child's death.

They would try again, Mary told me, but she worried. "If I can't name what I did wrong to cause the early birth and neither can Sebastian, it will happen again to us."

I wanted words to comfort her. "All we can do is ask forgiveness for whatever sins we commit, even the ones we can't name," I told her.

Mary's purest desire was to live her life so her children would be healthy and well and grow up strong. In my years of knowing her, she'd been close to that perfection, much closer than I'd ever be. She worked hard, lived cleanly, always sat attentively at the sermons, unlike me. She was even more generous than my mother, and my mother gave her all. She actually believed it important not only to give to others so they'd have what *they* needed, but also that in sharing into the common purse, what we gave became not just someone else's, but *ours*.

Unfortunately, considering Mary's virtues highlighted my less-than-angelic ways and our leader's dire warnings about childbirth. I might well be storing up some trouble of my own, when that day came, with my headstrong ways.

I pitched those thoughts aside while Willie walked with me to his father's home. He'd brought Gloriana with him, and we held the child's hands between us, lifting her every now and then into a swing. My arms ached, and I felt tired from all the nights of sleepless turning, trying to find a way for Christian to stay at home.

"My father said he only had a moment," Willie told his sister as we walked. "So not much time for swinging."

His sister giggled and leaned back, knowing we would catch her, knowing we'd both lift her up. "There's no sense in fighting it," I told him. "When a girl sets her mind to something…"

"*Ja,*" he said. "Especially a German girl."

I had one chance, I knew, one opportunity to convince our leader that I should be allowed to go along. I was certain such a request had not occurred to him. He'd be expecting me to beg him to let Christian remain behind. My husband would never raise the issue of my going west. He'd only do so if our leader thought it wise or if he ordered

Christian to do it. Christian would not directly disobey an order. If our leader had forbidden our marriage, I'd still be Emma Wagner with Christian a husband lost to me forever.

"So. We talk again, *Frau* Giesy," our leader said. He wore his long coat for the occasion, but he bent to work at his plants, mortar and pestle in hand. He hadn't motioned me to sit, so I came to stand across from him at the high table. Dried plants lay like corpses between us. "You have news to share with me?" he said. "I hear you share news with many."

I swallowed. "No, no news."

"*Ja,* you tell our new families it would be better to live elsewhere than at Bethel."

"I only discussed what people already spoke of," I defended, "after one of the Kentucky families left. I didn't know them and had nothing to do with their leaving."

"You want to leave yourself, *Frau* Giesy?" He raised both bushy eyebrows at me. He reminded me of a horned toad.

"I go where my husband goes," I said. " 'Whither thou goest, I will go.' I'm a faithful wife."

His voice softened. "Ruth of the Scriptures went with her mother-in-law, not her husband, Emma. Those are a widow's words you speak."

"I fear I might become a widow," I said, "should something happen to Christian on this journey west."

"Ah. You are fearful. This is why you ask to speak to me." He motioned for me to take a chair, and then he put away his plant musings and pulled a chair up before me. Not the inquisition format, but one of a father to a child. He acted the kindly *Belsnickel* who granted gifts at Christmas. He was the "Father Keil" my own father referred to, someone loving who cared for each of us as though we were his own. So many loved this man. Why was I so suspicious? "Tell me what is on your mind."

"I…I think it would be good for Christian, my husband, if I went with him on this journey west."

He raised his eyebrows again, assessing me as though I were an object in the distance he wasn't sure was friend or foe. "This is not even worth considering," he said then and started to rise.

"No, wait. Please, just entertain the possibility," I said. "You always tell us to think creatively, to use our God-given abilities to solve a problem. Remember when you came up with the plan to make a drill to go through the pine logs so they could act as pipes with seams tarred tight? No one had ever done such a thing before."

"It was ingenious, that plan for the fields."

"Yes. So just consider my going along. Please."

He took it as a puzzle, I think, a small challenge from a mosquito buzzing at his ear. "Vell, then. You'd slow them down, I think. This is one reason you cannot go."

"I'd cook their meals. It would free them to make better time."

"You'd tire and they would have to stop for you. You're tiny, Emma. Now your sister Catherine is a big girl—"

"I've never been ill, not once. I know remedies, too, so if one of them became ill, I could minister to them. Perhaps even help others we meet along the trail. Wouldn't this extend our Christian love, our Golden Rule, to serve strangers we find in need? We could even tell them of our mission. They might wish to join us. A woman's presence would suggest family, safety."

"*Our* mission," he said. "You assume much, *Frau* Giesy."

"Only that we are all communal here, so it is our mission whether we go or stay."

He stared at me. "The separation will make you grow fonder of each other, you and Christian, so your hearts will be fuller when you meet again."

"As it did this past year," I said. I paused. "You may be right. Our love just grows stronger as we're apart. Perhaps we should be separated and never discover each other's faults. We will always be on a bridal trip."

He considered that, tapped his finger against his thigh. "Where there are women, there is dissension. How would you explain away this fact, should you go with the scouts?"

"There'd be only one woman."

"And what of the others? What if all the spies wish to bring their wives or sisters or mothers, someone to take care of them, because you are going?"

"Have they brought this to you? No? Then it is safe to say they have no interest in traveling with their men. I do. My husband has been taken from me—sent out in service, I mean—for more months of our marriage than not. I miss him, Father Keil."

"What does Christian say of this?"

"He thinks you would not approve." I ignored the fact that Christian also thought it wasn't wise and that I was not to bring the subject up, ever. "But you know he wants a family and while he is your age, Father Keil, he is well behind you with your nine loving sons and daughters. How will we populate the new colony if not with the children of your loyal followers?"

He adjusted his glasses. "We will populate it by taking more than two hundred people from Bethel with us when the site is found out west and by gathering new followers to our way."

He had that finality to his tone, and I could feel myself losing him to some prepared text. I'd have to put my last ladle into the dutch oven.

"How am I ever to experience what God wants of my womanhood if my husband is never with me?" I wailed it almost. "It's what you said God required of a woman, to conceive so she can know such pain as to be reminded of her sins and save her soul."

"You remember our discussion, then, that you were meant to bear the turmoil as penance for Eve's sin?"

"Yes," I said. "You are wise, Father Keil." I bit my lip against the bile I felt rising in my stomach for my demure demeanor when what I wanted to do was shout.

"Perhaps you have learned something in these past months. I'll think about this," he said. "Then let Christian know."

"No, no!" I grabbed at his arm as he stood. "If your answer is no, please don't tell him I've come to you. Please. He'll be distressed that I've disobeyed him."

"He told you not to come here?"

"He told me not to even think about going with him. He never dreamed that I'd bother you with my concerns."

He pursed his lips, pressed his palms against his thighs, elbows out, and held them that way.

"Perhaps I erred in preventing you from knowing all that a woman's lot entails. Perhaps Christian needs to understand why I could not bless your marriage." He stood, paced back and forth, hands clasped behind his back. I sat still as one of his discarded stems. Then he said, "I *will* send you out with them. You will have the chance to bear him a child, though such a hard journey might cause you to…but both of you believed you were meant to be together. Now you will have the chance to know for certain."

―――――――

Would Christian blame me for my manipulation? Or would he celebrate that we now had what we both wanted with the direction, if not blessing, of our leader?

"I wouldn't consider it if Wilhelm hadn't suggested it himself,"

Christian said when we lay in bed that night. Our leader had called him into Elim, he told me, and with the others scouts gathered he'd affirmed Christian's leadership of the journey. "Then he said that you would be going with us. It's as though he read your mind, *Liebchen*. His kindness and his vision know no end."

"You don't object, then?" I asked.

"It's an answer to my prayer. He said we'd waited long enough to begin our family. This is a double blessing."

"The first being?"

"That Wilhelm thought of this on his own, that he understood then that ours is a marriage ordained by God." He kissed me. "Still, if you were already with child, I'd make you stay behind even with Wilhelm's suggestion that you could prepare meals for us and minister to any ills we have." He stroked my face. "The trial of the journey might make it difficult for you to conceive, but it will be good to travel with you, to share what we'll discover there together."

"Once in Oregon, we'll find shelter and the promised land our leader says is there, and all will be well," I said.

So Wilhelm had let a lie stand, or at least had let Christian think my going with them was our leader's idea. I wasn't sure I liked conspiring with our leader against my husband, nor discovering that our leader and I had something like a deception in common.

"All will be well, *Liebchen*," Christian said and snuggled close to me.

Within minutes I heard his breathing change to a man in restful sleep, but I lay awake for hours and wondered how far along the trail we should be before I told him we could expect an infant in October.

7

New Schooling

I enjoyed the attention offered me by this journey's twist. Some of the looks came with clicking tongues, as from Helena and *Frau* Giesy, though neither dared protest too much, since our leader had proposed this idea of my "being sent" as one of the scouts.

"Even ordered that you go, I heard," Helena said. "What strangeness. No woman has ever been told to go with scouts. Men have much to do to carry the message of our religion. Women will be in the way."

Her words reminded me of a time when I was thirteen and Christian Giesy had just returned from one of his journeys south. Perhaps I fell in love with him that hot September day, now that I think of it. We were all in the vineyard harvesting grapes, as the nights had been cool. Our baskets were full of the purple fruit, and several children swatted at bees to keep them from devouring our harvest. That was my task, too, to swat at bees.

Christian rode by on his big horse, and as people recognized him, they stopped working and shouted hellos, welcoming him back. He shook hands with the men, and I remember their grips left purple stains on his wide, soft palms. He dismounted and wiped his wide forehead with the back of his arm, adjusted his hat and pushed it back on his head. His teeth were naturally white, not yellowed as my father's, and his big smile seemed just for me when I handed him a tin cup of fresh water. "It's pleasant to be served on a hot day, *Fräulein* Wagner," he told me, treating me as though I was someone. "A traveler misses such tending when he has to look after things for himself day after day."

"It's a cup you made," I told him.

"So it is," he said, turning the tin in his large hands. His long fingers wrapped around the cup gently, as though he held an instrument. He started to put the cup to his lips, then stopped as a wide-eyed boy stepped up beside me. Christian said his name, squatted to his height, then offered the cup to him. The boy drank, handed the cup back to Christian, then scampered off. "His mother's a widow," he said, as though I didn't know. "Will you refill me?" He handed me his empty cup. I didn't correct him; no one can fill up another. But I did replenish the liquid. "We both do the Lord's work," he said after he finished drinking. He turned to talk with the men, then I eased to the sidelines, watching until Mary called me back to my task.

When I asked my father later what Christian meant by both of us doing the Lord's work, my father quoted Scripture to me, James 1:27: " 'Pure religion and undefiled before God and the Father is this, To visit the fatherless and widows in their affliction, and to keep himself unspotted from the world.' That's Christian Giesy for you, always serving. And you did too, offering cool water for that boy. Christian put the boy's needs first. That's what Father Keil wants for each of us, to serve in such ways."

I considered how I could serve on this trip despite the reservations some might have about my going along. Certainly, there wasn't a rule against having fun while being a servant, was there?

"You'll take herbs with you," *Frau* Giesy said. She became practical, accepting things without protest. She might have even enjoyed the challenge of preparing a woman for a scouting journey. She wore her hair braided three times like a crown on her head, unlike most of the women with chignons. But then her hair might have been quite curly, and such

gaudiness she would want to hide behind braids. "Herbs offer a service
you can provide, and will keep my son and the other scouts well." She
patted a loose hair into the braid ring. "I suppose he will worry less with
you along."

"My thoughts exactly," I agreed. "I'll make his long days light."

"*Ja,* I'm sure," she said.

"Let me show you about cold camps," Louisa Keil told me at the
storehouse one day, where I picked up flour for my mother. "You must
make meals quickly for them, often without a campfire. We will prepare pemmican and jerky before you go. Many dried peaches, too.
Willie I'll send to listen carefully when men arrive to pick up their wagons. He can tell what overlanders claim as critical to take with them
and what they think they can purchase in the West. Whatever else is
needed, we'll bring with us when we follow in a year or two." She
looked away, distracted. "Perhaps God wishes us to go around the
Horn, travel by ship to California, then north?" She put her fingers
over her mouth to silence herself. "What am I saying here? *Herr* Keil
will decide such things. He always tells me, 'You women stick to your
Strudels, and let us men deal with travel and theology.'" She dropped
her eyes, touched her fingers lightly to the part separating her hair, and
slipped away.

A part of me admired Louisa's devotion and acceptance. But
another part of me wondered if one day as a leader's wife I'd need to be
so docile. I pitched the thought.

"Oh my, oh my," Mary repeated, when we carried the milk bucket
together. She'd pulled her hair back so tight it made her eyes look like
almonds. "This is wise, you think? How can it be good? You with those
men, those spies?"

I wondered why some thought of us as spies, while others considered us scouts. Maybe it had to do with whether we were colonists seek-

ing asylum in a hostile land, or whether we went ahead as foot soldiers, pioneers, making a way for our friends. I preferred the latter.

"Our leader would not have suggested I go if it wasn't a good plan," I told her, already believing he had, in fact, presented the idea. *How quickly our minds tell the story we prefer to remember.*

"My husband says you've angered Father Keil, that he sends you along…as punishment."

I blinked. "Maybe your husband underestimates his brother. Christian approves of my going. Our leader must trust Christian's judgment and Christian trusts his. It's going to be fine, Mary." I took the heavy bucket from her to carry it on alone. "I'll have lots to tell you when we return."

She followed along behind. "Once you find a site, Christian will have to stay to start clearing the wilderness, that's what Sebastian says. I won't see you for a year or more, not until we come west and find you."

"Sebastian doesn't know everything about the future," I told her. "Christian is the spiritual leader, and he'll do what's best for us all. That might mean coming back so he can safely lead all of you from Bethel."

"*Ja,* maybe," Mary said.

My mother shook her head when I told her about my going and my joy in it, but she wiped the worry from her face. "I hoped you would outgrow your need to be…headstrong."

"You and Papa joined our leader when you were older than I am now. You followed him into a wilderness, and see what it gained you. A good home in Bethel."

"We followed our hearts, believing God called us to come here," she said. "Is God calling you to do this thing?"

I asked a question back, something I noticed men did when they wanted to avoid giving answers. "Papa's grandmother joined the Inspirationalists at the colony at Amana, isn't that so? Didn't she raise her voice and say what she thought best? She was accepted and respected. Men followed her inspirations. Maybe this desire to go with my husband into a wilderness is in my blood. Besides," I said, picking at a loose thread on my plain wool dress, "our leader did suggest that I go along."

The more one said a thing the more it turned to truth.

She smoothed my hair back into its chignon. "And did you protest to him, 'Don't send me west with my husband, I beg you'?"

I shook my head.

She sighed. "I suppose he did think of this himself. No woman has ever gone on any of the outreach missions before. Ever. Why *now* is the question. Unless Christian asked for it, but this I doubt based on his reservations."

"My husband spoke with you about this?"

She blushed then. "*Ach,* the walls are too tin in this house."

She turned her back to me, resumed rolling the pie dough I'd interrupted her from finishing. When she spoke again I could barely hear her. "I will miss you, Emma. I will miss you terribly, my daughter who wishes to be known."

"But you'll come when the others come in a year or so, after we send scouts back. You and Papa and Jonathan and David and everyone else. We'll find a place that suits you. We'll be a family again."

Her shoulders sank as she kneaded the dough. "Your father has moved enough, he says. And I am tired too. Too tired to start anew in a wild place." When she looked at me again, I saw that floured fingers had left white streaks on her cheeks when she wiped at her tears.

She wouldn't see her grandchild unless I came back with the scouts. Well, that would be my task then, to ensure that my child would know what it was like to be held by a loving grandmother's hands. Christian would have to assign someone else to stay in the Oregon Territory to begin building. He'd have to bring the news back himself, and me and his child with him.

I considered telling my mother about the baby, but if anyone knew that I expected a child, especially Christian, then everything would change. It wasn't enough that I wanted to begin our family for Christian's sake. I cherished something more.

"I'll have to be the adventurous one for us all," I told my mother. "And hope that Grandmother's spirit travels with me."

———

We would leave on April 23, the day after our wedding anniversary. Our plan included arriving at Independence Rock by the Fourth of July so we would miss any of the heavy mountain snowfalls. That was all I knew from my husband about the arrangements. I learned little more from the women. The scouts shared few tidbits with their wives, mothers, or sisters.

Louisa Keil, Mary Giesy, and I prepared beef pemmican we wrapped in canvas bags that could hang over a horse's neck just in front of the saddle.

"Will you ride sidesaddle all that way?" Mary asked.

"Of course she will," Louisa answered for me. "She wouldn't want to disgrace us by riding like a man would. What would people think?"

"Why would we care what strangers thought?" I asked. "We'll ride through groups of wagons and never see them again."

"Oh, but you might," Louisa said. "As a spiritual leader, Christian must be always at his best. He might recruit new members. You'll want to put your best foot forward, Emma."

"You think that would be the foot that hangs over that uncomfortable hook on the saddle all the way to the Oregon Territory?" I said but laughed. Louisa smiled like an indulgent mother at a challenging child.

We wrapped cheese in chunks and made hardtack, heavy biscuits that would go into tack boxes especially designed for packhorses the scouts would lead behind them. I wondered if I'd have one, too, but Louisa said she didn't know about that. She'd only been given instructions about the food. I thought she might know more, but Louisa supported our leader without question. She always had a response if someone raised a tiny question. He must confide in her to make her uphold his every word, but she shared little with me.

Frau Giesy wrapped dried herbs inside flat tins with tight covers. "Remember," she told me as I worked beside her, "ashes are a good way to stop blood flow from a cut."

My own mother gave me a sewing kit with several leather laces. "They can mend most anything," she told me. We sewed pockets into my skirt hems and placed in them soap cakes the women of the colony had made together the previous fall, following the rendering of hogs. "I see your crinoline has ruffles stitched to it," she said, raising an eyebrow. I started to explain, but she shushed me with her hand. "They'll make good bandages should you need them, as they're already cut in narrow strips."

"The underslip was a gift from Christian," I told her.

She patted my hand. "Even frills and needless adventures can be turned into something useful, Emma. If a person is willing to adapt and let the Lord lead."

Christian rose on Easter morning, then left without waking me up. I slept more soundly than I had before, and I wondered if dreamless rest helped me push away the little "strand of fear," as I called it, sinking in to sleep whenever I thought of telling Christian he'd soon be a father.

I dressed and met my parents downstairs, and with my arm wrapped through my brother's, we all left together in the dawn for the Easter service. Crows lifted against the pink sunrise as we walked toward the church, and the smell of wet earth and freshly turned soil rose to my nose, a comforting scent. My parents moved on ahead as a slight breeze blew, and I stopped to tighten my dark bonnet.

"Our last walk together for a while," Jonathan said, "and you make us late." He scolded, but when I looked up at him, he brushed at his eye. "Something blew in it," he said, turning away.

"I'll be back," I told him, catching up to him and grabbing at his elbow. I skipped out in front of him, all of them, and walked backward. "Next summer. After we find a place and return to get everyone here ready to come, we'll walk again then."

Jonathan shook his head, no. "Something will happen. It always does."

"You might marry by then," I said. "That would be a good something. We can write in between."

"The letters will take forever," Catherine piped in. "It won't be the same without you here, Emma. It just won't be."

I couldn't disagree with that.

"You have Willie and Jake Giesy and Rudy and each other. The boys are full of fun, Jonathan, and those terrible rhymes. You can make them up too. You'll be in the men's band before long and—"

He pushed past me, rushing ahead, leaving me behind to cover a distance that suddenly loomed desperately far and lonely.

Our leader chose texts for his sermon that told the Resurrection story, of the new life that each of us has and how Christ's ancient followers did not believe at first in the sighting of Him, or that He was no longer dead. Our leader even mentioned that a woman took the message first to the men, a fact of Scripture I had read but an admission that surprised me coming from our leader's lips. "*Ve* must always look for Him, alive," our leader concluded, "as Mary did."

It was a joyous sermon, one that reminded us that the Lord went before us and made our way, even when we sometimes had difficulty seeing His work within our lives.

Then he spoke of Joshua being sent out to discover what kind of land awaited the Israelites and urged those he sent into the wild to trust in Providence to guide and protect us. " 'As I was with Moses, so I will be with thee: I will not fail thee, nor forsake thee,' " quoted our leader.

Then he invited each of the scouts to stand before him. I started to stand, but my mother held me back and shook her head. "*Nein,*" she whispered. My face felt hot. I hiccupped once.

I wasn't really a scout; I understood that then. I was merely a guest on this journey, not one who had anything to offer, not one whose journey needed a blessing.

Our leader invited elders of the church to come forward. The men, my father included, placed their hands on the shoulders of the scouts while our leader prayed for their safety and safe return, referring to them all as spies going into the wilderness. I thought Christian would turn toward me, invite me up, but he didn't. I felt my shoulders droop. My mother put her arm around me and whispered the same words directly into my ear after our leader said them. When I looked across, Jonathan stared at me, but I couldn't read the message on his face.

Following the Easter sermon and prayers, the children looked for baskets of hardboiled eggs several of us had hidden in the churchyard the day before. The women baked ten-inch-long rabbit cookies, and I heard Louisa's youngest and my sister Louisa laugh in delight when they located the sweet treats. My mother said it reminded her of Easter celebrations in the old country: rabbit cookies and eggs, the laughter of family and friends. I'd miss this next spring, but I would plan an Easter hunt of my own for our child.

At the community meal held later, some outsiders came by. Having heard about our large meals on special days, people from Shelbina often rode in and were invited to stay. We welcomed curiosity seekers—or at least we had. We always made guests feel welcome. Our leader said they were all potential recruits, though when they later declined involvement, he often blamed outsiders for bringing into our midst moral decay and the longing for lavish ways. This day, the two young men ate well and talked with the colony men about horseflesh and tack. No one spoke about our impending journey with outsiders present, so it was not until late that evening, after Christian's final meeting with the spies, that I was alone with my husband.

Christian hardly spoke a word as he undressed in our room.

"Which horse will I ride?" I asked as we lay beside each other on the feather bed.

I received no answer. Instead, I heard the soft breathing of a man taken in sleep.

Is he angry with me? Will he be like our leader and share little with his wife? I told myself his silence grew from the journey's weight, but it occurred to me that I had much to learn about my husband's moods. Discovering them in the presence of eight other men on a cross-country journey might not be the place most young wives would choose to learn of their husbands' dispositions. Well, so be it. It was not my fault I knew so little of him; our leader had kept us separated from the start. At last, we'd be together, I the only woman on the journey west.

I pulled the quilt over my shoulder. I'd wanted to be singular and here I was. My husband snored softly, and I thought then as I drifted off to sleep that the schooling I'd just signed onto might be more than I had bargained for.

8

So Many Questions

We prepared to leave early, to the melody of songbirds and crows. That morning, I learned I'd ride sidesaddle on a sturdy chestnut-colored gelding named Fred. My father thought mules might be wise for the pack animals. Christian agreed and thanked my father for the suggestion, one we had no way of knowing would later serve us well.

I savored the flushed faces of friends there to see us off, knowing our leader approved of their delaying the start of their workday in order to celebrate this adventure. Well, he didn't call it an adventure. To our leader and his spies we performed the Lord's work, undertook a serious and purposeful activity. I tried to remember that, but the sweet scent of spring and the profusion of faces there to see us off kept bringing me back to joy.

Christian's somber face reminded me of the concern expressed by our elders about why we were making this journey. The evils of the outside world pushed us into it. Outsiders lured Bethelites away. The railroad threatened to steam through our town, bringing strangers from even farther off to wash away the established colony routines. Our leader worried that we young people were losing our piety and ability to follow God. Hadn't there been rumors of an unplanned infant born into the fold? Hadn't that young girl and her family moved away? These intrusions brought us to this day, not the adventure of a journey into the unknown. Yet that uncertain unknown called to me.

I took deep breaths, tried to soak up every sight and sound and smell of this stepping-off place. I would see things and hear things and know news no one here would learn of unless we told them. I coughed into my handkerchief to veil the grin that would not leave my face.

I learned then of more details worked out in advance by the many meetings Christian held with the others. Fred, my horse, would walk in front of Opal, a white mule I had sometimes walked behind when spelling my brother in the fields. Opal's packs carried a dutch oven and ten tin plates and cups that Christian, one of the colony's finest tin-smiths, had made himself. We scouts—as I preferred to think of us—packed pemmican made not of buffalo meat, but of beef cut into thin flakes and hung to dry before a smoking fire. Papa pounded it into a powder, then packed it into skin bags and poured grease in it to make it solid and sound. We could eat it raw or boil it with a little flour and have a nutritious meal quickly prepared. Flour, tea, sugar, biscuits, Edward's Preserved Potatoes, and cooking grease were packed in canvas bags, enough to take us all across, we hoped, knowing that as we moved west, the prices for products would go up.

Papa also suggested a mixture of cornmeal, cinnamon, and sugar, which he said I should stir into water for a good drink along the trail. His eyes teared up as he told me, a tenderness I'd savor as the miles between us grew.

My mother packed the mixture in an oversized oiled bag and pat-ted it as she pulled the flap over the side of the pack. "When it's empty, you can use it for so many tings," she told me.

Other items needed we planned to barter from better-stocked wagon trains or buy at the forts along the way; we expected to shoot deer or elk as the occasion arose. We'd need to be careful with ammunition, but being frugal and orderly were a Bethel colonist's middle name. Anything we couldn't get for a "good deal," we'd do without, though Christian said we had money enough to look prosperous to appeal to potential recruits, but not so wealthy we invited the attention of thieves.

Christian announced these arrangements to the entire crowd, as a way of engaging each of them in this journey and so they'd know how to pray for us in the days ahead.

We hoped for a wet spring in the prairies so by the time we rode through, the grass would be high and lush and our horses and mules able to feed. Michael Schaefer Sr. silenced anyone who aired concern about Indian troubles or disease we might encounter on the way. "We do the Lord's work," he said. "Worrying is not part of our labor."

"*Ja*," John Stauffer said. "If I thought it so, I would not have brought my son with me." Hans Stauffer was stockier and taller than his father, the son a security for his father and each of us.

My youngest sisters and littlest brother played and patted Sheppie. They didn't understand that I'd not be seeing them for months, though when the girls sprawled their elbows out at night, they might remember me with fondness by my absence. Catherine actually cried as she said good-bye, then pressed a small German Bible into my hands. "You'll need this," she said.

"Christian will have his along," I told her, attempting to hand it back. "We can only take so much."

"Take it," my mother said. "Each of us needs our own bowl of wisdom from which to draw without having to ask another."

Later I'd be more than grateful for both my mother's words and the book Catherine gave me.

Mother fussed at the cape she wore against the morning chill. My father shook young Joe Knight's hand, then turned to his old friend, Adam Schuele. "I remember when we were sent out those years ago." Adam nodded. "Your good judgment kept us from trouble more than once. This time you have my daughter to look after."

"*Ja,*" Joseph Knight interjected. "For better or worse." He looked at me but didn't smile.

"The prayers of the community, David," Adam Schuele said. "This is what will keep her safe. And us, too."

I tried not to think of the sadness in my father's eyes, focused instead on his hand gently resting on my mother's shoulder as she tried to untie her cape and keep William in check. Successful, she threw the dark green wool around my shoulders and pulled me to her. I felt the bones in her back, tried not to notice how she quivered in my arms. "When you need a mother's holding," she said, "you put this on and think of me, Emma." The cape hung longer than my own, since she stood taller than I.

"I will, Mama," I whispered, "I will."

Finally, it was time. I held each of my sisters and brothers in turn, told Mary I would write. Christian mounted without offering me assistance, so I led Fred to the riding stump and stepped onto the stirrup, swinging my leg high enough to hook my knee over the saddle hook. I had never felt secure on a sidesaddle and more than once had ventured through a field bareback on a nag, just to see what it would be like to ride with greater confidence. But this day I took it as a small sacrifice made to join my husband on this journey.

I adjusted my wrapper over my legs. The wrappers we women wore when we left the colony to go to Shelbina or Hannibal or other outside places served me well now. Made of wool the color of a wet ash, it folded in at a woman's waist and tied with a sash but had room for growth. The overfold prevented anyone from seeing a woman's curves or their absence when she lost them to a growing infant. Like a chrysalis, my wrapper kept the secret of my butterfly beneath its gray.

I laid Mama's cape out over the back of Fred, who pranced a bit, and I nearly dropped Catherine's Bible. I placed it in the saddle pack, then tied the front of the cape at my neck. My mother's hug wrapped me up in her lavender scent.

Adam Schuele's family waved good-bye. All the Giesy clan came out to say farewell to us, or at least to Christian, who steadied his horse next to mine now. Helena did pat my knee as it hung over the sidesaddle. She said she hoped I chose well and that it wasn't too late to change my mind.

"*Herr* Keil will understand if you decided to stay behind," she said quietly as she looked up at me. "He has a gentle heart and would listen to the pleas of a young woman."

"*Herr* Keil is the one who told me I should go. I wouldn't want to upset him," I said. "It's for the good of the colony," I added. "What a woman sees and sends back will reassure the rest of you when you follow. Besides"—I leaned over to her to keep my voice low—"I wouldn't want to challenge Father Keil."

Helena stepped back, her lips pursed. She folded her hands before her as though in prayer. Our leader stood in the center of the half circle we scouts formed around him. He draped his arm around Willie's shoulder. "Willie vill ride in the lead vagon when we leave Bethel to go to the place you choose for us. All of us depend on you now, each of you, to listen to God's Vord and His voice to lead you to the very best place for us to continue His vork. Pay attention to each other," our leader said. "Send back vord of vhat you've found and we vill follow. Be salt and light in this new world."

Following this he offered us a blessing general enough to include even me, and the brass band played a German marching song that made my eyes water, knowing it'd be months, maybe years, before I'd hear those horns again.

We started out, and then my brother Jonathan ran along beside us, as did several other young men, Sheppie, and a few other dogs, until we rode around the bend that marked the outskirts of Bethel. There Jonathan grabbed at Sheppie's collar, and the men stood and waved until my brother was nothing more than a tiny dark thread in the quilt that had been the comfort of the only home I'd known. I felt an awful chill.

———

The first day, Christian told me, would be our "rhythm day," finding the preferences of the animals, which horse needed to be in the lead, which could follow easily behind another without wanting to rush ahead, which pack mules would likely tangle us up if we didn't attend to their wishes. None of us owned the mules or the horses we rode, as they belonged to the colony, but Christian at least sat astride a horse familiar to him, unlike the rest of the men and me. The pack animals, too, needed time to adjust to their loads and the hitch of the ropes keeping everything even.

When the road toward St. Joseph narrowed, I brought up the rear, usually with Christian and his pack animal riding beside me. Opal, the mule, pulled against Fred at times, twisting the horse, but with occasional words from me to the mule, Fred was able to move along easily again. "Opal likes attention," I told Christian, who responded with something that sounded like, "She's in good company." But when I asked him to repeat it, he said, "She's in a good place in this company then. You can talk to her back here and keep her in line."

I'd vowed to be as quiet a scout as I could be, not to question what Christian did or directed, and to treat the men with deference and respect. They did know much more than I about being out in the world, and I vowed to watch them as I did my husband. Silence was my word for the day. Silence and listening and seeing so much I'd never seen before.

We rode on dusty trails northwest and passed small acreages with men and women already working their fields in the early spring. Cowbells joined the music of the lambs' bleating, and I could almost taste the feast of new life that always came with the melting of snow. We rested the animals ten minutes of each hour, allowing them to rip at grass while the men checked packs and took drinks of water. The other fifty minutes, we rode steady with little chatter.

It's what I wrote in my journal that evening: *silence*, the whisper of wind while I slept beneath the stars for the first time in my life, the quiet warmth rising as I lay next to my husband in a bedroll, the comforting noise of fingers scraping on tin plates and the smack of lips with our first meal of beef jerky and hard biscuits washed down with spring water. The men said nothing while we shared the meal that Adam Schuele prepared, not me. I wondered if it would be this way all the way to Oregon Territory, and if the meal was an offering of servanthood by Adam or a statement of no confidence in my abilities. When I tried to help he said, with gentle words, "I'm accustomed to this, Sister Giesy. Let me."

Following the meal, Christian offered a Scripture and words of prayer and encouragement—at least that was how I took them. The men nodded and kept their heads bowed as my husband spoke, rising as one to his "Amen," then moving in silence toward their bedrolls.

In the notepad I packed, I wrote of being away from the sounds of the shoe factory, the mill, church bells, the cackling of geese, the thump-thump of my mother kneading dough in the morning, my father sharpening a knife against a big strap of leather, Jonathan riding a horse down the streets of Bethel followed by yips from the dog, William's little snores that sounded like kitten whimpers. I wrote of hearing my husband preach for the first time—at least it seemed like a sermon—and how humble he acted, how willing he appeared to be molded by what the Lord should provide, and his trust in the mission our leader had set us all on.

The other men laid their bedrolls some distance from us, but I could hear an occasional cough and a mumble; a moment of laughter, too, and I wondered if Christian missed being with them, felt stuck here with me. He would have been lying next to them; perhaps they'd share ideas about the route, about the day, about life.

Yet here he was with me. I hoped he wouldn't come to resent my presence.

"I wish we'd brought a dog along," I told Christian in a whisper as I put my notepad away and crawled in beside him.

"*Ja*, Adam Knight said that too. A dog would let us know when trouble comes. We should have thought of it."

"There'll be dogs along the way," I said. "Maybe we could find one that would suit us."

"Unless he was a pup, he'd be loyal to another and eventually leave us anyway," he said. "And a pup would give us headaches getting into the packs at night, chewing the saddle strings."

"I'd watch him," I said.

He didn't respond.

"I would. It'd give me something to do while the rest of you are all working together so hard." He stayed silent, and then I realized by his slow breathing that he slept.

I wondered if our days would be like this: hard, silent rides with shared meals and prayers but few moments to truly be with my husband. And when I was, would not his mind be on the challenges of the mission or on seeking exhausted sleep?

His responsibility in this journey struck me for the first time as I watched the stars, and I hoped, even prayed before I slept, that I would do nothing to trouble him, nothing that would get in the way of my husband's success; though when I, warm beneath my sleeper, prayed those words, I felt a twinge of regret.

I turned over and decided then not to tell Christian anything about my carrying his child. Why worry him when he had so many other worries, and perhaps this one might never come to pass. It was possible I'd lose the child, a thought that sent more than threads of fear through me, threatening to knot up in tangles. That sort of thing happened even in our colony with good care and midwives to assist. *Look at Mary and Sebastian,* I told myself. Better to keep this all silent, wait and see what each day might bring. Besides, this day had already cracked me open, watching my brothers and sisters and parents disappear from my life; I couldn't afford to split my heart further.

I tossed and turned, trying to get comfortable. I slipped my hand up under the quilt rolled beneath my neck. I felt something cool there, hard. I pawed beneath it and pulled out a tin chatelaine. Slender as a finger, it had tiny designs on the side, a flower, a small bird. I removed the cap and inside were four sewing needles, the finest Shelbina had to offer.

Christian must have made it! But why didn't he give it to me? Why let me find it beneath my quilt? I held the gift in my hand. It had a ring so I could wear it around my neck. My husband gave me a gift both pragmatic and beautiful, and I, I kept secrets from him.

Our leader's words from Genesis of a woman's punishment came to me. But oddly, so did the words God said to Adam and Eve first: *Where art thou?*

Where was I, indeed, leaving the safety of my family, carrying secrets, hiding a possible harm from my husband whom I barely knew, who had dimensions and depth I was only now uncovering? What else was I hiding from, and what price would I eventually pay for my wanting to be known, to stand out in this monotony of colony I'd grown up in?

I'd have to eventually tell Christian about the baby. Would he forgive me for not telling him or our leader, who would surely not have sent me along if he had known? At least Christian would believe that of *Herr* Kiel.

I was not so sure. It might have made our leader more likely to have banished me to a wild place, to show me the power of God's words in Genesis that promised I'd bring forth children in sorrow. I tried to remember the rest of that verse: *Thy desire shall be to thy husband, and he shall rule over thee.*

But there'd been earlier words, spoken to Eve as she came out of the Garden, naked and ashamed, words that now spoke to me, a woman who had the will to choose her way. They were words not about the present, nor the future, or what my pushing to be here would eventually mean. They were words about my past. How had I gotten here? What price had I paid? What had I feared would happen if Christian had left me behind?

I prayed for sleep then and that I'd accept the answers to so many questions all begun with God's words to Eve: *What is this that thou hast done?*

9

As Singular
as Sunrise

I counted days by sunrises, noting their distinctive spread of dark to light, the way the pink gave way to ivory clouds against the morning blue. Each noon, Christian read from Lansford Hastings's *The Emigrants' Guide to Oregon and California* until we'd all heard every word written by this man through Christian's booming voice. He halted on occasion, translating from the author's English into the German we all spoke. Adam suggested we should hear the words in English to accustom ourselves to the language of the land we now lived in. The others nodded agreement. No one looked to me.

The writer of this guide blended his enthusiasm with details about river crossings and camping suggestions. But listening, even in the English I still struggled with, it gave me a sense of belonging, of hearing what they all heard at the same time even if some of the subject matter prickled. I hoped I'd find some small piece of information that I could later draw on that might save the day, that would please Christian, make him grateful I'd come along for more than someone to warm his bed. I didn't want to be a burden; truly I didn't. I wanted to belong and not stand out because of trouble, but from what I could offer. I wanted to be as reliable as sunrise, yet as singular.

Christian finished reading the Hastings book the day before we

reached St. Joseph, where we hoped to catch a ferry. Hastings had rec-
ommended this Missouri River crossing and the road that would take
us west, following the Platte River. He related details of what each
wagon should contain and what routes were wise and what to be wary
of at various watering places.

More than once in the few days we'd been on our way, I wished we
had a wagon hauling items such as kegs of water and stores of food and
extra clothing more easily reached than that tied up in the bedroll knots.
I had only one change of clothes—a woolen dress, another wrapper, and
my ruffled petticoat—and before the second day passed, as I watched
women doing laundry along the way, I realized I'd probably adjust to the
smell of my own perspiration rather than endure the effort of scrubbing
and pounding at rocks near streams along the trail. Doing my wash and
Christian's would be work enough. For a moment I longed for the large
group of women who scrubbed their laundry together at Bethel. I
pitched that thought. *No sense hanging on to what will not be.*

Most of all, I wished a wagon for the privacy it would have provided when I tended to my hygiene; in the shade of it, if not inside.
But a wagon would have slowed us, the men agreed, so during our ten-
minute respites for the animals, I found a tree or shrub and hoped such
sentinels of sanitation would continue to dot the landscape as we
crossed the continent. I imagined discovering shrubs with new kinds of
berries I could squat behind, increasing my understanding of botany
while managing bloat.

Hastings's book for emigrants did not promise such extensive trees
or shrubs once we reached the prairie country. His little book ignored
most of a woman's needs, so I hoped he might have misunderstood the
importance of mentioning such facts. Instead, Hastings wrote words
that encouraged early starts with longer rests at noon to manage the
daytime heat, or identifying prudent encampments and explaining how

to avoid "noxious airs" found near muddy waters. The author of Christian's noontime read spoke little of diseases and had written his book back in 1845, after the first cholera epidemic, but before this most recent scare that still plagued travelers' westward journeys. After reading the section about "muddy waters" and "noxious airs," Christian urged greater caution at watering sites. "We'll boil all drinking water not from springs," he said, so that we might all arrive healthy and well.

"We'll ask about illness on the wagons we encounter," he told John Stauffer, who patted his horse's neck as they spoke. "They'll have sent scouts ahead and may know of places we should avoid."

"Scouts sending out scouts," Hans Stauffer said. He removed his hat to scratch at his head where an early receding hairline made his hair look like a brown peninsula with white sandy beaches on either side. He scratched that spot so often that a callus formed on the right side.

"How I felt about you sometimes," Adam Knight told his brother, Joe. "When you'd run off as a *Dummkopf* and I'd have to catch you before Mama found out you'd left the yard or were so lost you whizzed your pants in fear."

"At least I explored a place or two over the years," Joe Knight said. A pink flush formed on his cheeks. "While you were busy chasing skirts."

"Joe!" Adam chastised. He nodded toward me.

"Oh, sorry, *Frau* Giesy. I forget you were here."

"I suppose that should be a compliment," I told him, curtsying as I handed him a refilled cup of corn juice. "I don't want to be a bother."

"No bother," Joe replied. He raised a single finger to the air, one of his habits when he spoke.

"I didn't wish you along, *Frau* Giesy," Adam said. "But you weren't no trouble this past week, and you even helped some."

"That might make a fine epitaph," I said. *"She weren't no trouble and she even helped some."*

"Let's not think morbid thoughts," Christian said. "Indeed, you'll help even more before long, become a true member of this scouting party." His words lifted my spirits.

"*Ja?* How will I do this?" Were they going to let me cook then at last?

"You'll be in charge of washing our clothes," Christian told me.

Unintended, my lower lip pouted out.

———

I confess, the excitement of wagons and horses and mules and oxen and people with accents closer to mine—*are they Swiss or maybe from Bavaria?*—intrigued me when we reached St. Joseph, Missouri, where Christian had said we would cross the great river. I heard French and what I assumed to be Spanish intermixed with English, and within an hour my ears hurt with the barrage, and my head ached from deciphering. What were all these people doing here? Where were they going? How would they know when they got there? I began to appreciate that we scouts had criteria, we knew what we needed to find and why we were seeking. Wilhelm held all of us together even in his absence, his words of life and death reminding us of the little time we had in the former and the encroaching hot breath of the latter. Did these others traveling west trust only Hastings's words? Or perhaps the leaders of their wagon groupings? I began to think about leadership and what it meant to the success of our task.

We had all we needed for our survival, were secure in our journey west.

We staked the horses above the ferry, awaiting passage while Christian and Adam Schuele, who understood English the best, prepared to venture forth to find out how long the wait for the ferry crossing would be. Adam headed south.

Christian asked, "Would you like to come along?" I beamed. "You'll need to watch where you walk to avoid horse apples and garbage plaguing the streets," he told me. I didn't mind. I could enter a world I'd never known. I'd love the confusion of people.

"I thank you for the gift," I said. "You were asleep when I found it. I didn't want to wake you."

Christian nodded. "You'll have need of it, mending our clothes."

"My mother sent her sewing kit with me. But this"—I patted the chatelaine hanging beneath my bodice—"the designs on the chatelaine make it more than just a tool. It's…art. Beauty for its own sake."

Christian's ear turned the color of tomatoes, and he seemed relieved when tent store hawkers offered meat on sticks and wild-eyed mountain men announced "essentials" for sale for the journey west. Christian's height caused people to step aside for us, though he never pushed or shoved his way. He tipped his hat to women and children, and I wondered what it would be like to understand all their English phrases as easily as Christian did.

A buxom woman with a painted face must have heard me talking to him in German, for she stepped out from the shade of her tent and smiled, boldly placing painted fingernails on his forearm. She said to me in German as she gazed up at Christian, "Your papa here is a handsome man, maybe in need of someone to look after his *kind*."

I frowned. "I'm not his *kind*." I added in English, "I'm his wife, not his child." Were these the kind of women that Willie and my brother spoke about in whispers after they'd come back from Hannibal?

She stepped closer to Christian and patted the lapel of his jacket as she inhaled his scent. The drift of her perfume rose over the garbage smells from piles around her. "*Ach,* my foul luck," she said, slapping Christian's lapel now in good humor.

I put my arm through Christian's, something I'd never have done in a crowd back in Bethel, where I'd have walked a pace or two behind.

She stepped away but kept eyeing him as though he were a good horse. "I always have an eye for the unavailable."

"Do you have an eye for the time of the crossing?" Christian asked her. "I suspect you've seen these lines before and know how long it'll take."

She stretched her neck to look at the rows of wagons and cattle, people and dogs, that crowded toward the narrow docking area. "Days, I'd say. By wagon?" she asked. "You go west by wagon?" Christian shook his head no. "Moving fast then. Someone on your tail." She leered at me.

I gripped Christian's arm. "*Ach,* you are a—"

"Our marriage is blessed," Christian said, "and our journey, too." She lowered her eyes just a moment, and Christian spoke into that interlude. "You could have such assurances too, *Fräulein.* There is someone always available, someone who would care for you as a parent loves a child. A whole community exists of people who love each other, who serve and demonstrate God's grace on this earth. No needs go unmet. It is a place of Eden."

"An Eden on earth," she snorted, then looked down, stuffed a handkerchief into the cleavage exposed at her breast. "There are always snakes in gardens."

"All the better then to enter all gardens with others."

"One day, perhaps." Her words softened. "If it were me, I'd go north to Harney's Landing. Takes you sooner to the Platte. It's about thirty miles south of Nebraska City, what they're calling it now. Used to be Old Fort Kearny. Ferry's good there, I'm told. Not so long a wait."

"I thank you for your help, *Fräulein.*" He tipped his hat to her again, as though she were a regal lady. "In a year or so, a larger colony will come this way, and you'd be welcome to join us. We're Bethelites. Mostly German, in service to each other as we're commanded."

"If they're as handsome as you, I might join up," she laughed.

"Not the best reason to come along, but God can use even that," he said.

"*Danke,*" she said. "I'll consider it if my fortunes don't pick up." Then she ducked back under her tent awning.

So this was how Christian won people over, not only with his smile and dazzling eyes but with his tenderness, his ability to see through the thick perfume, look past the sagging cleavage. He listened to what she didn't say and treated her with a dignity I hadn't thought she deserved, not with her suggestion that I was too young for Christian or that our marriage couldn't be real. He stepped over those things.

"What did you think of that woman?" I asked as we walked away.

"It doesn't matter what I thought," Christian said. "Like you, she is a child of God and therefore my sister. So I love her just the same."

The same as me? I felt a rush of some emotion I couldn't even name.

———

Christian and Adam Schuele compared notes upon our return to where the horses grazed. We'd made camp a good two miles out of town, as already the grass had been ripped clean by earlier wagons passing through with their stock. We agreed we'd head north, but Adam suggested we take the steamer *Mandan* up the Missouri River instead of going by land.

"We can afford this?" Hans asked John Genger.

John Genger frowned. I'd become aware of the separation of duties of the men. Hans Stauffer handled the stock. The Knights did the packing and cooking and determined when we needed to stop to check packs and ropes and seek supplies. The Stauffers were skilled at finding agreeable sites for our stock and for us to camp and seemed to have a unique understanding of landscape and weather. Adam Schuele and Christian did the negotiating with people along the way and brought into the open any issues needing decisions. George Link hunted and handled the weapons and ammunition. John Genger, the quiet one, kept the money and the records of expenditures.

Back in Bethel, I'd never even heard John Genger talk, and Mary Giesy once told me she thought he might be Jewish. At least one Jewish family lived within the colony, my father had told me, but he never would say who they were.

The unsavory task of laundry became my expertise, but fortunately, these were tidy men more interested in speed than in sanitizing often. Like me, they were anxious to enter land they'd never encountered before, land beyond the Missouri.

"I think we should not spend the money this way," John Genger answered.

"It'll save us time to go by steamer," John Stauffer said. "Our goal is to get west as fast as we can, find the site, and send some of us back to bring the main colony forward. The sooner we do this, the better, *ja?*"

"The steamer would rest the stock," Adam Knight said, nodding in agreement.

"We must save all the money we can in case we need to buy our land rather than get free Oregon Territory land," John Genger said. "This is not wise to spend so freely when we are only out a few weeks." He wore a small-brimmed hat that couldn't possibly shade his eyes from the sun, and he squinted as he spoke.

"You're the banker, John, and we value your advice," Christian said. "We'll pray about this tonight, and we will all decide in the morning."

We will all decide. I wondered if that meant my view would also be considered. If so, I'd vote with John, not because of the cost but because of the steamer. It was worrisome enough to think of crossing a swollen river, but to be on a larger body of water, well, the thought of that made my mouth dry. I hated the lurch of boats and their uncertainty, the need to place trust in the captains and pilots. I had to watch the weather more whenever we went somewhere by boat. I had to grip the sides and never rested, not once. I secretly thanked my parents, who preferred carriages over canoes.

But no one asked my opinion, and so I didn't have to disagree with my husband in front of the others.

In the morning, it was decided. Each man awoke to some assurance that taking the steamer north would be the wisest course. Even John Genger concurred. This surprised me. I hoped for a rousing debate with John taking my side, since my voice wasn't invited into the fray. But no, it appeared all were satisfied with the choice to spend the money and rest the stock. This consensus Christian labeled "God's will."

"Why are so many heading westward?" I asked Christian as we waited to board the steamer, my heart pounding, seeking diversions. The line for the steamer wasn't nearly so long as that of the ferry. "Were they all so unhappy where they were?"

"We didn't leave from unhappiness," he said. "We left because we were sent, for the good of those left behind. We have a privilege to prepare for the decisions that matter most in life, not just how to live, but where we go when we die. We listen to our leader and follow his advice. He leads us by his passion for keeping us from eternal damnation. I don't know whose advice all these other people follow."

"Aren't you frightened, even a little?" I asked.

He frowned. "Fear does not come from the Lord, *Liebchen.* I am cautious. We must be careful, *ja,* but not fearful." I rubbed my thumb and forefingers together. He held my hands in his. "Something bothers you? Your fingers tell me their story,"

I rolled my fingers into my palms, and shook my head no. "I feel a little ill. The water makes me dizzy, that's all. It will pass."

He pulled me to him, tucked me under his arm as a mother hen does her chicks. He patted my shoulder. I looked around to see if others frowned at this public display of affection. No one appeared to care. Worldly ways had merit.

"Perfect love casteth out fear," he said. "Perfect, as in complete. We have nothing to worry about."

Now was not the time to tell Christian that his wife objected to watercraft. I'd probably never be forced to take a steamer ever again. The prayers of the men had been answered, not mine. They had a more direct voice, I imagined, than a woman. That was a thought Helena Giesy might have. So this must be God's will, that they all agreed. Mine was a singular fear, one I'd have to swallow.

We were told to come back in the morning.

As we led our animals through the dust back to our camp, I decided it would be difficult to be a part of this jumble of wagons and horses and people and cows without knowing why we were leaving, or if we weren't well led. I had assurance to both of those questions, or so I thought. *Such assurance should help me overcome my fears.*

That's what I told myself as I took a deep breath and boarded the steamer the next morning.

10

Willing Things Well

My mouth watered, my fingernails burrowed into my palms, I felt ill and thought I'd lose my breakfast. I could barely keep my balance with the swirl and sway. But an hour or so out, I apparently got my sea legs, as George Link called it, his chipped tooth giving his words a kind of whooshing sound. I could walk along the deck without a wobble. The water pooling in my throat stayed swallowed, and I breathed in spring air. As the shore sped by, the wind dried my watery eyes. I could hear the steady swish of water rising up over the wheel, pushing us north. When I tired, I leaned up against our stack of packs and saddles piled on deck and pulled my notepad out to write in. I'd decided to describe the fearful parts, but list what went well, too.

I prepared a letter for Jonathan, and later, Hans loaned me a book he'd finished reading and said he wouldn't start it over for a time. I read, and the leather dropped into my apron when I slept as the afternoon heat warmed my face. I could still sleep.

When I awoke, I looked for Christian and found him engaged in animated conversation with a man. And another woman.

That feeling rose again, and I could name it now. Envy, what our leader once described as the greatest sin, for it announced awareness of the self; vanity—desiring more than God provided.

God had given me a good husband when we lived in the cocoon of the colony where each member understood our commitment to each other, would never think to flirt or interfere. Here, amidst the world where people spoke a different language than what I could understand, here the rules were different. Perhaps Christian might regret his vows spoken to a young girl. Perhaps he resented having to translate for me, felt embarrassed by a woman who could not speak English well or gather information that would ease our journey west. The buxom *fräulein* came to mind.

I jotted my worries into my journal and wrote to Mary then to take my mind from my sinful state. She would be working in the school in my place, I supposed, laughing with the children, suffering Helena, assisting Karl Ruge. I hoped we could post the letter somewhere along the way.

It would have been a placid journey if not for the weight of my worry. Not just about the river and how it could claim whole wagons, horses, and lives, but about my deception, for that was what it was. Christian loved Truth, changed his life for Truth, and here he was, unaware of a truth that would affect his life.

That evening, as Christian stood with his arm wrapped protectively around me, I considered again when to tell him. We curled up near our packs. John Genger had booked passage for us but no berth, no privacy. It saved money, and our exposure to the elements would be only for the night. Others, too, slept on the deck. I tried to imagine the best time to tell Christian so together we could enjoy the arrival of this child. But something told me I should wait. We were too close to Bethel here. I could too easily be sent back.

Nothing dreadful happened on the steamer north. It seemed sometimes the bad things I thought would happen didn't. Maybe by imagining the worst, I was able to keep them at bay. Helena said once, we should always think on worthy things, that Scripture encourages us toward joy not sorrow. But joy arrived to welcoming arms; sorrow needed reining in.

———

Instead of being bounced around and tussled, we eased through float-ing logs and flotsam, landing on the west side of the Missouri the next morning. At last we stood in "the West." We'd sleep this night in Indian Territory, as the scouts called it.

Maybe we were all regaining our land legs, but once on shore with the horses gathered together by the Stauffers and Knights, and Opal whinnying notice, we all stood silent for a time. The breeze played with my hair braids wrapped in swirls around my head now. I hoped the style made me look older. My bonnet hung loose at my back. I could say truthfully that I enjoyed this watery journey and wondered at such a change.

Around us, people bustled away, called out to friends and family, but we stayed silent, staring east. Maybe the men prayed.

Christian looked back across the water toward Nebraska City— what little there was of the town. I touched the sleeve of his coat. "What are you thinking of, husband?"

"Hmm?" He turned to me. The startling, longing look disap-peared. "Just saying good-bye," he said. "Foolish. Not to worry, *Lieb-chen*." He patted my hand.

"We'll be going back next year, and you'll see it all again," I told him cheerfully.

"Indeed," he said.

His absent-minded agreement made me wonder if he thought we might not return. "We thank God for our safe journey, ask Him to bless the remainder, and then we head west," he said to the group more than to me, his strong arms spread out wide as though he could take us all in, keep us all safe.

It must have worked—this plan of mine—to think of all that could go wrong to prevent its occurrence because little troubled us those first days. We rode our horses on the south side of the Platte and only had to hear about the rugged crossings of those who took the north side of the river. The men talked horseflesh with other travelers, and Hans even made a trade at a farmer's plot, turning over a tiring horse for a sturdier mount, a more willful mule who became a mate of Opal. We found good grass for them to graze on, and at least three times each week, we had wood to fire a hot meal in the evening.

Our camps were efficiently made, the beans cooked easily without sticking to the pan. Joseph Knight pulled out our Golden Rule Whiskey just once those first weeks to settle Michael Sr.'s stomach. We stopped on Sundays for a full day of rest, and Christian even helped me with the laundry on Saturday evenings if we were near water then.

Even the weather cooperated, though sometimes rain poured so hard we could barely see one another as we staked the tents. But my mother's wool cape kept me warm and nearly dry. Thunder boomed and lightning crackled and lifted the hair at the back of my neck, but the stock stayed together, and in the mornings, we repeated our routine of readying with minimal adjustment. Inconveniences, yes. Finding a private shrub when needed, biting my tongue when I'd rather have talked, sleeping without a down pillow at my head. But I held out the image of what we'd have one day when we arrived at wherever we were going: a roof over our heads, a permanent place to stay, sunshine to make the garden grow with just enough rain to keep it watered. Everything we heard of Oregon Territory made it sound like Eden. I could put up with temporary inconveniences knowing they'd be gone at the end of the trail. I vowed to share that with the Bethelites, to prepare them for the joys that would follow the trials of the journey.

As we could, we paralleled larger lines of wagons, camped at night close enough to hear their music and the mooing of their cows. We met a woman named Elliot traveling with her children to join her husband, and a young couple named Bond, all heading to the Willamette Valley ir. the southern part of the Territory. They eagerly looked forward to their new lives. They spoke slowly when I asked so I could understand them and smiled when my English broke through the German in an understandable way.

Most of the time, though, because we traveled faster than wagons could, we rode alone on the vast prairies, tiny pencil dashes against a slate of prairie green. A band of people so insignificant that even the Sioux took little notice of us, leaving us alone to contemplate the monotony of our days, the certainty of our future.

At one stop, Christian spoke with travelers who said they'd go north of the Columbia River once they arrived in the Oregon Territory, for the land there stood timbered and the Californians bought the logs as quick as they were cut. He shared this news with the scouts. "Timbered ground offers a ready market for logs. It leaves land remaining to farm. This has potential," John Genger said.

Dogs often barked in the distance when we nooned. No lost pups wandered in seeking scraps, though. Our stock became accustomed to the rhythm of our ways. I kept silent, trying to be that woman who "weren't no trouble and even helped some."

Just before Chimney Rock, some days out from Fort Laramie, George Link killed an antelope and brought it in to jerk. The rock pillar could be seen for miles before we reached it, and there we stayed a day beside a trickling spring that offered not enough water to wash clothes in, but ran fresh and not dirtied, unlike the rain-swollen Platte we'd been riding beside. We'd made good time, Joe Knight noted, his finger pointed to the air like the spire of Chimney Rock. "It's just June," he said.

"We are being tenderly led," Christian noted.

At Fort Laramie, we restocked beans and traded some of George Link's good jerked meat for sugar and tea and then left messages to be taken back by those heading east, most returning from the California gold fields or Oregonians bent on bringing the rest of their families out.

———

We were a day out of Laramie, whipped by late June winds that flapped at our tent in the night, when Christian let me know that he knew.

The intensity of his gaze must have awakened me as he leaned up on one elbow, gazing down at me when I opened my eyes. Moonbeams split the tent opening, giving a shadowed hue to his handsome face. "Can't you sleep?" I asked.

He remained silent for a time, then spoke. "I've lived around women all my life. Watched the moods of my mother and sisters and my sisters-in-law wax and wane with the moon." He combed hair from my face with the back of his fingers. He smelled of lye and vinegar from the soap we'd used to pound at the men's jeans.

I swallowed and beneath the blanket, my thumb and forefinger began their nervous rub.

"So I note," he said, "that something is amiss with you."

"I'm fine, husband. This clear air does me well. I may have lost a little weight with our spare servings, but I'm healthy. Soon we'll be in the mountains and—"

"Your face has gained fullness." He hesitated, then added, "And you've had no flow since we've left Bethel. None before that for a month or more, now that I pay attention. I've been remiss. But you, you have deceived me." I heard my heart pound in my ears. "Indeed. It's not a wife's place to keep secrets."

"I haven't *kept* it from you," I said. "I wasn't sure until recently. I didn't want to worry you. My mother lost two children. I might not have the stamina to carry this infant, and I didn't want you to—"

"All the more reason to tell me, Emma," he said. He'd stopped stroking my face. He sat up, lit the lamp, and then returned, his legs folded over, his hands clasped in his lap. He squeezed his hands together, open and closed, steady as a beating heart. "You should not be doing heavy work. The laundry." He shook his head. "Perhaps not even riding as you do, though how else we can do this now I don't know. Maybe you will need to walk more, but this will slow us. I will have to confer with the others."

"Why?" I whispered to him. "It's our baby, our family. It's none of their business. I can do the washing. You help me."

"What happens to them happens to us, and the same is true for them. We are on this journey together. It is not possible to survive it alone. This is our colony here, small as it is, and we must work as one."

"We don't share children," I hissed.

"Your needs and that of this baby now could compromise our task. Father Keil did not know of this or he would never have sent you with us."

I kept my expression unchanged. Our leader didn't know, but he sent me knowing that having a family was my intent. He knew there might be a child born in the Oregon Territory before the main colony came out. He knew I might have a difficult childbirth. He knew and sent me anyway, sent me *because* of the likelihood that I would at last know the results of Eve's sin in Eden and perhaps accept my place.

"Haven't I been helpful?" I put my cold hands over his clasped ones. "You didn't even know because I've been no trouble."

"It brings an issue we have not prepared for. I should have noticed before we left."

"You were busy, preparing. Even I wasn't sure."

"You should have told me." Christian looked lost in thought. He nodded his head as though in agreement, just once. "*Ja,* I'll send you back with Hans."

"No!" I withdrew my hands from his. "That would be wrong."

He was quiet, then, "*Ja,* you're right." I exhaled. "I should take you back. The hardest part of the trip is yet to come. It is my error. I should make the correction."

"No, no. This is your mission." My heart pounded, my mouth felt like fur. "Didn't you say we were tenderly led? This must be a part of it, a sign to show that even with an infant we can prepare for a new colony."

"The devil makes life easy, woos us to his ways so we forget that we are birthed in turmoil. We should not have welcomed such smoothness. I should have seen it as a distraction. So now I pay the price. You and our baby, too, unless we do the right thing now."

He attributes this easy journey to the devil's work; this infant, too?

"What is good comes from God. You told me this, Christian."

"Only when we are obedient, *Liebchen.* Only then."

If he took me back to Bethel, he'd blame me forever for depriving him of this response to his call. "Please listen, Christian." I knelt in front of him, pleading. "I'm healthy and strong. I'm young. There were other women with children traveling west. I saw them at the camps. The Elliots. That young couple, she could be carrying a child even now. Some even held newborns."

"Delivered with the help of midwives or other women, which we have none of."

"We'll be in Oregon Territory before the baby comes. There'll be people, neighbors."

"We seek isolation, Emma. We must prepare houses for ourselves and the others for when they come out. We have much to do before winter comes. A baby…in such wilderness…"

"It will break up the scouts and the success of the journey to go back now. We don't even need to share this with the others. We'll be in the Territory before it matters. Please, Christian. Don't send me back, and don't think of taking me back. I'll help make this work, I will. You'll be proud of me, as proud as any husband of a wife."

"You put yourself before the others in keeping this a secret. It is not a quality I noticed in you before we married. This is a difficult thing, Emma. Something I must pray about further." He unfolded his hands, pressed against his thighs as though to stand. "This is not your fault, Emma. It is mine. I must pay the price."

I'd expected his anger, prepared for it, delayed telling him in fear of it. I imagined it so it might not happen. I didn't expect self-reproach. He couldn't have found words to trouble me more than that he would bear the blame. Now I blamed myself, not for keeping the secret, but for not imagining the worst, and so it came to be.

He stood up then, pulled on his jeans and boots.

"Where are you going?"

"To decide, Emma."

"Can't we decide together?"

"Apparently not."

He stepped out through the tent flap. The whip of the wind blew out the light. When the flap closed behind him, the moonbeam no longer pierced the crack. Darkness hovered in the tent.

11

Open Places

In the morning, we gathered. A hawk of some kind soared above us, yet low enough I could see his yellow eye just before he dipped, then rose to catch a breeze. Even the bird accused. I'd spent the night in remorse, wishing I'd told Christian earlier, wanting to have shared this good godly gift with him, to let there be joy in the child's coming rather than discord. Some events never offer a second chance.

I vowed I wouldn't do this ever again. I'd be a wife who shared everything, a true helpmate instead of one looking out for her own…pleasure. My ears burned, thinking of what my father would say if he knew I'd kept such a secret only because I didn't want to be left behind. My mother's German proverb came to mind: I'd begun to weave, all right, with God's thread; but my tapestry had tears in it already.

The men gathered at the fire. I kept my red and puffy eyes lowered beneath my bonnet, raising them only to locate Christian finishing the tent packing. He would not look at me.

"What is it?" Adam Knight asked Christian. "We should be off now. We can talk at the evening camp, *ja?*"

"Something has…come up, something we need to discuss," Christian said. He motioned me forward then, and when I stopped behind him, he stepped back so I stood beside him, and I thus was ushered into the circle. At the oddest of times, I'd become one of them.

"My wife is with child," he said.

"Ach!" Adam Schuele said. He frowned.

"Oh, ho!" Joe Knight said, but he at least grinned.

I felt my face grow hot. I wanted to go back inside the tent, but Christian had already taken it down and rolled the pack onto Opal.

"It's nothing to cheer over," Christian said. "Not here. Not now. We have time to return, Emma and I. So she will be safe with family."

"You're my family," I said, biting my tongue as soon as I said it.

"*Ja.* We're all family," George said.

"Someone else can take her back," John Genger said. "This would be more practical. Not you. We need you. You've been anointed as leader."

"Anyone going back will compromise the mission," John Stauffer said. He pulled at a tobacco strip, then chewed. "We need all of us to build, all of us to decide the site. If one returns now, we'll have fewer to work and even less when we send men back to bring the rest out."

"Pa's right, Christian," Hans said.

"You knew?" Adam Knight asked me. "You didn't tell your husband?"

"I—"

"She told me when she was certain, but I should have known this," Christian said.

"She will slow us down," John Genger said.

"It hasn't—"

"If we are not here, there will be fewer to prepare for each day," Christian said. "You can make better time without us."

"You were chosen by Father Keil." This from Joe Knight's brother.

"We can make adjustments, brother," Joe Knight said. "All will work out well. Change doesn't mean we've erred."

"When? When can we expect this infant to join the scouts?" Hans asked as he scratched at his callus.

Christian turned to me, a puzzled look on his face.

"Am I allowed to speak at last?" Christian narrowed his eyes at me. "October," I told him, then said to the group, "Late in October."

We heard the oxen from a nearby camp being yoked. A child's cry rose and then silenced.

"Nine were chosen for a reason," Adam Schuele said at last. "Nine were commissioned by our leader. Nine plus this woman. She is one of us. She is here to discover her own part in God's plan for us. Her presence offers an opportunity to show the spirit of our colony, that we look after one another, that all needs are provided for with enough left to give away. We will look after you, too, Christian. It is how we do this. As community."

Adam Schuele had scouted for Bethel with my father, and his words now brought my father to mind. My father committed me to Adam's care in addition to my husband's; it had been my father's last request before we left.

The men remained silent after Adam spoke. I didn't know now if they'd take a vote or what would happen. Did Christian's word as leader carry more weight in this instance? Did his status as my husband matter? Was it a greater sin that I kept a secret from the scouts and the will of the colony, or from my husband?

The silence lasted a long time. I thought of words to fill the empty space, but something kept my mouth closed. Instead, I listened to the distant sounds of wagons coming forward, the stomps of impatience and snorts from our stock all packed up and ready to start out. The breeze dried the perspiration above my lip. I kicked at the edge of the fire and watched the sparks light up. The worst that could happen had been said out loud: sending me back.

No, the worst would be if Christian left to *take* me back. It would be years, if ever, before he'd forgive me for that. I poked in the dust with my boot, sending up dust puffs between Christian and me.

"By October we'll be well into Oregon Territory." Michael Sr. spoke at last. "You can winter in Portland or Dalles City if need be while the rest of us find the site and begin the work. This would be better than losing anyone to a return trip."

"Keeping her through the winter apart from us will cost," John Genger said. Then he shrugged. "But maybe some settler will take pity on us and sell out cheaper if they see we have a woman and babe to tend to."

"Oh, ho," Joe cleared his throat. "I say she stays. Who else says this?"

All the men concurred. Only Christian withheld his agreement nod.

"Can you live with this, Christian?" Adam Schuele asked. "Can you accept the consensus of the scouts and trust that what you have is what God wants for you?"

"*Ja*, I can," he said at last. "Though I will wonder always why He chose to let me lead this scouting party but not my own household."

The next days were silent ones between my husband and me. We did the work together that we needed, carried messages back and forth between the others and one another about how far we'd travel before nooning. We even washed clothes together in a dirty stream, and he answered me when I asked for the name of the land formation in the distance. We were civil to each other but spoke less than if we'd just recently met. At night, we slept side by side with his arm often draped over me as he snored. He would quickly remove it in the morning.

I wanted to talk with him about this infant. I wanted to ask how he might have rejoiced if we had been back in Bethel or already in Oregon sharing this news. It was this in-between state that bothered him, I told myself. He worried over our safety, about the journey between where we'd been and where we headed.

———

The snake rose up twisting and turning into itself, slithering like a thick rope through the landscape canvas of mountains and trees and rushing rivers until it hissed, "Traitor," its mouth wide and fangs wet.

"Traitor!" I shouted the word loud enough inside my dream that I woke Christian up.

"What is it? What's wrong?" he said, shaking my shoulder. When I couldn't stop the tears and frightened breathing from my nightmare, he folded me into his arms. "Rest now, *Liebchen.* You're all right, now. Shh. You'll wake the others."

"I'm sorry, so sorry, Christian. I should have told you. I feared you'd send me back. It was selfish. I'm so sorry."

"Shh, shh. I have my part in this, *Liebchen.* A man so busy with his work, he fails to notice when God has allowed him to co-create with Him, this is a man who needs forgiveness too."

"But you at least were doing good work. I…looked after my own."

He patted my back. "You're young, Emma. Let this be the only time you deceive me so you needn't have bad dreams."

I thought of staying silent about my other secret…but this might be my chance to truly wash away the deceptive stains I hid within my heart, the chance to change the fabric of my marriage. I took a deep breath. "Father Keil would not have sent me along if I hadn't begged him to," I whispered. I felt Christian's arms stiffen in their hold around me. "I went to him. I told him it wasn't fair that you and I were separated so much within our marriage and that you would want to start a family soon and how could you, with you gone for a year, maybe two or three before I'd see you again. And all because he sent you away each time."

"You went to him after I told you not to."

"Yes, but as Adam said and the scouts all agreed, he wouldn't have sent me along if he hadn't chosen to. No one can badger our leader into doing something he doesn't want to. No one ever has. And you prayed for this, you said that yourself."

"Indeed. He's human and can fall to deception too. Did he know you carried a child already? Did you tell him this?"

I shook my head. "He didn't know. But, Christian, I believe that if he had, he'd still have sent me with you. He told me that women will always be punished in childbirth, that it will be a hard state for us no matter where we are because of what Eve did. I think he hopes I'll find understanding within a difficult childbirth, my cries of pain to tell me of all I share with women through the ages, to remind us of our sins and that we are not unique at all, just one of many who need forgiveness."

Christian rested his chin on the top of my head. "You have a severe view of Wilhelm. I've known him many years. He doesn't dwell on sinfulness, Emma. He dwells on love, on sharing with others all we have, and holding us together so we will find that final respite in heaven. It's Christ's love displayed in his leadership that draws others to the colony. Not all of us could be so deceived to miss a man who harbors such harsh thoughts."

He leaned me away from him, then kissed me on the forehead, my eyes, my cheeks, and finally my lips. "We will start over," Christian said. "This will be a new time for us now." I nodded. *"Gut, gut."* He lay down and motioned to let my head rest on his chest. "We have both erred and been forgiven, *ja?* And we learn from this to talk when there are problems, lest the snake wake us in the night."

I climbed Independence Rock along with the rest of the scouts. We arrived there before the Fourth of July and celebrated the halfway mark of our journey west. Christian thought the rocks too smooth for me, that going up would be fine, but coming down would challenge and I might slip and fall. But I pleaded. I wanted to see the views from above, and finally he gave in.

Standing on top the hill as rounded as brown bread, a person could see forever. For the first time, I realized how the Missouri landscape had restricted my view, the eye, seeking distant vistas, always interrupted by trees and shrubbery and rolling hills. Atop Independence Rock, looking east, I felt as though I could see the bricks of Bethel. Previous travelers had carved names into the stone, witnesses to those pursuing wider horizons. The landscape west looked as still as a lake and twice as wide. The colony had restricted my vision, but perhaps that proved purposeful. They liked dips and valleys where people nestled apart from others, where they could believe they were the only ones in the world; intruders were kept out by clear boundaries and woods. Finding a site in the Oregon Territory with such isolation could prove challenging. I hoped a more open space in the wilderness would be where the Lord would lead.

"Careful now, *Liebchen*," Christian told me. He held my hand and caught me once when my smooth leather soles did slide on the rounded rock.

"The rest of the way looks…easy," I said. "Nothing in our way now. We can almost see the ocean from here."

"These western landscapes are like a woman's wrapper: deceiving," Christian said. He smiled.

He was right, of course, because not a few days later came Devil's Gate, a slice in a granite mountain that looked like a nasty wound. The

Sweetwater River ran through it. We would take the trail south, as the wagons did, even though Michael Sr. thought the animals could make it through the cut without a problem.

How the decisions were made in this community of scouts remained a mystery to me. I would have agreed with Michael Sr. True, the cut was narrow, but it would save time, something the scouts said must be a deciding factor if we found a good campsite and thought to lay over an extra day to rest the animals. "Got to make good time" was the motto, and so we'd head on out whether we were rested or not.

Yet here we could have saved time but didn't.

"Who decides whether we take a certain trail or not?" I asked Christian at noon while we ate jerked beef. "This road around the Devil's Gate took more time. We could have ridden through that cut in the rock."

"Our animals aren't so surefooted, though. If we had a problem in the narrow place, we'd have no help coming along behind us, as no wagons come that way."

"That's reasonable," I said. The breeze lifted my own scent to my nose. I needed to lay out my wrapper to air this night. "But who decided that? Hans makes some decisions about the stock. Wouldn't it have been his call about the ability of the animals?"

"We decide together."

But I hadn't seen it.

Neither did I see the discussion that led to my now riding Opal instead of my horse, Fred. One morning Fred stood packed and Opal saddled while Christian helped me up. Christian rode the traded-for-mule and had for several days.

"The mule's gait is better," he said. "It'll be an easier ride for you."

When we came to a gradual uphill slope some days later that Christian said must be South Pass, I didn't know how he knew that, either, until we reached the top, and I could see streams flowing west now instead of east. We'd arrived at the Continental Divide.

———

I noted graves along the trail, and further into the mountains, large granite boulders shaded a portion of our journey. I longed for the vista offered a few weeks back by Independence Rock. These rocks closed in. I had the fleeting thought that it might be a grand place for an ambush by Indians, something we were told to be wary of at each wagon stop, where we encountered the outside world. I preferred it when we camped away from that sort of thinking. Maybe, like me, travelers thought the worst in order to keep it from happening.

A few days later, we entered a narrow opening through the mountains. The horses and mules pulled back, sidestepped or tried to. They whinnied and strained against the reins. Hans's horse shied first and stumbled sideways, though it kept its footing. That abrupt action appeared to startle the horse behind him and then the one behind it, causing the pack animals to yank their lead ropes. Even steady Opal pranced and swished her tail. "*Ach,* be good now," I chastened her.

Hans Stauffer shouted to move the animals on out faster, if possible, to get into the wider opening where we could find out what troubled them. Perhaps a burr worked its way under a saddle, or maybe a pack slipped. Maybe they smelled an Indian ambush. I looked up. Bare, pinkish rocks rounded over us. I could see a patch of sky, but nothing out of the ordinary on the rock ledges.

Then Opal bolted, pushing her way along the narrow path occupied by the horses ahead. She attempted passage to the right of John Genger's horse directly ahead of me, so both my legs pushed against his horse rather than the rock wall that Opal grazed. I pushed back with my knees and my hands, but the sidesaddle pitched me forward, out of balance, and I let loose the pack animal and hung with both hands onto the pommel.

Unable to squeeze forward, Opal bolted back, making odd sounds of distress, attempting to rear up. Then she bucked, and before I knew what had happened, I'd landed on my back in the dust left behind by Opal, the packhorse running loose behind her. The world swam around as the packhorse's hooves threw pebbles at me as it tried to avoid me. I couldn't catch my breath. It felt like drowning, I imagined, with no way to take air.

Christian's mule barely avoided stepping on me as Christian raced up behind. He jumped off in an instant. "Emma!"

I waved at him, unable to get my breath.

"Stay calm. The air will return," he assured me. At last air filled my lungs, never more sweet, though it was laced with dust. He brushed the dirt from my wrapper as he helped me stand.

Christian's mule bolted past both of us now, the packhorse running loose behind it. "What's wrong with them? What's happening?"

We heard shouts and wailing animal screams coming from the area in front of us. Clouds of dust billowed like fog. Adam Knight shouted. Christian held my elbow and we stumbled forward.

Through the dust, the men had drawn their weapons, but I couldn't see the enemy. One of the packhorses lay on its side, breathing hard, blood in long scratches oozing from its neck.

Through the haze I spied Opal in erratic motions. She stomped with her front feet, pummeling something beige on the ground. Braying sounds pierced the air. "Oh, ho!" Joe Knight shouted.

The creature that lay before Opal attempted to get up, and she bit at its neck, then lifted it, and like a mother cat shaking a mouse to its death to provide lunch for her *Kinder*, she shook the animal back and forth until it hung limp. Then she dropped it.

A young mountain cat lay in the dust. Opal had stomped and bitten and shaken it to death.

I'd never seen a mountain lion before, let alone watched a mule kill one. The wind moved the fine hair of the lion. It had paws as big as my palm.

There were dangers in this landscape I had no knowledge of, dangers in confined spaces, in narrow places without vistas. I knew then that the Lord must lead us scouts to a landscape where we could see for miles, so we could always see ahead to dangers lurking.

12

The Wild of the Outside World

We made adjustments with one fewer pack animal, the cat's last prey. We dried the meat. It was my first taste of mule meat, but George Link said we must never waste what God provided. Piecing together what had happened, the men decided that the mountain lion must have lain in wait, hunkered down above us as we moved through the narrow place. The horses and the mules soon got its scent, and it was Opal who proved the most indignant at this interruption. Opal stood out.

The feast we held that night brought out harmonicas, and Hans and George Link and the Knight brothers danced jigs arm in arm to the sizzle of meat at the fire. Other scouts not dancing or playing clapped. We rejoiced in our safe keeping and our "guard mule," as we now called Opal. "Didn't need a dog to tree that cat," Joe Knight said, his finger held up to the wind.

"But a dog might have forewarned us," I said. "I still hope we can find a lost pup somewhere."

"At least we were spared," John Genger said. He sat with his ankles crossed, a cup of coffee in his hands and his Pennsylvania Long Rifle lying beside him. He didn't play the harmonica. I didn't disagree with him, though I had a bruise the size of Missouri—and still growing—on my backside, and the infant hadn't let me have more than a taste of the meat before it began its kicking again.

"We've been looked after," Christian said. And I agreed, even knowing he hadn't seen the bruise yet.

We headed north toward Fort Hall, where we hoped to restock our meager supply of cornmeal, among other things. At one point along the trail, a man with vegetables, onions and carrots and tomatoes, sat beneath a shaded tent. He smiled as he took our money, said something back to Christian, and they laughed. "He's Mormon, up from their place at the Salt Lake," Christian interpreted for us. Later Christian said they'd laughed because the Mormon said his vegetables were so good and so long-lasting that our baby would probably be holding a carrot in his hand when he arrived in this world.

"You told him about—"

"He can see, *Liebchen.* Your round face, the gap in your wrapper." He tugged at the gusset I'd had to sew in to ease the tightness across my breast. The infant had six months by my calculations and would be good size if these past weeks of his kicking and growing foretold it. "He's a man with a good eye." Christian winked, the first sign since I'd disclosed my deception that he found pleasure having with him a wife who would one day bear his child. He handed me many carrots, using one to shake his finger at me, the carrot as limp as resting reins.

After Fort Hall, we heard more rumors of Indian unrest, more than we'd heard on the plains during all the previous weeks. We could take no action, such a powerless state. I made myself think of more pleasant things—part of my new effort to control the future—and posted a letter back to my parents and to Mary and Sebastian Giesy, telling them about our child.

We headed on to Fort Boise, following the Snake River with its deep chasms and frothy, uncontrollable currents. All new things to see.

I tried not to think about crossing that wild stream, something Christian said we'd have to do, and we did when the time came. Here, too, rumors of drowning abounded, but we crossed without trial.

The number of rivers and streams needing fording increased as we headed west. We learned their names, later trying to match up Alder Springs and Burnt River, Mud Springs and the Powder, with stories told by other travelers we encountered.

Even the Blue Mountains gave us little to remember except for their beauty—a lovely spring at the summit, where other emigrants spent the night, and that hazy color people told us came from the Indians burning trees and shrubs to make way for spring grass for their horses. The Nez Perce were said to have many horses.

The terrain changed again after we crossed those mountains, winding down a long hill almost devoid of trees. At the base, it opened to expansive high plains. We encountered round, wide-faced Indians there who watched as we silently rode by. Sometimes in the mornings we'd see their camp smoke not far behind us. Christian said we'd double the evening guards, but they never shortened the distance between us, probably deciding wisely that we had little they might need for barter or theft. They never knew we carried medicinal whiskey, or that Opal was a guard mule of exceptional skill.

For several days we paralleled the river they called the Columbia, crossing the John Day River at Leonard's Ferry. I kept my eyes straight toward the willows fanned out on the far shore, my cheek tight against Opal's. I held my breath as the rickety craft pulled into the current and down to the landing, exhaling as I stepped on the muddy shore. We rode up another bare hill, rested at springs near the top, then headed west, spending the next night at the Des Chutes River, where the rolling water poured into the Columbia. Here we'd either need to swim or pay the ferryman. Fortunately, John Genger agreed we could pay. I was always so grateful when we could pay.

In late September, a snowcapped mountain became our beacon. After crossing Fifteen Mile Creek and then Eight Mile Creek, riding up to the top of a bluff that overlooked the Columbia, we reached Dalles City, right on the river, where the water spilled among huge rocks like strands of a woman's white hair draped in a man's knuckles. They called it Celilo Falls.

Dalles City, or Fort Dalles Landing as some called the town, grew around an army fort, as far as I could tell. Over the post office door a sign read Wascopam, and the postmaster told us in no uncertain terms that we should tell our friends to post letters to that name and no other. Since we didn't plan to stay, I let his invigorated opinion waft by along with his tobacco smoke. Apparently, there were arguments about what the town should be called. Later someone said it had endured ten different names already. At least our colonists never wasted time in such decisions; our leader decided the names.

Dozens of Indian people of various shapes and sizes wandered near the post office and in the town itself. A baker stepped out of a shop with the name *W. L. DeMoss* over the door and offered me a warm piece of soft saleratus bread, the first I'd had since we left Missouri. I took it as a gift divine, the dough as soft as angel's wings against my tongue. *What is it about fresh bread that brings peace to a woman's soul?* "Danke," I said, taking my husband's arm as we moved on.

Dogs sniffed from around various corners of framed buildings; their slender tails rose as they moved in small packs. I wondered out loud if we might rescue one to call our own, but Christian said, "We have enough to worry about just getting ourselves settled in with a babe without a pup in tow."

We passed a marketplace with Indians and others bartering baskets and dried fish, perhaps for canoe rides down the river. Some of the natives had foreheads pitched as steep as a cow's face, while many round-faced Indians stood heads down on a platform as men in the audience appeared to be shouting out bids. *Slavery, here? Wouldn't it be ironic if we colonists left Missouri to avoid a battle involving slaves only to step into another war right here?* I couldn't be sure what transpired, and I vowed to learn more English before the winter turned to spring. So much went on in this "outside world" that I couldn't decipher. To understand this new land and live well here, I needed to interpret for myself the words being said. I couldn't always rely on the interpretations of my husband.

The Indian bartering went on well into the night, along with drums and singing. We slept on the ground a little distance from the town, and Joe Knight suggested we all go down to where the music seemed to rise from. I thought that a grand idea, but this time the scouts reached the consensus that we remain safe where we were. I still didn't know how these things got decided, but Joe looked a little down as he pushed his night pack up against his saddle, punching it more than once for good measure.

Major Rains, the commander of the fort, had a doctor at his disposal. A family doctor also served the town, and in the morning, Christian insisted that I let myself be examined by Dr. C. W. Shaug, though I felt fine. The bruise that had spread like spilled ink across my back from when Opal upended me lingered. I still ached some at my lower back, but I decided it might be the baby protesting the long hours of riding even on a soft-gaited mule.

Dr. Shaug proved to be a big man, kindly, and he did all his examinations with a nurse present and with my wrapper on. Christian stayed to translate.

"I would say late November," he said. "Judging from the infant's size. Is this your calculation too?"

"No," I said, understanding the English name for the month. "October."

"The infant is small if it's to arrive a month away. Have you eaten well?"

"I've been in good health," I said. "Just one mishap on the trail, but otherwise enough to eat to fill me and not even sickness in the mornings, as I've heard can happen."

"Indeed," he said. "Well"—he put the end of his stethoscope into the pocket of his vest—"I'd suggest a physician be present. It could be your baby will need quick, professional decision-making when he arrives. Where do you intend to be in October? That's what you said, October?"

"We've yet to decide," Christian told him. "In the Willamette area. From what we've heard there is still good land available there."

"You're farmers? Yes? Well, that is rich soil country. How many sections are you hoping to file on?"

"Many," Christian told him. "We're the foot soldiers who make way for a large colony that will come out as soon as we get word back to them."

"Foot soldiers. Pioneers. From the Latin *pedant*. Well, then, Godspeed to you. There are good physicians there. Some in the French Prairie country, though little land's available there to claim. But make sure you winter near a doctor."

It was an unpleasant thought. I decided to pitch it.

———

We took a steamer downriver to Fort Vancouver. John Genger again said we could pay. It pushed its way along through pouring rain. Misty fog hugged the shoreline, forcing us to imagine the scenery, but I knew there must be high rocks and trees. I felt cold to the bone, my teeth chattering from the elements more than from the dizzying water. By the time we reached the landing at the former Hudson's Bay Company fort, my throat felt scratchy and I sneezed. I could see the buildings up a grassy slope. Here the men hoped they'd get good information about whether to go north or south to form the new colony. I hoped I'd find dryness and warmth.

Ulysses S. Grant, the senior officer who managed the well-laid-out fort, complained that high water would keep them from harvesting the potatoes that year. "But then, everyone appears to be raising potatoes around here to send to the California gold fields."

"At least the floodwaters have kept you from the labor of digging the potatoes up," Christian said. "Otherwise, you'd have watched them rot for lack of sales."

Grant laughed. "Good one," he said. "The silver lining in the darkest of clouds. You'll stay for supper," he ordered more than invited, clicking his heels and bending at his waist toward me. "I'll ask the fort physician to give you something for that cough."

Christian said the invitation would likely not have come without a woman present. I was pleased I could bring some respite to the scouts, who sat at the long table along with senior officers stationed at the fort. The conversation proved lively, and I could understand the hospitableness, if not all of the words.

I loved the lavishly painted dishes, the candelabra, and long-stemmed glassware that looked fit for a queen. Grant commented on the crystal goblets he said he always carried with him from fort to fort. "Something of my own to make a place like home," he told us. The food steamed with freshness, and my mouth watered just watching the platter of corn beef and cabbage move slowly toward my place, served by men with military precision. I wondered where the officers' wives might be, then heard women's chatter from an adjoining room. This would be what our life would be like if we were not bound to the colony. A life filled with worldly things, singular treasures, abundance, men perhaps waiting on women, and sometimes women sitting down beside men. Hadn't the Lord promised us such abundance?

I wondered if Christian might not entertain that idea too as he ran his finger around the lip of the crystal before bringing it to his mouth.

"Perhaps you should winter near here," Grant suggested. "Make your journey to mark land in the spring when the floodwaters recede and you can better see what you'll be getting."

"Indeed. Your suggestion bears some consideration," my husband said, then politely changed the subject. He told me later he didn't want to disagree with the commander, but he wanted to secure our site yet this fall so at the first sign of weather breaking, scouts could return to prepare the main party to come out.

"This might be a good place to winter, though," I offered.

"It would be easier for you and for the child."

"You could stay here too, make forays out north and south but come back here. The colony doesn't expect you to live in hardship. You were never asked to do so when you traveled into Kentucky, *ja?*" He nodded agreement. "You stayed as a guest, the way the disciples were told to receive what others offered, to take nothing with them. The commander offers us a place to winter. Is it not divine intervention?"

"*Nein.* Any area close to here will be too populated." He pulled on his reddish beard. "But you could stay, and in the spring, when the scouts head back, I could come to get you and bring you to wherever we have found a site."

A winter with a bed and roof did invite. But if I remained, Christian would miss the birth of his child. "I'm not staying here without you. I'm one of the scouts. I'll go where you go, as Ruth did." I wiped at my nose. "In sickness and in health," I reminded him.

That night as we slept on a feather bed at the fort, I wondered if I shouldn't urge us all to remain through the winter. Christian might come to see the merits of living closer to the real world of people finely dressed, eating at well-apportioned tables, learning to use English all the time. Maybe he'd see that we could live safely *in* the world while not being *of* it, as Scripture ordained us to be.

Here were many people who could be brought into our fold. Maybe we were being led to *this* place. Maybe we scouts needed to pay more attention to populated sites. *Perhaps isolation shouldn't be the most important factor to consider.* I'd find a way to mention that to Christian.

I watched the light flickering against the pewter and crystal, washing over the gray steins on the table. Our leader back in Missouri saw the heaviness of the world able to snuff out one's light, leaving people lost and alone in the darkness, and so we were advised to look to the colony, return to the colony, trust only in the colony. Our leader would have us isolate ourselves as the true way to resist the world.

But how could we light the world if we were so far from it? There were goodly people populating this country. The commander. The doctors we'd met. Even German women of negotiable affections provided assistance to us on our journey. What we needed had been provided. God was in the world. Surely God could look after us if we lived among others. Meanwhile, we scouts could offer another way to bring light to the wilderness, though it did require risk.

That was the challenge, I supposed, as I watched my husband talk with those worldly men in their uniforms: to be willing to enter the darkness of the unknown wilderness, the outside world, hoping the light one brought would be bright enough and warm enough that it would overcome darkness, and more, encourage others to light a candle there too.

13

Into the Wilderness

I woke up singing, as I understood Christian's mission better than I ever had before. With a little effort on my part, I thought he'd accept my observations about lack of merits within isolation. How could we expand the colony without more people around? If we lived here or near this Columbia River, Christian wouldn't have to travel as he had before to bring people in, as we'd be in the midst of people. All sorts of *Volk*, free and slaves, made their way here, and surely acts of charity toward them formed a part of our mission, to break the holds of bondage of all kinds while serving as the hands and feet of God within the world.

As in St. Joseph, Missouri, I'd already heard French and Spanish, and even some German spoken, and a tongue with clicks and rolls that crusty old mountain men used to converse with natives. Hadn't our Lord walked within the midst of common people? Didn't He appear to His disciples after His death in everyday places where His friends ate together or where they worked beside their fishing boats? This was the goal, then, to be among people, even buxom women attracted to my husband, but to not allow them to lead us astray. *Ja*, I'd have to learn to live with the monster of envy, but isolation would make that lesson more difficult to learn and wouldn't be any protection at all.

Even I could see that this Fort Vancouver and the town of Portland across the river would be where emigrants would come and want to stay. Vistas of green slopes and oats growing high rolled up onto craggy rocks with waterfalls. The weather felt mild, almost warm, even last evening. Timber soared into the skyline in this Columbia country, so all the other criteria except isolation were met. Surely isolation shouldn't be our chief desire. That's what I'd have to convince Christian of, and I intended to begin that morning.

But Christian had dressed early, and I never even heard his steady breathing as he did his pushing-ups. He left so quietly that I slept on. When he returned he expressed enthusiasm about a chance meeting that sealed our fate. Or perhaps where God's concerned, there is no chance at all.

"Get dressed," Christian said. He brushed at his hat, tossing rain-drops on the wood floor of the room we'd been given to sleep in at the fort. "We've found what we've been seeking."

"Near here? I'm so pleased," I said, pulling on my wrapper against the morning dampness. I sent a prayer of thanksgiving upward.

"No, not here. But not far away."

My husband had met an emigrant who'd come out from Iowa the year before, and the man, Ezra Meeker, said we should go north, farther north to a place of such mild weather, such beautiful meadows and prairies, that no one who ever saw it would ever choose to leave.

The walk across the wet grass brought a fresh scent to my nose. Christian and Adam Schuele and Ezra Meeker himself now shared this news with all of us as we stood inside the sutler's store, watching a driz-zling rain fall across the door opening. The sharp scent of salted hides waiting transport lifted from the bales around us.

"Emigrants from the Puget Sound Agricultural Company cleared land there and planted trees, had sheep and cattle, and did quite well. Some have been there since '48. They'd have done better if they could have kept the increase of their herds, but they were indentured, almost, to the Hudson's Bay Company. Now that they've sold out, those farms are available. The lands there are rich and fertile."

"Are there portions there for donation land claims?" asked Michael Schaefer Sr.

"That and to buy," Ezra Meeker told him. Christian raised his eyebrows. "Well, some are fixing to leave, so they'll sell; but more will come, you mark my words. The best part of the Oregon Territory is north of the Columbia."

Meeker looked not much older than I, and he told us he'd come south this past week to stock up on things from the fort's supply and to talk with emigrants recently arrived. He said he knew how hard it had been for him when his group reached Portland last November, trying to find the best place to settle. Meeker planned to head back, and we could travel with him if we wished. Or he'd give us good directions. He said he had intentions of returning east in the spring to guide other wagons out. "Puget Sound, part of the newly formed Washington Territory, that's where I hope they'll all settle."

"What do you think?" Christian asked the scouts as we stood inside the sutler's store. "This Meeker is a kindly sort. Youngish." He spoke in German in front of the man, and Meeker smiled as though accustomed to waiting through translations. Or perhaps he understood German. I couldn't tell.

"What's in it for him?" John Genger asked. "What does he get for guiding us north?"

"Nothing. Or at least he hasn't asked for a guide fee," Christian said. "He has a wife and baby girl, so he knows what a family would need."

"How do you know this about him?" Hans asked.

"He told me so. I trust him."

"How do we travel?" John asked.

"We could head on out to the mouth of the Columbia, catch a ship north that would drop us at Puget Sound. But it would be expensive."

The idea of an ocean voyage caused my stomach to flip. I swallowed and wrapped my mother's cape around me closer. Her lavender scent on the wool had nearly vanished into the wisp of her memory. I rubbed my cheek against the cloth, taking in its comfort, then said, "The ocean voyage would be more expensive than following him back north."

"We'd have to sell the stock to do it," Joe Knight said.

"We might have to sell them anyway, from what Meeker says," Christian told him.

"What sense does that make? We need the mules for farming, the other stock, too. Why did we hang on to pack animals at the Dalles Landing when so many offered to buy if we're only going to sell them now?" This from George Link, and I thoroughly agreed. I nodded my head.

"Meeker says the land is good there, that it's already been farmed in places," Adam Schuele affirmed. "He's introduced hops, so you know the soil is good. We can buy stock from those already there." As the other fluent English speaker, he alone could verify Christian's enthusiasm and assessment of Meeker's words.

I imagined having to part with Opal and didn't like that thought at all.

"Indeed," said Christian. "If we can buy some of those established farms and lay claim to adjoining land, we can have all we need for the colony."

"There are neighbors near?" I asked.

"Most of the travel is by walking or by boat," Christian continued, as though I hadn't spoken. "The woods are too tangled for wagons, but the rivers are perfect for bringing in supplies and for sending sold products out. We'd farm beside the rivers." A gleam formed in Christian's eyes.

There'd be few families there if wagons couldn't make it through the rough.

"Timber everywhere and a ready market for it in California in the gold fields. Indeed. I believe the Lord has led this Meeker into our midst as a beacon, the directional light we need."

Travel by boat? Rivers? Timber without wide open spaces and not even the comfort of the mount my father picked for me? Where were the women? I felt my stomach lurch.

"Wilhelm wanted separation," Adam Schuele reminded. "But there's a fort at Nisqually and another at a place called Steilacoom, so should there be Indian trouble we'd have a secure place to go to."

"Could we talk more about the need for separation?" I said. "Perhaps the way the colony is to grow isn't through new recruiting from far away, but by living closer to people, where they can see the caring in our lives and want that for themselves. Maybe the Lord has led us here to this Vancouver to do things differently than before, and this Meeker is a…distraction."

Only the steady thumping of the rain on the log roof filled the silence. Men moved their eyes to Christian, then to the floor. I might have fine ideas, but today I appeared to be invisible and my words as silent as a preacher's sin.

———

Against my better judgment (not that anyone asked), we sold the stock. How I hated parting with Opal, who'd become more of a pet than a work animal, a confidante for my unspeakable woes. Her new owner, a

Portland farmer, took Fred, too, but I spent most of my time with the man singing Opal's virtues, including her guardian tendencies. He smiled indulgently. At least he spoke German and so could communicate with the horses and mules.

Within two days, we took a scow north on the Columbia River to a landing at Monticello, where once Hudson's Bay people had a fur storage place. There, we were met by tall, somber men and their long cedar canoes. "Cowlitz Indians," Meeker said. "Friendly. They speak some English. Their name means 'seekers,' I'm told. As in a spiritual sense."

"We have that in common," Christian said, and he clicked his boots together and bent at his waist in recognition of their virtue.

They had that curious sloped forehead I'd seen at the Dalles Landing, and I wondered what could cause this but didn't know how to ask. Besides, I didn't want to be rude.

Meeker said we'd pay the Cowlitz in trade goods to take us all north, and I wondered what of our meager goods might appeal to these stately men or to the women who I noticed now sat in the bows of the crafts.

We moved by canoe up the Cowlitz River into the new Washington Territory.

Once again I watched the shoreline glide by, this time while seated with packs of our personal belongings like gray mushrooms at my feet. A Cowlitz woman and child were in our canoe, which held Christian and five other men besides the Cowlitz paddlers. A wooden cradle wrapped around one infant. A brace pressed against the infant's head, answering my question about what made the sharp angle to the forehead. I wondered if it hurt and wished again that I could speak another language. The baby cooed and his mother smiled.

Every now and then a woman reached into rectangular, oval-bottomed coiled baskets to give their babies something to chew. The honey-colored baskets were beautiful as well as practical. Whatever they held comforted the infants. It looked like thicknesses of fat.

The paddlers urged us past sand bars that speared the water, often poling and using ropes to pull us against the current. Occasionally, we got out so they could take their heavy canoes around fallen trees that blocked the waterway. Back in the canoe, I tried not to look at the water rushing by, grabbed the side of the canoe when a swift current caught the craft and might have sent it spinning but for the skill of our handlers. I noted how thin the sides of the boat were. I could find no seams, so the boat was formed of one continuous, long, red, fragrant cedar log.

I caught a glimpse of a huge bird with scarlet feathers that Ezra Meeker named a pileated woodpecker. "A shy bird," he told me through Christian. "One that doesn't like to be seen very often."

"That wouldn't be hard in those thickets," I said.

"Still, you've seen one, so that is something to remember," Christian said. "Meeker says that sightings are rare. A unique experience in this wilderness. You like unique things, if I remember." He patted my hand, stopped my thumb and finger from rubbing themselves raw.

The men spoke constantly of the timber, its size and girth, how dense and how abundant. The river meandered through lush prairies while I forced myself to think not of the possible problems with the water but to watch for dots of color, to let myself be taken in and comforted by the presence of flowers whose names I didn't know. We all marveled at the high, timbered ridges, much taller than the bluffs of Missouri; more foreboding, too. We swatted at mosquitoes, buzzing.

Wide prairies eased out from the water's edge, and we watched deer and sometimes elk tear at grasses. Despite the promise of lush soil for kitchen gardens, I noticed few clearings in this wild.

When we reached Toledo, another small landing with a few log homes and fenced gardens, we stepped out of the canoes and Meeker left us.

"His farm is near Puyallup, quite a bit farther northeast," Christian said. "But he thinks we should go on up to the Sound and see if we can winter at one of the forts there. They'll have doctors."

"But I thought we took this route because Meeker had neighbors that he knew of who had land we could acquire." I knew I sounded irritated, but when they included me in discussions, it was to eavesdrop more than participate. Issues weren't decided within my earshot. Within my presence they merely affirmed decisions already made.

"He's done what we asked of him," Christian told me. It seemed to me he bristled. "His advice has been good. We've seen abundance. We'll explore yet this fall and finalize our location, then send scouts back to Bethel. You have to agree, this is beautiful country."

Beautiful, ja, *but empty of all but tall trees.*

I assumed we'd walk the rest of the way to Puget Sound, to the promised "bustling" town of Olympia, but instead the Cowlitz paddlers had relatives who met us, and for another trade of red cloth bought just for this purpose back in Vancouver, we could ride their big horses behind them. We agreed, and for the first time since I was very young (when there'd been no one around to see), I sat astride a horse, my left knee no longer steadied by the lower hook. I put my arms around a perfect stranger. We were on solid ground, off of the water.

I could have stayed at Olympia forever. We spent our first night there at Edmund Sylvester's Olympia House Hotel. I heard even more strange languages spoken, including a high-pitched staccato chatter from the kitchen, where I caught a glimpse of an Asian man, his thin long braid swinging like a metronome as he bustled about. For dinner that evening we were served an appetizer Christian understood to be pickled blackberries. "A Chinese delicacy," he told me.

A newspaper lay on the hotel desk counter, and I read its name in English, the same as the river: *Columbia*.

Puget Sound lapped up to Olympia, a body of water as smooth as fine tin. Christian said, "It's the ocean," but it had none of the white-caps I expected from having seen paintings made by those who'd traveled west. The town stepped down from a timbered bluff toward the sea. Houses sat on flattened spots between sawed-off trunks still being pulled by horses and chains. It was a growing place. I loved seeing stumps with steps cut into them for ease in mounting a horse and the window boxes that dotted the few frame houses. Such sights promised the presence of women.

But we were not to stay here. We headed east the next day, merely checked in at Fort Nisqually, a former Hudson's Bay site. There we received directions to the place where Christian (or at least someone) had decided we would spend the winter.

Fort Steilacoom became my home. Located about four miles from the little town of Steilacoom, and some distance from Olympia, it boasted a few log buildings, fenced-in gardens, and an orchard with chickens pecking about. A man named Heath had farmed it for the Agricultural Company, then left when the Company sold it to the U.S. Army.

Most importantly, Christian told me, a doctor remained quartered at the fort. At least I believed he'd chosen for my benefit this little clearing in the timber separated from the town. I suppose he thought that having the doctor would give me peace about this birthing, or give him peace, as he had plans he just now decided to tell me about, plans that offered me no peace at all.

14

Accommodations

A three-story gristmill in Steilacoom promised wheat and population. A sawmill on a place called Chambers Creek meant frame houses rose here in a place named for a group of sturdy-looking Indians known as Steilacooms. The Indians lived in cedar houses nestled back from the shoreline like quiet beneath trees. I noticed their presence first from the smoke rising as if from blackberry brush, then looking closer, I could see the outlines of the houses. When I encountered one or two of the Steilacooms on the paths, they kept their eyes lowered and always stepped aside. They didn't look cowed as those at the auction in The Dalles or Wascopam or whatever they called that town that week. Neither did they look frightening or fierce. Polite. They were simply polite.

Fruit trees grew here—propagated they'd have to be because they couldn't be so large grown from seed. People hadn't been here all that long, at least not white people. The trees promised apples and pears, and I could taste the *Strudels* I'd bake. This would indeed be a good landscape for all of us. Not unlike Olympia, it boasted storefronts and a wagon maker and a church, and women with children walked on the board streets while white birds, seagulls Christian called them, dipped and cried overhead. Christian said there were two settlements here: a Port Steilacoom near the bottom of the bluff and a Chapman's Steilacoom farther up, though I couldn't tell where one began and the other ended. It was how I'd begun to think of our journey here, too. Had it ended? Or were we just beginning the next phase?

The scouts remained at Chapman's Steilacoom, talking to locals, I assumed, gathering new information with Adam Schuele to translate.

But Christian said that he and I needed to walk on through the cedars and blackberry bushes along a narrow trail to reach the fort before dark. We found it clearly defined not by fortlike walls, but by the split-rail fences surrounding large cultivated fields. This garrison didn't match what one might expect at an eastern fort. It consisted of a few log structures, one frame building under construction, barns, small outer buildings, and clothes hanging limply on a line.

Captain Bennett Hill once served as commanding officer, having taken over the land after the death some years earlier of the man who cleared these fields, 106 fenced acres planted in wheat, peas, and potatoes. That commander had been recently replaced by an Irishman, Captain Maurice Maloney. It seemed no one stayed at Fort Steilacoom for long.

Captain Maloney knew not a word of German. His dark blue uniform, frayed at the cuffs, merely heightened the red of his hair and the verdant green of his eyes.

"The accommodations aren't much for ladies," he told Christian. "But you're welcome." He said this with his eyes on me while Christian translated.

"It's the physician we're interested in most," Christian said.

The captain pulled at the sleeves of his military jacket, straightened his shoulders as he responded to my husband's words. "Aye, we have one. Frame building will be completed before long, and he'll have a surgery. Meantime, he's housed in that log one, along with his wife." He pointed to a structure that looked sturdy and stable, with moss growing on its wooden shakes.

"There are women posted here?" Christian asked.

"Aye. A few of the officers have their wives here. Even a child or two."

The captain led us to what I assumed would be our new home. We passed small log houses, and I could see easily that this had once been a farm, though someone's vision of a fort in the future rose too. Soldiers cleaned the barns while others carried buckets that frothed white with milk. Chickens scattered like seeds as we walked.

"What about the rest of the scouts?" I asked Christian. "Are they coming later? Will there be places for them to stay?"

Christian didn't answer. Instead, he took my arm in his and patted the back of my hand. I thought he might be pleased that I thought of someone other than myself.

We met the *gut* doctor, as I came to call him, at his office that was also his home. Christian explained our "circumstance," and I once again suffered an examination—with my clothes on, thank goodness. "November," the *gut* doctor said when he stepped from beneath my wrapper and I stepped down from his stool.

"Indeed. November," Christian said. He pointed his finger at me to remind me of his rightness.

"It should be sooner," I said. "Tell him it will be in October."

"Twice now these men of experience have said November, *Liebchen*. I think we can trust this. And it's good. You will have time now to rest, to settle in before the baby comes."

"I don't want to settle in. I want the baby to come and for us to stay the winter in a civilized place."

"Father Keil often said it is not wise to want or desire, Emma, but to accept what we're given."

"As if he ever did," I mumbled. If he had, we would still be in Bethel instead of here.

At the third log house, we were introduced to Nora, the *gut* doctor's wife, a tiny woman with dark curls peaking beneath a cap that otherwise covered her head. She had small eyes that sparkled like a kid goat's, with the same quick movements as she opened the door, invited us in. She wore a skirt full as a bell, and I wondered how many petticoats the material covered to make it sway so as she walked. Beside her, a child stood with hands akimbo; another, Nora balanced on her hip. I wished I'd known what all she said as she talked with quick, crisp words spoken through a mouth with all of her teeth. I deciphered only *baby* and *room*.

Nora led us to a windowless enclosure at the back of the cabin. A bed and bed stand marked the space. Still with the toddler on her hip, she picked up a ball and a small wooden horse from the floor, and I realized this must have been her son's playroom we'd now taken over. The baby leaned out as she knelt, then pulled in at her mother's neck when she stood up.

"Danke," I said. When she motioned for me to sit, I nearly collapsed onto the bed as Christian removed the pack from my back. We'd left Fort Nisqually early that morning, walked through the two towns of Steilacoom and the final four miles uphill to this fort, encountered Indians, met the commander and doctor and now his family. It was late afternoon. My limbs felt shaky and weak. The pillows, filled with feathers, were soft as lamb's wool on my cheeks.

"This will be a comfort while I'm gone, *Liebchen*," Christian said, looking around the room.

I yawned. "Are you going somewhere?"

"To arrange things," he said. He kissed my forehead and left, closing the door behind him.

I was too tired to ask for details and must have known by intuition that I wouldn't really like his answers.

———

The "perfect arrangement" is what Christian called it. A physician nearby; a woman to be with if trouble arose; a military fort safe and secure, set within timbered land in a climate so mild I almost felt as though I'd taken a fresh bath when I hadn't had one in weeks. I would have one this day, though, and that made the day seem blessed.

Then I learned what Christian was really up to, and no amount of my wailing or disagreeing budged him an inch. "You have miscalculated, Emma. I will make every effort to be back by the middle of November. That is your time. The captain says that the weather is rainy but mild well into December, so you are not to worry. All will be well."

"But why you? Can't Adam and the others find the place?"

He shook his head as at a recalcitrant child. His words were singsong, a repetition. "We are a team sent out, Emma. Finding a place for the colony, that is what matters most. You must remember this. I'll be back in due time."

I'd been a part of that team too, though he said nothing about that.

"I can't even make them understand me," I said. "How will I ever tell them what I need?"

"A good opportunity for you to learn English." He sat beside me on the narrow bed we'd slept one night in. *One night!* He hadn't even chosen to stay a week here, so anxious was he to complete his precious mission. "You said you could adapt, Emma, could make do, so we wouldn't have to turn back, wouldn't have to send someone chosen for this work on a detour. This is what you wanted, *ja?* You get what you want, now."

"You'd leave me? With strangers? In this…fallen world? What about my possible corruption? Aren't you worried about my becoming envious of the luxury here, unable to give it up when the time comes?"

He frowned. I realized I'd never mocked one of the reasons given for our needing to find a new site.

"Are you worried about people here making you do something you shouldn't? I don't believe this of them. They are soldiers. They'll protect you. You're safe here, from all kinds of harm. Even families are here."

I wept then. "I have nothing for the baby when he comes, no swaddling cloths. My own dresses are thin as spider webs."

"Ach," he said, patting my shoulder as we sat side by side on the bed. "I'll ask John Genger to leave an account with the captain. So you can purchase cloth to make a new dress and clothes for the baby. Purchase food for yourself, too, though the captain has said you can eat at his table. It will give you something to do while you wait for this one to arrive." He rubbed my belly with the palm of his hand. "You will contribute now to the Lord's work by waiting."

"I don't want to wait without you. It's why I came in the first place, so I wouldn't need to be alone when the baby came."

He leaned back. "You said you didn't know—"

"I meant when we talked about sending me back," I corrected. "Does the Lord call you to leave your wife behind like this? Isn't there a proverb about an unloved married woman being one of the three things no one can abide?"

"Liebchen, you are loved. You must learn not to rely on others to make you happy. Happiness comes from knowing what God calls us to and doing that. All else is false."

"So that's part of your, your…theology, deserting your wife in her hour of need? I thought our leader taught us to treat our neighbors as ourselves. This is not how to treat neighbors, Christian, deserting them when they need you most."

He stroked my hair as I leaned into his chest. "What one comes to believe, one's theology, is in large part what gets written on one's own heart in ways that are hard to describe to another. Like poetry it becomes. Like a beautiful dream that loses its depth in the daylight. Think of Martin Luther. Of John Calvin. Their everyday lives changed who they became and changed what they came to believe. And what others came to believe as well. Ask them about their theology, and they would talk to you of the struggles they had and the choices they had to make in their everyday lives, *ja?* Indeed. It's how they came to know that each of us can speak for ourselves to God." I nodded and sniffled. "I'm not called to abandon you and I don't. I'm called to do what is asked of me, to take care of you and to continue with the other scouts to accomplish what others are counting on us to do. It is why we are here, Emma. Because others are counting on us. You must do your part now."

"But what's wrong with all the scouts staying right here in Steilacoom? Why can't we find donation land claims near here? It's perfect, as you said Ezra Meeker described it. There are already people here and towns and the climate…" I breathed in deep. "It is perfect."

"Well, it may be, but we will not know until we survey more, look beyond what has already been carved out. We look for our own clearing in the wild, Emma. As each of us must do in our own hearts. Perhaps this time without me right at your side, where you are asked to do new things that might frighten you unless you lean onto the Lord, perhaps this is how you will begin to clear your wild."

"The baby really will come in October," I whispered.

"The doctors all say November, and I will be back in November. I always keep my promises to you, *Liebchen.* You can count on this."

My tears did not stop him. My prayers were rarely answered of late, so when he walked through the door away from me, I didn't bother to pray he would stay. Instead, I turned my back on him on the seventh day of October and buried my head in the feather pillow. I didn't know when I'd see my husband again.

The day darkened with rain that fell from a pewter sky. No one knocked on my door to see if I was alive or dead. I lay on my bed, staring up at the peeled logs, watching a spider weave its web. I tried to imagine what the scouts would be doing, how Christian would get along without his wife at his side as I'd been these last months. They'd see, those scouts, how much harder it would be to search for the right site without me along. They'd see. I pulled the wool blanket up around me, feeling suddenly chilled.

Who would fix Christian's corn drink on the trail?

The Knight brothers would.

Who would wash their heavy jeans and shirts?

Christian would, as he'd helped me perform that labor each time. He always acted as a servant, even though he was the chosen leader.

Who would encourage them?

It wouldn't be me even if I had been along. Hans made us all laugh. George kept us fed with fresh game. John Genger kept us solvent. The Stauffers read the landscapes. What had I contributed?

I'd given little with my presence. They'd had to accommodate me on the journey west. My absence offered more to the success of their venture. What kind of uniqueness was that? What kind of theology was I inventing?

"Challenges defined belief," he'd said. I looked back to see what evidence existed for that in my life. When I thought I'd be left behind in Bethel, I'd met that challenge by discounting the virtue of my childhood and lying my way onto this journey. At least, I'd omitted some truths and in that way betrayed those I said I loved most. What would it have hurt me to remain with my parents and travel out with Christian's family in a year or two when they'd found a site? What would I have lost in staying behind?

I felt my stomach knot. To be excluded from this, to be asked to continue on in the colony routine, to never question what our leader asked of us, was that a woman's lot? Was that the belief I couldn't accept? Tears dribbled down my cheeks and into my ears.

In German, the word *to believe* meant to feel deeply about a thing. I did believe in my husband and the work he was called to. I did feel deeply about the success of the journey and the ultimate goal of bringing the colony to a new and different place. But I felt deeply about my own needs, too, my own rights to pursue what I might be called to do. Helena Giesy would say wives were called to support their husbands. Our leader would say we are to shun the ways of the world and serve our Lord on the road our leader chose—the road of obedience to him, service to one another, and lives without envy.

My mother would likely concur with those virtues. I missed her this night. Though I did wonder, as I fell asleep, how that strand of pearls she wore hidden by her collar fit with her living a simple, devoted, colony life.

15

To Need Another

I'd have to ask for help for everything: where to empty my chamber pot, where to get water so I could heat it to bathe. He'd left me helpless as an infant, me who wished to be independent, to do things on my own. I'd become a bummer lamb, that smallest offspring sent for special handling because it couldn't survive on its own.

Worse was that I couldn't even ask without appearing like a *Dummkopf.* I'd have to fumble and mumble along like a toddler just learning to talk. My parents had never encouraged my learning English. They'd never stopped speaking German, even though they'd lived in America for years. Papa said it would make them too much like everyone else, that they'd just meld into the world around them if they spoke as the outside world did. Our leader never encouraged outside learning either, unless it offered practical advice about animals or grain, woolens or wagons. The Bible met our educational needs, he always said, and that book was written in German. Bethel didn't even have a library. Still, my father learned English in order to reach out to those beyond the colony, to recruit people, to buy land for the colony owned by "the world." He'd entered the world without becoming contaminated.

Christian learned English too, and I surmised that our teacher, Karl Ruge, owned a variety of books on more subjects than German or mathematics. I remembered seeing him read a book of plays once, written by someone named Shakespeare. The very tools that would let me survive in the world outside were seeds in my father's garden. I would become fluent in English, that would be my new vow.

Right now, I needed to meld into that outside place, watch and learn as I could, become someone who didn't stand out, at least not for what I lacked.

I slept off and on during that day that Christian left me. I'd awaken, startled by the unfamiliar setting, then think of his leaving me behind. My stomach felt as heavy as a rock plopped into water. *"Tschuess, Liebchen,"* he'd whispered before he left. "Good-bye, sweetheart," he'd repeated in English. I'd turned my back to him.

Hours later, though I needed a bath, I simply could not bring myself to ask where I could heat water or even to bother trying to explain myself. I'd just suffer for a time, scratch where the wool wrapper chafed at my neck and across my belly. I wrote a letter to Mary but couldn't begin to tell her of the awful thing Christian had done, leaving me here alone, putting his precious mission before anything else. Isolation. He'd certainly found that for me, and he didn't need colony wilderness to do it.

Sometime in the late afternoon, a loud thump hit my door, once, twice, three times. It wasn't a knock exactly, coming low on the door as it did. With a push of energy I got up from my bed and lifted the latch.

"Simmons," Nora said to her son, holding a hard leather ball. She shook her head at him, smiled at me with apologetic eyes. Nora motioned me out then and offered me a chair in an open room that housed Japanese prints on the whitewashed log wall. I'd spent the day alone, and now she had a tea service set up in the open room. I could hardly turn her invitation down.

After she poured me tea, she tended her youngest, whose name I didn't yet know, while I sat on an embroidered stool. My fingernails needed attention. My wrapper, all speckled with spots, looked like it had measles. Simmons now bounced the ball against the wall, watching me watching his mother.

Nora used the word *mess* when she changed the napkin of her youngest, a girl with just a fuzz of blond hair. *Could that be the child's name?* "Mess," Nora said with a bit of disgust in her voice, but she grinned at her daughter. I knew it couldn't be a name. But when she proposed we go to the "mess," I wasn't sure I wanted any part of it.

She motioned eating with her hands, and I nodded, though I did wonder if eating would end up in a "mess." My stomach growled with hunger. I'd spent most of my last twenty-four hours in my windowless room, since late afternoon of the day before. A charcoal dusk brushed the sky. I'd brooded and pouted with no one even seeing how I struggled. No wonder I felt hungry.

I should have bathed, should have combed my hair or at least rebraided it. But what did I care? It would serve Christian well if others judged his wife to be a "mess."

A knock on the door revealed a tidy-looking Indian woman, who took the towheaded child from Nora. She said something to Simmons and he laughed, but he put down the ball that he'd been bouncing in a steady rhythm against the wall, and instead from the Indian woman he accepted what looked like skin stretched across a narrow circle. It now assumed his attention as he struck it with his hand. *A drum.* The child played a drum. He made me think of my little brother William, who would have loved such a toy.

Nora motioned to me, then pulled me up from the stool. Her hands felt warm and smooth. She said something and with her eyes asked permission to do something to my face. I nodded, and she brushed the loose curls from around my ears, then led me to the wash basin in the room she and her husband must have shared. *"Danke,"* I said. I'd just do my face. I didn't care about the aroma of me at that moment.

The *gut* doctor came out from the other side of the cabin and bowed slightly to each of us. He pulled his wife's arm through one of his own, then offered me the other. I took it. It must be the custom in these parts, I decided as we walked to the next log cabin. Apparently, the officers and wives were served their evening meals, all taken together like a family.

Walking in to a room full of faces, five men and two other women besides Nora, was not my idea of pleasant. I wished now I had changed my clothes and asked for a garlic compress to reduce the puffiness in my eyes.

I hiccupped. One of the women giggled. My face felt hot. I had to find some way of turning this discomfort into grit. It would be my…theology. If Martin Luther and my husband found meaning in life by facing challenges they'd have preferred not to, then I would do so as well. I'd ask for no special attention, not that I could ask for anything with clarity. I'd listen carefully to what everyone said but watch what people did more. Maybe each day, I'd choose one word that I'd try to remember and write down, making it sound in a way that Nora could read it and say it out loud, and then I'd know I had written it well. I'd know I pronounced it correctly. *Superior.* I knew it as a word that meant someone above me, someone higher up. Why it came to me just then I do not know, but as I looked into the eyes of those women, I felt low and small, making them my superiors I was certain.

For this meal, I'd be lowly, quiet, not bring attention. I'd behave as a deaf woman, using my eyes to interpret whatever I could.

The *gut* doctor stood beside his wife while she made introductions. I heard my name spoken. A blond woman with a long, narrow face raised her eyebrows at my introduction, and I curtsied and repeated her name, as I understood it, with the title, "*Frau* Flint." She waved her hand as though dismissing me, and then whatever she said next made everyone laugh. My face felt as though I'd been sitting beside the fire all day. I caught the English words "emigrant" and "beefy." I knew what emigrant meant, but *beefy?* We'd jerked beef before we left Missouri to feed us along the way. Were they serving beef? I wished Christian were here to help me translate, though with that thought came outrage masquerading as an unexpected hiccup.

Nora patted my hand, then shook her finger at *Frau* Flint the way my mother often did at William when he was younger and avoiding his bath. It was done in jest, and I supposed someone had offered a tease spoken at my expense. I was glad I couldn't understand their comments about my uncontrollable stomach acids.

My brother teased me often at the table, his sign of affection, my mother said. Maybe it was *Frau* Flint's way of being friendly, too. I smiled at her, hoping to win her over.

Captain Maloney sat at the head of the table, and he jumped up to pull out my chair. His quick movement attracted the attention of the other table mates, so I sat while their eyes looked at him instead of at me.

Someone must have prayed a grace, as each one bowed their heads. I did as well, taking in a deep breath and praying for strength to survive this…mess.

I survived the mess—my word for the day—without spilling the juice from the venison onto the apron I'd pulled from my pack, still clean from its last washing the day we arrived at Toledo, the day we left the Cowlitz River behind. I ate the pink-fleshed fish they called salmon and let the white sauce swirl into the inside of my mouth. Butter, sweet butter, something I hadn't tasted for months. I savored it slowly. I listened to the barrage of sounds, knowing that my mother had been insulated from English by living within the colony. Her choice made it easier to remain as a German speaker only. This would not be the case if the colony moved here. We'd all have to learn English unless we settled in a place so remote no one lived there but us. We couldn't rely on just a few like my father or Christian or Adam Schuele to be the salt that seasoned the outside world.

I ate the fluffy white vegetables Nora called *wapato*. Words swirled around me like music sung in a language I didn't know. Eventually, the *gut* doctor stood and broke my reverie. He pulled Nora's chair out so she could stand. I lowered my napkin and started to stand too, but Nora waved me to remain. "Finish," she said, the meaning clear.

Captain Maloney then said something, and Nora spoke in a reassuring tone to me, pointing to the captain and adding the English word *home*. I watched *Frau* Flint elbow the woman seated next to her, and the two patted napkins to their lips but not before I saw the looks they exchanged.

Then my guardians left me.

I dropped my eyes, poked at the pudding a soldier now placed before me as he took my plate away. It wasn't supposed to be this way— me, alone, making a fool of myself with total strangers while my husband explored for new worlds. "Home," Nora had said. I missed being home. Even a windowless room with my husband in it would have been "home." I wanted to go home, but I had none, at least not here.

I had no strength for this.

Indigestion left a foul taste in my mouth. My food no longer appealed, and I could feel that prickle at my nose that told me tears threatened like a summer storm. There appeared to be no reason to continue to endure this. I stood abruptly, nodded at *Frau* Flint and the others and stepped behind my chair, my lumbering body pushing it up against the table. I turned to go unescorted back to my room, but the captain reached my side in seconds. I had no idea what he said, but his hand felt firm at my elbow, and I heard more laughter as we walked out the door, him straightening Nora's loaned shawl over my shoulders.

I said nothing. What could I say? He chattered, using words all foreign to me. He pulled me closer, maneuvered me past a rock in the path that he bent to pick up and toss. He patted my hand, smiled, pulled my arm through his. His voice came low and lilting. He leaned over me to pull my shawl tighter around me. "Chilly," I understood him to say, but his breath felt too warm at my cheek. I was a lamb alone in the wolves' quarters.

I pulled my arm free and set a faster pace, stepping ahead of him. He talked, using a tone like the petting of a frightened pup, as he hurried to catch up with me. My fury at my husband grew. I should not have been left in this kind of setting. I did not deserve to be treated as though I were some trollop free for the taking. What must the captain think of a man who would leave his wife behind?

I couldn't depend on Christian—or anyone else, for that matter.

The lamp in the window flickered as I opened Nora's door. I turned to curtsy to the captain, and before he could say anything either to me or to the *gut* doctor as he had answered my knock, I closed the door in the captain's astonished face.

If Christian wouldn't help me, I'd have to help myself.

———

Tending the children was something I could do. There were only Nora's, I discovered in the days that followed. All the other couples here either had grown families as the tiny drawings in their lockets showed, or they'd left their youngsters behind with relatives while their husbands served in this faraway place.

Simmons, the boy, had decided I could stay when I played ball with him one afternoon, never stopping, never tiring. I'd done such things with William and David Jr., and I found it a soothing thing to do. Nora kept saying, "Thank you, *danke*," and I realized that occupying Simmons allowed her to accomplish necessary tasks when Marie, her toddler, took her nap or when An-Gie, the Steilacoom woman, came to help. Simmons apparently did not nap.

Nora also taught her son and allowed me to sit in on the sessions. I picked up new words that way and found I could recognize some words in the Germanic language of English that sounded much like the German words. This made memorizing the words written down on Simmon's slate next to simple drawings much easier to learn. It also meant I could add to the list of English words I kept in a book I'd acquired on account at the sutler's store.

A few Indian words came into my vocabulary too, words An-Gie said more than once that I thought I understood. She called Simmons *tolo* when she nodded her chin toward the boy. I assumed it meant "boy." She'd call, *"Muck-a-muck!"* and he'd come running, so I guessed that word meant either "eat" or "the stew's getting cold" or something to do with food. She used the word *klose* often, too, and Nora even used it. I guessed that must mean *"gut"* or "fine" or "great," a word one should know in many languages, I decided.

In the afternoon when the women gathered together to stitch, Simmons and I played ball. I knew I should have been working on clothing for the baby, but I devoted my evenings to this task, stitching the flannel into a long dress that I could knot at his or her feet to keep the child warm. In the evenings, I took out my chatelaine and sewing kit to mend my own wrapper and let the pretty tin needle holder hang openly at my neck. The work served as backdrop to the evening time when I talked to the baby as though it could hear me. Listening to the chatter of all the women at the fort fatigued me. I learned better with just Nora or An-Gie to listen to.

So during the day, I played with Simmons. My afternoons with him were much more invigorating than listening to *Frau* Flint and *Frau* Madeleine—the other wife at the fort—gossip about me with words I couldn't understand.

Besides, I contributed more to their conversations by being gone. I wondered if I contributed to the conversations of the scouts. I missed the men. I wondered where they were, how far away, whether they'd found that perfect place they sought. I missed being with them, all of them.

I missed Christian most of all, especially at night when I could hear the muffled laughter of the *gut* doctor and Nora rising and falling as I sought sweet sleep.

Before long, the anger I carried at Christian's leaving me behind turned into aching and, I decided, a theology of unrequited longing.

———

It was while playing ball with Simmons on October 19 that I stumbled and fell. As An-Gie would say, this was not *klose*, not *gut* at all. I was careful how I fell, aware of my baby even while in slow motion I watched the spruce trees' branches sway above me as I reached for Simmon's ball and lost my footing.

I felt a single sharp thrust beneath my breast that made me gasp for air when I hit on my bottom, hard. Then a jolt at my wrist, where I tried to keep from falling backward. I felt dizzy sitting, holding my wrist. I must have cried out, because Simmons came running.

"Missis, Missis," he said, his small hand patting my shoulder.

"*Danke,*" I told him. I'd ripped the hem of my skirt and would now need to acquire more thread at the store. I smiled to reassure him but swallowed instead as water gathered at the back of my throat. I thought I might be sick. My face must have paled. I felt clammy, lightheaded.

"Mommy! Mommy!" he shouted as he ran to the cabin where the women stitched.

"No, no," I called to him. The last thing I needed was *Frau* Flint making some comment about my clumsiness or my beefy nature. I tried to stand, couldn't. My bulky body rolled on the dirt and spruce boughs I'd slipped on when I went to catch Simmons's tossed ball. I panted now, looked around for something to use to pull myself up with, but we'd been in a field and the tree that gave its boughs up kept its trunk beyond the fence, too far away for me to reach or lean against.

"*Ach,* Christian," I said, wanting to curse him for not being there. I supposed that even if he'd stayed with me, he could have been in Steilacoom for the day or back at Fort Nisqually and not been able to help me now, but I wouldn't let him off that uncomfortable hook when I saw him. I suppose I shouldn't have been playing ball, but it seemed a harmless-enough occupation.

Nora rushed out of the house then, followed by *Frau* Flint and *Frau* Madeleine. An-Gie rushed too, carrying Marie.

"*Ach,* I'm such a bother," I said. They each took an arm, and one got behind me to ease me up. "*Ja.* Good. *Klose,*" I said, nodding. I was still panting and lowered my head to keep the world from spinning. My mother said such behaviors often worked.

Nora on my right put her arm around my waist, *Frau* Flint did likewise on the other side, and with slow steps they took me to the side of the house, where Nora's husband worked in the infirmary. She shouted something to Simmons, and he dashed from the porch, where he'd been staring, and ran through the door to his father.

The *gut* doctor held a towel in his hands, sleeves rolled up, and he frowned as the women led me closer. "I'm good," I said. "*gut.*"

"Here," he said and motioned the women to help me inside.

I tried to pay attention, listen to what he might try to tell me I should do to ease the motion sickness. His kind face and gentle hands helped lay me on the cot. "Good," he said. "Very good."

At last something was *klose,* and I hadn't had to ask for help after all; it had been offered. It was the last thing I remembered before I fainted away.

16

Original Sin

I saw Christian's face in dreamlike motions leaning over me with gentle eyes, caring globes of sky above me that I fell deeply into. I wondered how they'd found him, told him of my need to have him near me, sighed with relief that he'd returned.

But his voice had changed, and when I focused, these were not Christian's azure eyes at all. The *gut* doctor stared at me instead. I pressed my eyelids closed against the disappointment.

Distant sounds of wind through trees rushed against my ears, so I heard little of whatever chatter there might have been within that room. The scent of Nora's lavender soap drifted past me as she placed a cool cloth on my head. Someone brushed glycerin on my lips, a woman's soft finger easing like a skater across my flesh.

I hadn't fallen on my stomach, I knew this. I had protected my baby even in my reaching for Simmons's throw. That was why my wrist hurt so. I'd turned it nearly backward to break my fall. I lifted my hands, opened my eyes to peek. Tiny bits of stone and dirt ground into the flesh of my palms, proof of how I'd kept my child free from harm.

Dirt on my hands.

My wrist throbbed. Nora washed my palms and then my fingers, massaging them, one by one. I flinched at the pain in my left hand, wondering why her touching my fingers should bring such pain to my wrist.

She replaced the cool cloth grown hot from my fevered head. The *gut* doctor left then, and Nora sat beside me, sometimes reading from her Bible words I couldn't understand; sometimes sewing tiny stitches on a quilt square. Simmons came in once and leaned against her, asked a question. His mother gave an answer. He sighed and left. I so wondered what they said.

The day went on in dreamy states and, except for my wrist, I felt no piercing pains, but my body felt as though it carried a rock dropped inside my pelvis. My child kicked once, and my back ached as it never had before. I breathed words of gentleness to him, and he rested for a time.

But in early evening a kind of motion sickness interrupted what had felt like troubled sleep. I sat up, must have cried out, that rock sinking in my pelvis pushing to get out, stretching flesh and searing through my body in an effort to be free. An ache rolled over me more frightening than painful in its change. I was alone, though Nora must have lit the lamp beside my bed. "*Frau* Nora!" I shouted. What was this? It couldn't be labor, could it? I remembered then our leader's admonition that women experience pain in childbirth as a universal act of remembering our Garden sins. Perhaps Fort Steilacoom was too far from Eve's Garden for God to care about my pain, this unusual pain. It was not as our leader foretold. I didn't feel cut in two. I didn't feel as though sin lay on me. I felt discomforted, yes. But it was pain hard to describe… distinctive. Unique. I panted.

I felt wetness beneath me, and then, as though I'd swallowed a horse, a burning pushed through my abdomen, but I swore I wouldn't cry out again. My husband abandoned me. My mother lived months away. No stranger offered comfort.

But then Nora scurried inside the room, took one look at me and left, returned in minutes behind her husband, her skirts swaying. I motioned with my hand to my abdomen, wondering how I might ask for soda for the burning there. A sting of pain rose over me then, followed by a climbing pain that arched above me and made me want to push my insides out. My eyes throbbed like a heartbeat. "Is this it?" I panted. "Does my baby come?"

Before the *gut* doctor could answer, he threw my skirt onto my abdomen. The pain crested. I shouted loud, a wail almost, and then this aching stretching as though I'd ridden through a rock cleft to the wide clearing on the other side.

"Boy, Mrs. Giesy. *Junge*," the doctor said.

"Es ist Junge?" I asked in German. "It's a boy?"

In response, I heard a baby's cry as he held the infant up for me to see. A twisting cord of flesh tied us together, and then I saw toes, then chubby legs and all the parts and hands and head that spoke of his completeness and perfection: our son. The doctor continued speaking, but all I really understood was *Junge*. Boy.

Heartburn. Stretching flesh. Not much to complain about. I lay stunned by the arrival of an infant with so little trouble. My wrist from the fall I took hurt more.

Our leader might say I'd slipped past sin.

As Nora laid the infant on my breast I sighed, so grateful, so amazed that I had given birth with so little fanfare. I felt no guilt at all, but rather joy that I had co-created with our Lord and brought new life into the colony!

The child's dark fuzz brushed against my face. Nora rolled a quilt behind me so I could sit up a bit, then I nestled the boy in the crook of my arm. The size of a watermelon, he promised as much sweetness. I gazed into his face. He'd be tall one day like his father. His hands were large, his fingers long. He was full term, arrived when he should have.

I'd tell them if I could. He wasn't a month early, as the two medical men predicted. I'd love to tell them they were wrong, but it would have to wait for Christian's arrival for that translation.

I wished my husband had been here. He'd missed his son's arrival. Otherwise, this child appeared on time, in October, just as I predicted, without tragedy or unbearable pain.

I named him Andrew Jackson Giesy for the president that Christian loved so much. Christian's grandfather carried the name too, but it was for the president I'd call our son. "A man of the people," my husband called Andrew Jackson, "who fought the banking institutions and other powered men in order to bring better lives to those who worked so hard." It didn't matter that the Senate later censured him. That act was led by his former rival, Henry Clay. Jackson said the banks monopolized and therefore hurt each small farmer. Being censured for seeking truth, my husband told me, was a badge of courage. Experiencing challenge and distress in the name of virtue was a virtue itself.

The year of my birth, Jackson was nearly assassinated for his views. He became even more worthy in Christian's eyes when he died ten years later, having never given up on his beliefs. I hadn't followed politics all that much until I married Christian, but he'd said if our child was a boy, we should call him Andrew Jackson.

As a dutiful wife, when the child opened his eyes to me, I did just that.

I stayed in a daze of wonder throughout that evening, considering our leader's predilections for my disaster. Except for my aching wrist, this childbearing had been an easy venture. Perhaps it was man's duty to imagine the worst and woman's duty to prove them wrong.

I slept with my son beside me, though I woke often to be sure he still breathed, those tiny lips like pumpkin seeds barely moving as air as soft as sunrise moved between them. I so wanted to share these moments with Christian, to have him see that I could do what he hoped: give birth without bother, tend to our child, and as Scripture advised, bring the baby up in the way that he should go so he would never depart from it. I'd begun that very morning saying prayers for Andrew—Andy, as I thought of him—someone firm and sweet and not needing the power of the former president, an infant basking in the love of his mother.

Andrew was the name of a disciple, too, the one who pointed out the boy with the basket of fish when our Lord gave His sermon on the hillside. An observer, that Andrew, and a good and loving man who noticed children and all they could contribute.

I showed my Andrew to Nora in the morning while he wore the long gown I'd made for him. *Frau* Madeleine tucked the blanket under his chest with her bony fingers, speaking in her high-pitched voice. Her words sounded joyous, and I heard her say "bright," a word I'd thought referred mostly to a bold dye or the sun.

I kept him tightly wrapped when I met *Frau* Flint at the sewing time, not certain what her English words might say. She didn't seem the least interested, merely lifted her glasses on her beaked nose to stare at him, grunted once, and returned to her stitching.

Nora brought An-Gie in. She looked at my child and smiled. "*Tolo,*" she said. "*Junge,*" Nora told me in German. An infant boy. Nora motioned for An-Gie to comb my hair. I'd purchased new combs, abalone shells that the sutler kindly said he would order in for the commissary store. I showed them to her, and An-Gie turned them over in her wide brown hands, then began the gentle tugging and pulling on my hair. I felt tended and closed my eyes and hummed as she worked.

Even Captain Maloney's somber face at dinner could not dissuade the joy I felt, showing the seated group my son, who by now had begun to share his own voice with this company. I suppose every new mother thinks her child is the loveliest and best, but I was sure of this. I set aside the ache of knowing others saw his son before Christian did.

The second morning my body felt sore in places I'd never known it to be before. Worse, my child wailed and couldn't be comforted for long, neither by my stroking his face nor planting tulip kisses on his brow, tiny smooches opening to larger ones if only he responded. Did children normally fall asleep even when they hadn't sucked nearly long enough? He cried until he slept, then woke to cry again. I couldn't comfort my son, though I walked him and patted him and changed him. I couldn't help him find nourishment at my breast.

Instead of looking plumper as I thought babies did after a day or so of living, his face narrowed. His skin felt loose around his jerking, slender legs.

I winced when Andy tugged at me and at first Nora smiled, as though this sort of behavior from an infant could be expected. But by the end of the third day when he seemed to sleep more than even attempt to eat, I somehow conveyed my breast pain to Nora. She nodded, then offered poultices of grain. She made motions that I should pump my breast, and I felt my face grow warm. This was the work of milkmaids, with goats or cows, not healthy young mothers wanting nothing more than to nourish their child.

A pale liquid, nearly clear, left my body, but even I knew it wasn't enough to nurture a life. I longed for my mother's wisdom of what to do and chastised Christian beneath my breath for his absence, his missing words that would bring help. Then I cursed myself for not knowing what I should have known, what all mothers surely knew.

It was *Frau* Flint who, with gestures firm and clear, her hands cupped beneath her own ample breasts, brought out bristling behavior from Nora. Nora shook her head. *Frau* Flint pointed to Nora's toddler and spoke. Nora dropped her eyes. They argued, at least the snapping of words, and the pursed lips in between them suggested an argument to me. Nora said, "No," and I knew somehow that *Frau* Flint wanted Nora to nurse my baby. For some reason, this kind woman resisted, but she left and returned with a cup of milk.

Cow's milk would rescue Andy, wouldn't it? *Frau* Flint scowled, as though to say "a waste of time," but Nora soaked a rag in the milk, then brought it to Andy's mouth.

He licked, then spit up over and over again until he fell into an exhausted sleep.

Would my child starve? Could that happen? Surely not with a healthy mother and a doctor right there to advise.

Simmons brought me a book to look at while I rocked my limp child. I hoped the pictures would engage my mind on something bright and pleasant. Instead, the book had strange line drawings of an organ grinder and a monkey, a scrawny, narrow-faced primate that made me gasp instead. It looked too much like Andy.

I pushed back tears and vowed to stay alone, enclosed in my room, dipping into the cow's milk to drip into Andy's mouth, even though he spit it up; even though he slept now most all of the time. Some small nourishment had to reach him. Surely, my milk would drop soon. I'd hold him in my private, windowless room to protect him from what others might say while I was forced to watch my child die; I couldn't begin to imagine what I'd tell Christian when he came back, if he came back.

Nora knocked quietly at the door and then entered. Her words were soft, and I could see she cried. She motioned that she'd take Andy, gestured she'd hold him to her breast. I'd seen Marie eat table foods, so perhaps Nora felt her toddler could survive and her milk was better given to Andy. But then I could see the tears in her eyes and somehow knew what *Frau* Flint didn't: Nora had not enough milk even for Marie anymore. She'd been weaning the child. She had nothing to offer. That was the cause of her tears, not her resistance to share what she had.

I would always remember that moment when I knew my child would die. Nothing stirred the air. My mouth felt dry. I understood then what our leader forewarned: not the physical pain of childbirth; not the agony of sore breasts or healing from the infant's passage from his watery world into our own; none of that was worthy pain to redeem the sin that Eve committed. But the searing wrench of powerlessness, of being unable to tend to one's child, to keep those we love from suffering, such was the curse of a woman's original sin. And I'd committed it.

17

Trees of Knowledge

How I longed for Christian's presence, to shatter all my fears, make them unfounded, reassure me that God would intervene and save Andy's life. Could God create a woman able to give birth without bother, but who then couldn't keep her child alive? What kind of God was that? What kind of mother was that?

I tried to remember the verses my father read about children, of God's love for them. Our leader adored children, gave them sweet treats when he met them on the street. He didn't talk about them much, and I wondered sometimes if he thought little ones kept their parents' eyes from him and he was envious of their interest going elsewhere. I chastened my thoughts. I couldn't afford to offend God by decrying one of his chosen servants.

Andy stopped smacking his lips when I brushed water against them. He looked wizened as an old squash sinking into itself.

I could not stand this, I could not!

I raged into the front parlor, paced before the window, where I watched a light falling snow. Were there no goats here? We hadn't tried goat milk. I pawed through the books on the shelves looking for a drawing of a goat so I could show them. What was the word in English? Might the sutler know of a goat? He'd been so helpful with all of my purchases; surely I could tell him what I needed.

I grabbed my mother's cape and wrapped it around me, leaving

Andy lying so still I leaned over him to make sure he breathed. "I'll bring back what you need, I promise," I whispered, then stepped outside, feeling the wet snow cold against my thin slippers.

The commissary stood at right angles to the officers' housing and the doctor's surgery. With my head down against the sleet, the mix of rain and snow, I nearly knocked over An-Gie. With her, a young woman carried an infant in a board. They appeared headed to the commissary. This plump and round-faced child with large liquid eyes blew satisfied bubbles from its lips. I knew what I had to do—if only I could make her understand.

———

The girl carried her baby wrapped in a board decorated with shells and colorful beads. I could smell the cedar wood. She never looked at me, and it was torture staring at this plump baby, smiling while my child lay motionless. Could she tell that my heart split open at the sight of a healthy, fat child?

I tugged on An-Gie's arm, motioned toward the young girl who might have been a granddaughter perhaps or a niece. I pulled her toward Nora's house. The girl held back, but I urged both her and An-Gie into my room where Andy lay.

I picked him up, held his face to mine to feel the small intake of his breath. Then I motioned to the girl to take him.

"No, no!" An-Gie said, standing between us. "No *omtz*. No *ho-ey-ho-ey*. No trade."

Trade? I knew that English word. I held Andy to my breast. *Does she think I would give my son away in exchange for hers?* I held the back of Andy's head with my hand. He still moved, shuddered almost. "No *ho-ey-ho-ey*," I said. "*Muck-a-muck*. Eat." I made the motion with my hand and lips. *"Cum'tux?"* I'd heard Nora use this word to verify that An-Gie understood. She had to understand.

What kind of mother was I to ask a total stranger to bare her breast to my infant and keep him alive? A desperate mother. A strong mother, that's what I was, doing something I had never imagined I would do.

An-Gie spoke to the girl, who at first shook her head. An-Gie clucked her words, repeated *muck-a-muck,* and eventually, the girl laid her baby down on the bed beside the shallow impression Andy's feathery body had left on the quilt. She opened her skin jacket and untied the strings across her chest. Then An-Gie took Andrew from me and placed the baby in this girl's arms.

My child suckled for the first time in three days.

"Klose," An-Gie said. She patted my arm.

He was weak, very weak. The girl kept touching his cheek, as though to remind him of what he needed to do to live. I heard a soft wail in between, a good sign I thought, that he could protest the delay in his eating.

Finally, both fatigued and satisfied, he calmed, his tiny fingers no longer lifting and bending like a waiting praying mantis's, but instead resting in serenity on the smoothness of his savior's breast.

I wept. *"Klose, klose,"* I repeated over and over, hoping that *good* also meant "thank you." Because of these native women, we both would live, for surely I'd have died along with Andy if he'd left this world.

From the parlor window in December, I saw the scouts ride through the cedars, ducking beneath the feathery boughs, stirring up thin layers of snow that turned brown grasses into white. I counted the scouts. There were only seven.

I grabbed a shawl against the cool dusk and raced outside, Andy in my arms. He'd gained weight and felt like the watermelon he'd arrived as. My eyes scanned, seeking my husband's. I didn't find him.

"Where's Christian?" I asked Adam Schuele as he tied up his mount to the hitching post. "What's happened?" The horses' breaths puffed into the cold air.

"Nothing happened, Emma. All goes well, though we still do not find the perfect place for our brothers and sisters in Missouri. We come back so Christian can be with you…at your time." He looked down. "I see we arrive too late."

"So he's safe?"

"Christian stops at the commissary to attend to your bills, and ours. John Genger goes with him to ensure the accounting."

I would deal with the dis-ease of those bills later. Instead, I let my rage rise. Christian might have come here first; he might have seen his son before worrying over obligations of the "mission." Hadn't our separation been sacrifice enough for his success?

"What do you bring us?" Adam nodded toward the bundle in my arms.

"A boy," I said. "Andrew Jackson Giesy. The first new member of the Bethel Colony in the West."

I held Andy up for Adam and the other scouts to see, then pulled him back into the warmth of my chest. Andy cried, and I patted his back while the men stood at a distance, nodding their heads in that way that men do with newborns, that mix of hesitancy wrapped in awe, humbled that women bring forth such lusty life and that they too had a part in it.

George Link made the only specific comment. "He has big hands. He'll carry the *Schellenbaum* well." The rest of the men mumbled agreement before they headed to the soldiers' barracks where they would spend their nights. They walked as though they carried extra weight, though their faces had all thinned since I'd seen them.

All the lamps were lit, and Pap, An-Gie's daughter, held Andy while I swayed her boy in his board by moving my knees as I sang. These two were brothers fed from the same breast. I'd decided not to run after Christian; the sutler would tell him of Andrew soon enough.

The abalone shell combs held my hair in the low knot at my neck. I'd embroidered a tiny white shell onto the otherwise plain woolen dress that I'd made while Christian was gone. I hoped Christian would like it. The wool had been expensive, but it would last a long time. I had never sewn an item from cloth made by someone I didn't personally know. I even knew the sheep back in Missouri and carded the wool with my own hands to tug at the sticks and burrs hidden there. I spun the wool into thread and finally into fiber. I thought of that now, the memory of spinning arriving as a soothing thought for the anxious waiting of my mind.

Like bursts of bubbles from Andrew's lips, little worries popped up. Would Christian be happy with this son? He was a bit thinner than I would have liked. Would he be pleased to see me? Had he missed me at all?

I stood up holding Pap's son, went to the window, sat back down. Where was Christian? Why didn't he come?

Nora's children played on the floor while she and An-Gie fixed their meals. In no time, the *muck-a-muck* call would come. I hoped Christian would be back here in time to walk me to the meal.

The clock ticked steadily, and I decided to give him five more minutes, and if he hadn't arrived, I'd find him even though my interrupting him at the commissary would annoy. I went into my room, patted fresh-scented water onto my neck and throat. It had been nearly two months since I'd seen him. Did I have new wrinkles? I returned, lifted

Pap's baby again, and sat back down. I unlaced Pap's child from his board. Soft moss served as both a pillow for his head and ballast beneath his knees, and as a diaper to keep him dry. I held this chubby child on my knees. Across from me, Andrew continued to suckle at Pap's breast.

I heard footsteps, and when Christian stepped onto the porch, night had already fallen. He wore an expression of dismay, almost irritation, as he eased through the door, head ducked to miss the top of the opening. He stomped muddy snow from his boots and caught my eyes. He moved to the child on my knees, bent down and smiled, a gesture that turned to confusion. "This is our boy? The sutler tells me he arrives ready to play music."

The German words fell across me like music, words I could understand after so much time in the darkness, so much time as though I were deaf. "Pap tends our child," I told him and nodded toward the girl breast-feeding. "She feeds our son, Andrew Jackson."

Christian startled, then took his eyes from the baby I swayed on my knees. He rested his eyes on the baby Pap fed. His cheeks burned red. *Because of the cold,* I thought. He cleared his throat and turned, offering his profile to the girl and our son. "I'll let her finish," he said, coughing, "while you tell me why you let another feed our son."

"*Ho-ey-ho-ey,*" I said, and Pap exchanged my baby for her own. A tiny drop of milk still lingered on Andrew's pink lip as I held him, slender arms akimbo like a spider's. He smelled of fresh milk. "I had no choice," I said. "I…couldn't make the milk he needed." I kissed his tiny mouth of the last drop of white.

Christian looked confused. "He comes too soon," he announced then. He stood, hands straight at his side. "You did something to make him arrive before he was ready." He stiffened his back as straight as a rifle, and I could almost see his finger shaking at me as though I were a wayward schoolgirl, though he held his hands into stiff fists.

"He arrived healthy, a chubby baby," I said. "He came when I expected him to. October 19. It was when I couldn't feed him that he wizened. Pap saved him."

"You fell, the doctor tells me."

I showed him my palms, the tiny pebbles now blue dots beneath my skin. "Yes, but I caught myself when I fell—"

"And injured our son."

"No, he—"

"*Ach*," he said, pushing his hand against the air, both silencing and dismissing me. "I had such hopes for you, Emma. But now you see the consequence of not behaving as a young wife should."

"Christian, please."

But he'd already stomped out the door.

Why was he so upset? Why didn't he give me time to explain?

———

I'd decided to go after him when Christian returned with the *gut* doctor. It seemed like hours but wasn't. Nora still stood patting my back; An-Gie now served stew to Simmons and Marie. Pap held her son, wrapping him back into his baby board.

"We go to eat now," Christian said. "Come."

I handed Andy back to Pap. I didn't look to my husband to see if I had permission for such an act. It was my duty to tend to my child, and I'd done it without him and still would. How dare he judge me while he was off with his precious mission that had once included me and now did not.

I shivered as we walked to the meal together, the silence murky and heavy as mud. Weeks of missing him and this is what returned? I tried to keep up with him, but I faltered, my slipper stuck in the snow-crusted mud. A cry escaped my lips. The sound slowed Christian. He turned. "*Ach, Liebchen,* how does this happen always to you?" He held his hand to mine and pulled me to him. He motioned for Nora and the *gut* doctor to continue on.

"My slipper stuck," I defended when the others disappeared inside the mess hall. But Christian shook his head.

"What trouble you bring upon yourself and others too, it appears."

"I behaved as any wife left behind with total strangers would have," I defended. "I made myself useful to Nora and her husband. I tended to their children to help pay my way."

"Indeed. But not completely, or so the sutler's account tells me."

"Oh," I said. Perhaps this is why he was so angry.

"*Ja,* oh. That's something else we must discuss."

"I was as frugal as I could be," I told him. "I even learned to find cedar bark that can be woven into hats that repel the rain. I let An-Gie introduce me to this landscape. I learned some Indian words that might be useful one day. I dealt with being alone where no one spoke my language, and you dare say I bring trouble on myself?" I crossed my arms. I would have tapped my foot in outrage except that the slipper would sink back into mud.

He picked me up to carry me over the mud then, his motion swift and sure. His arms wrapped warm and welcoming around me. He set me down at the steps, then held my slipper, wiping the mud off with the palm of his big hand.

"I took care of it," I continued my defense. "I found Pap to feed our son, told her what I desperately needed. Even without knowing her language. I did what I had to do, left here alone. I did it, and I'll not let you make me feel less for having done it."

I saw the clench of his jaw relax, though his next words were spoken with annoyance. "*Ach, ja,* I am the *Dummkopf,*" he said, "spending long days trying to find our new home while you are here…spending." He pushed the slipper back onto my foot.

"I needed things," I said.

"Hair combs. Fine wool. A silver spoon?"

"He is our first child. All firstborn sons need something special to announce their arrival. He didn't even have his father here to hold him to the stars and introduce him to God." I lowered my eyes. "I'll find a way to pay for it," I said, though the how of that was far from certain.

He pulled me to him then, snuggling the cape close to my neck. Tingles of connection quivered through me to my knees. "You're cold," he said, quiet. "We should go in to the meal."

"I'm sorry for the purchases. Was John Genger terribly angry with me?"

"More with me, that I left no good instructions for you." He sighed then. "But I am angry more at myself. I carried that into our argument earlier. That was a mistake. You did well to keep Andrew healthy and alive, and I am grateful to have a son. *Ach,*" he said. "We scouts, we spend good time and money and don't even find what will work, and then I come home and argue with my wife. An unloved married woman I do not want you to be."

I could see the upturn of his lips in the moonlight.

"Then let's stay here in Steilacoom," I said. "Let's see if we can buy up land here in this good place." I faced him, my hands on his chest. "Our grain could be shipped out by sea from here, and the weather, it isn't so cold. See?" I lifted my ungloved hands up as though to catch snowflakes, though none fell.

He shook his head. "We will talk of this later, *Liebchen.* For now, let me tell you of my sorrow that you were left alone to decide what was best for our child. This is not the way a man should treat his wife. I hoped to get back in time. This was my goal."

"I know. Adam told me. But Andy really did arrive at the right time."

"Everyone says November," he repeated, and I could hear an argument rising that could never be solved. I decided not to add to the fuel of that fire, one better put out. "It will not happen again," Christian continued. "Our next child and the next after that will be born with me at your side."

I should have said then that making such plans simply challenges the devil to interfere, but I wanted to hear those comforting words. With them, Christian lifted my chin and kissed me, stealing my breath and repairing my broken heart all in one act of forgiveness and love.

———

We spent three more months at the fort resisting the rains. A happier time in marriage I'd never had. Christian did explore land sites near Steilacoom. He walked to Olympia and looked at maps with coastlines and dots of towns, but few marks of trails and no roads to speak of. He returned, usually within a few days, telling me tales of what he saw and what he heard. The other scouts too fanned out, returning with crestfallen eyes, drenched to the bone from the rain.

Christian watched our son grow and came to accept Pap's presence in our days and her son, whom she called Nch'I-Wana for the name of the big river, the Columbia, where he'd been born. My husband was a loving father. He watched how Nch'I eased into sleep inside his board, then asked how he might make one. An-Gie giggled when she understood. "No men do," she said, but she showed him, and he cut the board while we women cut the hide that would wrap around Andy, gathered moss to serve as a pillow and to place behind his knees. I stitched tiny squares to make a covering for the boughs that arched out over his head to keep the sun from shining in come spring; to keep the rain out when we went outside. He rode on my back, looking out at the world while my hands were free to help Nora with the laundry or to sew, remaking my overland dress into a shirt and skirt for my son.

While Andrew slept, Christian taught me more English words, and I shared what I knew of the Chinook and Chehalis words Nora and An-Gie and Pap often used. Eventually, I could talk to Nora of places and people. It was she who told me Captain Maloney had merely wished to offer me safety when he'd walked me home after Christian left. My face burned with the memory. Nora and I also talked of something that truly mattered: her offer those months ago to feed my child even at the risk of not having enough for her own, and my wish to thank her for that gift of willingness she gave. She practiced the Diamond Rule, wanting my life to be better than her own.

Rain fell steadily with rarely a break those first months of 1854. The paths between the houses and the mess hall ran like streams despite the wagonloads of woodchips, brought from the mill in Lower Steilacoom, that the soldiers put on them. This land was made of mud. Rain and mud. And trees, trees so large that four men holding hands could not reach around the trunks. Sometimes my eyes traveled one hundred feet up the trunk before I saw branches spreading out.

Sometimes, while Christian traveled to the surrounding towns and while Andrew slept, I'd make my way into the stand of trees, grand fir and Sitka spruce and red cedar. I learned their names. Beneath them, I found the ground soft, but not as muddy as along the meadow trails. I could hear the rain drip on leaves, push through needles, falling soft as teardrops on the forest floor. I'd find a place to sit beneath tree-falls, what Christian said the men called the large trunks pushed over by winds or age against another, or caught up in tangled branches, sometimes crisscrossing narrow trails like sticks set to build a giant fire. I found respite in the cluster of these trees, in knowing I had a warm, dry place to return to. I prayed that Christian would find his mission here, close to Steilacoom.

A couple of the scouts went south into Oregon Territory seeking sites, but in early spring they returned, and at a meeting I was allowed to attend, they shared their news. Christian told them he'd talked to men from the Pacific coastlands who knew of a place with wide river bottoms rich for planting. Nearby, timber waited to be harvested for buildings. The logs offered pilings for shipment to San Francisco, and with the Bethel Colony bringing grist stones, there'd be water for a mill.

"Isolation, too," he told them.

"When do we go then, to see this land?" Hans asked.

"April. When the rain stops and the trails are not so bogged down in mud and the fallen trees are more easily crossed."

"We take axes then," John said.

Christian nodded. "And saws. Ropes. Those are our tools."

"When I look at these trees," Michael Sr. said, "I wonder how many days it will take us to cut one down or try to split it."

"When we find the right place," Christian said, "all will fall into place."

"We've looked at lots of land," Adam Knight said. I heard annoyance in his voice.

"We must all agree on the place," Christian said. "So far, each of us finds some fault with what we see."

"These coastlands you hear about, are they like Ezra Meeker's lands?"

"More isolated," Christian said. "Unlike Steilacoom." He looked at me. "We must not let the demands of the world encroach upon us. Here things are too easily purchased, life made too simple so we forget what we're about."

"Are you sure enough of the coastal site's potential that we could send men back now?" Adam Schuele said. "We've seen the terrain. Those south have too. Could we return to help prepare the rest? We'll be three, four months getting back. That would make it July when we arrive in Missouri."

"It's too late for them to come out this year, and the longer you stay, the more houses we can build. If you go back in August, there will be time to prepare the Bethel Colony for departure next spring."

"We could agree to meet here, then, in Steilacoom, and send word for you to come and get us." This from Joe Knight. I liked this plan. Perhaps I could remain here, too, until the larger colony arrived.

"You think you'd be one to go back?" his brother said with just a hint of teasing.

"No," Christian said, his words cutting off any jesting. "We must find the place together and all feel it is worthy before any return to Bethel. That way we'll know that God has chosen the site, not any of us."

"But not this place?" I interjected.

"No." All the scouts nodded agreement with my husband. "This is not the place we're called to."

I wondered why I felt such a calling here, and yet I was obviously the only one. Why did what I see differ from these men?

"You will have to enjoy your stay here, Emma, for a few more weeks, and then we will all load up, pack what we can carry on our backs and our new mules we've purchased. We'll make a new Bethel."

I nodded agreement. What more could I do?

When the men left in early June, I took a long walk into the cedar trees, Andrew on my back. I prided myself entering the dense trees and finding my way back. I remembered the tree with the moss patch on it that looked like a long, open wound, or the thick bark that had a design in it that resembled a face. My feet made no sounds in the wet woodland. Pap had made a pair of moccasins for me, much more practical than slippers, though I could still feel small cones when I stepped on them at the arch of my foot. I crawled under a new blow-down, careful to push Andrew in his board before me, located the game trail again, and this time walked farther than I ever had before. I made sure of my bearings, then continued on, not sure what I was looking for or how I'd know when I found it.

But I did. Deep into the trees I saw a shaft of sunlight making its way through the denseness. I walked toward it, chattering to Andy as I did, until there it was, taking my breath away.

A meadow. A wide, lush prairie filled with white flowers and pink dots of color. Deer nibbled at the tree line, and overhead large birds called out. It smelled earthy and fresh. I turned around and around, arms outstretched. "This is beautiful," I told Andy. I'd thought this whole country was nothing but trees where rivers cut through them on their way to the sea. All the small towns lick Puget Sound's shoreline. In all our traveling up the Cowlitz, I hadn't seen such wide meadows, such vast prairies. I took this discovery as a sign. There were clearings already prepared for us. We needed to pick one of those and not a place where we'd have to bring down tall, massive trees.

"This could be the land we farm and settle on," I told Andy. It would be the best of both worlds: dark earth easily plowed but isolated and yet close to the sea. And it was right here in a climate we'd already been introduced to, the land that Andy inhaled first. My heart pounded and I sat in the tall grasses, chewed on one long strand that smelled of onion.

I'd been led here, I was sure of it. No matter what the challenge, one just had to keep pushing through dark timbered places, trusting there'd be clearings in the light beyond.

I began my trek back, buoyed by my seeking and discovery, as hopeful as…as *Eve when she first ate of her fruit.*

18

The Winding Willapa

Something isn't right. It is hailing inside our tent. White rocks the size of Andy's fists pelt us. Christian scrambles to repair the torn canvas first, shoving me and Andy toward the back of the lean-to. I lay with my body arched over my son, oddly able to see Christian working frantically as the ice begins to melt and turns to torrents of water filling up our little place, and yet I can see my son beneath me, smiling up. The rain pours down now, and my baby is lifted by the torrent, torn away from me while I grasp, shouting for Christian to stop worrying about the holes in the tent and see what's happening to his family instead. "Christian, help!" I scream, but my words fall on deaf ears while my son floats beyond my reach. I grope! We've camped too close to a river, and now we are a part of. The landscape's chosen us, picked us out to die. Now we're in a craft, a small troubling craft taking on water. I know we have to go under the water to get where we need to be. "Christian, do you know how to get there safely?" He shouts back, "No! I don't have a compass." Andrew cries, and I feel pain in my shoulders.

"No compass? No compass?"

"Emma, you will wake the others."

I opened my eyes, gasping. My husband is arched over me. "You have bad dreams, *ja?*"

My body shook while I reached for Andy, held him close to my chest, slowing my breathing. Then I came fully awake to a storm wail-

ing around us. Wind mostly, not rain. What sounded like hail on top
of our canvas tent must've been branches and needles torn loose. Puffs
of wind pushed the walls of the tent out like a bloated frog, then sucked
them back in. We heard roars like the steam engine at Shelbina. "The
trees…?"

"This is an odd storm for August," Christian told me. "The man,
Swan, said the weather stayed mild through the summer. High winds
didn't come before October maybe. I think we'll be all right." I couldn't
stop shaking from the dream. I kept kissing Andy's forehead, and then
I remembered Opal, the goat. "Is the goat still tethered?" I asked. Maybe
that's what the dream meant, that I'd lose my son because the food he
needed had torn loose in the night. Or maybe it meant we didn't really
know where we were going, and the weight of this journey would sink
us in the end.

The goat bleated then, and Christian lit a lantern, though the wind
blew out the light as soon as he opened the flap. *"Verdammt!"* he said,
the first curse I'd ever heard from my husband's mouth.

"I find her, Emma. Don't worry," and with that he stepped out into
the darkness.

I rocked my son, back and forth. Christian had discounted my
grand prairie plan; instead, he and the scouts went west and found what
they said was the perfect place. We'd said our good-byes to Steilacoom
ten days before, now here we were, in the densest of forests.

Opal's bleating came closer, and then as though the Lord Himself
acted as shepherd that night, the goat nearly ran Christian over, pushing back into the tent. It shook its tail of the wet and the wind, its little
bell tinkling.

Christian relit the lantern. "I need to make a casing for this light,"
he said. "To keep the wind from having its way with the oil."

"We need a shelter," I said. "A casing for us. A real home with

walls." I stroked the goat with one hand, rocking Andy on my knees.
He slept now, and I marveled at his comfort in the midst of chaos.
"We'll need a root cellar to hide in if these kinds of storms happen
often."

"I tell you, they won't. This is a freak storm, Emma. Don't worry
now. Where we go, this will not be so bad. Swan's been here three years.
He says the climate is mild not hostile. We'll be all right, and see, the
goat finds its own way to safety."

I gripped the goat's rope collar with its tiny bell still dangling from
it. "We'll have to hold his collar as his rope's been torn," I said.

"*Ja*," Christian said. "I'll hold him until daylight, when we can sal-
vage the tether and then move on. "It will be well. You'll see. The place
we chose is perfect."

I felt powerless to calm the rush of wind which, as I listened to it,
probably wasn't any worse than a rainstorm in Missouri. The dream
had heightened my fright.

I held tight to Christian's words. The scouts' unanimity of choice
gave me comfort. How could every last scout—save one, me—favor
the landscape unless God Himself had spoken to their hearts?

"You rest now, *Liebchen*. With sunlight, the day will be better. We
are almost home."

He patted my knee and lay back down under the tarp. He fell
instantly asleep, leaving me to grab for the gray goat's collar before it
bolted out of the tent opening. It bleated until I spoke to it of the home
I imagined in my mind, the words like prayers taking me through the
darkness and residue of dreams into a morning calm.

My husband was right. Sunlight made life better.

I stepped outside to see little had changed in the landscape. I saw
timbers split and felled months before like some giant hand had flicked
its fingers against the forest. Tall firs leaned against others still standing;

more crashed to the ground, their root balls like crones' hands struggling out of forest graves. I squinted. The root balls looked old. The trees that leaned against each other already had moss growing where they met. These trees hadn't blown down in the past night's storm. They'd been down a long time; I just hadn't noticed them when we'd made our evening camp.

"See how the Lord looked over us," my husband said, standing behind me. "Everyone slept well." We watched as the Knights and Michael Sr. and the Stauffers moved from their tents. The only real damage was a tarp with a tear that John Genger set about repairing with the paraffin he carried with him, but I remembered that tear had been there before, too.

I filled Andy's tin cup, fortunately only partway as he batted my hand and whined, letting me know he wanted to do it himself. We spilled less when I'd fed him through the fingertip of a leather glove. I'd poked a hole in the glove to manage the flow. He slapped at my wrist as he reached for it. It had been nearly a year since I'd fallen on that wrist, and still at times it shot pains through my arm. Our son, however, didn't notice. I wondered if every mother experienced pain as we stretched to learn new things, to do things by ourselves. Maybe pain rode before a lesson.

We set out again carrying large packs on our backs as well as on our mules. I carried Andy on my back and walked, draping a bag of items hung by a rope over my shoulders and around my neck. I tugged at the goat, too, as we followed what Christian said was the trail the scouts had cut through this land earlier that spring. I did see evidence of their chopping, but even in the short time since they'd been through here, young shrubs and vines won back the trail. Trees newly fallen across it made us have to choose to either take a day to chop and saw the trees to make an opening or try to go around and make a different trail.

Would we find such signs of effort where we headed? Would one log consume a day to get it where we needed? We'd built brick houses in Bethel. I saw no evidence of material for such here. I couldn't imagine how the wagons coming out from Bethel would make it through here, but I didn't say a word. The scouts chose this. Even practical John Genger and the wise Adam Schuele claimed that God had chosen this site for them all. They could see through these tree-falls and a landscape so big we were all ants in a field of grasses pushing our way through.

Ferns shot up from the forest soil, their fronds edged with tiny dots that looked like perfect black knots of thread. They reminded me of stitching, and I wondered if I'd ever have time for such pleasant needle-work again.

This landscape was such a contrast to the meadow outside of Steila-coom that was so open, so easily plowed. But Christian had not even walked there with me, saying he'd been all around, and nothing in that area appealed until this place we were heading to.

Rustling sounds in the distance made the goat pull back on her tether. "Bears," Christian said over his shoulder.

I looked around for bears as I followed him. *A new danger.*

"We're making good noise, so I don't think they bother. I can hardly wait for you to see this new land, *Liebchen*."

As we walked, I wondered if Moses felt this way leading his people through the desert, sure of the destination but uncertain of the people's readiness for what goodness and trials lay beyond. I thought to mention this perspective to Christian but abstained. He seemed so happy even as the sweat dripped from him and tiny gnats pushed at his face.

"This is a land worthy of God's work," he said as we chewed on hard biscuits when we nooned.

What was one woman's cautious voice against such enthusiasms? I had nothing to say. The scouts' confidence carried me along on this craft without a compass.

———

Twelve days after leaving Steilacoom, we reached the Willapa River. We approached the stream from the east near a bend, so at first it looked tame enough and not particularly swift. A flat spread out from the water's edge, and with sweeping arms, Christian told me, "Here's where we'll make our mark then."

"Right on this bend? This river?"

Narrow meadows, what was once the river's bed, no doubt, lined the river, bearing tall grass and purple flowers. The land we could cultivate at least. The soil looked black when I kicked at a clump of the grass to smell and taste the earth.

"And see, there are plenty of trees to log, for building houses. All we need is here," Christian said.

I looked up at the tops of the trees, nearly stumbling backward. Some stood more than two hundred feet high, making my neck ache as I gazed at their tops. Our tiny saws and axes would be but mosquito bites to the tough, long arms of the trunks that rose before us.

"And this river goes right to the sea, maybe fifteen or twenty miles west at most. We can float logs down, dig for clams at the ocean, have plenty of seafood to add to game. This river lures fish in during the season, Swan tells us. The bounty God has led us to…" Christian stood teary-eyed.

He's in love with this landscape, this formidable, dark, dense landscape.

Christian had no doubts, and the man Swan was spoken of as someone wiser than Moses had been. When we made our way toward a small clearing cut back into timber around the bend, my doubts lessened a little as well. For there rose a sturdy log house almost as large as the surgeon's quarters at the fort. Best of all, a woman holding a bucket in her hand stood before it.

———

Her name was Sarah Woodard. She was but a child, maybe fifteen, with hair the color of pale butter and eyes such a deep blue they looked black at times. Her muscled arms reflected hard work. Sarah and her husband invited us to stay with them at this river crossing for the night. Christian hesitated. In German he said, "We should not get too close to those around here." But Adam said accepting generosity was a kindness in return. I rejoiced. Here lay a feather tick to lie on. We herded the goat in with the Woodard cow and its calf. *They own a cow!*

"We brought it up from California, put onto a ship, and here it is," Sarah's husband said when I commented about the animal. "A brute bred her back so we have another increase next year. We get to keep what we raise, not like those folks who worked for Hudson's Bay Company."

I vowed to have Christian order a cow from California for us. If he intended to send products out on the tide, then south by ship, then we could get them north to ease our lives too. I never thought I'd say it, but travel by ship would be so much easier than what we'd been through overland on what Christian called our "Dutch Trail."

"Why didn't you propose to have the Bethel Colony come out by ship?" I asked Christian. We leaned against a tree at Woodard's Landing, as the place was known. Andy played with the Woodards' dog. The pup brought sticks to him that Andy threw, the makeshift toy landing not far beyond his toes. I shooed the dog back when it started to lick Andy's hair as he sat. "It would be so much easier than to come overland with wagons and stock." I hesitated, then said, "I wonder how the wagons will come through that trail we made. At the first windstorm, you'll have to go back and reopen it."

"You worry over much," he told me. "We'll bring them up the Cowlitz River, as we came in canoes, but only as far north as the Chehalis River. Then it's a short portage onto the Willapa, and they'll be right here, just as we need them to be." I still didn't see how the wagons would come up that Cowlitz trail, but Christian's tone suggested little patience for my questions.

I changed my son's diaper. At least the area offered an abundance of moss for his diaper. I walked to the river and rinsed the cloth, then laid it over a blackberry bramble to dry, checking the ripeness of the berries as I did. It was August. They were ripe enough for pies.

"They'll have no need for wagons here," Christian said when I came back. He'd been thinking of our conversation. He used his preacher voice. "Indeed. All produce and people will go by water to market. Wilhelm's group can sell their wagons in Portland. It will mean more money to purchase grain and other things needed to tide us through the winter."

"But if we've no need for wagons, why not tell the colony to come by ship?"

"Too expensive. Besides, we can use the plows and other personal items they bring. The returning scouts will tell them what we need. Axes, saws, hammers, plows, scythes, seeds."

I wondered if someone would bring out trunks of clothing for us and the other scouts who remained here. *Or perhaps we will return.* That thought proved fleeting as I watched my husband scan this landscape, take some measure of contentment that he had found what he considered the perfect place for the colony.

Whichever scouts returned would have to start back soon in order to be in Missouri before the snow fell. I wanted to talk about that but instead I asked, "And what will the wagon makers do here when they arrive?"

I thought of my brother Jonathan apprenticing as a wagon maker. That had been his plan, to make wagons and sell them to those coming west, his contribution to the colony an important one.

"Maybe they'll build boats," Christian said, his annoyance obvious in his tone. "Or furniture. Each house will need furniture. We adapt in the colony, *Liebchen.*"

Would wintering with the Woodards be an adaptation? We surely couldn't work through the wind and rains of winter to build. But if I said that now, he'd think I coveted comfort. I didn't want any suggestion of weakness, or Christian might consider sending Andy and me back with the scouts—without him.

———

Living in Bethel I knew most everyone. Maybe due to my father's influence, or perhaps because I paid attention to new babies born and did what I could to help at the harvests, adapted, and went where I was told. They were like a family, each willing to help the other no matter what. We were asked to be in service to others, to be ready on Judgment Day to face our Maker and say we had tended to widows and orphans and brought in new sheep to the flock.

Since we'd left Bethel, I'd met dozens of people, some with names I now couldn't remember and some on the wagon trains we briefly joined. We might have nooned with them, listened to their stories and then moved on. The names and faces ran together for me like birds along a rock fence. Maybe our journey intrigued them; maybe they found sojourners in the Lord's vineyard to be of interest. I didn't feel a part of any community with them because we didn't stay in one place together, we didn't share both hardships and joys. A community, even a colony, needed those shared times to bind it together.

I hoped there would be a kind of town when we finally settled. One family named Woodard, a woman plus nine scouts, and a child hardly seemed enough to make up a town. Christian would say our community would arrive full force with the Bethelites and that I must be patient and wait.

But then one morning in late August 1854, even this small fragile community changed.

"Reasonably, it must be George Link," Adam Schuele said in response to the question Christian posed that morning about who would return. "George has a hunter's eye and can repair anything, wagon wheels especially. He can bring the others here safely."

John Genger was chosen along with George, or at least his name came next and he nodded. "We've spent what we must to secure the land, and we will depend on the bounty here for the rest. Essentials you can purchase from Woodards' store, but keep it minimal. There'll be little accounting needed for a time. We need to be sure to have money to bring the first group out while the rest remain at their posts, working."

"Perhaps you should go back with them," Christian said.

Andy rode on my knee, and I bounced him before looking to see who the third person chosen would be. When I lifted my eyes I saw that that the scouts looked at me.

"You'd consider returning?" I asked my husband. He shook his head, no, and in an instant I realized I'd become complacent with my plans. I remembered my earlier vow to do what I could to get Christian to be one of the scouts to go back to Bethel, but the months across the trail and the month here at this Willapa site told me my husband's devotion went to the success of the western colony and that required his effort here. This was his mission, his passion. He'd never desert it, not even for a season. I hadn't imagined that he'd try to send me away.

I took a risk. "Will the scouts return by ship?" I asked. I swallowed hard.

"Maybe we should reconsider returning by sea," Joe Knight said. "It would be less dangerous, perhaps even quicker." He raised his pointing finger to emphasize his point.

"There, you see?" I said. "A sea voyage would shorten time."

"*Nein,*" Christian said. "The expense is too great. Indeed, I'm surprised you'd suggest an ocean voyage knowing how you feel about water."

"I only want to be…cooperative."

"You raise unnecessary issues."

Adam Knight, his eyes cast down, waited to speak. These men were not accustomed to overhearing disagreements between husbands and wives. "Overland is best," Adam said then. "So the Bethelites will have the latest information about the travel. Some may come back to Willapa by ship, and this is good. But to return, the expense is less to go back the way we came."

"It would be better if you returned, Emma," Christian said. "This will be a harsh winter here, everything unsettled. We may need to live in tent houses. Perhaps we could find the resources, John, for fare back by ship?"

The mere thought of me riding those ocean waves without my husband at my side churned my stomach.

"We could consider—"

"No, please," I said. My husband prepared to send me back, get me out of his way so he could stay devoted to his first love and, worse, would take the idea of a trip around the Horn as suddenly legitimate.

"It wouldn't be good. I can help here, I can, Christian. Wasn't I strong along the plains?" I imagined more river crossings and rickety ferries on any return trip; I imagined a long journey back in silence with men perhaps resentful that a woman and child rode with them. I imagined a ship in a windstorm with me and my son all alone. "I could stay with the Woodards. That way I wouldn't be a worry to you."

"No," Christian said, his voice nonnegotiable. "We will not impose."

"We'll have to hunt for ourselves now without George's fine eye," Hans Stauffer said, changing the subject as he scratched that place on his head.

"You've been itching to try," Adam Knight told him.

"*Ja,* now I'll be the hunter," Hans said.

"We'll all have to hunt, and we'll all have to fell trees," Christian said. "You see how much work there is." He stared at me. Did he think that I would agree so he could devote his entire life to this mission, so he'd have no guilt about the conditions he asked me to live in?

"I'll not go, Christian," I said. " 'Whither thou goest, I will go', remember? I can be of use here. I can prepare meals. You will simply have to let me do my share." Andy cried now. He did this at the worst times. "A child needs both his parents," I said. "Surely this is God's order of things. How could you even suggest separating a father from his son, a wife from her husband, when it is not necessary?"

"I believe it is," he said.

The men kept their eyes from us, and finally Adam Schuele said, "Her return could be dangerous, Christian. For her and the boy. I made a vow to her father, to keep her safe. I can't do that if she is on a horse riding sidesaddle back to the States."

"It's not good for a married woman to travel without her husband, not even on board ship, not without at least another woman. These men who stay know their wives and sisters will travel with many others. What would our leader think if you sent me back among men whom I'm not related to?"

Christian might have heard my heart pound, considering how it filled my ears as I waited, my fingers and thumbs making circles on the pads as I wrapped my arms around my son. He fussed and pushed to be set down.

"I decide," Christian said. "Hans and Adam and me, we remain. Then you Knights, you stay too. But in a few months, you go back around the Horn. That way we have both kinds of trips covered. Michael Sr., George, John Genger, John Stauffer, you return now. You'll need safety in numbers; we'll be in this isolated place, which will be our protection. A woman and child would hold you back. We will miss you men, but God goes with you. You bring our families to a good place, the place God chose for our colony."

"We'll build here," Adam Schuele added. "Our colony will keep us spiritually prepared for the end yet allow us to prepare others we come in contact with."

He looked at Christian, whose set jaw locked tight as a closed fist. "Indeed," he said at last. "You're our return scouts. You have special rewards waiting in heaven for your obedient service." It seemed to me he emphasized *obedient* before he turned his back on me.

"Do you agree that I should remain here?" I asked.

"Obedience," he said, "applies even to me."

———

We had a rousing send-off in the morning with prayers and a little music from Hans's harmonica playing. *"Auf Wiedersehen,"* we shouted our good-byes. Christian acted not unlike our leader when he sent the scouts from Bethel, offering up wisdom and guidance, and at that moment, I was as proud of my husband as I had ever been. He forgave my challenging him in front of others. He would perhaps allow me to assist as I could. "We will all sacrifice here as you are sacrificing to return back," he said. "Remember us in your prayers as we remember you in ours."

"Remember our empty stomachs," Hans said. We all laughed, but there was truth to what Hans said. Who knew if we'd have enough ammunition to take the meat we needed? Who knew if we could build three dozen structures within a year so there would be houses for the Bethelites? Who knew if I had just made the best choice for my son and my husband?

I slipped a letter to my parents into John Genger's hand. He tipped his hat as we waved good-bye. Watching their hats disappear through the timber, I thought how a year from now, this would be a new place. What seemed a strange and foreign land would be familiar, and when it was filled with friends and family, it would be the delight of my husband's heart, and I would have played a part in it. I'd been chosen to be here just as the other scouts had been chosen to return.

My heart sang as I turned to begin my new work beside the winding Willapa River.

19

The Giesy Place

We began building on the "Giesy place" about a mile south of Wood-ard's Landing. I picked berries, dried the meat that Hans brought in, shooed away seagulls who pecked at the deer entrails, milked the goat, and while Andy slept, I chopped at slender willow branches—*withes* Christian called them—that could be braided into rope or used for binding while the men felled with their saws.

The timber, both tall and stately, took days to chop through the trunks. I stood in awe of the size of the red cedar they selected first. Smaller than the towering firs and spruce, its long flat needles sagged toward the earth. The tree did not easily succumb. Both its wide girth and the sweat off Christian's brow surprised me. I listened to the chink, chink sound of the axes making their wedge around the base of the trunk. And when the sun set, only small indentations of the axe marked their day's work. Standing inside that forest felt as peaceful as being in the church at Bethel when our leader was absent. Light filtered through the branches. Echoes of bird calls trembled in the silence when the men rested their tools. The air smelled moist, and the forest floor acted spongy against my moccasins, the cedar liking damp, it seemed. I set Andy down and brushed away the needles and picked up a handful of soil to inhale it. Later when a squall moved through, dropping rain on us, we stood with Andy beneath weepy boughs, barely getting wet. I leaned against that dark grain of a thousand years of growing undisturbed until we came and wondered how it was we had found this Eden of our own.

It took the men three days to chop that first tree down.

When at last it cracked and sounds of falling splintered through the forest, Adam shouted to get back. The tree's heaviness lingered in the woods as it sighed against another taller tree and hung there, unwilling to lie down. Sam Woodard called such trees "widow-makers" when Christian rode to get him, seeking advice. Sam offered suggestions to get it down without a death. It required skill and God's blessing, but they accomplished the task.

"Maybe it would be good if you looked for downfalls," Sam suggested. "Find some not rotted. It might be easier."

I thought that good advice, but the men still looked for trees they felled themselves.

By the end of the first week since the scouts had left, they'd felled two huge cedar trees and prepared to cut them into ten-foot lengths for walls. The bark stripped off easily, and Sarah Woodard said she'd seen the Indians pound the bark until it was almost like a cloth. The bark looked fuzzy with fibers floating from it. I pulled some free and found they might work as thread to repair Christian's socks.

The men harnessed two mules brought from Steilacoom and drove them into the forest, and while it may have seemed a good idea, and would be in time, the mules resisted pulling the logs behind them. They startled and reared and snapped ropes, and I could tell that even getting the logs to a building site could take days of wrestling them over brambles and vines into the small clearing at the edge of these trees.

My stomach ached with the possibilities of injury, the snail's pace of the work.

Sometimes, if the men chopped a tree near the top of a ridge, they would try to roll it down, but the tree often hung on another tree felled by a previous storm. The men did then consider chopping and using downed trees, but many rotted in place. They wanted strong, sturdy logs to house us. Cedar, they said, would last forever.

It took a month for the small squat hut we called the Giesy house to rise up at the forest's edge. It needed caulking, something I could do, but the men decided this could be done later. For now, they would set a ridge pole and some cross rafters for later roofing. In time, they'd draw a canvas across it for a winter's roof.

"As the Israelites lived in tents to remember their harvests and all God provided, so will we live," Christian said. The cost of bringing milled lumber from Olympia, or even from a mill Christian learned was built closer to the ocean, meant an expense so great none of the scouts felt it justified. Secretly, I thought they didn't want to have to explain to John Genger where the money went when he returned.

"It'll be easier now that we know how to do it," Hans said when they prepared to move on to build another hut.

Adam Schuele said, "We must show that we can build in this place and live from it as we are asking our brothers and sisters from Bethel to do."

"The weather's mild," Christian noted. "By the time they arrive here next fall, we will have two dozen log homes for them to winter in. Maybe three dozen." It sounded more like a wish than a promise.

I couldn't see how. It was September and we'd only finished one. At one a month we'd only have a dozen by the time the Bethel group arrived.

"Might we stay with the Woodards when the weather keeps us from building this winter?" I asked Christian one night when we lay in a lean-to with our canvas acting as our roof. I could see the stars like white knots of thread in an indigo cloth appearing in a tiny patch of sky not covered by treetops.

"Nein," Christian said. "What would it look like for the leader of the scouts to stay in a soft place with feather ticks while the others make their way beneath a canvas tent? We will all stay at the Giesy place if we are unable to build where we need to, but I don't expect that. Last year was mild, Sam said. We can work in the rain."

"At least we'll be in our own place," I said. He didn't correct me.

———

As the weeks wore on, I wondered how these men convinced themselves that they could build enough houses in time for the arrival of the Bethel group. Weren't they counting the days and weeks and months that one small hut required, and it still needing a roof and caulking? They had to hunt for food, which took time too, and we needed to graze the mules closer to the river and give them more rest time. They looked thin from all their efforts. We'd need to gather firewood, dry more deer meat, and perhaps even fish before winter so we'd have food enough to last us.

Once when the work slowed and I couldn't watch any longer as they swung their axes against so noble a tree, I took Andy and walked to the Woodards'. Andy sat playing with clamshells and a knobby shell Sarah called "an oyster house." Andy was nearly a year old, and Sarah had made a cake for him, which we ate on the porch of her house. I loved her view with a small grassy area surrounded by split cedar rails that eventually disappeared into trees. The house sat in a clearing that felt open and wide even with the darkness of the trees beyond. I could hear the Willapa River swishing its way to the sea, pulled there by the tide.

"How long did it take you to build this house?" I asked Sarah. She brought the churn to turn as we finished up Andy's cake.

"It stood here when Mr. Woodard brought me to it," she said. "We added on a room that took a little time, but I don't know how many days the house took to raise."

"What does your husband say about our efforts?" I asked. I knew men gossiped as much as women, though they claimed to be above such matters.

She smiled. "How do you know we talk of this?"

My English had gotten better every day as I made myself use it with Christian and with the Woodards. "My husband talks with me about the world around; yours, too?"

She lowered those dark blue eyes. "He says you Germans are stubborn, that you should live with us while you build. It is the Christian thing to do to make that offer and Christian to accept. But your husband does not do this."

"He gives," I said. "If ever you have need of something, my Christian will provide it if he can. But receiving is harder for him."

"He is generous to his family," she said.

I nodded agreement, wondering what she'd seen that made her say that.

"He names the Giesy place and says it will be for his parents and brothers and sisters."

I felt an envy pang, or was it disappointment? "He takes care of his own, *ja,*" I said. I took Sarah's place at the churn, pounding with vigor though I didn't know why.

"Mr. Woodard says your plan to build right on through the winter is also a…crock full of wish. A dream, my words for it," she said. "Instead, the mud will keep you in one place. Venturing out or chopping trees will be too difficult. My husband says you should be preparing food for winter storage now. Chopping wood and keeping it dry for firewood." She stopped my hand and lifted the plunger. "I think it is churned enough." She finished the butter, and we pasted it into wooden molds. "Do you have candles for the winter?"

"Some." I thought of our lantern and how easily that light blew out.

"Plan to stay with us. We'll read and tell stories and sing and maybe even dance while the rains come down."

It had been a long time since we'd danced.

"My husband is determined to have three dozen structures by next fall for when our friends join us."

Sarah nodded her head. "This is the stubborn part my husband says defines yours. You won't be able to work so hard through the rains, and the trees…the trees demand respect and are not easily changed."

"You make it sound as though trees have a soul," I said.

"The Indians say they do. The trees give them so much—canoes and clothes and houses and tools." She showed me a deep scoop spoon made of wood the color of my sister's chestnut-colored hair. "Smell it," she said, and when I did I knew it was a cedar burl. "Something that gives so much needs to be noticed, witnessed to," Sarah said. "It gives up in its own time, giving itself as a gift rather than a taking."

"People are counting on us to have homes when they arrive," I defended.

"This forest and river land will be their home," she said. "People here just take temporary cover inside their houses."

———

Christian's constant enthusiasm and my commitment to be his helpmate silenced me. Even when we poled upriver in the Woodards' boat so Christian could show me another piece of property he'd claimed for the colony, I kept my tongue about whom he built for and whether we could accomplish all he'd set to do so we could make a life here.

It wasn't that the land near the river wasn't lush and laid out for easy tilling, but that these meanders of river were separated by ghastly tangles of vines and trees and sometimes close-in hills that seemed to suck the air from my throat. We could cut trails along the river through those sections, but most likely living here, we would use the boats often, ride in small crafts that were not nearly as grand nor as sleek or as stable as those used by the Cowlitz people. We'd be dependent on this river, to go from here to there. I'd be on water nearly every day of my life if I wanted to visit someone, or become a hermit connected only to my husband and my children.

"I've purchased these three hundred twenty acres," Christian told me when we'd beached the boat and climbed up a high bank. "It was a donation land claim of a man who is prepared to leave."

"But it's so far from Woodard's Landing and our place," I said. "Won't we all want to be close, the way we were in Bethel?"

"This is maybe seven miles, nothing more." He bristled.

"I only meant that in Bethel we all lived close together. In a town, with streets that—"

"Some stayed in Nineveh, you forget. We can have settlements separated by a few miles and still remain true to our cause. We all agreed to settle along the Willapa, Emma. We will need to do things differently in the West. Around us is free land if a family lives on it for five years and improves it. It's theirs. There is no such thing as this in Bethel. We cannot afford to drain the entire treasury there to buy land for us, *Liebchen*." He patted my shoulder.

"I've seen no buggies, or even people except for the Woodards."

"I told you. Here we walk or go by water. It is the way. There's a post office in Bruceport and warehouses, so there are people closer to the bay. We'll go there one day. You'll see. This will be the route nearest to the Cowlitz, and those from Bethel will come across our trail, and maybe by then we'll have time to clear it further so the stock can be driven across too. The returning scouts will advise that we bring only mules or oxen to drive the wagons. Our farm will be along the way for people heading to the coast."

"Whose name is this property in?" I asked, changing the subject.

"In the Territory's eyes, it is ours," he said. "But it belongs to the colony, all held in common as in Bethel."

"Then who owns the Giesy place with the one nearly finished house?"

He cleared his throat. "I claim that for my parents. This section, distant but not so far away, this one will be ours to farm."

Andy shouted, then pointed at a squirrel and took my attention.

"You let us men attend to these things," he said, following me as I changed Andy's diaper. I grabbed at some cedar duff as an absorbent. "Your job is to make what we will build into a home to raise our sons in. Wait here."

He walked down the riverbank and leaned into the wobbly craft we'd pulled up onto the shoreline. From it he took a pack with a shovel pitched over his back. "I begin," he said.

He lifted the sod from a square, pushing and scraping the tall meadow grasses. Sweat dripped from his forehead, but he whistled as he worked. I gingerly walked through the grasses, felt the sun warm my face and knew it must be warm on Andy's too, though I'd set him in the shade. I took his hand and he waddled upright. He still hadn't taken his first steps alone, but with help he grinned at his success. "We may as well see if there are late-blooming berries, since your father is so occupied in digging."

I'd filled my apron with flowers instead, sticking one behind Andy's ear, tickling him as he sat. I slapped at mosquitoes. They'd be swarming by sunset. Andy pulled against my skirt to raise himself and stay balanced. Finally, Christian whistled his single loud tone and motioned me to return to the square he'd scraped out. Across it, he'd spread the canvas. Come," he said. "Let's christen this land we've been given to turn into service to our Lord."

The look in his eye told me he had more than the Lord's service in mind at that moment. I felt a stirring in my own heart. My face grew warm. I marveled that his hours of intense labor poling upriver, then clearing the sod, hadn't weakened him in the least. If anything, it seemed to fire his desire.

"When do we begin work on our house?" I said as he reached to untie my bonnet.

"Don't worry about that now." He pulled me to him.

I said, "Right here? Won't it tire you for the return trip? And what about Andy?"

Christian smiled as he lifted his son still clinging to my skirt, laced him into the board leaned against the tree. His wide fingers wove the rawhide strings through the buckskin covering, then tied them neatly in a bow. Something about the movement softened me.

"Andrew has perfect timing," he said. "See? He sleeps."

Swaddling did usually put Andy to sleep. His father laid the board propped up against the shovel base, but in a shaded area beneath some arching vines. On his cheeks I wiped the mud paste to counter mosquito attacks. Christian replaced the flower behind Andy's ear, and our son took two quick breaths but didn't awaken.

"As for me being too tired to love my wife and then take her safely back to the landing, you forget." He grinned now and began untying my wrapper at the bodice. "Do you still wear the petticoat with the ruffles?" I nodded. "Then here is another occasion to mark your uniqueness on *our* Giesy place." With Christian, life felt right, even in this place so far upriver from the others. Geese called above us on their way south for the winter.

"Trust me, *Liebchen*," he whispered as he led me onto the canvas he'd unfurled on the ground. "It's an easy ride downriver to wherever you wish to go from here."

He kissed my neck, and I felt like a tall cedar going slowly down.

20

Duty-Bound Steps

Fog, like a faithful scout sent ahead to survey the land, eased into the Willapa Valley. Behind it came the storms.

At first we crunched our necks into our shoulders, doing our best to ignore the rains, my mother's wool cape no longer spotted with water but soaked instead. Our lack of attention to the rain must have angered it, for soon it came down harder, and the lean-to Andy and I huddled in beneath a cedar while the men worked in the trees on another Giesy house, not ours, could not keep out the damp. The fire I kept going at the entrance of the lean-to billowed smoke back into our faces. We coughed but chose that discomfort over being drenched.

One or two seagulls continued to seek us out, which surprised me, as we had little to offer them. I now used the deer bladders—the rounded organ that I learned to pick out quickly from the entrails—to hold dried berries. Sarah said she'd seen Chehalis people dry deer ears and later boil them with roots and little plops of flour. That sounded like a dumpling stew, so I did that too. She told me to save the brains for tanning hides (we'd done that back in Bethel) and that the broth from boiled tongue helped people with a cough. I even kept the sinew away from the seagulls, that stringy part along the deer's back strap that proved as tough as any thread I'd ever used before. One day I boiled the shinbones and found the tallow a palatable fat. Even the antlers became digging tools, not that the seagulls hungered after them. The birds had all looked alike to me, but when Andy and I sat in the lean-to and watched them screech at one another, lifting up and settling back, I did notice one with a chip out of his flattened bill. He returned often enough we named him Charlie. He became a friend for Andy.

Opal, the goat, bleated protests, lifting her right leg up onto my squatting knees as I cooked. I protested too when I had to clean out the area of the shelter where I milked her and where she stood during the night. How she must have resented my cold hands on her bag in the morning, but she never kicked. A docile female indeed—as I was becoming.

I considered building a corral for Opal using abandoned branches from the trees but wasn't sure she'd stay in it. And besides, I'd be leaving that corral for Christian's sisters or brothers. It wasn't as though we were establishing the home we'd be staying on. That was selfish of me, I knew, but I'd endure the weather better, I thought, if I knew that one day soon I'd have a place to call our own.

By December, with every day crying rain and a coldness I didn't remember while I lived at the fort, I risked again urging Christian to reconsider staying with the Woodards at least until March, when the rains tended to come more intermittently—or so I remembered Sarah saying.

"You're soaked all the time. I've given up washing, or have you noticed? The mud clutches at clothes, and they're dirty before I even finish, and they never dry. You've started to cough. We'll all be sick, and when spring comes you won't be able to make up for the time you're losing now."

"We have to keep going, *Liebchen*. They count on us. So many count on us." He coughed a racking cough, bent over, barking like a sea lion. When it stopped he said, "In November next year, if all goes well, they'll arrive. How will they live through the winter if we have no houses for them?"

"They'll do what we've done. Live in lean-tos and under canvas."

"They count on us for better, *Liebchen*."

"Andy and I count on you too," I said. I saw the pain in his eyes and I softened. "Please. Let's stay with the Woodards. They've offered this to us, and you always say the receiving of gifts is as important in the Christian way as giving is. Why shouldn't we learn to receive? Accepting their generosity would be a good witness, wouldn't it?"

"If we stay at Woodard's Landing when the weather is good, we'll lose precious daylight making our way to the woods. Here, we can get up in the morning, and our work is before us, as the Lord provides."

"He provides more work than necessary," I said under my breath.

"Your being here helps," Christian said. He patted my shoulder, then coughed again.

He'd never said such a thing to me before. "You're pleased I stayed despite my...ways?" I said.

He nodded. Dirt caked the lines in his eyes, and for the first time he looked old, my husband did. Old and tired. And sick. I thought back. He'd stopped doing his pushing-ups.

"Why don't you build more homes on the original Giesy place, then?" I said. "We could stay at the Landing and you'd still be close to your work."

"Each claim needs a house or we will lose the deed."

"There's time," I said. "Isn't it five years to develop the land before the risk of loss?" He took a drink of the hot tea I'd made and pulled a piece of tea leaf from his lower lip. *Is he considering my idea?* "At the least, why not roof one house to make it livable? One house we could all stay in and be dry. The one you're working on now, maybe. It's as though you're putting together puzzles, but you don't stay long enough to finish even one."

He shook his head. "You don't understand. When we are all here, we can more easily do the roofs, Emma. We need to keep building walls as we can." His voice had that final note he gave when he'd bear no more protest. "You talked your way into being here. You must now make being here your way."

———

"Can you talk to him, *Frau* Giesy?" Hans said. I patched the scab on his head with a paste of herbs. A light snow fell outside the lean-to while I tended him. My hands were cold even wearing gloves. I'd wrapped Andy in his board to keep him from wandering off while I helped Hans. I didn't want my child getting wet or colder than he already was—than we all were. Even Hans's teeth chattered as I ministered.

"Emma, Hans. It's all right to call me by my Christian name."

"*Ja*, Emma." Hans had scratched until the place on his head bled nearly every day, but this day he'd scraped that spot as well when he crawled under a tree-fall looking for a deer he thought he'd downed. "It rains so hard a man can hardly see to shoot straight," he said. "We really need two men hunting together, one to help the other."

"That'll mean even fewer to haul the logs," I said, dabbing again at his wound.

"I saw some Indians out there too," he said, his voice a whisper then.

"My husband says we're perfectly safe here. I've seen only friendly Indians willing to show me how to make a spoon from a burl. They're very kind."

"But I hear—"

"They're as cold and hungry as we are, I suspect." I'd been startled myself coming upon what Christian said were Chehalis men at the river when I went to rinse out clothes before I stopped bothering. A man batted with a club at large fish coming up the river while the women with him cut them lengthwise into long filets. They'd arranged a kind of dam that appeared to divert fish into a holding pond where they were easily taken. They'd built a fire beneath a lofty cedar and skewered the filets with long sticks they poked into the ground, holding the fish's pink flesh toward the fire. The men wore reddish-colored capes that looked like woven reeds or even bark and basket hats that shed the rain. They didn't seem the least interested in me. When I approached, the women noticed me and offered that cedar burl spoon.

"Still, *Frau* Giesy—Emma—he would listen to you. We'll all be getting sicker if we don't bring in more meat and get out of this wet. Look at us!" He held up his arm and reached his hands around his wrist. "Thin as a cane and barely as useful." He lowered his voice even more. "We should not have sent so many back to bring the rest out. Two would have been enough."

Should I defend my husband's leadership? I wanted to, but Hans did look thinner. We needed fat; we had all lost weight. My wrapper ties circled twice around me now, but I assumed my weight loss came from doing my best to make sure Andy and the men had sufficient food as they were working the hardest. Opal's milk kept me fit. Or so I thought. But I was hungry more often than not. These men must be too.

"We all think we should finish one house, cover it, and wait out this rain. Then we can start in earnest in the spring."

"You've spoken to Christian about this?"

Hans shook his head. "Bring it up even sideways, and he turns us around with those staring eyes. He is a taskmaster, that one."

"He stares at me, too," I said, the most critical of my husband I preferred to get in the presence of Hans.

"*Ja,* but he pays attention."

"Does he?"

———

Adam Schuele sought me out for his cough next. He needed something more than the boiled deer tongue syrup. I made a pepper and sugar tea, having him sip it slowly as the pepper clustered at the bottom of the mug. "It burns," he said. But the cough lessoned for the moment.

"We don't have much sugar left," I said. "I hope the Knight boys don't get that cough."

Hans caught it, too, and Christian's never did go away, though it wasn't as wracking as it had been. But my husband wouldn't hear of leaving or even roofing the hut they worked on. He'd already planned to move on to another Giesy claim, this one for Sebastian and Mary, and haul logs for that house. "Discomfort is part of our mission," he said. "No disciples ever found following the Lord easy. It is how He works out our character, through these trials."

"But the men—look at them." The men stood inside a rotted tree trunk out of the rain, so Christian and I talked in private. "They're ill. They're tired. They're weary of all this. You're thin as a reed. Surely God did not intend for us to kill ourselves in pursuit of this new colony."

"We all chose this place."

"*Ach, ja,* I know. But things change. We have new information now. The trees aren't easily harnessed. There are too few of us working on the huts, so you push too hard."

"Are you saying I shouldn't have sent so many back?"

"No, I… It's just that there aren't people here for us to recruit or to serve, and we're devoting so much time to housing there's no energy left for…listening to God's Word or bringing it to others. Even those who've lived here three or four years before us in the Territory are leaving. Isn't it true you bought out their claims? Perhaps this isn't the way we were supposed to prepare for the others, perhaps we've lost the heart of this mission, the soul of—"

"I'll not hear any more dissension," he shouted. Andy stopped his playing at my feet and looked up at his father. His eyes filled with tears. The goat scratched with her back leg at her bag. "No more," he said, quieting. "We will do it this way and the Lord will keep us. You must not be like Job's wife who did not support her husband in his hour of trial. You must have faith."

That night I dreamed that my soul woke up. The stretching of my stomach seeking food elbowed it awake. My heart pounded fast, then slow, pushing blood into my head to get my brain to work, feeding it thoughts. My bones ached but exerted strength as they poked at my organs, swimming around inside me until my soul awoke. It had been asleep too long while the other parts of me took over. It was the oddest dream, but when I awoke I knew what I needed to do.

———

The tarp must have weighed fifty pounds or more, and as I dragged it, it began to collect mud, adding to my effort. "We'll find fir boughs to lay it on, and I'll haul that," I told my wide-eyed son, who sat staring back at me from a distant tree. I'd wrapped him in a larger board I'd made, liking the security it afforded me at times, tying him in. With my small axe, I chopped a bough from a fallen tree. I did imagine Christian's look when he returned to our lean-to and found us gone. But he'd roll in with Adam Schuele and the others so he'd not sleep in the wet, though they could all cough together once they consumed the pepper-and-sugar tea I'd left for them. And maybe, just maybe, then he'd follow me, and if nothing else, the men would have a few days' rest while he searched.

My routine involved walking ahead through the mud with Andy on my back while I tugged at the goat. Christian once said the goat would follow me anywhere, but I couldn't take that chance. I would set down the small pack I carried around my neck, lean Andy's board against it, tie the goat, then head back to the tarp that lay like a giant gray slug in the rain some distance behind me.

Back at the tarp, I would roll it onto a flat cedar bough, which seemed to reduce the muddy drag. Cedar needles were softer, not as prickly as the fir, but the bark still chaffed against my hands as I dragged. When I would reach Andy again, I'd rest for a bit, say a prayer, take a breath, then put my son on my back, place the bag around my neck and grab for the goat, leaving the canvas behind. If I began to think about how far I'd have to go like this, I'd make myself concentrate on something else. Reality would strip me bare, and I might simply stop. All I would think about was the next step and conserving energy for my work, wasting no effort on future foes I faced nor past disasters. My soul kept me awake.

Carrying my son ahead helped me find the best path and gave me short respite from the aching of my shoulders and my legs that hauling the tarp induced. I'd settle Andy down while I could still see the slug, as I called the canvas; then when I returned for it, I was never far from Andy should danger work its way toward him. We made enough noise with my grunting and his crying out for me "Mama, Mama" off and on that I couldn't imagine any self-respecting cougar or bear would even be in the region, let alone curious enough to try to find us or do us harm. I did once wonder if the goat might attract them as a perfect noontime meal. And once when Andy cried, I remembered Sarah telling me that Indian children are kept quiet during berry-picking because their cries sound much like bear cubs, and a mother bear might seek out the sounds.

I pitched those thoughts away.

I pitched many thoughts away. Thoughts about what my action might mean to my marriage, thoughts about where I was and what had I done. The trees did offer solace as I made my way through them in the mist and rain. Their stillness and stability made me almost worshipful. We hadn't had a church or any fellowship or any time to even read the Scripture because we all fell wet and tired onto our moss beds. I vowed to change that once I reached my destination.

Near the riverbank, Andy and I fell into a mud hole up to my knees. The goat bleated as he jerked the rope out of my hand. The weight of the mud and its sucking felt like a too-tight cape around me. I thought then that maybe I'd made a mistake. Maybe we were meant to endure hardships, and it didn't matter where we endured them: in a lean-to or in a mud hole. Maybe Christian was right about trials gouging out our character and that avoiding them just made the next carving more grievous.

Would we be stuck here? Would Andy and I sink, then be consumed by bears? That thought gave me new energy, and I grabbed at shrubs and vines at the river's bank, yanking at them until I pulled myself free. I lay on my stomach, panting with effort, the sound of the river rushing behind me.

There had to be more than one way to carry out God's plans. That's all I was doing: finding another way. It had been my way that once set upon a course I found turning back a trouble. I believed Christian and I shared that trait. I was doing this not just for the men but for my husband. I, too, like Job's wife, was duty-bound.

———

Dusk greeted us as we made our final approach toward the four walls of the first hut of the Giesy place. When I'd left that morning, after the men headed into the woods, I thought I'd go to Woodard's Landing. But once on my way I believed going to the Giesy place would make more sense. It was the same distance from where the men worked, and it offered opportunities to redeem myself once my husband came after us. I hadn't yet entertained the idea that he might not.

I'd come three miles from where the men worked, though I'd walked it twice, pulled myself through knee-deep mud carrying Andy, found a different route back for the tarp. Even the goat stayed close to Andy, and by the last half mile or so, I didn't have to take the time to tether it; it trusted I'd be returning.

"At least they weren't working on our site, Andy, or we'd have had to come seven miles or more through brambles and trees." Opal bleated and butted, jerking both Andy and me to my knees. "We're almost there," I scolded.

When I arrived, I stood in the doorway of the hut, the sound of my own voice an icy slice into silence. It was not the quiet that invigorated, I decided, that tingled one's toes or lightened the spirit. It was heavy and dense, as weighted as an anchor. Dark trees towered over us, filling the sky except for the clearing where the hut stood, its uncaulked walls and open rafters making it look like an animal carcass of ribs more than a possible home.

But we'd made it.

In that heavy silence I unrolled the small canvas that held our personal things as rain dribbled off my cape hood. I found sticks to hold the canvas up enough to keep the rain from our faces through the night. We ate jerky and I milked Opal, and both Andy and I drank our fill of sweet milk. In an odd sort of way, it felt homey here. The accomplishment of a thing, even so simple as milking a goat, could give pleasure.

My mother's face came to me, her standing at the doughboy preparing bread, a fire in the fireplace, my brother bent over his studies awaiting my father's return for the day, my sisters chattering as they tied one another's braids into loops that hung at their backs. It had been a simple life in Bethel but a good one.

A dry life too.

What was the point of our being in this Willapa place so far from those we loved, so engaged in a labor that even when completed would seem primitive to those who led orderly, tidy lives back in Bethel? Our brick homes there seemed luxurious compared to these humble dwellings. And where were the people we hoped to influence with our ways? The Woodards thought we were stubborn, maybe even *Dummkopf.* People lived in Bruceport off the bay, Christian said, but we wouldn't go there much except for supplies now and then. We rarely saw anyone else, rarely took time to know what filled the lives of our distant neighbors. We focused only on "the mission," securing an isolated place where we'd be safe when God brought about the destruction of the world. But what if we destroyed ourselves in the process? What if we only saw one another and never touched the world around us at all? If this was the site chosen for us, then where were the people we were to touch with our lives?

I quickly tossed that disloyal thought. My husband would find a way to make sense of this work—if he didn't die of consumption or exhaustion first. I pushed aside the ache of his absence.

One of the true blessings of physical work is that it presses a body to the point of fatigue, so sleep falls upon one like a brick against the hearth. Andy snored softly, our first night alone inside four walls since we'd left Fort Steilacoom. I laid my head down with images of my family dancing in my dreams and, blessedly, fell asleep.

In the morning, I shoved aside the tarp and looked up through the open rafters of the log house. I wondered if Jonah felt like this inside that whale, the rib cage arching over him, his fate to wait.

To wait was a luxury I didn't have. I lifted my arms above my head to stretch and felt my shoulders protest. My whole body ached in new places, my sides, my forearms, my thighs. All the dragging and hauling told this morning story. Maybe I should rest today, I thought. But no, the muscles would only groan again when I began the work of covering the ridge pole, and I wanted it finished when Christian found me. I knew he would; just not when. I'd left a note to say I'd gone to a drier place and for him not to worry. He'd assume the Woodards' but he'd be wrong. I wouldn't take the feather tick Sarah offered either, but I'd make a home in this wet weald, and in so doing maybe Christian would see that resting until spring made sense.

While Andy slept, I milked the goat who'd bedded down beside us. The elk bladder Hans had given me to hold water and milk held most of what Opal gave, and it would stay fresh until we could drink it later. For now, I needed to see what it would take for me to get the tarp up onto the rib cage of this hut to form a roof.

As I stepped outside the four walls, I pulled my mother's cape around my shoulders, surveying my task. The goat followed me out, butted against the back of my knees, but I kept my balance. At least my physical balance. Imagining the work ahead threatened my emotional one. *Begin to weave / God provides the thread.* I smiled to myself at that thought. Weaving was about balance. I had to find that kind of equilibrium in my life.

21

Just a Woman

The drizzle continued as I worked to find two poles. I wanted them ten to twenty feet long. *Surely it won't keep raining every day until Christmas.* Even angels' tears had to stop sometime. But I couldn't let the climate change my course.

Andy wailed to be set free, but I kept him in his board. He drank his milk, which quieted him. "As soon as I figure out what to do about the roof," I told him, "I'll put dough on a stick and cook it." I thought about trying to bat at one of the big fish, as I'd seen the Indians do, but the river ran high and swift with rains, and I didn't want to go anywhere near it.

A strip of venison jerky quieted Andy as I freed his arms from the board, tying the rawhide across his chest. He chewed. I roped Opal to a tree near some brush she promptly ripped at. "I wish our keep were as easy," I told the goat.

The design of the Indian board with its woven shelf out over Andy's head acted like the brim of a hat and kept rain from his face. His eyes followed my movements, and I could see both my brothers in them and Christian, too. "Mama, look," he'd say, and I'd turn to his pointing. "What's that?" he'd ask, and I'd tell him in English and German, sometimes even using Swiss words. But mostly I told him to wait because I was busy. And I was.

The axe weighed heavily against my legs as I walked. I'd taken the tool with me, though I risked Christian's upset. But I needed it for the windfalls I hoped to find, something slender, maybe a tree pushed over or snapped off by a larger one. I entered the edge of the forest, then heard the rustling, though I couldn't see it. No snorts, just the sounds of something moving through the trees. Maybe Christian had already caught up with us!

I eased my way back, picking up Andy with the goat following as we returned to the inside of the log walls to wait.

When Christian didn't appear, I began to worry about the noise. The activity of the men working each day kept the bears and other would-be predators away. Safety lived inside that colony corral. We were alone here, at my choosing.

I considered praying for our safety. The colony teacher, Karl Ruge, had told us we could pray for anything, that we didn't need a priest, as in times of old, to intercede. But surely God would frown at my putting ourselves in injury's clutches, then asking for reprieve.

"You'll have to stay in here, Andy. You too, Opal," I said. I piled sticks and boughs up against the doorway that lacked any other kind of covering. Building a permanent door would be a new task too, but first, a roof. That's what we needed.

I reentered the forest. To make more noise, hoping to stave off unwieldy beasts, I sang old German songs and hymns my mother taught me, though all singing stopped when I spotted a fallen tree I thought I could manage.

I chopped at the side branches and then began the work of pulling the log through the woods toward the cabin. I looked for the axe marks on the trees I'd made to note my way in and then back out. It was noon when I dragged the log to the cabin and let it lie. One log, really just a branch. A half a day. I pulled away the branches from the doorway and set my son free from his board. Then I took my flint and burned some cedar duff, establishing a cooking fire.

I took water from the small canvas set to catch the rain. After drinking hot tea, I returned to my work. By the time I got that slender log braced up against the wall of the cabin, I hungered for food. I told time by my stomach rather than any sight of the sun. Andy screamed his protest at being confined for so long, but I had to put him back into the board. I wondered how Pap had taught her child to be so quiet in his. A better mother she was than I. Hearing my son's wails, I knew that wouldn't be hard.

I untied the rawhide strips that kept him secure and lifted him from the board, holding him close to me. His cheeks felt cold, and I realized the fire had died while I'd been dragging in the tree. I may have been successful at one of my tasks, but the second long branch I needed would have to wait until we were warm once again.

———

The work fatigued, reminded me of how weak I had become. I puffed hard as I braced the second log at an angle up against the wall of the cabin, felt my legs wobble as I headed back into the trees to look for a third. This one would be longer, and by the time I found it and dragged it close, dusk had fallen and I collapsed. We'd have to spend another night beneath the small canvas.

I'd never ached so much nor been as tired. Tears squeezed from my eyes, and I hoped as I fell asleep that the branches filling the doorway would be enough to keep us safe. Andy coughed once and I held my breath. *Please don't let him get sick. Please just let him sleep.*

In the morning, it snowed, the flakes falling through the open rafters and covering the muddy floor. I felt defeated until Andy stuck his tongue out to capture them and he giggled. His joy tweaked my own. "It's not often it snows inside a house, is it?" I asked. He laughed again and raised his hands to catch more.

I could see my breath as I puffed to build up the fire that had stayed through the night. Such small blessings gave me joy, and I decided that was how I'd restore my vigor, reminding myself of what God had provided and what I'd already accomplished, and that I did this thing for the good of the colony, for the good of my husband.

My son and the goat settled, I rolled the canvas out full, laid the log at one end, then rolled the wet canvas up around it. It lay as a crossbeam on the ground, against the two logs leaned against the wall of the cabin. Now the work truly began. My goal was to somehow push the rolled tarp up onto the leaning logs, and when it reached the roof edge, to unfurl the tarp which was wrapped around the log, pushing it up over the ridgepole and letting it fall down over the far side, unfurling the canvas with it. It would be my roof. If I could make it work.

Early efforts frustrated. I rolled it halfway up the leaning poles with little trouble. But once it hit a certain pitch, it slid back down, and my weakness prevented me from stopping it. I had to start again. I didn't want it unrolling onto the leaning poles, and that became a problem as well. A Greek myth came to mind, of a god sentenced to push a piece of dung up a hill and having it roll back over him so he had to start again. I even tried to pull the rolled tarp up by wrapping a rope around the cylinder I'd formed, climbing up the leaning poles to the top of the walls, and tossing the rope over the top to pull it from the other side. But it was too short. Some tasks needed more than one person to complete them.

After the fourth try, this time using another short log to push up against the tarp only to have it nearly reach the edge before it fell back against me, I simply sat in the melting snow and cried. Maybe I wasn't large enough to do this; maybe I wasn't strong enough. Every muscle protested. I kept looking in the direction I'd come from, hoping Christian would soon figure out where we'd gone.

"Mama, look!" Andy said, spying something out through the uncaulked walls.

"Your papa?" I said.

But it wasn't Christian.

Two Indian men appeared, dressed well against the weather with bark capes that draped over their shoulders and hung down to their knees. A fur of some kind showed beneath the cape. They wore hats the color of cedar and simply appeared through the mist. I moved away from the hut, hoping they'd follow me and not find my son.

But Andy shouted again. "*Ja,*" I whispered, "I see." I tried to keep my words calm, though my heart pounded.

They stood at the cabin's edge. "How can I help you?" I said in German. "Maybe some biscuits?" I had a little more flour and could mix it with water and bake it in the fire. I'd have to go inside the hut for that, and then they might take Andy or the goat. I looked at my makeshift door. They could dismantle it with a sneeze.

Instead, their eyes moved to the tarp. "Oh, please don't want that, please," I pleaded. If they took my tarp, this would all be for nothing!

One said something to the other. "I need it," I said, wishing I knew Chinook or Chehalis or Shoalwater or whatever language they spoke. Words could be such bridges, but the lack of them built walls.

They moved toward the tarp and I wailed. "*Nein,* please!" They squatted at the tarp, each at one end, and they lifted. *They are taking my tarp!* But instead of walking off with it, they lifted the tarp rolled around the log, and the two of them hoisted it up over the top, then let it finish rolling over the other side. I heard my long branch drop with a thud on the soft ground. One of the men held the tarp near the leaning poles to keep it from being pulled up and over. It was just as I'd imagined it would work.

The taller of the two men said something to the other, who disappeared into the trees for a time, then returned with long strands of some kind of vine that he'd cut with a knife he carried at his waist. I hadn't noticed the knife before. *Sometimes it's good to be blinded by fear.*

Then they did something I wouldn't have thought to do: they lifted one of the leaning logs up onto the roof the length of the tarp. With the vines, they lashed the tarp to the edges of the outside rafters and used the log to secure the length of the tarp. It would prevent the wind from lifting it up, and it hadn't occurred to me to do that—not that I could have by myself. They repeated their effort on the other side, and I stood back when they finished, amazed at this gift in the middle of nowhere. I didn't mind in the least that I hadn't done it all by myself.

"How can I ever thank you?" I said, smiling, bowing, hoping my actions told them how grateful I was, how embarrassed that I'd thought they were thieves. *"Kloss,"* I remembered. "Good. *Danke.* I'll fix tea for you, *ja?*" I motioned with my hands as though to drink, and they looked at each other and the taller one shook his head. They both had round faces, their woven hats arched out to keep rain from their eyes.

I wanted to know how to make those hats. I'd have to ask Sarah Woodard, who knew so much about this landscape and its people.

They wouldn't let me prepare tea or anything else for them. Instead, they grunted as though satisfied with their work and then moved into the trees.

I stepped inside and felt the dryness, the slight darkness with a tarp now over our heads. We were in a cave of our making, and I did a little dance, swirling around, singing to Andy. "We have a roof over our heads, we have a roof over our heads. We entertained angels unaware as Scripture tells us."

"Mama," Andy said when I danced dizzily past him. I was too lightheaded from the lack of strong food to dance for long.

"What?" I said, catching myself before I fell.

"Look."

One of the Indians stood in the doorway; he was naked from his shoulders to his waist.

"Did you want tea after all?"

He stared at me, then stepped aside while his friend hung the coat-like skin cape he'd worn over the door opening, darkening our log cave further. The fur side faced in. Elk hair moved in the breeze that seeped in through the openings between the side logs. The jagged cut of the elk skin was long enough; it nearly reached the bottom of the doorway. I could stitch a piece of hide to it, maybe even take Andy's board apart to completely cover the opening. Once caulked, this house would be snug as a mouse in a wheat barrel.

Then the other Chehalis man stepped inside. The sight of this bare-chested man standing in the cold brought me to my senses. "No," I said. "You will be sick if you give us this." I made a motion of being cold, flapping my arms, then pointing to him. "You take," I said, stepping around him to touch the hide. The fur felt so heavy and soft and smelled of smoked wood.

He struck his hand against his chest and said a word that might have meant "strong" or "a gift, don't reject it" or "we're going." At least I hoped that was what he was saying. He stood close to me. Did he want something in payment for the hide?

Before I could do anything else, he pushed the hide aside and stepped out, letting it flap behind him. I squinted through the logs and watched as the one man pulled his cedar bark cape over his shoulder, and the two men left, moving at a steady trot past the cabin, back toward the river until they disappeared.

Our leader had told us colonists long ago that we must not only live the Golden Rule, of doing unto others as we would have them do unto us, but to go further, to live with the Diamond Rule, where we gave so that another's life wasn't just like ours but was better. To give in this way was the mark of true Christian love. This was the first time I'd really understood.

———

It felt like heaven to be out of the rain and the wind, to have places dry enough to sit without globs of mud attaching themselves like ticks to my skirt and Andy's pants. The ground remained wet, but piles of moss provided a soft carpet. The elk hide deterred wind at the doorway, even though it blew in through the wide cracks of the walls. The hide looked so heavy and warm I considered taking it down and wrapping us up in it, hanging our blanket over the doorway instead. But by the time the fire merely glowed as an ember, I felt warmer than I'd been in weeks, and I trusted it was due to the gift of the roof and the draft-stopping hide.

I used the boughs that had once filled the doorway to make a kind of lean-to for the goat and tethered her outside, at least for part of the day. Eventually, her bleating became so constant I returned her inside. She wasn't a dog, but she served as good company for Andy, I decided, and we'd seen nothing of Charlie, the seagull. Opal's body heat warmed up our house. *Our house.* As I milked her, I felt a twinge of guilt that I'd deprived the men of this white gold, not acting the Diamond Rule at all.

It had been four days since we'd left, and I confess I expected my husband long before this. He could have been at the Woodards' in but a short hike, discovered I wasn't there, then surely he'd know I was here. Where else might I go? *Will he think I tried to make my way back to Fort Steilacoom?* I hadn't thought of that before. He'd be outraged if he arrived back at the fort after several days only to find I wasn't there either to greet him. No, that trip from the Fort had been troubling in summer; he'd know I'd never attempt it in the winter. I circled my fingers and thumbs, trying to rub away some of that uncertainty.

I would do what I could do. I would make a caulking and secure this cabin even tighter.

Finding mud was no problem, but what to mix with it to make it strong and harden, that was a question. I'd known of houses caulked with mud and straw, but we had no straw here.

But we had forest duff, needles and vines and small dead branches and moss, lots of moss, for the taking. I put Andy in the board, though he cried to be set free, and put him on my back. I donned my mother's cape and set out for the woods, returning with an apron full of small twigs and forest discards and moss. I dug a hole, let it fill partway with rain, broke the side walls of dirt into it, adding forest duff, wet grasses, brambles, and branches. Then I stirred, hoping the twigs and such would be enough to thicken it. I had no idea what men used to do this. I kept stirring and adding until my mixture felt thick as cold pea soup and my stirring stick stood upright in the goop. Then I spread the mixture on the lowest log wall, stacking it between the logs, filling in the missing spaces, slapping moss onto the wet glob. I let Andy help with the stirring. We worked the day and rested in the night, warmed by a small fire I made inside, letting the smoke drift out through the top layers of logs. The fire offered small light in the darkness.

In the morning we began again. It would take many days at this rate, but the work filled a hole growing in my heart. It kept me from thinking of what I would do when we ran out of flour and jerky; from imagining Christian's first words when he found me. The effort held at bay the worrisome thoughts of what my life might be like from now on, pushed back the fear that my husband might not seek me at all.

22

Last Times

"Last times" take on new meaning once we admit they exist. I remember the last time I wrapped my arms around my mother. I cherish the memory of the last time my father lifted his eyebrow to wink at me before we headed west; the last time Jonathan ran along the boardwalk chasing a ring with a stick while Sheppie barked behind him; the last night I slept with my sisters; the last warm kisses from my two youngest brothers. They are bittersweet memories claimed as markers of my life.

Last times began to cloud my days. Rain poured down in sheets as I tried to remember the last time I'd slept totally warmed, wrapped up against my husband, not worrying over a small cut in a canvas that unless I repaired it soon would force rain inside this finally dried-out place.

This day was a marker, too, as Andy and I ate the last of the jerky I'd brought with us. "We can live on Opal's milk for quite a long time," I told Andy. "But then I guess I'll have to take the axe to club those fish and hope that I can land one or two." I didn't say out loud that I might have to return to face my husband's wrath. Or lack of it. Perhaps I was so insignificant against the mission of his life that he hadn't noticed yet I'd gone.

Today was the last day I could put off clubbing a fish, the last time I dared tell myself that Christian would find me, that he'd want to find us. By my counting, I'd been here nearly three weeks, listening to the rain, trying to stay out from under the holes in the canvas, bringing the goat in from her grazing, reworking my caulking recipe, adding mosses with the hope they one day would harden to snug these walls into a home.

The last time. I hadn't thought that the last time I'd kissed Christian good-bye that it might truly be the last time.

I had to toss that thought, or I'd fall into a morass of misery more engulfing than the mud.

Instead, I considered my monthly flow. I'd completed it, though it was barely noticeable. *My last flow? No more chance of a child?*

I needed to eat more. I'd have to try hitting those fish if I could see them in the water…if I could get close enough to the river to see. The Indians I'd watched doing this actually stood in the water, the harsh current pushing against them so hard they sometimes lost their balance, though they laughed as they splashed, something I was sure I wouldn't do. The thought of that rush against my legs while I struck a fish in such a way as to throw it onto the bank tired more than frightened me. But I had to eat more to keep Andy alive; Andy had to eat more too. We needed fat from the fish. The Lord had provided a stream and the abundance of fish, but that stream, rolling and swift… I swallowed back nausea just thinking of it.

I entertained the thought of going back. Such a groveling that would be, admitting that I needed help in surviving, though didn't we all? Worse would be telling myself the truth that preparing this colony truly was the most important thing in my husband's life, more important than locating his family, making sure they were safe. He would do anything to serve, but it looked to me that he served the colony over anyone else.

That was sacrilege, I was sure. Fortunately, our leader couldn't see inside my head, and he lived several thousand miles away, so even his dark eyes weren't here to accuse. *The last time he accused me...* I drove away that thought too.

"Mama, look," Andy said.

I wondered what my son saw now, annoyed that he hadn't found any new words to share with me. "Mama, look" greeted my every moment or so it seemed. Or maybe I felt put upon because he'd been waddling behind me poking the caulking with a stick all morning, saying "Mama, look!" showing me a bug or a twisted root or stopping to look and giggle when his slender belly made gurgling sounds.

"I'll look later," I told him.

I'd gone too far this last time with Christian. Perhaps I should have stayed with him longer while I prodded him to be a leader who tended to the needs of his men and still found a way to be a husband aware of his wife. But I had tried. Hans had asked that I try to make Christian see the men's need for rest. And I had. Even coming here had been a part of that effort; that was all it really was. I'd manipulated for the last time when I'd talked my way into coming along, when I'd kept our son a secret for a time. I might not always make the best choices, but they weren't meant to deceive or get my way, only to be of help.

"Trial," I said out loud. "A word with two meanings. Someone being judged and someone being challenged. As you are at this moment, poking at my hard labor and telling me that my caulking is inferior." I patted Andy's head, then returned to my work.

I'd had no more dreams about my soul awaking or going to sleep. Now my dreams were of food, luscious roasts and steamed yams and corn boiled and spread with fresh butter. When was the last time I'd eaten that well?

But in daylight, my soul did sleep. I couldn't find a way to reach within me, to recall the Scripture verses that might have brought me ease, or to concentrate long enough to read from Catherine's Bible. Our leader rarely emphasized hopeful verses; my mother told me of them, words that promised help in times of trial. I tried to remember some of those. Christian would be angry with me if he knew how weak my faith was, how I struggled to find meaning in this effort.

"Mama, look," Andy repeated.

"What is it?" I sounded harsh; I knew it and felt instantly sorry. I turned and squatted to him, apologized. "Mama's a real trial this morning, isn't she? Let me just finish this little dab here, please." He leaned his head into my chest, bunting me just a bit. He pointed behind me. He probably wanted to show me yet another hole he'd poked into the caulking. My temper was frazzled as an old rope. Did the lack of food make me irritable?

"Papa. Papa."

"Papa is a new word for you," I said, standing and lifting him onto my chest. "Good for you!"

As I turned, there stood Christian, the hide door pushed back.

I could see his hair, a mass of wet locks, his jaw squared and set.

"Woman," Christian said, "what have you done?"

I rushed into his arms before he could say another word, handed him his son.

"Your woman," I told him. He grunted, but his arm closed around me while he held Andy with his other.

From behind him I heard coughing, and there stood Adam, Hans, and Joe and Adam Knight.

"Come in, come in," I urged them. They all had longer hair and scratched at their arms.

"We have wasted days looking for you," Christian said gruffly, stepping back from me to let the others pass inside. "Worried days." He sounded cross, but I also heard a catch in his throat.

"We were sure you were at the Woodards', so we didn't even start to look until last week," Joe said.

"Don't ever do this again to me," Christian said, leaning toward me. "You will remain with me to work things out. You won't run off like a wayward child and risk yourself and my son. We will do what must be done together."

I bristled. Did I look like I'd risked his son, whose arms draped around his father's neck? Did I look like a wayward child running off, only hoping to be found? I started to challenge him, but instead I took a deep breath and chose to be happy rather than right.

"I've provided a house with a roof on it," I said. "I've kept me and my son out of the rain, and I didn't mean to—"

"You disobeyed."

Adam coughed then, a hard racking sound. "I brought pepper," he croaked. "Will you make us tea?"

"*Ja*," I said. "Be dry and warmed by the fire, and I'll fix you some. We have a roof," I said, pointing upward. "You'll not believe how the Lord provided it."

They all crowded inside the hut they'd built, the men squatting on their heels, leaning against the walls, slipping their wet caps off, looking around for pegs. Their rain slickers were soaked, and the room felt humid. "No pegs," I said. "And I haven't gotten the walls all caulked either, but a good start."

"Where'd you get the elk hide?" Hans asked. He fingered the fine fur at the doorway.

"Some Chehalis or Quinaults. They helped me with the tarp and then left me that hide. One took it right off his back. They acted the Diamond Rule."

"They made your life better than their own," Hans said, nodding.

"They're acclimated," Adam said. "They can handle this weather bare chested." He wiped at his mustache that dropped nearly to his jaw line. His beard had filled in over his chin and onto his cheeks. His hand quivered. He coughed. *Maybe I shouldn't have left them; maybe I could have kept them from getting so ill.*

"We'll be accustomed to the rain in time," Christian said.

I watched as Adam glanced at Hans, who shook his head, as though warning not to press the matter further. Christian's tired eyes lifted to the tarp roof and the sound of the steady rain. "But for now, we will rest," he said. "We will hunt together and smoke the meat and gain some strength. We'll repair that split in the canvas before it grows longer." His eyes lifted to the canvas top. "Small fractures should always be fixed before they become too large." He stared at me when he said this. "Indeed. This is good common sense."

Adam's wracking cough interrupted Christian. When he'd stopped, Christian continued. "We will get well. And when the weather lets up, we'll build another hut, *ja?*" He looked at me. "But we'll build it where the land borders this claim, at the corner, so there will be closer neighbors and so we can come back here each night for a dry place to rest." He lifted Andy up into his arms. Andy's head touched the tarp, he sat so high on his father's shoulders.

"We might even finish our next one with a wooden roof before moving on to another. The Lord led us here. He provides. This is what we must remember. He'll make the way for us to prepare for our brothers and sisters. On time."

"You've made a wise choice in coming here now, husband."

Christian grunted. "I have a…creative teacher."

I leaned into him, patting Andy's legs that hung like two sausages on Christian's chest. "And your teacher learned a lesson too," I whispered.

He furrowed his brow but didn't pursue what I'd said.

That night, curled into our bedroll, Christian asked me, "What lesson is it that you learned, *Liebchen?*"

"Sometimes I should act even when my husband thinks I shouldn't, and not wait so long before I do."

He grunted. "You could have told me where you went. I assumed you went to Woodard's Landing and allowed you a few days to come to your senses and return. When you didn't and when you weren't there, then I worried. There was no need for that."

"You'd forbidden it. And would anything less have gotten you to tend to your men, let alone me?" He didn't answer. "You're a good leader, Christian. You've set the task the men can respond to. You decided as you did about resting here, getting strong, that is a good sign."

He grunted, then lay quiet for a time. We could hear the cadence of the men's breathing as they entered into sleep. Andy made little wheezing sounds, and I gently squeezed at his nose that had started to run.

"But you have to notice others, what they need. It can't all be for the colony," I said. "Men work harder and longer when they know the task has meaning and gives to others. We can't just say that's so; we have to act it, even here so far from home."

"You defied me, *Liebchen.* You risked our son and your own life. This is not the way to be heard."

"You risked us, too," I said. Then added quickly, "You're here now. Let's let it end there."

"*Ja,* because the men tell me I'm foolish to give up a bed warmed by my wife."

"That's the reason you came to find me? Because you wanted a convenient bed warmer?"

"Shh. I came because I love you and our son. But I carry with me the knowledge of a failing." It took a strong man to admit a mistake. "I need to believe that God's Spirit speaks not just to me but to you as well, though you are just a woman."

"I am just a woman," I said. "But I'm a dry woman lying beneath a roof. And I'm a woman willing to share her bed with a stubborn husband."

"And I with a stubborn wife."

We celebrated Christmas with a goose Hans brought down, whose feathers I stuffed into a dried elk's bladder that I softened with the animal's own fat. No *Belsnickel* brought gifts by as he did at Bethel, but I had enough sinew thread left to sew the elk bladder into the perfect pillow for Christian's head. I took my precious needles from the chatelaine that hung around my neck. Christian winked as I did.

A couple of the men had whittled toys for Andy, which he played with now, the wooden horse in one hand chasing after the wooden goat of almost the same size in another. I did not expect nor did I receive any tangible gift from my husband. That we were all together with food in our stomachs and aware of the Lord's presence in His provision was present enough. That and our own Christmas service reading from the Bible. Christian ended the day saying we must make more time for prayer and worship. Our lack of such, he said, explained why our efforts moved so slowly and with such turmoil.

The Knight brothers surprised, saying that if they left now they could return to Bethel in time to help bring the larger group out. Joe wanted to go by ship to San Francisco.

"But we need help here," Christian said.

"You'll do little till spring. Then in summer, maybe you could hire the Indians," Joe replied.

I thought, *It must've been hard for boys Jonathan's age to be isolated for so long.*

"Indeed," Christian grunted. "And if I say no?"

The brothers looked at each other.

"Maybe we'd leave anyway," Joe said.

That night, I knew Christian lay awake, his Bible open in his hands. In the morning he gave his consent to the Knights, who headed back after the first of the year, the tide taking them out to sea.

———

Through January the men hunted together, once bringing home a bear whose hide became a welcome blanket on the coldest nights. We had meat we smoked inside a branch-covered lean-to. The smell of meat made my mouth water sometimes, even in the night. Stews were frequent, and all of us regained some strength. We read together, finding Scriptures our leader had never preached on, wondering if we had the right to say what we thought the words meant. We were not learned, after all; we merely lived and hoped our lives reflected what we loved.

One day when I went into the woods to graze the goat, I startled several Indian women gathering cedar root and bark. I motioned to ask what they'd do with their bounty, and one of them made a pounding motion against the bark, then pointed to her cape. I could pound it into a mat to cover the floor or perhaps make a cape for Andy, even for the men. This might be the last winter when we were so wet because we lacked the proper clothing.

I nudged Christian into making a trip to Woodard's Landing.

"We're not asking them for anything," I said. "We're just being good neighbors to visit." He finally agreed, and we spent the day in each other's company, talking and singing. Sarah had an angel's voice, and her singing taught me new English words. I considered her my friend and overlooked her clucking tongue when I told her of my leaving Christian for a time and living in the woods alone.

"The Indians…," she said. "You took a terrible risk."

"Either way," I said, "if I hadn't gone, I'm not sure we'd all still be alive. The men needed rest."

"You are overly dramatic, Emma," Christian said, overhearing us.

"You were all sick. I made a way for us to have a roof over our heads."

"No, *Liebchen*. That was God's work, not yours."

How I hated it when he defined anything good I did as something brought about by intervention. Did I offer nothing? Did I not at least act in concert with God, sometimes? Or was that route only possible through the works of men?

At times, there were slight breaks in the rain, or it drizzled more than poured. After the men began to feel better, on those still days with the weather offering fog rather than rain, they'd work in the woods, bringing out the logs they needed and stacking them. When it drizzled, they'd work on the structures, Christian still bent on having three dozen houses roofed and ready by the time the larger group arrived.

I still didn't see how we could accomplish this. The Bethelites might not understand the primitiveness of this place. What had the Knights and Michael Sr. and John Genger and George and John Stauffer said to them by now? Would they be enthusiastic? What would they say about a place where horses bogged down in mud and people used the river if they wanted to truly go somewhere? Would the promised richness of the soil and the bounty in the woods be enough to overcome the challenges?

I calmed my unease about the arrival of the others by remembering that the more experienced colonists had been through this all before. Helena Giesy, Christian's sister, would likely say this was an easier creation of a colony than when they moved to Missouri, conquering hardwood trees and plowing meadows. Missouri was a wilderness of sorts in the 1840s, and there were Indian scares there, too, with Andrew Jackson's Removal Act forcing the natives onto reservations far from their home lands.

I'd arrived in my parents' home well after those early years. I didn't know the trials they might have lived through. Maybe all new adventures had missteps and trials and, as Christian said, I was merely being dramatic.

Spring arrived, and with it improved health for us all. Even the goat gained weight. I watched my husband lash a log behind a mule to pull it to a clearing. We Germans were accustomed to hard work. It was what defined us. It's what helped carve a Bethelite's faith. Hard work and a hope we walked on God's path.

Now began the work in earnest. The Bethelites would be here in less than six months.

Part II

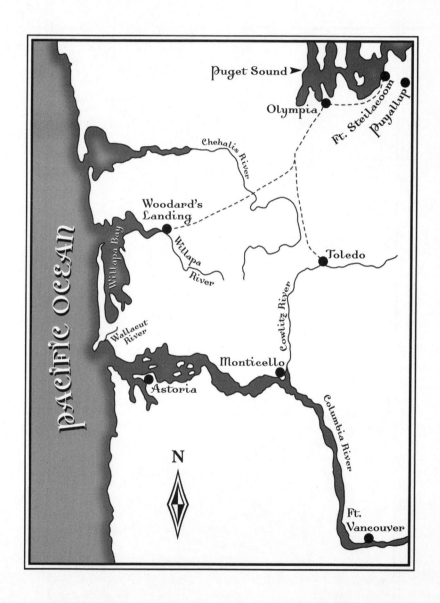

Puget Sound ➤

Olympia

Ft. Steilacoom

Puyallup

Chehalis River

Woodard's Landing

Willapa Bay

Willapa River

Toledo

Cowlitz River

Wallacut River

PACIFIC OCEAN

Monticello

Astoria

Columbia River

N

Ft. Vancouver

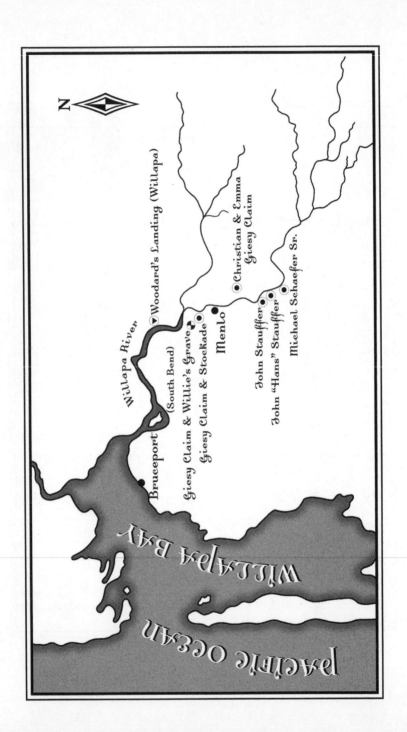

23

Virtue and Vice

"Mama," Andy said, and he handed me a clutch of wildflowers as white as chalk. Spring 1855, and I pitched any worrisome thoughts away. White trillium carpeting the forest floor distracted me. Pink and white orchids grew on tree trunks, or so it appeared; flowers with podlike blooms turned the meadows beside the rivers blue. Moss green as cats' eyes lay curled around tree roots, waiting to be patted. This valley formed a tapestry, a quilt of such richness I wondered that I ever questioned my husband's choice to come here. The air smelled fresh each morning, and the river, raging as it did carrying all that rain to the sea, kept within its banks, and I felt blessed.

I walked the tall grass meadows with Andy running now before me, still falling down sometimes but always picking himself up to carry on. The goat trotted after him like a dog. I could hear the sounds of hammering, the grunts of men raising logs to rafters. They coughed less now, the lingering illness of the winter fading. Still, each night I heard Christian's lament about their lack of progress. "Soon we'll have to send someone out to meet Wilhelm's group," he told me. "That will leave fewer of us to work the logs."

"Maybe, with so few of us here, you could wait and hope that Michael Sr. or George will be coming with them and can lead them here."

"*Nein*. We should have them come a different way, across the bay. We'll need to send someone out to lead them."

While I questioned that wisdom, I kept silent. I could do little to speed the progress except dig roots, pick berries when they were ripe, tan the hides as best I could, boil river water for drinking now that the rains had ceased, and watch after Andy. An-Gie had showed me how to find the *wapato* and a few other roots to dry. Christian called one camass and said we could cook them, which I did. And once, startling me in the woods, two Chehalis women showed me mushrooms they motioned for me to pluck from the forest floor and eat. They were white as beach sand and tasted like sponge, it seemed to me.

This Willapa Valley offered such abundance of cedar and fir and hemlock and yew, and yet we paled against the requirements to rein such bounty in. We had fewer than five huts built, and those would be roofed with tarps from the wagons of the Bethelites once they arrived. Knowing that a large wagon train would soon bring 150 people or more into this clearing pushed at the men, but they could work no harder than they already did. It fell to me to raise their spirits, to force them to look at what they'd done rather than what was left to do. "You've bought the land. You've befriended Indians. You've staked out boundaries. You've met townspeople, you've spent money wisely to keep us fed, you've sent off the scouts on time. You've kept your wife and son close by, and on top of that you've built huts. Houses," I told Christian one dawn. I took a breath.

Christian held a chunk of biscuit out for the seagull to peck at. This new bird still wouldn't take anything from Christian's hand, only mine and Andy's. He didn't have the chip from his bill, but a hole in his webbed foot marked him as unique. We called this one Charlie too.

"And on top of that, you've been as faithful a man as I've ever known, trusting always that you were doing the Lord's work, never putting yourself first in anything. You are a good man, Christian Giesy, and this place will one day reflect all that you have done to take it from the wild into a welcoming place."

He dropped the breadcrumb. "Yet the bird does not trust me."

"What does a bird know anyway?"

He grinned. "Your passion and vision remind me of Wilhelm's."

"I'm nothing like our leader," I retorted. The thought startled. I picked up the crumb and held it out. Charlie waddled over, his beak never touching my finger as he lifted the bread from me as I squatted. "Wilhelm is…visionary, I agree. But he's also…selfish."

Christian frowned. "That's not a word I'd use to describe either of you."

"Don't compare us," I said. My voice shook. I wondered where this trembling came from.

"I only meant that both of you use words that change the minds of people, take them from lowly places onto hilltops where they can see farther than they did before. I see compassion in both of you, too. *Ja,* I know how you feel about Wilhelm." He'd raised his hand to silence my open mouth to protest. "But sometimes when we see only another's faults, we ignore the other side of those flaws. He's driven, yes, but also passionate. He acts boldly when needed, though you'd say arrogant. He's a leader, and sometimes that makes a man single-minded. But that's you, too, Emma." My face felt hot with such words. "You must be careful you don't define our leader with such a narrow view that you become more like those negative qualities you claim he has and ignore the strengths on the opposite sides that each of you share. Virtue and vice, they live together."

I blinked, at least a dozen times. Charlie pecked at my wrist, wanting more food, but I had none in my hand. Food for thought is what Christian gave me, and I found it hard to swallow.

———

Andy and I often went out with the men, me serving food to them with some hope that it sped their days. It also gave me opportunity to walk what would someday be fields of grain. I imagined our fields with wheat bending in the breeze. I squeezed my eyes shut to picture our house built one day. I visualized my son growing up to work beside his father. Imagining what might be gave me respite.

The colors in this landscape took my breath away. All the fresh green of moss and trees, the still wet, black vines, the reddish bark of cedars, a rushing river, browned by the tumbling banks of mud that tried to define it, a sky a staggering blue, all acted as an admiring audience for the promise of the meadow's performance. *Lavish*, I thought. *This is lavish.* Certainly a God who could create such as this would not protest displays of beauty on a person or a place. I wondered if my mother had come to that conclusion and that was why she kept the strand of pearls about her neck.

For some reason an old sermon of our leader's came to mind, in which he spoke of the prodigal son. He said the word *prodigal* had more than one meaning, and one of its meanings was "lavish, abundant." That wayward son's father lavished him with good things, so surely wishing to have abundance was scriptural, wasn't it? Surely wanting abundance couldn't be prideful. Why would God have created all that lush growth and glorious land if not for us to experience the fullness of it all? *What good is creation if one doesn't find awe and joy in it?*

I thought back to Bethel. Filigrees and fluff had been permitted on our houses. Elim, Wilhelm and Louisa's home, stood recognized from the other homes with its size, its many chimneys, and wide porches framed with gingerbread cutouts. Perhaps lavishness was permitted in places other than on an individual person.

I loosened the tie on my worn wrapper, let the warm breeze flow through to dry the perspiration on my skin. I heard the men shout to one another and direct the mules, who jerked against the straps as they hauled another log out of the woods. Perhaps we could be ready for those coming behind us, ready not with physical things like houses but ready to receive them into an abundant place. Maybe Christian was right about my ability to express myself. I could use words to help them see the bounty here, to trust that this was a place chosen for us. Perhaps this bountiful place would be enough to meet all the needs of these people. A house to live in wasn't nearly as critical as land that could raise grain.

Christian's parents would bring the grist stones, coming by ship around the Horn; they'd make it possible for us to have flour before the year was out. Wheat of our own grinding, if we got some planted. I needed to honor all that we scouts had done surviving in the Oregon Territory for two winters, keeping always focused on meeting the needs of the colony. Well, almost always.

Andy raced ahead of me, running without falling for his longest time yet. He'd grown. I counted his months. Nineteen. I thought back to the time I carried him. Under other circumstances, another brother or sister would be good for him. But here, with such work to do, it would be better to wait until we were settled into our own hut. I thought to the last time I'd had my monthly flow. It had come back with the good food of the hunters. But I had not known it now for three months. *Three months.* This was already May.

I looked down at my abdomen, ran my hands around it in a warm circle of affection. It was already too late to wait: if I counted right, this baby would arrive in...December. The wettest, coldest, and dreariest month, but also the most prodigal time.

———

Mules can be a trouble at times, but they are more reliable than a horse. We scouts had moved ourselves and were back living in lean-tos to be closer to the work sites while the men labored at their tasks. I assured Christian that the exercise of plowing would be good for the baby I carried, since I could do little to help them in the woods.

After a time of cleaning his ear with his finger, his newest sign of being in thought, he consented, saying we'd repay the Woodards for the use of their mule by giving them wheat. We couldn't spare any of our animals; they were needed for dragging logs.

"It would be better to plant oats," Sarah told me. "Wheat doesn't grow well here. We usually order flour in."

"They grew wheat near Steilacoom," I remembered.

"Even in a short distance the climate affects what grows."

"We have wheat seed," I said. "No oats."

She shrugged.

I didn't share the conversation with Christian. But we borrowed the Woodards' plow and mule, and I began the work, pulling the heavy straps over my shoulder, gripping the plow handles while wearing my leather gloves. The Woodards' mule had plowed fields before. I could tell he didn't like it.

A mule being asked to do what he doesn't like consumes one's energy completely, allowing little time to think of anything deeper than how far the wheat field furrows sink. I longed for that distraction as I watched the men begin to question once again their ability to complete their labors in time. Plowing fields kept my mind from disappointing thinking.

I'd seen the men plow fields back in Bethel. And I knew it would take me long hours of being jerked by the single-bottom plow when it might strike a rock or it would pitch over and fall, and I'd have to hoist the handles and blade up, hoping the mule would stand firm. We put blinders on him to avoid distractions from birds swooping overhead or any other skittering thing that might shake an animal's confidence and make it bolt. A dried leaf could do it; a bear would surely cause a stir. Both the mule and I did best when kept from distractions.

I'd tethered Andy with a long vine of cedar root I braided into a sturdy rope so he wouldn't go wandering off too far from the edge of the field I worked on. The rope was another gift of the landscape brought to my attention by the Chehalis women I saw now and then. Maybe when they'd seen my makeshift cedar cape, they'd decided I had potential and shared bits of their experience with me.

Andy explored the ground for ants and salamanders and other insects with names I didn't know. He particularly liked the slugs, the slimy finger-length creatures the color of the scorched flour I used to treat Andy's diaper rash. Their little antenna broke the monotony of their bodies, and Andy loved to touch them. Slugs and his wooden toy horse and goat, Charlie and the live goat kept him company. He even napped in the shade of the tree he was tethered to. At least we'd never found a snake here; only spiders kept us on our toes.

I'd pounded cedar bark with a rock into a kind of mat. He lay on that now as I worked. I found that the best time, his napping time, when I didn't carry this nudging worry over him in the back of my mind. The river flowed close, and while it no longer crested near the banks, it was still wide and hungry and would easily consume an adventurous child. I wondered if my mother had worried like that when I was little and Bethel was being built. I planned to write her when the others arrived, bringing precious paper with them. What paper we had we'd used up, so I couldn't even make the notes I wanted, to remind myself of how I felt with all we did here. I'd have to be like the Indians and memorize the tales. At least that's what An-Gie said they did, and thus she'd found little need to read or write.

The mule's tail swatted at flies and tiny bugs, and the animal occasionally looked back toward me, though I knew he couldn't see me with the blinders on. I'd "gee" and "haw" him to turn right or left, and we'd jerk forward. Sometimes I sprawled in the earth as he'd skip ahead before I was ready; sometimes I'd fall into the furrow and have to shove the plow off of my leg, then sweat and ache to get it upright again. My left wrist still gave me sharp pains when I tried to lift or twist with it too much, a remembrance of our Andy's birth.

The soil beside the river was rich and dark, and the plow turned over deep chunks of dirt within the furrows. I'd sink down nearly to my knees at times. I'd pulled the wrapper up between my legs and tucked it into my apron's belt so I wouldn't trip on the hem. The dress was threadbare, though I washed it only once a week, grateful that the breezes dried it through the night.

By June we'd returned the mule, and I'd broadcast the seed. I convinced my husband we were sending it out the way Christians and Muslims of old must have done it. If all went well, we'd have a crop by fall, and the gristmill stones Christian's parents were bringing would grind our own wheat first.

The men slept out under the stars now as they worked on huts yet farther away from the original Giesy claims. Christian and I slept again in a lean-to so we could see the moon as it slivered through the tree tops. We spoke of our own growing family and how pleased his parents would be when they arrived, knowing that at last their firstborn son had made them grandparents and would soon do so again. It was almost like being in Bethel.

"When will you begin our home?" I asked one noon while I fed Christian hard biscuits and a jerky stew with mushrooms and *wapato* chopped in. The field I'd plowed was on the Giesy claim he'd singled out for his parents and brother. I would have plowed "our" fields, but the seven miles between the sites made that difficult. There were two river crossings needed to reach our claim even riding the mule, something I didn't relish with Andy, the mule, and a plow to manage too.

"Time enough to build ours," he said. "There'll be more hands here by October, and we'll build ours then. Not before."

"Can we go back so I can see where our hut might sit? I like to imagine what it will look like and what the view through the windows might be."

"Women," he snorted. "What does the view matter?"

"Each window offers something special; each woman's home will be different from the others, individual. I like thinking of how we'll place things there. Besides, we take little time for imagining, for doing anything except work. This can't be good, not in a land that is as flashy as a feather cape."

Christian dipped the hard biscuit into the stew, sucked on it. "Why is it so important for you to stand out? Perhaps we should consider building one large house for several families. That way there'll be no argument about who got the best site, whose house is bigger or better. It borders on envy to want such things."

I knew our leader thought envy to be one of the deadliest of sins. Now my husband swirled my opinions into our leader's stream, combining desire with sin rather than with imagination. I wished I'd kept my thoughts to myself. Living in one large family house forever did not seem like a wise idea to me. Envy wouldn't be the only deadly sin that would ripple the surface of that river if that were to be my fate.

"The other side of envy is…compassion," I told him. "Being aware of what others need."

"*Ja,*" he said after a moment's thought.

"I simply wish to be the wife of Proverbs 31," I continued. "She bought fields, burned a late candle on behalf of her family, and was praised for clothing her household with scarlet and having coverings of tapestry and her clothes made of silk and purple. Her children sang her praises and so did her husband."

"Proverbs 31 also says, 'Favor is deceitful, and beauty is vain: but a woman that feareth the LORD, she shall be praised.'" He could always silence me with his better understanding of Scripture. He continued. "I worry that at times you seek favor from the wrong places, Emma. Favor is deceitful."

I felt my face grow warm despite the cooling breeze. *Should I simply suffer in silence or should I speak a piece?* I took a deep breath.

"This place is rich with beautiful flowers, with trees that tower so high I get dizzy looking up at their tops reaching to the sky. Game is plentiful for food and skins, and even the river that I give wide berth to, even it offers up those things we need: fish and a way to get from here to there when the vines tangle our paths. I can't believe such abundance is meant not to be noticed. You sing the praises of the timber and the soil that will grow grain that we'll grind and sell to others, people living on Puget Sound, people coming here because of this land's rich re- sources. I can't believe I was created to pretend I don't notice that these gifts are wrapped in a landscape of loveliness."

"*Ja,* you notice. But then you start to compare, to put your own mark on the landscape by saying, 'Here is my view. It is prettier than your view.' Or 'Here is my house. Even the pegs are sturdier than yours' or 'My door is wider' or... *Ach.*" He brushed the air in disgust. "It is dumb talk you make. We are called to live together, one as the other, no one standing out. We have come here to prepare a way for others. We will be as one, brothers and sisters together."

"Chosen," I said. "Does God not pick us out then, see us as special? How can recognizing what makes us different be sinful?"

"He chooses us to serve Him," Christian said.

I could hear the irritation in his voice and knew I should stay quiet, bite my tongue, pitch the thoughts of what I'd say next and would likely later regret. But it was not my way to remain silent, not my way to be like other community women, and I couldn't help but believe that Christian knew that of me and had "chosen" me because of it.

"So some are not selected. How do we know? How do I know if I'm of the elect if I don't name the things that make me stand apart from…unbelievers, from those not chosen?"

"Those selected for His service have trials," he said. "Remember Moses. Remember Mary and Jacob and Ruth. They all found trouble as a part of their decisions to be obedient."

"But see, they stand out, those men and women of the Bible, and we don't think unkindly of them," I said.

He coughed. "They weren't selected for their talents, nor for the best of anything they made nor for the most exquisite view nor for gathering the most people around themselves. They were and are unique, *Liebchen*, because of what they lived through, because of how their faith deepened by the things they faced and overcame. Our Lord reminds us that we do not choose Him, but He chooses us. He's chosen us to follow Him here to Willapa to be in service to Him. And when the others arrive, they too will see that we are all chosen to be together."

I wanted to believe that this place was specifically meant for us, but I didn't want to be "chosen" for the trials I had to face. We'd had our share of them already, with the weeks of dreary weather, heavy rains, and dark skies that stole our energy like maple sap taken from its tree.

"The Lord uses trials to turn people around, Emma."

"I wonder, then," I ventured, "if He wants us to leave here, since progress has been so slow on the huts. Maybe it's His way of turning us around?"

Christian stared at me.

I remembered what our leader told me, about women needing to support their husbands, that suffering in childbirth was our penance for disobedience and betrayal. "Maybe we've taken a side road and are here in Willapa not to serve God but to serve our leader. Maybe that's why things have gone so slowly." My heart pounded. It was the most direct I'd been with Christian in challenging his thinking.

"We have lessons to learn from this time, Emma. Remember, all the scouts chose this place. All agreed as we have worked: agreed on which huts to build, even when to wait out the weather. We even agreed on who should go back to bring out the other Bethelites and how they should return. We discuss, and then the Lord moves us toward His way."

He swirled the water of our uncertainty now, convincing me where I'd earlier encouraged him. I supposed that is what marriage looks like, that exchange of hope between people who love.

"*Liebchen,* whenever you doubt that we belong in this place, you make yourself think of those early signs of certainty. They are memories that not only comfort but help move us ever forward."

"As when I stumble behind the mule in the field."

"*Ja.*" His voice had softened. "You don't question whether you should be behind that plow. You pick yourself up and keep going. That is what we faithful Germans know to do."

24

Natural Wealth

"Emma, bring the corn drink," Christian shouted to me.

"Can it wait?"

"No," he said. "Bring it now."

I had enough to do at the river, washing the men's shirts. I'd spent the day chopping at weeds in the grain field, a lost cause. Fall approached, and I wondered if we'd even have a crop given the strength of the weeds and the short stems. And I hadn't seen Charlie the seagull all morning, and Andy kept asking, "Charlie? Charlie?"

My husband's words annoyed. Why bother me when I worked, making me pull the rope on the corn drink to bring it to the men? Surely they could get it themselves. I pushed against my knees and stood. That's when I noticed we had company.

The men arrived with furtive eyes, silent as snails. They were Americans, they said. They spoke only English but told us that from now on, we should only speak our German so if the Indians approached they'd think we were French or British, anything but American. They'd come through the eastern part of the Territory and told stories of the Yakima tribe's uprising. "Dozens of other tribes are angry with the wagons pulling across the mountains and taking their lands. Government won't protect us. You'd best use what resources you've got to secure your people. Your strange language. That's a weapon here."

"Is it just in the western territories?" Hans asked. "Not a problem in the prairie places, then?" I knew he thought of the Bethelites making their way from Missouri.

"Everywhere." The American took a swallow, letting the corn drink pour down like streams separating his thick beard. He wiped his face with his palm. "You folks got people coming across?" I nodded. "Worry for 'em," he said. "Unless they act like foreigners, French or Germans or whatevers, they'll arrive without their hair if they arrive at all."

The men quenched their thirsts, then informed us of the failed treaty negotiations in this Washington Territory, as it was called now, and the government's plan to get all the tribes to sign a new treaty that would place all Indians on land set aside for them. Reservations. "Even the Shoalwaters of this country resist. I guess cuz they weren't named specific and given their own place." Only the Nez Perce remained calm, they told us. "But don't worry; they'll war against Americans too. The Cayuse have already joined up. What horrors they heaped on those poor Whitmans. Don't have to wonder what atrocities they're capable of."

I frowned. I hadn't heard of the Whitmans' trouble. I'd have to ask Sarah to see what she knew of them, but for now I could only imagine the trials being experienced by our colony heading west. What if they were attacked? What if they never arrived? Maybe it was good that my parents and brother weren't coming west, but Christian's brothers were, and Mary and Sebastian would be making their way.

The Yakima, the men told us in hurried conversation over a campfire, had killed a miner making his way from Puget Sound across the northern part of the Territory into Colville country. "Took all his gold," they said. "Slaughtered him up and down. Then more Americans were found dead. Never Frenchies or Brits," the men complained. "Watch your backs, you Germans, living out here close to Nisqually and those Hudson's Bay folks. Those Brits don't want others coming here either, messing up their trading. They'll get those Indians riled as they did back in New York years ago." He patted his sidearm. "Be ready to shoot first."

I remembered the Chehalis men who gave us the elk hide door, who'd roofed our very house. I'd seen a few Shoalwater people at Woodards' who seemed friendly enough. In my halting English I suggested as much, but the Americans cut me off. No woman would have sway with them, I guessed, especially one who spoke with any kindness toward the natives. The men sat on mats of cedar bark that Indian women had shown me how to make. Cedar capes made from the pattern of a gift lay stacked ready for winter's use. Surely these were peaceful people, even those charged with warring.

The Americans hitched a ride on the mail boat heading out from Woodard's Landing toward the sea. At the Bay they planned to catch a ship back to the States, and if we were smart we'd do the same, they told us. Those were the last things they said before parting.

"Are you worried?" I asked Christian that night. A spider tickled a slender strand across my arm, and I brushed at it.

"Only about the colony. Here, we're safe enough," he said.

But something in the night must have caused Christian to reconsider the men's words. He told Hans and Adam that he'd head to Woodards' to see if any letters had arrived from the colony. I asked to go along, but he refused. "You'll be safer here," he said, so I knew something troubled him. Signs of autumn appeared in the foliage. Geese already flew south. While my pregnancy had been fine so far, my wrapper had to be extended farther than before, and when I walked, I floated like a boat shifting from side to side. I'd miss seeing Sarah, but today staying behind didn't bother. Christian pushed the small boat with a sail into the water. He'd bought it on account. I didn't mind not being on the Willapa, but I did miss my husband that night.

When he returned in the morning, he came with news that would change our direction. He said an agent named Bolen, sent to investigate the miner's murder, had been killed by Indians too. The Shoalwaters had been left out of the treaty and were using their hatchets and guns to protest. An outraged Governor Stevens called the Indians defiant and ordered the military to shoot to kill. Added to this, several of the plains-area Indians said they'd seen enough of wagons coming across their lands and wanted no part of this proposed federal treaty. That angered the governor even more so that he called for war against all Indians.

My palms grew wet as I wondered how our leader's wagon train fared.

"They'll come this way, too," Christian said. "We're on their land, even though we've gained it fair and square from the government. But it won't be ours if we can't hold it against an uprising."

"Maybe we shouldn't have claimed it," I said.

He ignored me.

I thought about the words our leader said to us, that we would go west to find a place where the world could not encroach upon us, where we could take care of our own without harm to others and be able to give back in return. Give back on our terms. But there was no place like that.

"We'll build a blockhouse to defend ourselves," Christian told us. "We have no one here to protect us except us, except the work of our hands."

"It'll delay the hut-building even further," Adam complained.

"*Ja.* But protection for the larger body will be necessary once they arrive. We must fortify now." Christian put his little finger into his ear, thinking as he scratched it. "Maybe we were meant to do this now, to better prepare for the time when all will end."

He hadn't spoken much about the *last days,* not since we'd arrived.

I didn't like talking about it now, but I did notice that when he did, when Christian asked us to think about our own possible deaths, that the scouts appeared more encouraged rather than fearful. They worked with greater enthusiasm. They questioned his decisions less. I wondered if that was something Wilhelm understood, that we follow a leader more faithfully when we're reminded of encroaching death.

As though to prove me right, we woke with urgency. Christian said we'd build the stockade wall on top of the hill of the Giesy claim, near where we'd first built our completed log house. No one disagreed. Christian and Hans and Adam cut logs fifteen feet long while I dug at the trench as I could. After the others joined me, we dug the trench three feet deep in an area around the house and then wider—to encompass another house Christian said we'd need to build as soon as we finished the stockade.

I rubbed tallow onto my hands to counter the blisters, thinking how nice it would be when the others arrived with amenities we hadn't had for so long. My lanolin and lemon were long used up. My hands were rough as cedar bark and nearly as red. *Ach!* I chided myself for longing for small bits of luxury in the midst of preparing a safe place for others.

Andy found all the activity joyous, climbing down into the trench and walking his way along it, his towhead like a dandelion floating on a sea of dirt.

"Keep him out of there," Christian shouted to me. "The sides could cave in, and we don't know where he is when we bring the logs to stand."

I pulled him up and then found myself accomplishing no work at all until he slept, for he headed for the trench each time I loosed his hand. I wondered why it is we are pulled to that which is dangerous, to places we should best leave alone. As I watched Andy return time after time to the trench, then look back to see if I would catch him before he jumped in, I wondered about this challenging nature we were born with and what kind of God kept calling us back when we were wayward so often.

On September 12, 1855, we heard voices and the sounds of animals crashing through the timber. Christian shouted, "To the stockade!" and ran toward me. I grabbed Andy and scooped him into my arms, lumbering like an old boat. The stockade remained unfinished, but at least there were three sides completed. My heart pounded. The sounds couldn't come from the Bethel group. It was too early. We didn't expect them until late October, maybe even in November. We mustn't panic. Perhaps another group of Americans headed toward the Bay to leave this territory behind. I'd think it was that, hoped only good would soon charge through that brush.

And then I heard German. Was it? *Ja!* And the cries of a child, and then through the openings of the timber and the vines came Peter Klein, a Bethelite, and a dozen others, twenty-five in all, men, women and children weighted down with packs on their backs and driving a few cows before them.

"From what George told us, I knew we couldn't make the trail with wagons," Peter said. He laughed and his eyes sparkled. "But the cows helped thrash it down for us—those we didn't lose."

I named the people who'd come, hugging the women and children, getting their stories of when they'd left, the trials they'd had along the way. Andy clutched my knees as I walked, and I realized he hadn't ever seen children before, had never gazed into the eyes of one his size.

My greatest joy was when I reached Mary Giesy. I held her in my arms with just the hint of guilt that I had a child of my own and would soon produce another, when last I'd seen her, she grieved the loss of her son.

"Did you have trouble? With Indians?"

Mary shook her head. "No. It was almost…boring," she said. "Day after day of walking, sleeping out under the stars. We were just anxious to leave Bethel, and with Willie turning ill, the rest of the party decided to wait for him to improve. We came on ahead. Michael Schaefer Sr. drew maps and told stories until we felt we'd been with you all coming across."

"Willie's ill? Something bad?"

"The malaria. He gets it every year, remember? It's one reason *Herr* Kiel wants to come west, to have his children in a healthy place."

"Except for mosquitoes, spiders, and an occasional bear, this is a heavenly place," I said. I hugged her again. "I'm so glad you came with Peter's group, before all the rest."

"*Ja,* me, too," she whispered in my ear. "I wanted my baby to be born in this Washington Territory and not somewhere along the way."

Her dark eyes danced with her news. She hardly looked pregnant, and when I stood back to gaze at her, she giggled. "We have until next year to prepare," she said. "The baby isn't due until January."

I calculated.

Mary smiled. "*Ja,* the first week away from Bethel I conceived. On the trail."

"Is it sacrilege," I whispered, leaning in to her, "to think we all might do better away from our leader?"

Her eyes grew large and then she laughed. "At least you haven't changed," she said. "That's comforting when everything else surely has."

But I had changed, at least inside. I was stronger and more aware of my husband, more willing to help him succeed. And one way was to celebrate the arrival of this first group. He'd pay attention to the task, but joy fueled the laborers. Oh, how we sang and celebrated in the September air so crisp, with the spruce trees in their prime, of full brush of branches arching out over the forest floor. The hemlock and fir, even a tree Christian called yew, stood in their glory, piercing the perfect blue sky. I loved the looks of the children as they eyed those massive trees, saw the thickness of such timber; ignored the catch in my stomach as the women looked upward, shaking their heads at the treetops. Mary nearly fell over backward trying to see the top. I caught her before she fell.

"It can be tamed," I told Mary when she said she'd never seen anything so dense, so foreboding.

I took in with good cheer the approval of Peter's wife and some young girls as they noted my pregnancy and patted my Andy's head as I held him on my hip.

"*Ja,* it is good to be here," they told me.

"What is the three-sided yard?" one asked.

"Part of a stockade," I said. "Just a precaution. Against Indian trouble."

They looked with judging eyes at the log house with its pitiful canvas roof. They didn't seem pleased at the height of the riverbanks where we'd have to slide down to pull up buckets of water. The amenities they'd left behind loomed larger. I knew those looks. Yes, they were grateful to be at the end of their journey, but alarmed perhaps at what this next step in the journey entailed. I tried not to dwell on their expressions, the looks that said, "Where are we? And what have we done?"

"They left Bethel early," Christian told me that evening. He wasn't telling me anything Mary hadn't already said. As we talked, he walked with me to the river, reached down, and pulled up the bucket with corn juice from where I tied it to keep cool. We didn't purchase much corn, just enough to make the drink that I swirled round with my long burl spoon. I imagined how many new things I'd have once Christian's parents arrived with our trunks. "They came overland," Christian said. "Wilhelm is but a few weeks behind. We'll need to send Hans or Adam out to meet him and bring him on up."

His words held…caution, I suppose, perhaps a wariness that he'd be judged by that man. But no, those would be my thoughts pushing their way through like an unruly toddler. Christian would be worried about their safety, about having enough for them to eat once they arrived, about having shelter and safety from any uprisings.

"Joe Knight never made it back with them," he said then.

"He didn't? What happened?"

Christian shook his head. "He…made his own way, going to California, Peter tells me. Adam returned, said they were but a day out when Joe announced he wanted to work for a while, maybe in California. There were words exchanged and then they separated."

"Maybe he met up with them. Maybe he's with Wilhelm's group now," I said, chirped almost.

"They argued. The scouts separated. They didn't agree once they left here. This is not a good sign."

"But now you'll have help to build the houses," I said. "All those men. You'll have them built in no time."

He hesitated before taking my lead away from the discomforting news about Joe Knight. "*Ja*, we finish the stockade, then build a gun house, high so we can see all around. Peter thinks it necessary, as all they heard along the way were rumors of massacres." He looked away from me.

"But with all this help—"

"Peter says our leader brings thirty-seven wagons, more than I thought for this first journey. I figure six people to a wagon. That's two hundred and twenty people who will arrive here in less than two months."

I swallowed. He didn't need to say more. The rains would come soon. The cool air promised that. And now there was a defection, a hole in the tapestry of the scouts. I had nothing to say to bring comfort.

In the morning, the men finished the stockade wall with the logs stood up on end, side by side like little fishes in those metal tins I'd once seen. The stockade surrounded the house we'd built. Then the men enclosed it with a heavy log gate hung on leather straps and began chopping more logs to build the gun turret area while other men began another hut inside the stockade.

I kept my voice light for the women, to reassure them. I showed them how we would have enough to eat to feed their children. "Food is the servant of the heart," I said. "We can go to the ocean and dig for clams. They try to hide but we find them. We might buy an oyster or two as well."

"You've done this?" Mary asked.

I shook my head, no. "But my friend Sarah digs for clams and she eats the oysters, and there are fish in the river, and elk and deer and even bear in the forest. We won't go hungry," I assured them. I showed them my dried berries. I suggested that we could all sleep under one roof but that we had so little rain in these months that their canvas tarps would protect them against the elements until all had houses. I made sure to call them houses—not huts.

As the men worked on the houses, we dug potatoes I'd planted and roasted them. Hans had help now and brought in good-sized deer. We all had fresh meat, and I showed them how to dry it.

Then later in the week, with the scythes they brought with them, we women cut the skimpy grain and talked as we worked, like women of old who bent to their harvest. It felt good to be in the company of women again. I looked out over the heads wrapped in dark scarves tied at the back of the neck, and for the first time I didn't mind that I wore one too, for it made me one of them again. To be able to answer their questions, to calm their worries, to offer comfort in this wilderness, that was what love was. Noticing another's need and tending it.

The Wolfer girls looked after the younger children as we tied the shocks, then broke the small heads into our aprons. We'd grind the grain on river rocks until the grist stones arrived and we had a mill of our own. The other women followed suit, and it seemed to ease the fears of the uprisings, of all the unknowns that face anyone who enters a wilderness place. Acting together to help others forestalled our deeper fears.

We had grain for our children to eat, enough for ourselves and one another, at least for a time. Our men prepared a safe place for us. We had friends and family together for the first time in more than a year. What more could we ask for?

Karl Ruge, our teacher, had once quoted Socrates, who said contentment was natural wealth; luxury, artificial poverty. I saw natural wealth here. I wanted to believe that everything would be well. We'd been chosen to come here. All had agreed. We had nothing to fear.

25

The Confluence of Streams

"Emma," Christian shouted. He looked happy. "Michael's here."

Michael Sr. rubbed his chin. Before we could send anyone out, Michael Sr. had left Keil's train to come ahead, letting us know they were close. George Link and John Genger would bring them on in the rest of the way. We gathered around him, breezes swirling our thin dresses. Wilhelm's wagon train was somewhere east of The Dalles along the Columbia River. Instead of telling us how they all fared, he told us rumors of the Indian wars and the soldiers who dotted the river passages with troop transports. I tried not to feel nervous about the possibility of attack. No Indians here had frightened us. Our remoteness probably helped, I decided. They'd have to come looking for us; we wouldn't likely stumble upon trouble. We'd built that stockade. But that was cautionary, something a good leader would do.

"Your brother travels with Keil," Michael Sr. said and nodded to me.

"He and Willie just couldn't be separated now, could they?" I said. "Thank goodness, or my brother would have stayed home." *Jonathan traveled with them.* My brother, soon here holding his nephew, telling me how Mama and Papa were, the girls and little boys, what the journey had *really* been like. I could hardly wait.

"Ah…*ja*," Michael Sr. said. He cleared his throat, turned back to the others. He changed the subject then, but not without leaving me wondering at the wariness in his voice. "Their journey west has been uneventful," Michael Sr. continued, then said that our leader was primed to love this place because of the ease of the overland passage. "When I left them at The Dalles, they'd had gifts of horses given to them by Cayuse, and they'd been treated like royalty by the Indians coming across, or so Wilhelm tells it. It's only since they reached Oregon Territory that there are Indian worries. On the plains, sometimes whole deer would be killed, dressed, and left for our arrival at an evening camp." Entire Indian families came in more than once and were fed by the colonists. "One night we were joined by thirty braves and their wives and children and their dogs, too." He grinned. "Of course, Wilhelm had invited them, although he never once said anything to Louisa or the others, so we thought we were under attack at first."

I could imagine the fear and then surprise Louisa, Keil's wife, must have felt, taking a deep breath and finding a way to feed those additional people without even the benefit of preparation. "Keil, he is ready to love this place because I tell him of all the possibilities. He is excited, I can tell you that," Michael Sr. told us. His eyes scanned our progress, and I thought I saw a small frown. "At one point on the journey Keil was burdened, but he separated himself and went to a high mound, and there he wrestled with the enemy, and God said He'd walk with him."

"Does he think the game left by the Indians is an example of that?" Peter Klein asked.

"Maybe. And Adam's letters reached home ahead of time to raise their enthusiasm. But more, the Indians were subdued by the…hearse," he said. "I've come ahead to tell so we can send a delegation to the Columbia River to bring them here."

At last they would see what my husband had contended with and how well he'd done despite the trials. The stockade had a blockhouse within it and gun turrets at the top. The fields of grain were harvested, and we had plenty of potatoes. Christian had hoped we'd even sell some and ship them south, our first produce sale. But the Californians apparently planted their own this year and weren't interested in any of ours. Still, anyone could see that love and labor had gone into this clearing to prepare for the community. I loved Michael Sr.'s enthusiasm. The safe trip by the main colony affirmed that the journey west was of divine calling.

But what was this hearse?

Already a light rain dribbled over us as we talked, the drops of water on my husband's hair like light spots of diamonds flashing when sun broke through the clouds. The air smelled sweet, and the contrasts between the dark trunks of trees and the needles of green stood crisp against the mist. I wanted the new arrivals to see what we saw, this beauty and not the challenges still to be faced.

"What is this hearse you speak of?" Sebastian Giesy asked.

Michael Sr. looked around then and nodded toward the stockade. "A sturdy blockhouse. Good. We'll be safe here. When the Indian things calm down, we can move to our houses."

"We didn't expect so many," Christian said. He added, his voice low, "We have fewer houses ready than planned, but not for lack of work. You know of our challenges here. Wilhelm will understand."

Michael Sr. averted his eyes. "He may expect more from us. He's… not always realistic." He pulled at his beard. "When I told him you had a son, he groused and said, 'That's not what I sent him out there to do.'"

The men chuckled low, all except Christian. I felt my cheeks grow warm and was grateful when Peter Klein said, "Why do we send men to the Columbia River to meet them? Won't they sell their wagons in Portland and come the way we did?"

Michael Sr. shook his head and then looked cautiously at me. He took in a deep breath. "They have a hearse. Willie died before they left. Wilhelm's beloved son."

This was news even Peter Klein's early-leaving train had not known. Our leader loved that boy more than anyone—more than Louisa, I thought, though I'd never said as much. I wondered how he'd dealt with the loss of *his* son. Did he blame himself, his own sinful state, as he had with Sebastian and Mary? Or did he blame Louisa? I shivered for her. How hard to leave behind a loved one deep in Missouri soil.

"*Ja,*" Michael Sr. continued. "It was a big loss. Malaria. Your brother grieves, *Frau* Giesy. They delayed starting west because of Willie's death."

"To take time to bury him," I said.

"No." He swallowed. "To bring Willie with them."

"What nonsense is that?" Christian said. "They brought Willie's body across the mountains, the plains, through Indian country?"

"*Ja.* Keil had a lead- and tin-lined casket made. He would have asked you with your skills, but you were here. So it took a little longer to make. Then he placed the body inside. He steeped it in our Golden Rule Whiskey. He composed songs sung each morning by the colonists walking behind the *Schellenbaum. Herr* Keil believes it is that which kept the Indians from harassing them. The Indians saw their journey as a sacred one, that our people tend well to the dead. Adam says Indians came in and looked at the hearse. *Ja, Herr* Keil wanted to bury his son here in this place that calls us all. Well, almost all. He names this place Aurora for his daughter without even seeing it."

He'd brought his dead son all the way across the mountains. I couldn't imagine how hard that must have been for Louisa, and for the colonists, each morning following that hearse carried in an open ambulance with fluttering black fringe around the top. Keil would have made it big and ornamental, I had no doubt about that.

"Hopefully nothing bad has happened to the wagons after you left, Michael," Christian said. "It will be good if all things continue to go well. It will make him more understanding of our...of our progress here."

It was the first indication I had that my husband worried.

"Our leader will see that this is the place we were meant to be, or he wouldn't have had such an untroubled journey here," I said. That became my prayer. "Moving a hearse across the country. *Ja,* that is quite a feat."

While Christian prepared to leave to meet Wilhelm's group, I busied myself quizzing Michael Sr. about who else had come, which families, and who remained behind. Certain families were more easy-going than others, less dependent on sturdy roofs over their head, I imagined, more able to bundle up with another family and make a joy of it rather than a misery. "At least they'll have wagons to spend the winter in," I told Michael Sr. as he looked around the stockade. "We can pull quite a few inside the perimeter."

"Tents. They'll have to live in tents or inside the stockade house," he said. "Most of the wagons were ordered sold in Portland. I told them they can't easily come across the trail where the younger men will push the cows through. You say we're to go farther down the Columbia toward the old Astorian fort and have Keil come up the Wallacut River?"

Christian nodded. "It's closer to the coast. We'll cross the Bay and finish here on the Willapa River. The portage at the Wallacut will challenge them, with that hearse. Moving that wagon will be the worst. It's a heavy thing."

"You bought boats with sails, *ja?*"

"One or two," Christian answered. "And there are larger boats that come in as far as Woodard's Landing."

"*Ja,* then everything will go well."

"I hope," I said. *It must.*

———

"Why can't I go with you to meet them? I haven't seen my brother for nearly two years." I bounced Andy on the side of my hip. He fussed. While I didn't relish the trip across the Shoalwater Bay or down the Wallacut River to the Columbia, I did like the idea of standing beside Christian with our son in my arms when we greeted our leader.

"Because you and Andy will be more people to transport back and portage."

"I could help," I said.

"You would bounce our next child to arrive early?" Christian stopped his packing and patted my stomach. "We'll be on the river and then the bay more than not, and you don't like water travel, if I remember. We may have to wait for transport. Besides, who will feed the goat and that bird?"

"If needed I can take the boat," I said. "I took it with you to look at our land not long ago."

"*Ja,* you did," he said and grinned, his eyebrow lifted with the memory.

We'd gone alone and marked the outline of our house with logs so I could see the view, a prairie view that bled into timber with willows lining the river and a big leafed maple I recognized as similar to trees at Bethel. We'd spread an elk hide and placed it where the rope bed would stand. Andy had stayed with Mary and Sebastian, so we were alone for the first time in years. I lay on my back next to him, looking up at a bird's-egg-blue sky. He'd rolled on his side, his arm draped over my growing belly. My husband then kissed me sweetly. I'd teased him that he lay down on his job, skipping away for an afternoon while there was work yet to do. He'd laughed. "Our leader will know when he sees you and Andy that I lay down more than once." He kissed me again. "I love you, Emma Wagner Giesy. I love you and am grateful you came to this valley with me to begin a new life for us and for the colony."

I cherished the moment, a rare respite for Christian, one I knew wouldn't be repeated once our leader and the remainder of the group arrived. Especially now that Keil had spoken with some disdain about my pregnancy and Andy's arrival. But I held the memory of that languid afternoon in my heart because Christian saw me as doing something worthy despite my willful ways.

I smiled even as Andy pulled on my ear and said, "Down, Mama. Want down."

Christian brushed his beard against my cheek. "Your mind wanders," he said. "Or do you plot?"

"Me?" I said.

He laughed, then sobered. "I'll be back as soon as I can. We have a heavy hearse to bring and many people, and they are tired from their journey and grieving as well. It makes sense that you stay here to prepare to welcome them."

"Imagine, bringing a hearse across those mountains," I said. "What makes that man's mind work? Surely he knows that Willie's soul isn't in that body. Do you suppose he wanted to show everyone that once he says, 'You can ride in the lead wagon, Willie,' that he keeps his promises, no matter what?"

"Indeed. Strong-willed is the other side of stubborn."

"But imagine what that must have been like for Louisa. To watch this hearse that holds your firstborn rumble out every day. To follow it and be reminded every single morning that the child you loved is dead, gone forever. Would she go to it every night and pray over him? Would she listen for the sound of the wind in the *Schellenbaum* or whatever bells he probably put on it? How could you sleep? And Michael said Keil composed funeral dirges, German songs that everyone sang each morning as they set out. For five months! Think of that, Christian. The man…spurs himself."

"Or finds his own way to grieve," Christian said.

"But at what cost? That's a nearly impossible feat, to bring such a heavy thing. His success will only serve to make him think anyone can do anything if they simply set their minds to it." That thought spilling into my words caused a grimace to form on Christian's face. "And he names this place Aurora, for his *daughter*. How must that make Louisa feel?"

"Maybe she suggested it," he said. Then, "You remain. Make those here on the Willapa continue to feel welcome, *ja?* As a good wife should. As the wife of a leader should."

We'd spent so much time being equals here, me doing what I could without regard for whether it was a woman's place to speak or stay silent, whether something was women's work or not. I wondered if that would all change, if what we'd come to cherish in our time together would now be set aside.

"Maybe if I joined you, Keil would see that here we stand side by side to do the work we're called to. There's no need to separate men from women either in the worship house or in our labor."

"That isn't what they'd see, *Liebchen*. They'd see a foolish man who couldn't control his wife and brought her along at the risk of her state. What kind of leader would that make me?"

"You draw out the strengths of all of us," I said. "That's the kind of man you are. Not one who would put an entire colony at risk by bringing the body of his son across the mountains."

He grunted, but I saw the corners of his mouth rise up, and I knew then that he agreed with me, prideful as it might be. He acknowledged that he had led this small colony of scouts well. We claimed him as our leader, and Peter Klein's advance group of colonists deferred to him with respect. With the arrival of *Herr* Keil would come the story of how two strong streams of men came together. I could almost imagine the froth that would rise from that joining, prayed for the settling of it in a hopeful manner.

26

What We Set Aside

Christian insisted I remain, but he couldn't prevent me from meeting him first at his return with our…with Wilhelm. And so with Andy, I made my way to Woodard's Landing to wait. Louisa rode heavy on my thoughts. I knew she'd be critical of the primitive houses here, but she'd stay silent unless her husband spoke. That was her way. But perhaps the pain of her child's death blanketed her, too, with change on this journey west. Maybe she would speak up and influence the others in negative ways.

A west wind tugged at the braids I'd twisted into a crown at the top of my head. My cedar cape kept the drizzle at bay. My eyelashes caught droplets I blinked away. The air held a chill, and I lifted Andy to my widening hip both to rest his weary legs and for the added warmth seeping into my bones.

I'd make a treat of this day with Sarah, I decided, and set aside my worries about Louisa and the rest as I waited for my husband's return. Christian had left spirited, pleased that soon he'd show our leader all we'd accomplished. I wanted their return to be an eventful day, and I calculated that if all went well, they should arrive this afternoon.

Sarah and I spoke of my baby coming, and she smiled wistfully when I teased her that she'd have one before long too.

"I lost a child this spring," she said, her voice as quiet as a pine needle falling to the forest floor. She'd never told me of her loss, nor had

I noticed, always consumed with my own life. My face flushed with regret. "We'll wait now, my husband says, until I'm stronger." *Stronger?* She was one of the strongest women I knew. She shrugged, then added, "All things happen for a reason, don't you know? We don't always see it in our time."

She didn't equate suffering with evil, or pain with sin. The wisdom from someone so young humbled, left me unsure how to comfort her.

"There'll be a midwife for you next time," I said. "Or you must tell me. I think I could midwife. My mother did." Andy played with the Woodard dog that rolled a ball with his nose, back and forth between them.

"Will your mother be here for you?" she said.

I sighed, picked up needlework, and began to stitch on her sampler. Apparently, she didn't have a chatelaine to hold her needles, as she kept her needle stitched onto the cloth. I missed using needle and thread for pretty things, and not just to mend a shirt or draw bear grass through cedar to make a basket, but who had time for such? "My parents already said they wouldn't come. But my brother's with the colonists. So that's almost as good, though not for midwifery."

She smiled. "Things will all change now, Emma." Her doelike eyes dropped to her hands clasped in her lap. "You'll have your German friends to speak with soon, women and children to fill your days. You won't come this way so much."

Would we be pulled into a ball of colony yarn wrapped tightly around one another, never letting our threads roll out toward our neighbors? "I will," I promised. "Once we finish the houses, it will be like a real village. You'll have more neighbors, not fewer; more people coming for the mail boats. We'll travel in for supplies and to ship things out. We'll have big picnics and our band will play again." I was surprised by the joys I could name from my time in Bethel and equally pleased that I hoped they'd be repeated here.

Then in a moment, I wondered if they would. No clearing stood wide enough to make a town here, such as we had in Bethel with room for house-lined streets. Worse, Wilhelm might insist we not associate with our neighbors except in commerce for fear they'd corrupt us the way one bad potato can spoil the lot.

Ach, no. I couldn't let myself worry over such thoughts. With all the people here at last, the building would go more quickly, and each family could work on its own house. We'd be constructing ours, and now I liked the idea of its separation from the others. I could visit Sarah as I wished without colony eyes watching. I wondered why I'd fussed at Christian about the distance. Except for the river passage required at certain times of the year, and the river crossing when we wanted to travel north, we'd be out from under the scrutinizing eyes of our leader, Christian's parents, everyone. It would take more effort to visit friends like Sarah. But if Mary and Sebastian took a claim close to ours rather than on the Giesy site, where the blockade house sat, I'd have friends close. We'd have our own lives and yet have the advantage of giving to and sharing with the colony. It would be better than when we were in Bethel, each looking over the shoulders of another, each feeling guilty when our eyes might move from the pull of our leader to something of our own interest.

"Will the new families be disappointed that they must build their own homes?" Sarah asked.

"Only some," I said. I looked away, poked the needle into the cloth, and set it down. "They'll see that even our home is left for last and that we put the needs of the elders first. They'll understand." I said the last as a hope as much as a promise.

Toward the end of that afternoon, we spied Christian's boat. Tears of hope welled up inside me, though a drizzle welcomed their arrival. I stood on my tiptoes at the wharf, Andy's hand gripped in mine, looking for Christian and my brother. I found my husband's hat bobbing above the others, but it was our leader who stepped off first, his brow furrowed.

His scowl reminded me of Andy when he did not get his way.

———

"Jonathan?" I asked Christian when I caught up with him. I peered behind him.

"Wilhelm sent him back to Portland with most of the wagons," Christian said. "Wilhelm said we needed the money we'd get for them there, and we have little need of so many wagons here." His voice sounded cheerful within the earshot of others; but a caution formed in the lines of his eyes, a pained look that only an attentive wife might notice.

Then Louisa walked down the gangplank, her hands carrying an infant, holding on to a toddler. Next came Aurora. *Aurora.* The child had grown. Kindly, she tended to a younger brother. Louisa nodded to me, then stood to the side while they harnessed the mules and pulled off the hearse carrying their Willie.

The casket was massive. I marveled again that something so large and cumbersome could have come all the way from Missouri. The challenges must have been immense.

"He can rest now," I told Louisa, walking up beside her and patting her arm. She held her brown cape tight around her. "And you, too."

She nodded her head. "It's been a long journey." She looked around. I hoped Woodard's Landing appeared inviting with its tidiness behind the picket fence Sam built. How organized and civilized it all looked to me with the small warehouse, store, and post office all under one roof. Prosperous, I decided. Large sunflowers still bloomed beside the Woodard house, though it was nearly Thanksgiving. Surely Louisa and Wilhelm would see the promise here; surely being thankful for all we'd done would come as easily as the autumn rains. "My husband is tired and weary," Louisa said then. "I must help him find rest."

"Where are our lodgings, Chris?" our leader asked.

I saw in Keil's eyes that engaging intensity that brought people to him. But I also saw the tiredness mentioned by his wife. Something else, too: sadness perhaps, which sloped onto his shoulders and showed in the downturned lines around his mouth. He looked older than when we'd left him, while Christian appeared carved by the elements and stood leaner and more muscular than when we'd left Missouri.

"We'll take advantage of the Woodards' hospitality and spend the night here at their request," Christian said. "In the morning, we'll make our way to the claims I've purchased."

"I'd prefer to go to our own homes now," our leader said.

"A fresh start will be better in the morning," Christian insisted, and to my surprise, after a hesitation, our leader agreed.

"And the others…?" I said.

"In their tents this night," Christian said. "That's how they've slept along the trail. They understand the vigor of building a new community."

I watched as the men moved to set their tents in the potato fields. The women huddled in small groups, some waiting out of the rain on the Woodards' porch, then moving to shelter under their canvases. I counted as I could. It looked like seventy, and with the Klein group, more than one hundred people were here already. But more than twice that number were yet to come.

The women didn't raise their eyes to mine, busying themselves with the solidness of land after their days on the boats. They were tired, I decided. It would be better when we were together tomorrow at the stockade and they met up again with Peter Klein's group, who would tell them of how hard we'd worked and how the land demanded more than we'd imagined. The scouts would all be here again save two, claiming as we had before that this was our promised land. We would have a gathering in worship led by…Christian, perhaps, or our leader. All would be well.

It had to be well.

———

"Let's walk, then," our leader said to my husband in the morning. "Show me this place you all chose." His words chopped like an axe to a tree trunk. He'd grown stronger with rest under the Woodards' feather tick. Voices echoed in the relentless rain, which I prayed would stop so they could see the grandeur of the trees instead of the misty fog veiling their tops. My teeth chattered, from the cold, I assumed. Our leader acted like a man who had to be convinced instead of a man grateful for what God had provided. I wanted him to see the possibilities here as my husband saw them; not the way I'd first seen it and only later been wooed over to my husband's view.

Our leader impatiently grabbed at his hat while ordering Louisa to bring him a hard biscuit and jerky, as though she was a servant instead of a wife. Christian would have to win him over quickly. Something had changed from the time Michael Schaefer Sr. reported on our leader's optimism over the journey to what I saw now.

Louisa pulled her cape up over her head and rushed out to their wagon to bring back a cold breakfast for her husband. I opened my tied bag and gave Christian jerked meat, a piece of dried fruit, and a biscuit. "I planted and ground the wheat for this myself," I told the new arrivals.

Louisa frowned, and I wondered if she thought me prideful.

"We'll take the mules, Wilhelm," Christian said. "The road is too muddy this time of year to try to walk it."

"*Ach,*" our leader said, striking the air with his hand, but he followed Christian out into the rain to saddle the mules.

I made it my duty to raise my own spirits as well as those of the others while we waited at Woodards'. I told them stories of our time here, making the tales light, about the goat's antics or the delight of watching bobcat kits racing in the spring sun or how moss made the perfect bed matting and it was free for the plucking. The women warmed up more, and I told them that the earthen floors of the houses were nearly as hard as the tile back in Bethel, that in summer, berries literally dropped their fruit at our doors. We'd found a wild honey tree and so had sweetness. I assured them of this land's sweetness.

We were joined by several of the Klein group then, too impatient to wait for us, and so the gathering increased with German words chattering through the forest like chickadees. Soon both men and women were together in the warehouse Sam opened for us so we'd have a drier, though no less crowded, place to wait.

I listened more now and learned of events along the trail, and that's when Karl Ruge told of Keil's strange arrest and trial. The Klein group hadn't heard of it either, and as Karl spoke, I wondered if the arrest and brief trial of our leader in The Dalles had caused the change in his attitude from one of happy assurance to what I saw as discouraged doubt.

"They accused him of disloyalty to the American government in a time of war with the Indians," Karl told us. "He was arrested for treason."

"For treason?" Peter said.

Karl nodded. "*Ja,* but it was all a mistake. Some Americans reported that Wilhelm said such things when it was another, one of the Indians who befriended us, who said Americans were bad."

"They arrested him for disagreeing with the government?" I said.

Karl blinked as he turned to me, surprised I guess that a woman raised her voice in this mixed group.

He hesitated only a moment. "*Ja,* by golly. Wilhelm sent the rest of the group ahead while he and I tried to get to the bottom. We did, though they paid no heed to what either of us reported about our loyalty. Instead, another American came to our rescue, testifying that he'd heard the exact same words spoken by this same Indian. The court took the word of that American over anything Wilhelm or I could say."

"I'll bet Wilhelm hated that," I said, then clasped my hand over my mouth. Wilhelm Keil demanded recognition, acclamation almost; he hadn't had it in this territory so far. But I didn't need to announce it. I looked for Louisa. Her sunken cheeks burned red.

"It…grieved him," Karl said, his eyes resting with kindness on Louisa.

Late in the day, one of the colonists who'd remained at the stockade came through the forest and said we were to bring the hearse and come to the stockade. I saw this as a hopeful sign that our leader had seen our land and approved and now we could move toward home. *Home.*

"No. I don't think my husband would want the hearse hauled by any but our two mules," Louisa said. "And they are being ridden by our…by Wilhelm and Chris." She crossed her arms over her narrow chest. "I'll wait here with the hearse until he brings the mules back." She wrapped her cape around herself, an immovable log.

"We must take people to the stockade area," Peter said. "We will wear out our welcome at the Woodards'. Wilhelm wants this done."

Louisa hesitated, bit her lower lip, but then the lessons ingrained to women, that we must follow our men, overtook her and she nodded. Peter and the other men harnessed two oxen to haul the hearse the last mile or so to the Giesy claim and stockade. The rest of us would form the funeral march that followed.

I helped pull up tents and talked with several of the women, assuring them that there were roofs, at least a few, so we could get in out of the rain once we arrived at the Giesy site.

And we did so, many of us huddling into the log house I'd spent the last winter in, more pitching tents outside.

I'd claimed this hut as my own last winter and noticed anew the hides that I'd helped tan, the sleeping mats that bore our blankets, the moss that I'd cleaned the slugs from. It now belonged to…all of us. My stomach knotted. I wondered if Christian and I would be allowed to take the elk hide gift when we moved, or would that now remain as a part of the house rather than a part of our lives?

Louisa sat down on my blanket, pushed it back behind her so she could lean against it. She patted the soft bedding, looked around. She nodded approval. Her eyes met mine. Once again all that we had would have to be shared with everyone else.

In that moment I knew that the colony had truly arrived.

———

"He's taken Wilhelm to your claim," Adam Schuele told me. "He wanted him to see the widest prairie and where the gristmill could be placed. All our ideas Chris wants to share with him."

"What has our leader said?" I whispered. We stood in a large tree-fall that some of the men had scraped out for a dry place to sleep. "Does he give an indication of his approval from this morning's trip?"

Adam looked away, picked at some pitch stuck on his hand. "He spent a good amount of time on the hill behind the stockade overlooking the valley." Adam shook his head. "I don't know. We were all so sure…"

"Because it is a good place," I said, certain. "I struggled at first, remember? I didn't think this land could support us all. It took so much work just to build, but Christian assured me. You assured me. That all the scouts agreed, that's the true sign that we have chosen well, that it was chosen for us. Surely our leader will not dispute that?"

Adam said nothing, walked over to take the blinders from the horses he said were given as gifts to only Keil's sons. They were chestnuts with white spots spattered across their sides. Adam tied the horses at young trees far enough apart that they didn't entangle each other. The goat ran around trying to decide if all the additional dogs were pets or peril.

Work would set my mind at rest, quell my imaginings of what occurred between Christian and our leader. I helped milk the few cows that Peter's group had driven down the trail. I showed the new women the latrine area, commented on the berries we could eat to supplement our diet. "You can squat and eat," I said, grateful for their chuckles. I urged them not to hunch their shoulders against the rain, as it did no good and only caused later aches. "We can weave capes," I said. "Right from this land. What we know of wefts and warps serves us here." I showed them where I kept food cool in the river, the large drums that we collected rainwater in for drinking and washing. They peered at the meager grain storage. "I know there isn't much, but we can buy flour through the winter from the ships coming in." Potatoes were plentiful. We'd have a little milk now with the few cows here, though not enough for all these people. We could perhaps buy a few more of Sarah's eggs, maybe even some of her chickens. "We have plenty of ammunition, so we can have game to eat. We won't go hungry, that's certain," I told them.

Christian had planned well, considering he never knew how many people would actually come here or the circumstances when they did.

"It'll be a bit squeezed in together, and we'll need the tents still," I told the women. And maybe a few more of these rotted logs carved out for people to stay in. "It doesn't snow much here at all, and by February, the sun comes out more often and flowers begin to bloom. By March, this is an Eden, it truly is. Even I plowed and seeded the grain field, the soil is so easily broken."

"Will we rotate being able to sleep under the roof?" one of the women asked.

"The doctor will need *this* roofed house," Louisa told her. It was the first time she'd engaged in the conversations, and I noted that she referred to Wilhelm as the doctor. "Or had you planned that for yourselves, Emma?"

My faced burned. "We'll live in a tent through this winter as we did most of the last," I said. "All the scouts lived in this house; it wasn't 'ours.' We built it for the colony."

"*Ja*, well, you call it the Giesy place, so I assume," Louisa said.

"Christian claimed the land in his parents' names, as the law requires, but of course it is for the colony."

"The land in Bethel is in my husband's name."

"But here, the free land needs specific people named," I said. I was even more grateful that Christian had made it clear where our claim would be...far down the road, seven miles down the road, and we'd spent no time at all on building it at the expense of building for others. He'd sacrificed a dry home for us to make homes for others. Couldn't they see his generosity?

"I note there is no Keil place," Louisa said. "Or does my husband go there with your husband, and you have saved the best for last?"

She grieved; I needed to remember that, to chalk away the blemish of her words.

"This stockade, this roofed house will house you as it does all of us. It isn't Elim yet, I know. But once we have a mill, we'll have all the timber we could need to build grand houses just as we had in Bethel, just not with brick." Even Christian's parents would not assume they alone would have a roof over their heads. "There are some other structures on adjoining claims, a few, with canvas roofs. With so many of us, now we will be able to finish those."

It flashed through my mind that with so many people here we'd also be spending more time hunting, more time handling food than we had before. I hoped that Christian had put in a large-enough order for wheat to come into Woodards' warehouse, and I wondered if some of the party still to arrive might come up the Cowlitz and take the trail as Peter Klein had and bring sheep. Mutton would taste good, and we could use the wool to spin to replace our threadbare clothes. That reminded me that I hadn't noticed that our leader's group included any trunks marked with our name on them. So it would be Christian's parents I'd have to count on. They carried the grist stones and were coming by ship. Surely they would have our trunks and bring our personal effects.

When Christian and Wilhelm returned, I could tell that something was very wrong. Our leader walked with his shoulders bent, striding well in front of Christian, who slowly unsaddled the mules. Wilhelm walked purposefully. He stopped at the hearse standing beside the log house and gazed around, finally pointing at Louisa that she should follow him, and they disappeared behind the hearse.

"What does he think?" I asked Christian. Andy patted the mule's front leg. "Did he approve of God's choice?"

"Take the boy. He could get hurt." I reached for Andy, lifted him. "Well?"

"He does not," Christian answered me then. "But he says he has no choice but to bury his son here." He wouldn't look at me, just started brushing the mule.

"But that's good. He'll want a home close to where his son is buried."

Christian turned to me, his eyes like my old dog's when I'd refused to give him a bone. "He's telling people to head back south, into Oregon Territory. He's sending Michael to stop the rest from coming here. He wants them to find jobs in Portland through the winter. He says the women can clean and cook, and maybe there is work for the men there. He's sure there is nothing here."

"Jonathan won't even come north, then?" I asked.

"Don't cry over your brother," Christian snapped.

"I…I hadn't meant to. I'm just disappointed."

"*Ja*," he said, leading the mule away from me. "You and *Herr* Keil have that in common."

27

Drowning in Bounty

In the midst of people deciding who would leave first and who would remain, leaving in the spring instead of this winter, Sam Woodard told us, "The army says we should all move into an area that can be defended well. Sarah and I will come here if that's agreeable. The stockade, it's more isolated. A few others in the valley are being urged to come this way too."

"More outsiders in this small space?" Louisa said. Wilhelm frowned at her. Probably more for having expressed an opinion than for what she said. She stepped back and clasped her hands before her now-bowed head.

"How good we have a place of safety you can come to," I noted. "And that we can share it with others, as good Christians, as we did in Bethel."

"*Ja*, come here," Wilhelm said, speaking to Sam as though Christian weren't even present, as though I hadn't even spoken.

"What we have is always available to you, Sam," Christian said. "Did the army say what the new threat was, or how long it might be, all of us here together?"

Sam shook his head. "Only that the whole region is a prime target. The governor's dislike of all Indians has fired even the friendlier ones. The Shoalwaters feel left out of the negotiations, so they're refusing to go to another tribe's designated reserve. Governor Stevens wants no negotiating with anyone. So the Indians have nothing to lose by attacking whenever they wish."

One of the men who'd traveled with Wilhelm said, "Our leader charms the Indians. We had no trouble coming across, did we, Wilhelm?"

"No," Wilhelm said. "No trouble. But here is different. Ve have trouble here."

So we would all be housed inside the stockade walls with our tents and a few under roof. Christian assigned men to rotate watch at the guardhouse; Wilhelm voiced his opinion about who would follow whom. I noticed that the men took orders given by either Christian or *Herr* Keil.

Inside the house that evening, several of us scrunched together at one end, the smells of wet wool and smoke filling our heads. Adam and Michael Sr. and other scouts who'd been a part of this journey from the beginning stayed close together. I wished that the Knights were here, but Adam had signed up for the military when they'd reached The Dalles with Keil's group and was said to be fighting the Cayuse. How strange that was to me with Wilhelm speaking pacifism, at least before we left Bethel. No one knew where Joe Knight was. I longed to know what had happened and why after all this distance and all we'd done together that the Knights had decided to separate.

I poured hot tea into mugs while Hans spoke with several men about heading out in the morning as a group to bring in meat. John Genger had acted as a hunter on the trip out, and he oiled his gun as Hans spoke.

"Didn't you hear Woodard say we're not to go into the woods?" Wilhelm said. "Too dangerous."

"I think he meant alone and to fell trees," Hans said.

John Genger stopped, his oil rag midair. "We have to eat, Wilhelm."

"I saw a few deer when we brought the hearse here yesterday," Hans told him. "Off by that ravine, where we took out the big root ball, remember?" Michael Sr. nodded.

"We must preserve the ammunition now so ve can defend ourselves," Wilhelm said. "How foolish it would be to use it all up gathering food. Ve must think ahead. We are planners, we Germans."

"The people need food, Wilhelm," Christian said, his hand resting on our leader's forearm. "And we're still quite a distance from the trouble farther east. It's good to be here together and be cautious, but we have hungry children."

"Did I not see fish jumping in that river?" Wilhelm countered. "If this is such a promised land as you have dubbed it, Chris, then let us fish. Let us club them as you say the Indians do."

"To supplement the meat, yes, but to—"

"There will be no using the ammunition except for defense." Wilhelm's voice boomed, silencing even the children whimpering as they tried to fall asleep. Rain pattered on the peeled logs, and the pitch in the cook fire flames hissed like huddled witches.

"Wilhelm, my friend and leader," Christian said, his voice like the stroke of a gentle hand on a skittish cat. "In this clearing there are different ways of doing things. It is not a challenge to you that I tell you that having meat makes sense. We will be frugal with the ammunition. Hans knows this."

Wilhelm's eyes grew large, the white around them reminding me of a buffalo's eyes. Christian dared challenge him in front of all of us, and challenge he must, or we could all die of starvation.

"I have paid the bills," Wilhelm began. "The one thousand dollars you charged for this and that; it has cost us almost eight hundred dollars just to bring these few people from Portland to this godforsaken place. To pay off the claims you've bought will deplete us even more. I need to make these decisions now, Chris. No ammunition for hunting.

I'll not risk the loss of ammunition when we may need it to defend ourselves against those Indians. You have brought us to a hellish place, Chris. Now I must get us out."

———

"Send a letter to Bethel," Keil directed Karl Ruge. It was the third day behind the stockade. At least fifty people remained; the others had risked the river and the bay to return to Portland as Keil directed. The rain fell steadily. Andy hadn't seen the seagull for several days, but he'd stopped asking when I'd snapped at him. I tried to imagine myself alone, in my own home, but Keil's voice took me from my escapist thoughts. "Tell them we will bury Willie here, on the hill just beyond the stockade walls. Then we will all go to Portland and spend the winter in better conditions." I watched the pain in my husband's eyes, moved to stand beside him.

"We will do what Judge John Walker Grimm suggests," he dictated to Karl. He'd apparently met this man in Portland while the judge shipped apples to California. Grimm sold fifty-six apple trees to a man named Adair while Keil watched. Pippins and Winesaps and Northern Spy apples (such detail our leader recalled and had Karl Ruge put into the Bethelites' letter), and the judge told the colonists where the trees were grown, somewhere in an area on the Pudding River in Oregon Territory. Our leader saw hope in such trees for the colony; he didn't see hope in this clearing.

If such a man can ship apples south, why can't we ship our grain south and other products we grow, just as we did in Bethel? I hoped Christian would say such things, but he didn't. He stayed silent as a saw leaned against the wall.

Then Keil began what to me was a tirade against this landscape. He had Karl write terrible things about this valley, about how long it took them to ride a mule seven miles, of how he had to cross the Willapa six or seven times to get from one claim to another, and that the road to our claim had been the most dangerous trail he'd taken since he'd left Bethel. "The soil may be rich, but it is covered with three to four feet of decaying tree trunks," he dictated. "The land grows anything, but there is no one here to buy it except ourselves. There is no prospect of more people coming here, as the rain sends everyone away, everyone with any sense; and everything we need is too far away and too expensive to get. A barrel of flour in Oregon costs three dollars and fifty cents, while here it costs fifteen to twenty dollars, and it will be impossible much of the year to even get it here by boat. There is no good farm land and can never be." He looked up at me. "Little fields cleared beside the river. A pittance. There is no fodder for cattle or sheep; the land is covered with trees or what is left of them. If we built a distillery, only a few oystermen would consume our product. In one day I can see the problem of this place, and yet the scouts, they claim this as God's land. They were not listening to the voice of our Lord, our Savior." He took in a deep breath. "They listened to one another."

My husband sank into himself. I couldn't bear to look at him.

I stared instead across the room at Louisa. *Does Louisa look proud?* No, it was another emotion I saw there in the eyes that gazed back at mine. Pity, perhaps, that emotion that covers fear.

Keil finished with the admonition to any Bethelites still in Missouri to remain there. "You are a poor, unbelieving people without me," he dictated so each of us could hear. "Like Moses, I've led my people through the desert, and no one has sacrificed his firstborn to the Lord except me, myself." *He left out Louisa's sacrifice.* "But God has called us to be at peace." His words were full of consuming fire, not a word of peace except the word itself.

He finished by having Karl tell them that when they wrote, they must send their letters to the Portland post office, Oregon Territory, and a copy to Bruceport post office, as he wasn't sure when the weather would let them bury Willie or when the army would release us from this stockade so we could all leave this hellish Willapa Valley. As a last act of control, he ordered cattle, mules, and oxen to be taken to Portland to be held there or sold. Once Willie was buried, those favorite mules of Wilhelm's would be taken south as well.

Christian got up and left. I wanted him to fight, to send another letter, to see what he had seen before, in the beginning. I followed him out as Mary reached to distract Andy. Outside, I couldn't see him, as he'd walked into the foggy mist. At the brush-covered lean-to where the cows lay, I found the goat tethered near the outside. Even she had been asked to share her space. I put my arms around her neck and felt hot tears pour out onto her musty hair. We'd waited for this day, this time, with such anticipation. All our efforts for nearly two years had been for the benefit of the colony, and it had abandoned us. *Poor Christian.* I didn't know how I could comfort him. I mumbled a prayer for him, not sure if we'd moved away from God or if God had stepped away from us.

How could we not have seen what Wilhelm saw in just a few days here? Maybe because he was a visionary, had always seen more than others. But we'd followed his directions and listened, believing God spoke to us as well. Had our souls slept while our hearts worked long hours?

I had once seen this place as Keil did. I'd seen the troubles he wrote of but told myself, for Christian's sake, that they could be overcome. I hated that I hadn't stood my ground with Christian and the other scouts and insisted that we leave, that we find a landscape more hospitable to clearing, to building, to life.

But more, I hated having anything in common with *Herr* Keil.

———

At dusk on the afternoon of November 26, 1855, we sang the funeral dirge *Herr* Keil composed for his son's burial. We followed Willie's hearse to the gravesite on the hill, the bells of the *Schellenbaum* tinkling in the rain, the majority of us carrying small candles that flickered as we walked. It took the mules and men to push the heavy casket up the hill and roll it over tangled vines and small fallen logs. How they had ever brought this boy's body all that distance, all that way, was a feat few would ever attempt, let alone achieve. Couldn't Keil see that his very act of doing the impossible was but a forerunner for what we could do here in this bountiful place?

With ropes, the men lowered the casket into the ground as we sang our German dirge. Then Keil spoke, our faces shadowed by the candle-light. He reminded us that light would overcome darkness; Christ's light would shine above all. His words heartened me, spoken in German. Everyone spoke in German now. What was American, even English, was being set aside.

But as we filed back down the hill toward the stockade, I knew we'd buried more than this boy. We buried promises, efforts, and our future.

———

The Woodards joined those of us at the stockade, and then began the strangest time in Willapa that I could remember. The first nights were chaotic and close. Children cried, and the smells of their dirtied napkins permeated the air. Thank goodness for abundant moss that all the women soon used. Old men sweating and women perspiring in the damp heat added to the mixture of scents strong enough to make a pregnant woman ill. Rain dribbled in through slits in the canvas roof when we bedded down that first night with townspeople and us Germans together, with growls in our stomachs. A few people had come inland from Bruceport on the Shoalwater Bay, having been told of our isolated encampment.

I pushed back hot tears while my husband snored into my neck, his arm across my chest. I longed for escape in his whispered words of love; I longed to feel hopeful once more. As I lay, eyes resisting sleep, I recalled Christian's return from his walk in the mist. Since then, he'd turned inside himself, his eyes empty as the grain bucket.

By the second night, it was decided the men would risk time in the woods in order to build another house so those staying in tents outside would have better shelter.

I wondered how Sarah felt with this German spoken all around. She'd so often opened her home to us; we had so little to offer back.

Bickering broke out. Hunger takes away one's patience. People moved into tents to have time alone. Smoke from the cooking fires—with little to cook—permeated the entire area.

The Woodards remained but a week, deciding to take their chances back at the wharf. "We can't help you," Sarah told me as I begged her to stay. "We add to your trials. So many of you to feed, and the rule you have about saving ammunition will only keep you hungry while there is game available." She shook her head. "Maybe it isn't so bad with the Indians. Maybe the military exaggerates."

"I'll miss your company," I told her.

She patted my hand. "My husband says we'll send peas to you and a bag of potatoes from the warehouse. We'll pray the ships will come before long and bring the flour you ordered."

After a day of trying to finish another house, Christian said, "Tomorrow, you must club fish." His voice was low, but everything was easily overheard. There was no escaping unless we went outside and stood beneath a cedar tree. Andy cried and I rocked him as we sat our backs against the logs. *Herr* Keil played scales on his harmonica, up and down, like a bad whistler who refuses to stop.

"Just send Hans and John out into the woods," I whispered. "There is plenty of meat. Keil doesn't have to know. Why—"

"*Nein.* We are not to use the ammunition. Wilhelm forbids it."

"Overrule him," I said.

"We'll club fish. All of us, though the more we men can work in the woods, the better. So you must set the tone and get the women to help."

My face grew hot. It was insane, this thought of clubbing fish when we could feed ourselves well with game. What was my husband thinking? What was *Herr* Keil thinking?

I shook my head, too outraged to even argue with words.

In the morning, Christian reached for my hand. "I'll show you how to do it," he said. "Let Andy sleep."

We eased our way past sleeping bodies. Louisa, awake, followed our movements as we made our way out through the door.

The rain had stopped, though a heavy mist sifted around the stockade. I could make out the men in the gun turret area and felt a flash of outrage that they would stand there with ammunition while we would club fish for our food.

"Like this, watch now, Emma," Christian said. He'd picked up an oar for each of us, then he let himself slide down the side of the bank, taking dirt with him. His feet sank into the mud, and the edge of the river filled in around him up to his calves. "Come." He held out his hand to me.

The water mesmerized, swiftly flowing along, carrying branches and leaves. But within its roiling it carried food for the taking. I could see the fish roll, giving up flashes of silver and blood red. I hiked my skirt up between my legs and hooked it into my apron belt, then used my oar to balance myself as I slid down the bank and sank, the wet squishiness against my moccasins, cold on my feet, my ankles. I shivered.

Christian moved a few feet away from me so as not to hit me by accident when he struck at the fish. "See," he pointed. And then with a loud slap and whack, he hit a dog-head salmon swimming upstream. He slammed it into the bank. "One chub," he shouted, then unstuck himself enough to strike the fish before it flailed and tossed itself back into the water. He grabbed it by the gills, and from the effort it took to hold it up, it must have weighed what a wagon hub weighed, several pounds. "Now you."

What did this man think? It took all my effort to maintain my balance, standing, with the pressure of the water against my legs, let alone strike at a fish. My belly threatened to get into the way of my oar swing. Bile rose against my wishes. I spit, took a deep breath, and then whacked but only hit the water, splashing cold onto my chest and face. I struck again and again. What would my baby think, getting baptized early with splashes from the Willapa River?

"Try to reach underneath one," Christian said. "Use the wide end of the oar to lift and then throw the chub out."

I glared at him. "Why don't you just shoot it?" I said. "Why don't you shoot a deer or an elk? Butcher one of the oxen. This is—why are you letting him do this to you, to us?"

"Lift it out. Hit it. Like this," he said, sliding back down into the water. "Can't you do anything I tell you?" He struck at the fish, the river, sliced the oar into the water's rush, and the silvery flesh rose from the river and soared into the air, where he struck it again and again, then tossed it up high on the bank. He returned like a madman, I thought, pushing and clubbing. I pulled away, clawed my way back up to the top of the bank. My heart pounded as I watched this man I didn't know. The curls of his hair were matted with the rain, and bits of mud speckled his face like freckles. He walloped and whacked until he had fifteen of the fish, their tails still swishing and jerking on the bank. He slid back down into the stream, a grunt coming from him with each blow. Sweat poured off him.

"Enough," I shouted. "It's enough, Christian."

He struck the water, even though there were no fish being lifted out. How he must ache. Despite the current and the depth, I slid back down and pushed my way over to him, touched his shoulder. He shivered.

This was what love was then: meeting another's need, not our own.

"Christian," I said. He jerked and stared at me, his eyes vacant and filled with such sadness I thought if I stared longer I'd sink away. "Christian," I whispered to him and opened my arms. He leaned into me then, and we stood in the rush of the water while I felt more than heard my husband's deep sobs.

———

"They'll make good eating," I told the women. "See how we clean them." I stabbed the head with a knife, asked Mary to hold it tight to the wood slab. Then with another knife I filleted them, cutting lengthwise from the head to the tail, then turning them over and slicing another long side, piling the bones with tiny bits of flesh left on them beneath the rough table we used. "We can make fish soup from the heads and bury the bones in the garden. My friend Sarah said not to let the dogs eat the raw flesh. It will kill them. The fish tails and bones will make everything grow better come spring."

"We'll not be here to see that," Louisa said, her arms crossed over her chest.

I ignored her comment, kept helping the women. Mary gouged

out the side of a chub, nearly cutting it in two. "It takes practice," I told her, wiping the slimy film from the fish off my hands in the dirt.

There were no fish left to smoke after that first meal. I tried to make light of it, that wasn't it grand we had bounty from the water for our bellies and bounty from the forest to cover our heads. The thought of going out again in the morning sent chills down my back, but if we women killed the fish, the men would be free to build. And if they built, perhaps Wilhelm would change his mind and want to remain.

I wanted so much for people to see the good in this place, to not question what God had provided for us. How could this not be the chosen place when each of the scouts had concurred?

But one had defected. Now the whole colony planned to leave. I wondered if we would.

"We'll go out tomorrow, and we can bring back enough for two or three meals," I told the women.

"Should you be doing that?" Mary asked. "Might you hurt the baby?"

I shook my head. "Christian showed me how. I'm healthy, though a little weak. But the fish will be good for us. It has fat, and if we can find a dry place to smoke, we can pound some into pemmican like we do dried venison or beef. It'll be good for the men to have when they work so hard."

"It's terribly oily," one of the women noted as she wiped her hands on her apron. "It almost looks like wax. And they stink." She wrinkled her nose.

"Maybe we can burn the oil," I said. I wondered why I hadn't thought of that before. We could put the oil into tin cups and burn it for light. Another bounty.

That's what I told Christian that night when he returned with thirteen other men who had been working to build another house.

"Some bounty," he said.

"But it is, just as you said it was." Even though we'd moved into a tent outside so one of the other families could sleep within walls, we spoke in low whispers. *No need for everyone to hear our business.*

Christian lay silent, but I knew he didn't sleep. "Our leader is right, *Liebchen.* How could I not have seen that what is here is not enough to sustain us all? I should have sent word when I realized how long it took to build one house. Or we should have looked elsewhere, maybe closer to your Steilacoom. I should have diverted them in The Dalles, given them a better choice. A good leader would have. That's what Wilhelm is doing now, giving people a better choice."

"To die of starvation because he's afraid of Indians?" I said.

"The fish will be enough. And the ships will come in, and Sam Woodard will send word that flour is here. We'll count on that. Until spring."

I thought of taking a rifle and trying to bring a deer down myself. I thought of what that act would do to my husband. I decided against it.

———

After three weeks, the men had completed one more house. We did not celebrate, as I thought we should have, marking a good thing, a met goal. We didn't even pray over the safety of the men as they'd worked in the woods and built another house within the stockade. Even the band instruments stayed silent. The children complained about the fish and potatoes, fish and potatoes, all we had to eat. The close quarters railed against our good natures, and people snapped at one another. To find privacy, we might leave one of the two houses within the stockade, but just outside were people in tents to maneuver around; others camped beneath cedar trees outside the stockade but close enough to seek cover if needed. The path to the latrines grew muddy and slick, and even the constant rain did not cleanse the stench.

Then the fish stopped swimming upriver. We were left with potatoes and a few of the Woodards' peas and the small amounts of milk that the cows and goat gave up. We divided all of it among the children.

"Perhaps when the flour arrives," Louisa said when I commented out loud inside one of the houses that it would be nice to celebrate the addition of the house, since we hadn't celebrated much at Christmas. We hadn't broken bread together in any special way; in fact, we had no bread to break.

"The band played in Bethel whenever we completed a new home," I said. "Will we not keep the same customs in our new colony?"

"This will never be our colony," Wilhelm said, in a rare act of speaking directly to a subject I'd raised. His voice silenced even the children. He sighed then. "Please will you write another letter, Karl?"

Dictating letters seemed to be all Wilhelm did now that Willie was buried and several had gone south with the cattle. Now the weather appeared too inclement for Wilhelm to head south to Portland himself.

Karl Ruge brought out paper and lead. He was such a kindly man with his graying beard and no mustache, his cheeks reddened from the wind and rain as he helped with the building. He was of an elder's age and could have simply stayed back with Wilhelm and the women and children, teaching, one might have said. But he chose to participate in my husband's efforts to ease the discomforts of this place. He rolled the lead across his knuckles while he awaited Wilhelm's dictation. He winked at Andy, who watched Karl's hands with careful eyes.

In this latest letter sent to the Bethelites, Keil reported on how long it took us to build the house and then announced that next week he would leave for Portland to see how the rest of the colony fared. "Take your time in coming out," he said. "Until we find the place the Lord has called us to, I wouldn't leave my home in Bethel."

The Lord had called us here. How was it that one man could change that? What about the voice *we* heard? I started to speak, but Christian anticipated and squeezed my arm as he stood behind me. I turned to look at him, and he shook his head. *Silence,* he mouthed. *Silence.* My greatest challenge.

Would it be so sinful to ask for help, maybe from people at the coast town of Bruceport, I wondered. They might have flour we could buy now. Keil wouldn't let us, I supposed. He was the keel, the wedge in this ship.

I dreamed that night of water, of Wilhelm taking me on a small boat across the Shoalwater Bay to the Wallacut River, then upriver on the Columbia and into Portland. At least that had been his plan. I ate from the leg of a deer in my dream but didn't swallow it. My hunger continued. Then the ship capsized in the bay, and I couldn't reach Wilhelm; I was too frightened to throw him a rope, too frightened to help him, and so he had drowned.

I woke up with a start, my heart pounding. What kind of mind did I have, dreaming of the death of Keil? Christian patted my arm. "Water," I said. "I dreamed of swirling water."

I shivered and felt wet. My whole mat was wet. I looked up. No leaks. And then I knew: my water had broken. My second child pressed its way into this chaotic world.

28

It Is Finished

"Get Mary," I told Christian. "My baby comes."

"I'm already here," Louisa said. She'd slipped into the corner of the Giesy House that now belonged to everyone. "Let's not bother Mary or alarm her. In case something goes wrong."

"Something goes wrong?" I croaked. *Why bring in the ghost of suffering at such a time like this?* "I've been through this," I said, firm. "Maybe I don't even need a midwife. Christian will help me."

"*Ach,* it's no job for a man. He has things to do, don't you, Chris?" She shooed her arms at him as though he was the goat. "Don't be selfish and risk your baby," Louisa said, patting my arm. "We women must suffer the pangs of childbirth together. Leave now, Christian."

"I missed Andrew being born," he said.

"Men usually do," she said. "Well, then. If we need you, we'll send someone." She pushed him aside.

I wanted him to stay, to resist the push and pull of others, but he stepped away. Louisa hung a quilt for privacy, which I later appreciated when the waves rose and ebbed through my body, carrying me up and over the pain. I didn't cry out, though, at least not that I remembered. Muffled conversations of others in the house drifted to me as did the smell of the cooking, the crying of a child. I tasted sweat on my upper lip and welcomed the wet cloth Louisa placed on my forehead as I waited for the next cry of my child's journey into life.

Christian didn't go far. I could hear his voice as he spoke to others, commented on the leather hinges he'd made for doors. He waited within earshot. Had I told him that Louisa made me nervous? Knowing he waited just outside the door comforted. I'd tell him that when this was over.

This infant wouldn't come as swiftly as Andy had. The day waned as the baby pushed its way closer to arriving into the world. Then we heard shouts from the gun turrets announcing an alarm.

I struggled to sit up. Louisa helped steady my shoulders. "I'll see what it is. You wait here."

"Did you think I planned to take a walk?" I snapped.

I heard her say in English, "No. She is indisposed," but then she stumbled aside, and Sarah Woodard bent through the opening of the door. I sighed relief. Even if she brought news of Indian attacks it would be good to have her here.

"What news?" I said between pants.

"No attacks," she said. "But the first ship of the New Year arrived."

I leaned back against Louisa. "Good. There'll be bread, then, grain for us all."

With full stomachs and a greater variety of food, tempers would cool. Maybe playing music would be considered acceptable. Karl Ruge could return to reading nightly to us from his books while smoking his long clay pipe. Our hungry stomachs had elbowed our souls, and many of us couldn't listen for long. Music would soothe. Surely any hostile Indians wouldn't mind the sound of trumpets and horns. Maybe we'd begin thanking God again as a group for all He had done. My husband would be vindicated. Flour, as he'd ordered it, well in advance of the arrival of this many people, would mean nourishment and a sign that my husband was a good leader, someone who could anticipate and provide, with God's help. Always with God's help.

Sarah looked down, then wiped my sweaty forehead. Rain dripped from her cape, and steam rose up from the moist wool already warming within the close heat of the house. "Your family arrives," she said. "They say they are Giesys, and they bring grist stones."

"Christian's parents." We'd have more to feed, but we'd also have more support for Christian. They'd see the possibilities here. They'd want to remain where Christian and the scouts had done so much to prepare for their coming. And there'd be flour. Food. Our hunger filled at last.

"We'll have a big meal," I panted. "With bread and cakes maybe. And the band will play."

Sarah's eyes went to Louisa's. She leaned into Louisa and whispered something. Louisa shook her head, no. "What is it?" I asked. "Tell me what's wrong."

"No," Louisa said. "You don't need to know."

"Here we share good news and bad," I panted.

Sarah nodded. "The ship brought only one small bag of flour. Sam and I will ration what we can and share what we have with you."

"One bag of flour? Didn't they understand the order?"

"Maybe a mix-up, my husband tells me. It happens," Sarah said.

"Or maybe your husband did not order as much as needed, thinking you would have grain here to grind," Louisa said.

"He would have done what he thought was right," I defended. The pain began its rise. I gasped.

"Nothing good comes of this place," Louisa announced. "But we will help with this baby. Then you'll travel better to a new place, one my husband picks that will be good for all of us."

"One small bag," I cried, then gripped Sarah's hand as Catherina, my daughter, arrived without further fuss into the promised land of the Willapa Valley.

The first months of 1856 were marked by the cold, icy winds and incessant rains, but with small signs that we were still blessed, still under the shelter of our Father. I found myself clinging more often to the words of faith that Karl Ruge dispensed in nightly prayers for us all. Wilhelm remained distant, aloof; my husband acted faded and fatigued. I hoped that my leaning on faith wasn't temporary, that perhaps I had learned how to trust even in the midst of disaster. The Israelite tents pitched before they crossed into the Promised Land were reminders of where our shelter truly came from. I waited each day to hear Karl Ruge's gentle teaching, his encouraging words of *"Ja,* by golly, that's right!" that followed a positive comment or small success.

The goat kept my babies alive as Andy drank goat milk and ate the lumps of cheese we made, dripping the rich milk through Mary's petticoat, the cloth as close to muslin as we could find. The other colonists allowed our baby and other young children to drink the milk first, but when Mary's baby, Elizabeth, arrived in February, we rationed ourselves even more to ensure that Mary had enough to eat to make milk for her baby. When she offered to nurse Catherina, too, I whispered gratitude and remembered how An-Gie had found help for Andy. My daughter would have the blessing of a friend.

Wilhelm had yet to head south. He stayed and continued his insistence about Indian troubles, so we could not bring in game. I missed the cows and mules. We could have sent men and cattle into the prairies, where they would have had plenty of grass to consume, but Wilhelm didn't trust that the men watching them would be safe. While I rocked my infant to sleep, I imagined the rich prairies south, where one day Christian and I had hoped to build our home. I remembered walking that prairie, sitting in the quiet of the trees, listening to rain patter onto the needles that carpeted the ground. The silence would be broken only by the cry of a pileated woodpecker or a deer stepping on a fallen branch as it made its way past.

At night, I dreamed of food that I just couldn't swallow.

Potatoes baked in the coals soon lost their flavor. The same meal we'd had for weeks lacked both savor and salt. We caught very few fish now.

Barbara, my mother-in-law, busied herself with her grandchildren. She rocked them, and though she was skinny as a bedpost, she never mentioned how hungry she must have been. I hoped she noticed that I never complained about food, either, except in my sleep.

At least my mother-in-law had brought a trunk with our name on it, and at last I had a fresh change of clothes, a dress with a plain petticoat. Tenderly lifting items from the trunk served as a distraction from the ache in my stomach. I could grab a handful at the waistband of my petticoat, I'd lost so much weight. My old under slip with the ruffles had been stripped long ago into bandages for wounds and washed over and over to manage my monthly flow. My mother had made a baby's quilt and a small dress that might have been used for a christening, if we had such things. We would dedicate the baby to the Lord in time, maybe when we had a church or Wilhelm felt the occasion was right. Karl Ruge, who remained a Lutheran, spoke of christenings, and I thought the idea of it a lovely thing and wished we'd do it as a colony. When this time of want had passed, I'd talk to Christian about it, if he'd hear me. More and more he spent time staring, having little to say, carrying the weight of this starvation into a dark solitude.

Starvation. It was the first time I'd thought the word. Even thinking it made me feel disloyal to my husband.

I smelled each item I pulled from the trunk, imagining my mother's hands on each one, my father's eyes looking over them as she wrapped the child's gown in precious paper I'd use to write to them to tell them of Catherina. Inhaling deeply took away the dizziness I assumed came with the hunger. One last quilt made of red and black squares lay folded at the bottom of the chest. I lifted it out and something dropped on the ground beside my foot. My mother's pearl necklace.

Why had she sent it? Was she telling me that a luxury was acceptable, or that as one matured, one no longer needed such things?

"What's that?" Louisa asked. The woman was like the mist, appearing quiet and cold.

"Something my mother sent me." I folded it back into the quilt, liking the feel of the smooth round stones, perfectly strung. I'd look at it later.

"Your mother," Louisa said.

"Ja?" I prepared to defend.

"She found a way to be...noticed without taking away from anyone else."

A compliment? "We all need to be noticed," I said, stuffing the quilt into the corner of the trunk.

"Ja," she said, looking at her husband who slept, his head bobbed forward onto his chest, his arm wrapped around Aurora, who slept seated beside him. "There you and me, we agree."

———

Through the drizzle of March, a letter arrived in Bruceport on the coast, and Sam Woodard brought it to us. One of Keil's nieces, Fredricka, had married Benjamin Brown, a man she'd met in The Dalles, in the Skamania country east of where we were. The couple had met again in Portland and married January 3, 1856, beginning their new year in the Washington Territory. They'd decided to live separate from the colony, an act I thought very brave for Fredricka. I'd tell her so whenever I got to see her again. Her father, Keil's brother, had remained in the area with them, but when someone commented on his following in his daughter's footsteps, leaving the fold, Wilhelm announced, "He looks for a place for our colony. He's still engaged in the Lord's work."

The Lord's work. The words sounded empty. It seemed all of us were engaged in Wilhelm Keil's work, trying to find a place to serve him. If it were otherwise, we'd be discussing how to move forward here, how to make what the scouts had chosen *here* into the service we'd set out to perform. We'd be hunting and feeding our people. There were a few other English-speaking people besides the Woodards who might come to join us if we demonstrated strength, showed ourselves to be loving and generous rather than stingy with our hope.

"Do you think this time here might change Wilhelm's mind?" I asked Christian. "Maybe seeing that we survive even with little grain and without using ammunition to hunt will help him think differently. Maybe he would bring everyone from Portland after all in the spring."

Christian said nothing.

"We still have the promise of a spring to win him," I said. "Even I long for the prairie and when we can begin building on our place." I patted Catherina's bottom as I rocked her to sleep.

He turned to me then, my husband, his handsome face marked now by puffy skin beneath his eyes, the bones of his cheeks sharp as elbows, the hollows near his mouth as cavernous as caves. He'd lost teeth. So had I. Many of us had. We'd had a last apple peel sometime in January. I couldn't remember. But what he said then was more frightening than any of the physical fears we'd faced and overcome. "There is no future here, Emma. Father Keil is right."

By mid-March, Wilhelm decided the weather was agreeable enough that he would now act according to the letters he'd had Karl Ruge write. There'd been no more messages of Indian attacks and, in fact, we'd not heard of one person dying in the region due to hostile natives. Wilhelm's coat hung on him like a jacket slipped over a chair, waiting for someone to put it on and give it substance. But his voice still boomed.

"I will leave for Portland and from there onto a new life. A place has been found, according to the Bruceport letter. You are all good people," he said then, giving up a small crumb of praise. "Some of you may wish to stay until you can sell your claims, but the rest should be prepared to go with me before the week is out." He'd gathered everyone into the largest of the houses inside the stockade.

Coughs and muffled cries of children answered him first. Then Hans Stauffer said, "I'm staying here. I never once thought the Lord wasn't in this place, and I think we can still make a go of it. With ammunition—no offense, Wilhelm—we can eat well and have skins to put into service."

Adam Schuele nodded agreement. Michael Sr. and the Stauffers did too. "We all believed it was a good place when we found it. Even a woman could plow the soil here, and that means with more hands, we can have more ground planted. We can sell the grain and—"

"To whom?" Wilhelm asked. "And the grain, it's puny. Besides, you'll eat up your own profits."

"Near the bay, a man named White, who is a former Indian agent, he buys property, and those from San Francisco will come north to live here, for the climate. We'll sell to them," Hans said.

"The climate!" Wilhelm laughed at that, a big deep laugh without joy in it. His bushy eyebrows raised, then lowered into a scowl.

I hoped Christian would stand and speak. Here were two men agreeing that remaining was worthy work.

"It is a fine climate in the spring and summer and fall," I said, finally.

Wilhelm turned to me. "It is a place that encourages women to go beyond their position."

"Our Lord never asked women to take a place behind," I said quietly. Louisa gasped. "I know the apostle Paul had many thoughts of how women should be in the worship, but work is worship, too, and we women always served where we were called to work back in Bethel. We worked side by side with men. We do that here, too. But in deciding things, we were silenced, though not by our Lord."

"There are flowers blooming in the woods already," Mary said. I turned to her and smiled at her gift of support. "I would like to see how this landscape changes when the rain is replaced by more of the sun." Her eyes met mine.

"You, Christian," Wilhelm said. "You have your hands full enough with this woman of yours. I will understand your wish to remain here with her."

If Wilhelm couldn't see the good in this place, then we'd just let him leave. Without him here, Christian's waned confidence could return. We'd have a life again, not one focused on what was good for the colony but for our own families.

"And you make my point, Mary Giesy," Wilhelm said. "This place encourages defiance. The landscape itself commands too much. Ve learn to protest against it and mistakenly believe ve must protest against our leaders."

Louisa's eyes watched the floor, but I noticed that her hands folded in prayer had turned her knuckles white. *Does she wish to speak? She won't, not here, not now.*

"Who leaves with me?" Wilhelm asked. "And who wants to remain?"

Peter Klein and several others said then that they would leave. They looked apologetically at Christian as they spoke. One by one the group expressed their wishes until we got to the part of the circle where Christian and I stood. I waited to hear my husband say that we would stay; we'd build our Giesy place upriver. Wilhelm had even approved of it.

"We do," Christian said. "My family and I go with you."

I turned to him. "We can't abandon all you've done here."

He shook his head at me, signaled silence.

"No," I said. "It'll destroy you."

"We do not need to heed the voices of women," Wilhelm said gently. A man who had won could afford to be gracious. "I believe you have made a good choice, Chris. In some things, at least." He turned away from me. "Who else?"

"You can't, Christian," I pleaded. "You can't turn your back on all this. You did well. It is an Eden, it is. How can you say God acted wrongly?"

Wilhelm turned back to me to answer. "In Eden, God asked, 'Where are you?' and 'What have you done?' He punished Eve for being independent, for pushing beyond. God gave the Garden, *ja*, but then He removed people from it. He changed His mind."

"God is unchanging," I hissed at him.

"So then, you have come to accept your role, that God made woman of man and that you bear the sins of what happened. Your punishment will be always as a mother in peril at childbirth, at the mercy of her husband, never to make her own choices. Never," he said. "A good woman knows her place and stays there. She goes where her husband tells her." He turned to Louisa. She smiled at him, but I thought I saw something besides docility in her eyes, something I couldn't name.

I felt my hands grow wet with sweat. Catherina squirmed. *Not now, not now.* This was not about me being submissive; it was about supporting my husband. "Even when God removed them from Eden," I said, "He provided for them. He made clothes for them from animal skins, from the very bounty of the Garden. He was tender and loving and forgiving."

Mary had her arm crooked, holding her infant. She bore a healthy baby here, even with the trials of coming across the plains. "Don't you want your baby to grow up where she was born?" I asked Sebastian. Mary had expressed her wishes openly, but so far Christian's brothers had not.

I turned to *Frau* Giesy, Christian's mother. Surely she'd know that leaving now would be a final defeat for her son. It would deplete him. I pleaded with my eyes. She said nothing.

"Don't you want to finish what you started?" I asked my husband. "You're the one who convinced me of the merits of this clearing. You told me to put aside our own wishes for what God wants of us. Wasn't this colony to be in service to others? Who's to say that there aren't many in need of His love here? The settlers, though not many, might be soil we can plant seed in. Each other." I whispered that last. "We can be salt and light to the world around us if we open our arms wide. Even to each other."

"We have no need of a world so large around us," Wilhelm said. "Such intrusions only bring trials. Wars."

"You sent us out to find an isolated place, to find one where our faith could take root. But there is no isolated place, not really. And now you abandon your own mission? For…comfort?" I said.

"Emma—," Christian said.

"But you said this place was chosen for us, that we were chosen. When I struggled with the rain and mud, you're the one who reminded me."

"There are no people here, Emma," Christian said. He had tears in his eyes. "Father Keil is right. There are none to buy our products, none to bring into the fold. Only us, and we cannot feed ourselves, let alone those around us. Maybe some oystermen on the coast who are lost, maybe to those few we can bring the message of love and compassion, but not if we cannot survive."

"Perhaps we are the lost." I cried now, the words suffering through sobs. "Maybe we are the ones who need someone to reach out to us. Maybe what Wilhelm preaches isn't all that we're to understand. Perhaps this is the very place we were led to, so we could discover Him for ourselves before we attempt to tell others how He is."

"Stop now," Christian said. "It's no good, Emma. No good. It is finished." Christian took me in his arms and held me. His tears on my cheeks mingled with my own.

29

No Salve, Save Love

Word reached us of the death of Jacob Keil, Wilhelm's brother, and then of Fredricka and Benjamin, in an Indian massacre near Skamania on the Columbia. Not three months of marriage living outside the colony, and Fredricka and Benjamin's lives were over. So there had been Indian attacks in the world around us, but we'd been safe in our Giesy stockade.

I thought of our colony in Bethel, how it had been insulated from the world around it, but not for long. We needed that outside world, too, in order to survive. Nonbelievers bought our furniture and wagons, our whiskey and quilts. It was an intricate task blending isolation with protection, melding worldliness with spiritual calm, and Wilhelm must have done it well in the beginning to have so many remain with him for so long.

Or perhaps it was his talk of our deaths that kept us looking into his eyes, finding solace and obedience in his fold.

Had we spent so much time only with one another that young souls like Fredricka and her husband had no skills to make it in that outside world? These were questions I wanted to talk about with Christian but couldn't. I watched him suffer hopelessness, feeling that he had no meaning now, his inability to forgive himself, and worse, how separated he was from those who loved him. These were wounds as deep as if he'd sliced himself with a butchering knife, and I had no salve—save love—to offer to heal the wound.

Christian said what brought us together in the beginning was our wish to be in service, to treat one another with the Golden and the Diamond Rules. I wanted to make Christian's life better than my own, but I couldn't.

He'd committed to taking Wilhelm back to Portland.

A ship arrived, bringing us many sacks of grain. It was the same ship Christian and Wilhelm would leave for Portland on. We baked bread and packed it into the trunks of those heading into Oregon Territory. Christian suggested we prepare to leave too, but Wilhelm hedged. "You've endured this long. A few months more vill make no difference to you, *ja*, Chris? Until the site is ready, Louisa and I will rent a place in Portland, and when ve find the colony is ready, ve send for you. It's unfortunate, this kind of…separation," he said. "A better site would have prevented these adjustments needed now. *Ja*, that's so, Chris?" My husband nodded his head as Keil patted his back. It didn't look like brotherly love.

I seethed for my husband. Wilhelm didn't even want us with him while we waited. He treated us like children sent to the back of the room for our misbehavior while everyone else played outside. We'd been asked to wait until *Herr* Keil determined the perfect place…when we were already there. I could hardly stand it.

"We won't leave now either, then," Andreas, Christian's father, said. "No reason to find yet another place to wait while Wilhelm seeks out a new site." Sebastian Giesy nodded agreement. So at least I'd have company waiting. I smiled at that wish, when once I'd only wanted to be left alone.

"The rest of us will travel together for safety," Wilhelm said. "It was good we saved ammunition."

I wondered if Christian would decide that protecting Wilhelm would still be reason to go to Portland with him now when his parents said they'd wait in Willapa. Or would he think risking us, Andy and the baby and me, on this trip south might not be wise?

"You stay with my parents, here, Emma. You and the children."

"No. I'm sorry that I am always saying no to you, husband, but we need you here if we're here. Wilhelm does not ask his wife to remain away from him while he waits for their new home to be readied."

"I'll come back for you. I need to do this, Emma. It is the least that I can do for Wilhelm, considering." He gave me the look that said he'd bear no more dissent from me, so I waited until evening and asked him to walk with me to the far corner of the stockade area. Willie's grave overlooked us from the hill beyond. I carried Catherina in the board on my back, and Andy chased field mice before us. Dogs fought over a deer antler shed the previous winter that lay among needles and leaves. They growled and barked in the distance, and I wrapped my shawl around me against the evening chill. We hadn't had rain all day. White trillium bloomed on the forest floor. A spider busied itself with a web against the cedar's bark.

"Don't you see?" I said. "Wilhelm could go alone and let everyone wait here now that we have grain. No one needs to be uprooted while he finds the perfect place. But the truth is, he will take a group with him, and then while he waits in Portland, he'll disrupt them again, send others out as he did the scouts while he waits in luxury until they've built his *gross Haus,* his grand house," I said, repeating it in English.

"I doubt there are many grand houses for rent in Portland," Christian said.

"He isn't thinking about the colony's needs, not now. He's thinking of his own. He talks about his sacrifice with the death of Willie, but it was he who said we should leave Bethel, leave the simple yet contented lives we had there. He bears no responsibility for the hardships we've endured for the sake of the colony. He might accept your protection while he travels south, but he doesn't need to travel at all, and he doesn't seem all that concerned for those of us left here."

"It's a terrible thing to lose a child."

"It is! But Willie died in Bethel, not as a result of his sacrifice to come here. And think of what the colonists endured traveling with that hearse. That journey was made harder because of Wilhelm's…tending. He didn't think anything of the challenges others faced because of his orders. And now he will take us away from what we believed was God's calling for the colony and for us. Can this be right, husband?"

Andy chased a dog and rolled with the puppy belonging to one of the arrivals of Klein's train. Christian dug in his ear, so I knew he was thinking. "I know you didn't come here to please yourself, Christian. You came because of what you believed was good for all of us. That's true leadership, it is. Being faithful to your beliefs for the good of everyone."

"Indeed." He sighed. "I'll be back, and then we'll make our way together to the new colony. My father will look after you until then."

"You see? You think of us, of who remains behind. He doesn't. He thinks only of himself."

Christian shook his head. That pain of helplessness settled in the lines of his eyes. "That's not true, Emma. He's a good man, has always been so. This is…this is an unusual time. New nails have been pounded into his life, and like us, they stand out a little. This is something I can do, to help now. I need to do that." I pouted, I knew. "What we did here, Emma, is done."

My husband was falling into Wilhelm's way. Soon he'd want me to walk behind him on that path again. I could do that, and would, if it kept Christian from seeing himself as a failure, this place only as a sign of lost dreams, just a memory of a clearing he once made in the wild. "If Wilhelm was a true follower of our Lord," I said, "he'd be preparing other leaders now to take his place. He'd begin to trust others and not only his own visions. I thought he'd chosen you, but he won't relinquish control. But you would. You're the better leader, Christian."

"You say this because you want your own way, Emma."

His words stung, but I let them sink in to find their truth before I answered. "We are all entitled to want things to go well with us. That's not un-Christian. But what I want most of all is for you to believe in what you're doing. I confess I don't hold Wilhelm in the esteem you do, so you're right to sift through what I say about him. Nothing he's done since he arrived has made me trust him more. If you go with him, I'll follow you, Christian. But I want to follow the husband who saw the possibilities here, not the man who walks with the slumped shoulders of defeat. You changed my mind, husband; now I want to change yours."

———

What do men do while they wait? They whittle. They plow. They build. They talk of the future. At least that's what Christian's brothers and parents did, working together to finish a roof or push with their adzes to smooth a wooden doorway. They considered gristmill sites as though they might stay on here along the Willapa River. The plow my in-laws brought on their ship turned soil. They planted oats, as Christian's father thought it had a better chance than wheat of maturing in the cool climate. I wondered why they bothered when it was clear Christian accepted Wilhelm's decision that the Willapa Valley was a mistake. He intended to follow *Herr* Keil to wherever it was he might go. Christian even traveled with him, left us here to…wait. There'd be no one to harvest the oats.

At least we had food now, with the shipment of grain and Wilhelm no longer limiting the use of ammunition. Hans stayed with us, and so did his father, who had arrived with Keil and Christian and the hearse. All the scouts were accounted for now except Joseph Knight. For the rest of us, we simply waited for the perfect place to go to, the one Wilhelm would find for us. Except for me.

Louisa's last words before they left stayed with me. "We women are asked to support our husbands," she said. "Even when it may not be the best decisions that they make."

"Are you talking about our living on fish all winter while your husband prevented us from hunting?"

She straightened her shoulders. "That too." She tickled Catherina's chin, and my daughter jerked in my arms, flailing to reach out to Louisa. "She reminds me of Aurora at that age, all eyes and mouth, so ready for living." I nodded. *Louisa talks as though we might be…equals, even friends.* She reached for my daughter, who went willingly to her. "I referred to our coming here and then leaving here," she said. "I can see why your husband chose this place and how you found contentment here."

"You see contentment?" That wasn't a word I would use to describe my current state, but I had found gratitude here. Peacefulness did come floating to me when I walked the prairie, when I huddled in the trees to think, when Mary and her family arrived with the Klein train, when we'd worked together to bring in our meager grain, when Catherina had been born healthy and strong. A double rainbow colored the sky.

She continued. "I would be content to stay here, to walk daily to my son's grave. I'll miss not being able to do that. And here," she looked up at me, paused. "Here, the weight of decisions would not lie only on my husband's shoulders but on all the men's, especially your husband's shoulders. It would relieve my husband of much strain." Her dark coal eyes stared into mine. "When things did not go well here, my husband wouldn't need to bear all the weight. There is something good in that."

Louisa knelt and fussed at the mud caked on Aurora's skirt. All I could see was the white scalp that lined the part in her graying hair. "It is a sadness that either of them bears it," she said. "They follow our Lord, and yet they refuse to let Him carry their burdens."

I'd never heard Louisa express such thoughts, nor any colony woman for that matter. Did she question her husband's choices? Yet she followed him.

It didn't have to be that way for me, for us. Why should Christian bear the responsibility for this failed venture? It was only a failure if we defined it so, not because our Lord did. It was another part of a journey, not something so disastrous nothing good could come from it.

"Maybe we refuse to let Him carry our burdens too," I said. She nodded, and it came to me that if this landscape was truly what we'd been led to, there had to be a way to make our being here successful despite Wilhelm's pronouncement about it. I didn't know how that could be, but for the first time since my husband said we'd be leaving, I felt light as the orange butterfly that landed only for a moment on Louisa's shoulder.

———

Sarah had asked for goat's milk in exchange for eggs, and I carried it to her with Catherina on my back. With Andy in Mary's good hands back at the stockade, I made my way through the spring forest to the landing, walking the nearly dried-up path beside the Willapa. There had to be something we could do here, something that might intrigue Christian enough to make him remain. It had to be a new thought, a new way. I remembered hearing of the Rappist Colony back in Pennsylvania discovering silkworms as a way to contribute to colony funds. Maybe mulberry trees would grow here, and we could become a western silk-growing group. In Bethel, it was furniture-building and wagon-making and Golden Rule Whiskey that brought in money to serve the colony. Those needed people to purchase them, and as Wilhelm noted, we had few people here able to do that.

If the whole colony couldn't be supported in this valley, perhaps a small portion could. That smaller group could contribute to the larger group wherever we ended up. No, wherever *they* might end up. Wilhelm saw our success here as a challenge to him; that's why he twisted my husband into the ground beneath his boots like the remains of old tobacco. I couldn't stand by and let that happen.

If Christian moved us south, if we followed Wilhelm, my husband would forever carry the stigma of failure. *A man's heart deviseth his way: but the LORD directeth his steps.* I had to trust that proverb.

I reached Woodard's Landing, and Sarah motioned for us to sit. She lifted Catherina in her cradle board and braced her upward at the corner of her chair. I was tired and not expecting answers to the voiceless prayers lifted while I walked. *Show me the way. Show me the way.*

A warm fire crackled in the fireplace, and beside Sarah on the rough plank table laid an open book. *Shakespeare,* a word I sounded out in English. Karl Ruge had such a set of books that he'd brought with him, and through the waiting months stuffed together in the stockade houses, he often read to us using different voices for all the parts. We'd scoffed when he said all the roles had once been played by men. Wilhelm snubbed books and said there was no book but the Bible with anything to offer. Still, he listened when Karl read.

"*The Merry Wives of Windsor,*" Sarah said when I picked up the book. It smelled musty and damp, but most things did here.

"What makes the wives merry?"

"I'm not sure," Sarah said. "He talks about oysters, so it's fitting for this Willapa place." She laughed, then quoted, " 'Why, then the world's mine oyster / Which I with sword will open.' I think it will have a happy ending."

"Oysters are so hard to open he needs a sword?" I said. I'd eaten one or two oysters at Woodards'. Christian had opened the shell, then dug around and removed the meat. He opened his mouth, and the slimy white strip slipped down his throat. We'd boiled the remainder, as the oysters didn't easily give themselves up from their safe little shells. I found them tasty but not particularly filling.

"I think it means the world is rich and wonderful and can be tasted like a good oyster, and the character in the play plans to do that with his power, his might. The Californians must think a little like that. They order so many oysters and pay so much for them."

"This is part of Shakespeare's writing?"

She shook her head. "Our oysters here are as good as those anywhere in the world—even from the Orient, my husband says. I always thought it amazing that right in the middle of those ugly-looking oysters grow pearls. They grow out of irritations, things that don't belong, and yet they make themselves a part of the oyster. I like those little treasures in a story."

I thought of my mother's pearls. I had no idea they came from the misshapen, craggy shells called oysters, oysters that grew just downstream.

"Our Willapa oysters don't offer up lovely pearls," Sarah told me. "They're dull in color and uneven. Not nice and round. But they're pretty to me." She pulled a slender strand up over her collar. "See? They're not perfect but each is unique. Each one individual. I like that better than the perfect ones that I've seen that all look alike."

Unique. Formed out of irritation. I asked her to tell me more.

"They grow them in beds, like farmers do their wheat," she continued. She unwound Catherina from her board and held her firmly at her shoulder, patting her back as she talked. "Only in ocean water and in the tide flats. It takes a hardy soul to be an oysterman, someone who can work in the wet and up to their knees in mud or out on the skiffs, yanking and raking up clusters of shells, and yet can wait. They have to keep guard against predators, just like farmers have to keep birds from their fields. That's what my husband says."

What kind of predator would harm an oyster? Their shells looked like long tongues with bumps, and if what Sarah said was right, they were impossible to get inside of without a knife or some large rock to break them open. What could harm something so hard and well defended?

"People rob oyster beds," she said. "And there are green things in the ocean that can kill them. Things you'd never expect. They have to be tended. Everything has something wanting to destroy it.

"Only the faithful watchman can prevent it," I said.

Sarah nodded. "In San Francisco restaurants and saloons, raw oysters sell for one dollar apiece on the half shell. Same as what an egg costs there. Gold miners think nothing of celebrating their new wealth with extravagant dinners that always include fresh raw oysters."

Was it really just like farming? We Bethelites knew about farming. Perhaps the Willapa Colony could remain here yet. We could earn our way to repay what Wilhelm had invested in us. Our market didn't need to live close to us; we could ship our wares. Willapa could become the world that was "mine oyster" for those who chose to stay in the place the scouts had staked out. We'd simply have to learn something new from this Edenlike place.

"Should you go alone?" Karl Ruge asked me. He wore a dark suit coat that made his white attachable collar look all the whiter. He folded back a shock of silver hair with his hands as he talked. During all the rains and time of mud, Karl had always looked tidy, and he'd done his own wash, never asking any of the women to do it for him. "Maybe you should wait until Christian comes back. This would be better, by golly?"

"I need to find out about oyster farming. A dollar apiece. Think of that."

"For fresh ones, *ja*, shipped across the Bay and into the ocean. But most go for a penny, boiled on the streets of mining towns, or so I'm told. It is not a gold strike, Emma Giesy. This is not an easy thing you think of."

"It's farming. We know how to do that," I said. "We know about planting and tending and praying over the harvest."

"The oysters must be planted and grown," Karl said. "That means more investment. And learning how to replant, to not overharvest. In-vestments in ships to send them south. One still needs to find a way to live while the oystermen wait. All that will cost money, Emma."

"But if we were successful, we could pay off what the land has cost us and even contribute to the new colony when Wilhelm decides where that will be. We can still be a part of it but…separate." Oyster farming would make us unique, but I knew that was a word that also meant "extraordinary," a concept perhaps too close to "prideful" for Karl Ruge's simple ways.

"It is still not good that you travel by yourself. Your in-laws would not approve."

Karl was right about that. Barbara and Andreas, Christian's parents, had raised their eyebrows at me on more than one occasion since Christian left with Wilhelm: when I spoke up in a gathering, when I went alone to see Sarah, when I acted like myself.

"Do you have a reason to go to Bruceport?" I asked Karl.

He rubbed his white chin hair. "The post office there is where Wilhelm said for mail to come from Bethel. There and Portland. I should see if he's sent us word of where we are to find him or if there are letters from Bethel that need answering."

Karl hadn't gone with Wilhelm. I was curious about that, though it was none of my affair. He'd begun teaching the children of those who had decided to wait until Keil actually found a new place rather than adjust once again for a few weeks or months and then move to the more permanent site. Maybe Karl felt useful here.

The weather turned balmy, as it usually did in April, and with men able to hunt now, the cries of hungry children no longer pushed at us. Karl instructed out under the trees, using sticks and hard red berries to teach math and the beauty of the landscape to teach English. He said it was the finest schoolhouse he'd ever taught in.

Being in the Willapa Valley may not have been luxurious, but it was familiar, and with the rain ceasing it was gloriously pleasant. Perhaps Karl, too, wanted to move only once more and would take in the bounty of this place before choosing something else.

"*Ja*, by golly. I have reason to go to Bruceport," he said finally. "To get the mail."

"Christian might have sent me a letter. His parents would understand my wish to go there with Sam Woodard and be unconcerned if you came too, Karl. We'll do this together."

———

The Willapa ran full and wide, but I could see both shorelines, a comfort to me. I took deep breaths and made myself exhale so as not to get dizzy. Sam Woodard and Karl handled the oars and the sails. I could hang on tight to my son and daughter. Oystering would mean more time on water, more time *in* water, I realized. I'd need to have the children stay with their grandparents so I could help with the harvest, or maybe we'd need to move closer to the oyster beds so I could learn to open the shells or prepare them for shipping. *Closer to the water?* In Bruceport, I was told, the tide came in under the boardwalks. What could be closer than that? There'd be water everywhere, seagulls chattering to us every day, and not just Charlie appearing every now and then for scraps.

I took a deep breath. If this would be a way to bring my husband's confidence back, then overcoming my fear of water would be worth it. *Show me the path. Show me the path.*

Long-handled rakes leaned against log sheds as we eased closer toward the bay. Low flat boats, skiffs Sam called them, piled high with oyster shells, moved across the water toward the open sea and a large ship waiting there. Near a cluster of buildings, native women bent over piles of shells, sifting and sorting, their scarves tight around their heads. They stood and stared as we slipped by. I waved. They didn't wave back. Where the tide had gone out, beyond the buildings, I watched more native women stand in the low tidewater beside their baskets. They looked as though they walked on water, the mud slithered with a film that reflected them as they worked. Stacks of discarded oyster shells pocked the shoreline like a chain of small white mountains.

We anchored our boat, and carrying Andy, Sam splashed toward shore. I lifted my skirts and followed. I asked Sam if he could recommend an oysterman that I might talk with.

"You didn't come to get the mail?" he said.

"That, too, but I also want to talk oysters." I sat to put my shoes back on.

"Lots of folks do," he said. "They'll be nearing the end of their harvest soon. Never eat an oyster in a month that doesn't have an *r* in it," he advised. He scanned the wooden fronts of oystering warehouses. "I'd try that last place there, not far from the mouth. Supposed to be an American from San Francisco. He might answer your questions."

"Joe Knight! You're here? You've been here all along?"

"Not all the time," he said sheepishly. "Now let me answer your questions. They're middens, those discarded shells," he told Andy, who pointed at the piles of nubby shells. "Middens are what's left after we cull the good ones and then take out the meat to dry. The Indians do it that way mostly, drying the meat for use later. We like them fresh, of course. Earn more money that way." He pointed with that finger in the air and winked. He lived in a small log house set with a walkway to the beach, and he had opened his arms wide to Karl Ruge when we found him. To me he tipped his hat, shook Andy's little hand, and smiled at Catherina. It wasn't until I heard his German-accented English and saw that finger pointing that I knew for sure who he was.

"How long have you been here?" I asked.

"This time? About six months."

"You never went back to Bethel," I said. I bounced the baby on my hip. "You left the Willapa River but never returned. People wonder where you are. You need to let your brother know you're all right."

"I started to," he said. "But the two of us split after we worked on a bridge." His blond hair poked out from under his narrow-brimmed hat. He had a tiny mustache but no beard now at all. He still poked with his fingers when he talked. "I went to San Francisco and then came back. This was as far as I got."

"But why didn't you let us know? Why not return to help us?"

"*Ja,*" he said, looking down. "I wasn't sure colonists would understand my journeying into San Francisco. Then once the weather changed and I decided to come back, I thought maybe oystering would be a good thing for me, better than chopping trees so tall you can't see their tops without lying flat on your back. I was going to help you build through the winter. But I stopped here." His face colored. "I'd worked in California, so I had a little money and invested in an oyster claim. Right here," he said, waving his arm. Apparently, right at the mouth of the Willapa River lay a natural bed of oysters. "It has everything I need. Even people to show me how to do it. The Indians, mostly."

"You had no scares of massacres?" I asked.

He shook his head. "They might have been scared at what a bad oysterman I was. The women laughed at a man gathering oysters at first, but I notice lots of white men do it. We float along in the skiffs dragging our tongs until we stumble onto something that feels right. Then we grab with those tongs and, hand over hand, pull up whatever we've caught onto: rocks and broken shells and mud and clusters of oysters. We sort through it until we find just what we're looking for. The pearl, the best oysters. We dry or ship the rest for boiling, then discard the shells."

"The pearls here are not as large or perfect, I hear," Karl Ruge said.

Joe nodded agreement. "Perfection isn't my aim. Never was. Living full, that's what I wanted. I still share," he said. He sounded defensive just a bit. "I give back. Don't have to belong to a colony to do that."

Karl nodded.

"The Indian women say we should put the shells back into the water," Joe said, returning to a safer subject. "As a protected place for the young oysters to grow up in. No one else does it, though. It's hard work but I like it."

I wondered what he'd say when I proposed he needed a partner.

———

On the boat ride back, my mind raced with possibilities. Here, Christian could find meaning and good work; here, he could perhaps forgive himself for being human, for doing the best he could, though all hadn't turned out as he'd once hoped. But how to convince him that such a move could be a statement of faith?

"You are in deep thought, *Frau* Giesy," Karl said.

I nodded. "I want to find a way to help my husband see oystering as a buttress to his faith. And I want to be sure I'm not making my own religion up, as I sometimes think *Herr* Keil has, while I wrangle with how we should be in this western place."

"There is an old Norse word for religion that translates in the English as 'tying again,' " he said. He gazed out across the water, the silence broken only by the swish of the boat cutting through the water. "Somehow I think those Norsemen must have realized that life unravels us at times. It is the way of things. It is our faith, our religion, I believe, that then binds us together."

" 'Begin to weave / God provides the thread,' " I said. "My mother gave that German proverb to me." It came to me then what that proverb meant: that life is a weaving with our fine threads being broken and stretched. It's our calling to keep weaving, find ways to tie things together again.

30

A Pearl Unique

"The band played in Portland," Christian said. "March 22, 1856, our first performance in all these years."

"You played?"

He shook his head no, his enthusiasm apparently coming from the association with the players, not anything he did himself. "Jonathan played."

"You saw my brother? Is he well?" I clutched at his arm. "I wish he'd come back with you."

"He seemed content to be with the band and those who wintered in Portland. They played at the request of someone named Grimm, the same one who told Wilhelm about the apples. He sold us 256 bushels of oats at forty cents a bushel and 165 bushels of wheat at seventy cents each. They can begin grinding flour, and best of all, I've brought apples and more flour to tide us over until we leave. They'll take the grain to Aurora Mills; that's what Wilhelm calls the land they purchased. He's named it for Aurora."

Not for Louisa, I thought.

"It's a rolling piece of prairie south of Portland. Many acres. It already has a gristmill on it. Their neighbors are from French Prairie, named for all the retired Frenchies of Hudson's Bay and their Indian wives."

"So we can keep the grist stones your parents brought here, then."

Christian looked puzzled. "We won't be here, so why would we leave them?" He looked around. "In fact, I wonder why they've wasted time plowing up the soil and planting oats here."

"Have they already begun to build Wilhelm's *gross Haus* at Aurora Mills?" I asked.

He looked away.

"I suspect Keil and company wait in Portland in a nice warm house where food is plenty and he can hold court—I mean preach—to many, while my brother and others like him build his house for him. My own brother who doesn't even make a way to see me or his niece and nephew. Well, so be it." I brushed at my apron, though I saw nothing there.

"You can see him when we join them in Oregon, *Liebchen*," Christian said.

"I don't plan to go to Oregon, Christian. And when I tell you what I've found and who agrees with me, you won't want to leave here either."

"Emma…"

———

We took our small boat to our claim, seven miles up the Willapa from Woodard's Landing. I wanted a pleasant place to talk to Christian, and he was willing to take me to the site he'd once picked for us to build on. He was saying good-bye to the landscape, he said; I was beginning to say hello. We stood there now, overlooking the four logs we'd left last fall to outline the house. They'd been pushed and tossed in different directions. Maybe from stout winds. I hoped not from high water or flooding. Andy whined to be carried on his father's shoulders, and he did, riding high while reaching for the leaves of trees. I held Catherina in my arms. We ate biscuits with butter, a luxury, then sat on a quilt my mother had sent in the trunk.

It was now or never. "The scouts were right, husband. The Willapa Valley will provide everything we need if we're patient and are willing to accept not the perfect pearl but one that is distinctive."

"Indeed."

"Karl thinks that oystering can work," I said, after telling him about Joe Knight and our trip to Bruceport. "He's willing to remain here to make it happen and teach any children who stay here too."

"Karl is? He's so…loyal to Wilhelm. Always has been. And Joe…" He shook his head.

"It isn't disloyal to follow your heart," I said. "Karl didn't go with Wilhelm to Portland because he believes there is something here worth staying for. Everything about it here, except the rainy winters, is an Eden. We'd appreciate the blooms and beauty less if we had nothing to contrast it with, and therein lies the joy of the rainy winter months, the dark heavy clouds that shadow our days and promise sunshine in due time. I never thought I'd say such a thing, but I mean it, Christian. I do."

"Wilhelm is right, though. There is still no market here for whatever we might produce."

"But you were right too. We're on rivers and near oceans, so we can ship things to markets." He shook his head, still not convinced. I tried another tactic. "It doesn't mean that Wilhelm was wrong about this place. It just means others can listen and hear something else. Wilhelm has done that. He's decided to go somewhere else. Neither of you made a mistake. Each is free to make other choices. We just have to make a change in what we thought we'd do. Less grain farming and more… oyster farming."

"Emma, I—"

"At least until we get field crops established. We can cherish what we have, still be a part of the colony if you wish, but separated. Maybe the way Nineveh was back in Missouri."

"Nineveh grew just a few miles down the road. We'll be a hundred and thirty miles distant from Aurora Mills. It'll make decision-making difficult."

"Not if we're really…separate." Andy draped his arms around his father's neck as the child stood behind him. "He missed you terribly," I said, then continued. "We can pay off the land claims with what we sell. And maybe, just maybe, living communally isn't what we were called to do. We can still be faithful to our beliefs even if we don't have a common fund."

Christian shook his head. "What beliefs are there except to follow Wilhelm's way of serving? I have trouble seeing anything else."

"But that's it, Christian. Maybe, like Wilhelm, you too are vision-ary and you can see things differently if you can stop blaming yourself for what happened here. We don't need to separate our hearts from the other colonists nor from our neighbors to be in service. We can look at what our neighbors might need. Your recruitment brought in good people like Karl Ruge, but most were people who just made the colony bigger and produced more work. It didn't bring people in who had needs that we could meet. We tended one another, but isn't giving to those truly hurting what service is all about?"

He dug at his ears. He was thinking.

"Oystering, if we're successful, would allow us to be good neigh-bors to the colonists and to those here."

I decided to be still. My father said to sell a wagon, one needed to sing its virtues and then be quiet and listen to how the customer would then tell him why he needed that very wagon, how he had a big family and could use a sturdy vehicle, or how his wife was sickly and needed one that handled the ruts well. The rest would be simple.

Christian stayed silent a very long time. I'd probably strained my threads in trying to describe what I meant, in trying to tie things, again. He stayed quiet too long.

"We could share the costs and profits of those at Willapa, maybe send a percentage each year on to Aurora Mills. Tithe our harvest. But there won't need to be *one* leader with all the weight of the success or failure on his shoulders. We can decide as a family what to do, or as a group of families. We don't need to wait for just one ruler."

A seagull, probably not Charlie, flew overhead with several others. "Bread, Papa. I want to throw him bread," Andy said. I overlooked the fact that my son asked his father and not me for bread and handed a biscuit to Christian who gave it to Andy. The child threw up bread-crumbs and squealed in delight when a bird swooped down to catch a crumb in midair.

"Even the seagulls adapt to new opportunities," I said. "You know Wilhelm will never let another lead while he's alive, and he won't pre-pare another to take his place. So we should listen to our hearts, listen to what we think we're hearing and follow that."

Christian played with a long strand of grass, running it through his wide fingers. He watched Andy's interest in the root of a cedar tree. Catherina had decided to nap.

"We came to serve people, *Liebchen*. Wilhelm was right about that. This place has no people to recruit or bring into the fold, none to help prepare for the last days ahead."

"We don't bring them in, God brings them. Didn't you tell me this once? And we don't have to be so separated from our neighbors. Look at all those oystermen. Look at Joe. I think he feels a bit guilty for having left us. If we join him, you could help relieve that. There are dozens of people suffering in silence. We might hear them if we weren't listening to the chop of trees building the colony for the sake of...the colony. We can't just worry about our little group, Christian. How else can we be salt and light?"

"Father Keil sent us west to protect us from the world."

"Maybe we'll best prepare for the end times by behaving as though we can't control their coming. Because we can't. We can only love one another, trust we're not alone here. We can be good neighbors to people like Sarah and Sam. Remember how the Chehalis offered us hides and house-building help? Perhaps there are things we can do for those people whose lives are changing with these treaties and with us being here. Perhaps living in the world instead of apart from it will make us better servants in the end."

"My parents will want to go with Wilhelm. They've followed him their whole lives. From Pennsylvania to Missouri—"

"If you said you were staying and that you wanted something a little different from what we had at Bethel, I think they'd remain. They've already finished the log house they started for Mary and Sebastian. They're even going to roof it." He raised his eyebrows in surprise. "They trusted your judgment. So does Karl. So do I."

He leaned over Catherina, brushed a spider making its way toward her neck. "You think I can be an oysterman." He shook his head. "I can't believe Joe Knight is. He never seemed the type to branch out on his own."

"We never know what we'll do," I said, "when challenged. We're like oysters sometimes, I think. Trying to stay deep in the mud, out of the way, but then we get selected. But we're not alone, even in the worst of storms."

"I doubt Joe was 'challenged' by some storm to become an oysterman," he said.

"How can you know?" I asked him. "There he was all that time, and we didn't know it because we never ventured far outside our own little world."

He rose to follow Andy. He lifted the child onto his shoulders once again. He stood above me, and I shaded my eyes with my hand. "We can't know for certain about anything," I continued. "We listen, try to do our best to help our families and our neighbors, that's all we can do. Here, Andy. A little more bread for you to toss." I handed it to him and Christian set him down. I picked up the picnic things, started to carry them to the boat. "I'd like to ask Jonathan to come stay with us. At least make the offer. He might not come, of course."

"*Ja*," he said. "All we ever wanted to do was to take care of those we loved. It was all we did, we scouts. You included, Emma."

"Love's the thread. Then listen," I said. I put my finger to my lips. We could hear the wind through the treetops, the soft breathing of a baby, the shouts of a child racing a seagull, the rush of the river water behind us.

"I like what I hear," he said.

"We can go with you to the coast, maybe sell the claim," I ventured. "Or we can build our house, and I'll remain with the children while you're oystering."

"I don't like being separated from you."

"Seasons," I said. "There'll be seasons when we're apart, as when we were first married, but I won't long for you so much because I know you'll be doing something you've chosen to do, not something you do because you felt yourself a failure."

"You think we Giesys and Stauffers and Schaefers can survive not as colonists but as friends and family, together? Neighbors, too?"

"It's a path that has meaning, Christian. I truly believe that."

"I listen to you," Christian said. He reached his arm around me, pulled me close.

"Does that mean you'll stay?" I sank into his eyes, as inviting as a warm bath in winter. I was sure I knew the answer.

———

Christian woke me in the morning. "I do my seventy-six pushing-ups, and then we go down to see Joe Knight," he said. "I want to know that this is part of what was to happen here, not just the hardships, but the unexpected turn of events." For the first time since Wilhelm had arrived in November, my husband had a sparkle in his eye. I recalled a psalm where the speaker asked that he not be ashamed in God's sight for what he had done, and God answered. So He'd answered again. I nearly cried watching my husband lift and lower himself on the moss-covered floor. He did seventy-seven. "One for good measure."

We took our boat with the small white sail on it out onto the Willapa River, heading for the bay, and worked our way around the point to where Bruceport thrived. The wind and tide worked with us. Karl Ruge came along. I held my breath as the boat lifted onto a swell, then slapped down hard. Working with oysters would surely take the fear of water from me. Familiarity breeds freedom, I decided.

On this trip, the children stayed with their grandparents so I could concentrate on the details Joe could tell us about this work we were stepping into. I wanted to listen and look and smell what would become the way of our lives.

A Chehalis woman ran the trading post right on the bay. Her husband had died the year Andy was born. "Drowned in the Wallacut River, Captain Russell did," Joe Knight told us. "But in 1851 he introduced the first Shoalwater oysters from here to the San Francisco merchants. We can thank him for that and for what we do because of it."

"I'll thank the Provider of the oysters," Christian said.

Joe dropped his eyes, ran his hands through his thick blond hair. "*Ja,*" he said. "Him too."

So on this day at the Willapa Bay, Joe Knight and Christian and Karl discussed how they would work together as oystermen. I watched as oyster boats came alongside schooners out in the bay and men handed up their baskets of oysters. I counted twenty-eight boats, twenty-one scows, and thirteen canoes coming and going out to the huge schooner. "Some of the holds have timber in them too," Joe told us. "It's a lucrative place with gold from the forests and ocean here for the mining."

Christian would stay with Joe and work the oyster beds; Karl's investment came from money he had saved on his own as a teacher before he became a part of the colony. His contribution would pay wages for workers, and one day, the children and I would work in the oyster beds, filling up baskets to be taken out to schooners.

I'd remain on our Giesy place once we finished our log home. I'd be within a few hours' travel downriver to see Mary and Christian's parents, less time than that when the paths were dry and the mule surefooted. I could see Sarah and be there for her when she had need of help to deliver her baby. I'd make quilts again. We'd get sheep and weave when I wasn't plowing or milking or planting oats and peas.

The wind whipped Christian's hair as we made our way back toward the landing. His hair looked thinner, but his thick reddish beard framed his face. We'd spend the night at the stockade and then move the few things we had to the site he'd chosen for us long before, seven miles up the Willapa. We'd live in that tent a few more weeks, until his father, brothers, and nephews helped finish our house at last.

"I hope during the winter months if I have to be gone, that you and the children will stay with my parents or with Sebastian and Mary," Christian said.

"If it will make you feel better, we will," I told him.

Christian helped any of those who'd stayed behind to make their way to Aurora Mills, the site where Wilhelm would soon take up residence. As he talked with his family, his brothers and his parents, he found each wanted to remain in the place Christian had chosen, the place all the scouts had selected. "What is the likelihood that all nine men—and one woman—would be duped by the devil?" Christian's father said. "This must be a good place."

I didn't suggest that he used a poor standard, since hundreds of Bethelites were scattered throughout the Oregon Territory because of *one* man. Had we all been duped? Or was God still in charge of the colony, even our Willapa splinter, no matter what we humans chose to do?

Michael Schaefer Sr. and his son and children did stay. Even John Genger and the Becks, who came out with Wilhelm, presented their decisions at a gathering at the stockade that June. The Stauffers remained too. The tents of those leaving were all rolled up and ready to board the ship that would take them to the Columbia River and the Oregon Territory and Keil.

"We don't do it for you, Christian," his father said. "Though we are glad it is you who found this site first and put your sweat into building us a house. We stay because of the promise here. Yes, it will be hard to clear the ground, but what else do we have to do in this life? Yes, it will be difficult to build more houses, but we have many hands now. And there is something…pleasant about living close but not so close to one another as we did in Bethel. We can build a school and gather for worship. We depend on one another for help. We'll look to the Lord for guidance instead of just Wilhelm."

"We might have baptisms and communion," Karl Ruge said.

"Without Father Keil, we have no leader for those," Mary said.

"We didn't do it when we did have a leader," Sebastian reminded her. He didn't even seem surprised that his wife spoke up in this gathering of women and men.

"*Ja,* by golly. We'll celebrate the sacraments as they did in the early church," Karl Ruge said, clapping his hands. "We'll share the duties and the joys together."

"We can begin with my Elizabeth and your Catherina," Mary said. "We have a christening to look forward to. Maybe we can invite Sarah and Sam."

Christian then brought out a basket of oysters, and the men with their knives cut the membranes to open the shells. "Show me," I asked Christian. "I want to be able to do that."

He stood behind me and placed his warm hands around mine. I could feel the heat of his chest as he leaned against my back. Then with the knife I held, his hand clasped over mine, we sawed back and forth until the oyster shell cracked and I could twist it open with the tip of my knife. Inside was the white flesh of the oyster, moist and lying like a shimmering jewel on the half shell. And in the corner was a surprise: the tiniest gem, a pearl.

It was more the color of earth than ivory.

"Indeed. Did you know that pearls come from irritations, from something like sand gritting its way into the oyster, and it wants to get it out? It forms this shell within a shell," Christian said. "A little protective covering to keep the sand from doing damage to the oyster. In the end, it gets picked up for its singular beauty and becomes more a part of the world than it ever imagined." He was already becoming an expert on his new calling.

I had known. But this first pearl my husband gave me marked a new beginning in our lives, one I'd thought might never come about. My husband leaned on his faith and his family just a little more than he ever had before.

Best of all, when I later placed that little pearl on the thread of the dozen pearls of my mother's and hung it openly at my neck, I knew it would always stand out as unique and singular, though clearly, it belonged.

Discussion Questions

1. How would you characterize the role of women within the Bethel Colony? What changes occurred in the Willapa Valley that redefined the role of the women there? Who or what brought about those changes?

2. It's said that feeling unique and being acknowledged for that uniqueness is a prerequisite for a healthy sense of self. Do you agree or disagree? Can you identify something that is unique about you? Has that gift/talent/behavior ever been noticed by others? Is receiving appreciation for that recognition an act of vanity? What was unique about Emma?

3. After their marriage, why didn't Emma attempt to go with her husband on his recruiting into Kentucky or other places in the Southwest? If she had, would that have changed her desire to go west with the scouts?

4. Was Emma's decision to travel to the west with the scouts an act of love for her husband or the result of her own wish to be independent of the colony? Was she a scout?

5. What were some of Wilhelm Keil's strengths as a leader? How did he hold so large a colony together for such a long time? What were his flaws as a leader?

6. What did Wilhelm and Emma have in common? Did those qualities tend to help them or get in the way of what they said they wanted for themselves and their families?

7. What were some of Emma's growing pains? Was leaving her husband while they were building that first winter her only

choice? How might she have accomplished the same result with different actions?

8. What do you think the German proverb "Begin to weave / God provides the thread" means?

9. What tied the Bethel Colony together? What held the Willapa scouts together? What threats worked against the success of the Willapa Colony? Are there similar threats to communities of faith today? What helps them continue on?

10. Are there any parallels in our contemporary time to what Emma refers to when she says, "It was an intricate task blending isolation with protection, melding worldliness with spiritual calm"?

11. What was the Diamond Rule practiced by the Bethel Colony? Is such a rule substantiated scripturally for Christians? other world faiths? Did Wilhelm Keil demonstrate the Diamond Rule in his reaction to the scouts at Willapa?

12. Did Emma manipulate Christian to remain in Willapa? Was her interest in staying on after their harsh winter an act of love for her husband, a desire to be free of the colony, or from a new belief that she followed God's direction for her life? Do you think Emma would have remained in Willapa without Christian if he hadn't agreed with the possibilities of her plan?

13. Why did Christian concur with Wilhelm about the need to leave the valley? What made Christian change his mind? Are there likely to be conflicts between Emma and Christian in the years ahead, and if so, what do you think will enable them to accommodate each other in helpful ways?

14. Though we see the other women in this story through the eyes of Emma, what are Mary's strengths? Sarah's? Louisa's? Emma's mother's? her sister Catherine's? Do these women change

throughout the story, or are they static characters acting as back-drops for Emma's choice and change?

15. Toward the end, the author has Emma identify four spiritual pains* that she sees plaguing her husband, keeping him from seeking healing solace and from making the choice that Emma hopes he will: hopelessness, unforgiveness, separation from those who love him, and lack of meaning. What examples of Christian's behavior does the reader have that help define these four areas of Christian's struggle? How does Emma attempt to help him throughout their marriage?

*These four spiritual pains are described in greater detail in Richard Groves and Henriette Anne Klauser, *The American Book of Dying, Lessons in Healing Spiritual Pain* (Berkeley, CA: Celestial Arts, 2005).

An Interview with
Author Jane Kirkpatrick

How did you decide to write A Clearing in the Wild, *the first book in the Change and Cherish Historical Series?*

I'd visited the Old Aurora Colony Museum a number of times and found the lives of this utopian community of interest. But it wasn't until I read a brief mention in a quilting book, *Treasures in the Trunk,* written by a friend, Mary Bywater Cross, that Emma Wagner Giesy came into my life. She wrote, "1853. Emma Giesy came as the only woman in a party of ten Bethel, Missouri, scouts to find an Oregon site for their communal society." Little did I know that this sentence would take me from a communal world of nineteenth-century Missouri to one in the Washington Territory and eventually Oregon, introducing intrigue and unanswered questions along the way.

How much of this story is history, and how much is fictional?

"Between history and story lies memory," one sage wrote. Our memories of events are retold like a story, but they claim us as history, as fact. So two people can be absolutely certain of an event but carry opposing memories of it. I try to remember that when I'm researching and discovering diverse accounts of similar events. I tried, through reading descendant accounts and historical material about the Bethelites and where they came from, and through letters left behind, to create an accurate account of the colony, the faith that defined it, and the place of women within it. I had to sort through many accounts of which scouts actually came west and who returned to help bring the large group out in 1855. Opposing accounts and names and numbers exist between eight and nine, not counting Emma. I finally settled on nine men and one woman, using material from Clark Moor Will, a descendant. I knew Emma was pregnant when they left Missouri and where Andrew was born. I have genealogy information about family lines, children, and so on, and kept that factual. Christian was considered the leader of the scouts, or spies, as they're sometimes called. He had been a tinsmith and a recruiter, traveling outside Missouri to bring in new converts. Much has been written about Keil's history and his views, which could be described as autocratic at times. (He once broke away from a church because they planned to pay the pastor a salary, and Keil felt the pastor should live by the charity of his parishioners.) Letters by Keil that were translated from the German reveal his views of Willapa, and the chaos that reigned once the group arrived there. The difficult winter of 1855–56 is based on these letters and other historical accounts, so as much as possible, I've remained true to the "shared knowings," the facts that most people agree on, as I call them. He did limit the use of ammunition. He did require them to club fish to survive. The reports of others in the region at that time describe the German community as nearly starving to death that winter. Keil's letters provide clarity about his worries of Indian wars and the seeming impossibility of the colony being successful if they remained at the scouts' chosen site. He was quite vocal about his unhappiness with Willapa.

In the obituary of Andrew, we know he was born at Ft. Steilacoom. Catherina was born in the Washington Territory and not identified as having been born at Ft. Steilacoom, so by then the whole family was in the Willapa Valley.

Did Wilhelm Keil actually bring a hearse with his son in it across the continent?

Yes. No reporters or descendants dispute the relative ease of Keil's journey west in 1855, even with the presence of Willie Keil's hearse, and yes, they did use Golden Rule Whiskey to fill the casket. That something happened to change Keil's buoyant mood once he reached The Dalles is also agreed upon, including the report of the arrest and circumstances of the trial. Historians and family members also agree on the strain placed on the entire group while at Willapa, though they chose to bury Willie there. There are two accounts of the dates of that burial: one in November, the other December. They did carry candles at dusk to place him in the ground. A highway marker notes the site.

What was the position of women in that German community?

At Bethel, women and men were separated during worship. They worked with men, however, in the fields, in the tanneries, or wherever they were needed. Men were the leaders, and Wilhelm Keil was the unchallenged leader of the colony from the beginning until its dissolution in Oregon in the 1870s after his death. As was traditional in most societies of the era—and especially so of German American communities—women supported men and did not assume positions of leadership within a community. But this should not suggest that they had no desires to be known, nor should it be assumed that women within a Christian community, such as Bethel, would not have been aware of efforts within the United States to raise the awareness of women's rights, just as there were discussions related to slave and free men prior to the outbreak of the Civil War. Missourians were well aware of the tension related to free states or slave states. Men who were unhappy with Keil's leadership could leave; women had fewer choices and may have found more subtle ways to challenge that leadership, such as finding a way to participate in a scouting trip west. Women and men did mix at dances and at the many festival days for which the German community was well known.

Was Emma as independent as she seemed?

I think so. Certainly, she was as strong. None of the accounts dispute the hardships endured during those first winters in the Willapa Valley, which must have been extraordinary with an infant to care for and the knowledge that the small group prepared for the arrival of 250 people in just a few months. Winters in that region are legendary for the rainfall. The old growth timber that the scouts encountered soared hundreds of feet into the air. The scouts found isolation and timber, but harnessing both for their purposes proved a daunting challenge, and yet their decisions as portrayed at the end of this first book are accurate. Emma had to be a strong woman to find a new way to see the possibilities there and support her husband in the process.

Would Emma have challenged Keil's biblical interpretation of the role of women?

Here, too, I believe she would have. She may have known of the Seneca Falls Convention of 1848, where American women openly spoke and wrote of their beliefs and rights. There is evidence that her grandmother or perhaps a great aunt was the "Inspirationalist" leader whom men came to for religious advice over a number of years. Her parents had left their religious tradition to follow Keil. She therefore had a family model of a strong woman who felt called by God directly, not only through a male pastor's direction, but also of a family who questioned traditional religious authority. Once Emma was in a new territory, given her intelligence, family history—her uncle was an ambassador to France, Germany, and England—and Keil's absence, if she did not change how she made decisions and question traditional views, she may well have been unable to allow an Indian woman to nurse her child, for example, or support her husband's spiritual trials in the way she did. I saw her as a kind woman, spirited, who only became challenging of Keil when he proposed barriers to what she wanted: to have her voice heard within the community as a unique child of God and to support her family without losing herself.

Were the secondary characters—such as the Woodards, Mary and Sebastian Giesy, Louisa Keil, Karl Ruge, and Joe Knight—actual people?

Yes. Genealogy records and census records, Pacific County Historical Society material, and material from the Aurora Colony Museum in Aurora, Oregon, offered information about who lived close to whom; who remained in Bethel, who left the Willapa Valley, and who ultimately went to Aurora, the site chosen by Keil once he left Willapa via Portland. Emma did have several siblings who will appear in the next book. Joe Knight did take his little side trip. Keil's niece and brother did die in Oregon Territory. Karl Ruge, as the teacher, was especially important, I think, as Keil objected to education unless it was practical information. To my knowledge, there was no library—which is a common characteristic of many settlements—in Bethel or at Aurora, so Karl's presence carried additional importance within the community. That Karl stayed with the Willapa group intrigues me, and he'll add much to the continuing story.

Did you characterize Emma and Christian's relationship from letters or diaries, or did you create it?

I had no letters or diaries to rely on in creating these characters, but I did locate a drawing of Christian made from a portrait, so I had a sense of what he looked like. A great-nephew, David Wagner, provided treasured photographs of Emma in later life. There is really little written record about any of the colony women, and most of what was written down about them was written down by men. I had to track her movements by researching Emma's parents, brothers, her husband, and later, her sons. I don't think of it as "making things up" so much as trying to get inside the minds of people to tell a truthful story. I speculated about whether Emma would have told her husband of her pregnancy or not, as he was the leader, and politically, it might have been better for him not to have known. I speculated about why she had even been allowed to go along. A descendant's letter suggested that she and Christian had defied the leader, Wilhelm Keil, by getting married, and that he had "sent her along" perhaps as punishment. One comment suggested that "both had been exiled to the west." Those letters opened the door to that possibility and thus made the difficulties at the Willapa site have more tension with the nearing arrival of the main party.

Were there any surprises discovered as you wrote?
One thing I noted is how interconnected the earliest settlers in the Oregon Territory were—and are to my own writing experience. In Pacific County census records, I came across the name Soule, which is a family name I also found when I researched *A Gathering of Finches*. When I posted my interest on a Web site in Pacific County, I heard from Pat Smith, a woman in Utah who had helped me research the Marie Dorion story in *A Name of Her Own*, as Pat is a descendant of Marie. It turns out that relatives of Madame Dorion made their place in the southern part of Pacific County. Of course, Astoria played a big part in the Tender Ties Historical Series, and once again, I found myself researching right across the Columbia from that city. I also found the history of Washington Territory and the governor's hostility to natives

especially interesting. The effects of the Treaty of 1855 in Oregon versus the trials in Washington also added to my collection of historical facts I'd never encountered before. I was surprised to encounter Ezra Meeker once again, a man whose 1852 diary inspired my Kinship and Courage Series and especially Book One, *All Together in One Place*. I am also learning a little more about quilting and am grateful for the creativity and patience of my quilting friends.

What's going to happen in the second book?
Ah, that would be telling. But it is a series called "Change and Cherish," so I can assure you that Emma's journey of discovery continues. She'll be "weaving" and "tying" again, faithfully believing that God provides her thread—as do I.

―――――

You may join Jane and view her schedule at her Web site, www.jk books.com. Jane is also available by phone for book group gatherings, presentations, or signings by e-mailing her at jane@jkbooks.com or writing to her at 99997 Starvation Lane, Moro, Oregon, 97039.

ACKNOWLEDGMENTS

While I alone am responsible for this story and its speculations and errors, I could not have come close to authenticity without the help of many. I gratefully acknowledge the help of director Bruce Weilepp and other members of the Pacific County Historical Society in South Bend, Washington, for their assistance in gathering material about the early colony. Bruce's enthusiasm for my fictionalizing this story was of great support in the early collecting of information. It was while visiting the museum in South Bend and touring the old sites—Willie's grave, Old Willapa, and other Territory places—that I also found James G. Swan's book written in 1857, which provided detailed information about life during Emma's time.

I give special thanks to Erhard Gross of Astoria, Oregon, who not only offered specific advice about the flora and fauna of the Pacific Coast country, but walked me through the German language used in this story. He conferred with me about the nature of such a German society in the middle 1800s in America, and his careful reading of an advanced copy and his conversations with me about the role of women and religion and Christianity were always thought-provoking and appreciated, as were the conversations and fine German meals prepared by his wife and my friend, Elfi, at their bed-and-breakfast.

James J. Kopp, PhD, director of Aubrey R. Watzek Library at Lewis and Clark College and a scholar of utopian societies, made himself accessible for a variety of questions about community and specifically the Aurora settlement. He has a special interest in Aurora, is a board member of the Old Aurora Colony Museum and Aurora Historical Society, and lives in Aurora. I am especially grateful for his index of material, his willingness to spend time with me to explore the archives, and for his kind speculation with me about the lives of women at Bethel, Willapa, and Aurora.

I thank as well the Aurora Colony Historical Society for their maintaining of the facility where I've spent many days as a tourist hearing the stories, seeing the quilts, and wondering what life back then was really like, long before Emma's story called my name. I give special thanks to Alan Guggenheim, director of the Old Aurora Colony Museum, and his staff, board, and volunteers, especially Irene Westwood, for allowing me access to archival material and making me feel welcome even while they prepared for their annual quilt show at the museum and for the sesquicentennial celebration of the beginning of the Aurora Colony scheduled for 2006.

David and Pat Wagner opened their family files, and I am deeply indebted to their kindness and their passion for history. Annabell Prantl, author and historian, deserves thanks for locating several articles from the Marion County Historical Society in Salem, Oregon, and providing them to me. As an octogenarian, she is an inspiration and encouragement to my work and has connections to Pacific County.

Karla and Peter Nelson of Time Enough Books in Ilwaco, Washington, offered assistance about Pacific County and life in that landscape, including oystering, as well as reading an advanced copy of *A Clearing in the Wild*. They also obviously love books, something else we hold in common, and they understand the beauty of the landscape despite its demands.

The Fort Steilacoom Historical Society provided important information, as did the Steilacoom Historical Society. I'm especially grateful to Susan and Milt Davidson of Steilacoom for meeting me at the museum on a blustery Sunday afternoon and answering questions and "speculating" with me.

I thank Blair Fredstrom, who used her days to search genealogy connections, and for being willing to explore with me the lives of strong women and their challenges in territorial times. I thank Sandy Maynard for helping me type when I broke my arm early in the writing of this book and her later support during the deaths and illnesses that challenged the telling of this story. Carol Tedder is a prayer partner extraordinaire, and I have "groupies" who appear to help me at the most needful times. They are angels each one, and I thank them.

To my writing team in Oregon, Washington, Wisconsin, Pennsylvania, and Florida and at WaterBrook Press, a special thanks for your support and encouragement and prayers, especially during the writing of this book. You all know who you are and why you are appreciated so much.

A special acknowledgment goes to readers everywhere who find these stories and allow them to nurture them. Thank you for sharing with me through your letters, e-mails, and presence at events how these stories have touched your lives. I thank you for carrying me and these stories in your hearts.

Finally, to Jerry for his patience, his love of history, his mapmaking, and his willingness to live for twenty-nine years with a girl of German descent who some might say is both stubborn and strong-willed: Thank you. You are my clearing in this world's wild.

jane@jkbooks.com

Suggested Additional Resources

Allen, Douglas. *Shoalwater Willapa*. South Bend, WA: Snoose Peak
Publishing, 2004.

Arndt, Karl J. R. *George Rapp's Harmony Society 1785–1847,* rev. ed.
Cranbury, NJ: Associated University Presses, 1972.

Barthel, Diane L. *Amana, From Pietist Sect to American Community.*
Lincoln, Nebraska: University of Nebraska Press, 1982.

Bek, William G. "The Community at Bethel, Missouri, and Its Offspring
at Aurora, Oregon" (Part 1). *German-American Annals,* vol. 7, 1909.

———. "A German Communistic Society in Missouri." *Missouri Historical Review.* October, 1908.

Blankenship, Russell. *And There Were Men.* New York: Alfred A. Knopf,
1942.

Buell, Hulda May Giesy. "The Giesy Family." *Pacific County Rural
Library District,* memoir. Raymond, WA, 1953.

———. "The Giesy Family Cemetery." *The Sou'wester.* Pacific County
Historical Society, vol. 21, no. 2, 1986.

Cross, Mary Bywater. *Treasures in the Trunk: Memories, Dreams, and
Accomplishments of the Pioneer Women Who Traveled the Oregon Trail.*
Nashville: Rutledge Hill, 1993.

Curtis, Joan, Alice Watson, and Bette Bradley, eds. *Town on the Sound,
Stories of Steilacoom.* Steilacoom, WA: Steilacoom Historical Museum
Association, 1988.

Dole, Phillip. "Aurora Colony Architecture: Building in a Nineteenth-
Century Cooperative Society." *Oregon Historical Quarterly,* vol. 92,
no. 4, 1992.

Dietrich, William. *Natural Grace: The Charm, Wonder and Lessons of Pacific Northwest Animals and Plants.* Seattle: University of Washington Press, 2003.

Duke, David Nelson. "A Profile of Religion in the Bethel-Aurora Colonies." *Oregon Historical Quarterly,* vol. 92, no. 4, 1992.

Ficken, Robert E. *Washington Territory.* Pullman, WA: Washington State University Press, 2002.

Gordon, David G., Nancy Blanton, and Terry Nosho. *Heaven on the Half Shell: The Story of the Northwest's Love Affair with the Oyster.* Portland, OR: Washington Sea Grant Program and WestWinds Press, 2001.

Hendricks, Robert J. *Bethel and Aurora: An Experiment in Communism as Practical Christianity.* New York: Press of the Pioneers, 1933.

Keil, William. "The Letters of Dr. William Keil." *The Sou'wester.* Pacific County Historical Society, vol. 28, no. 4, 1993.

Nash, Tom, and Twilo Scofield. *The Well-Traveled Casket.* Eugene, OR: Meadowlark, 1999.

Nordhoff, Charles. *The Communistic Societies of the United States.* New York: Hillary House, 1960.

Olsen, Deborah M. "The *Schellenbaum:* A Communal Society's Symbol of Allegiance." *Oregon Historical Quarterly,* vol. 92, no. 4, 1992.

Simon, John E. "William Keil and Communist Colonies." *Oregon Historical Quarterly,* vol. 36, no. 2, 1935.

Strong, Thomas Nelson. *Cathlamet on the Columbia.* Portland, OR: Holly Press, 1906.

Swan, James G. *The Northwest Coast or Three Years' Residence in Washington Territory.* Harper and Brothers, 1857.

Swanson, Kimberly. " 'The Young People Became Restless:' Marriage Patterns Before and After Dissolution of the Aurora Colony." *Oregon Historical Quarterly,* vol. 92, no. 4, 1992.

Snyder, Eugene Edmund. *Aurora, Their Last Utopia, Oregon's Christian Commune, 1856–1883*. Portland, OR: Binford and Mort, 1993.

Weathers, Larry, ed. *The Sou'wester*. South Bend, WA: Pacific County Historical Society, 1967, 1970, 1972, 1974, 1979, 1986, 1989, 1993.

Will, Clark Moor. "An Omnivorous Collector Discovers Aurora!" *Marion County History, School Days I, 1971–1982,* vol. 13, Marion County Historical Society, 1979.

———. *The Sou'wester*. Several letters between descendant Will and Ruth Dixon, plus notations, essays, correspondence, and drawings of the Old Aurora Colony Museum, Aurora, Oregon. Raymond, WA: Pacific County Historical Society collection, May 29, 1967.

GLOSSARY OF GERMAN
AND CHINOOK WORDS

German

ach	oh no!
auf Wiedersehen, or informally, *tschuess*	good-bye
Belsnickel	a traditional Christmas persona bringing gifts
Peltz Nickel	a punishing companion of *Belsnickel*
Christkind	Christ child
Dummkopf	dummy or stupid
Frau	Mrs.
Fräulein	Miss
gross Haus	grand house
gut	good
Herr	Mr.
ja	yes, pronounced "ya"
Junge	boy
Kind	child
Kinder	children
Liebchen	darling or sweetheart
nein	no
nicht jetzt	not now
Schellenbaum	A bell-like instrument known in English as the "Turkish Crescent." Popular in the eighteenth and early nineteenth centuries, the large instrument combined music with a symbol of authority or standard of allegiance.

Tannenbaum	a tree, especially at Christmastime
Ve	we
verdammt	damn
Volk	folks

Chinook/Chehalis

cum'tux	understand, as in, "Do you understand?"
ho-ey-ho-ey	exchange or trade
klose	good
muck-a-muck	eat
Nch'I-Wana	Columbia River
omtz	give
tolo	boy